Lily Barlow

THE MYSTERY OF JANE DOUGH

a novel

Carla Vergot

BOOK ONE

NEW YORK

LONDON • NASHVILLE • MELBOURNE • VANCOUVER

Lily Barlow - BOOK ONE
THE MYSTERY OF JANE DOUGH

© 2024 Carla Vergot

Published in New York, New York, by Morgan James Publishing. Morgan James is a trademark of Morgan James, LLC. www.MorganJamesPublishing.com

Publisher's Note: This novel is a work of fiction. Names, characters, places, and incidents are either products of the author's imagination or used fictitiously. All characters are fictional, and any similarity to people living or dead is purely coincidental.

Proudly distributed by Publishers Group West®

A FREE ebook edition is available for you or a friend with the purchase of this print book.

CLEARLY SIGN YOUR NAME ABOVE

Instructions to claim your free ebook edition:
1. Visit MorganJamesBOGO.com
2. Sign your name CLEARLY in the space above
3. Complete the form and submit a photo of this entire page
4. You or your friend can download the ebook to your preferred device

ISBN 9781636981901 paperback
ISBN 9781636981918 ebook
Library of Congress Control Number: 2023935626

Cover and Interior Design by:
Chris Treccani
www.3dogcreative.net

Morgan James is a proud partner of Habitat for Humanity Peninsula and Greater Williamsburg. Partners in building since 2006.

Get involved today! Visit: www.morgan-james-publishing.com/giving-back

PG-13 | PARENTAL GUIDANCE SUGGESTED
SOME MATERIAL MAY NOT BE SUITABLE FOR CHILDREN UNDER 13

Lily Barlow

BOOK ONE

Still for Ricky

Acknowledgments

I'd like to thank the following people for making this journey possible: My husband and the patron of my work, Rick Vergot; my new publisher, David Hancock and the incredible team at Morgan James Publishing; my first publisher, Jesse Krieger, for getting *Lily Barlow* into the world; my superhero, Janet Evanovich, for her grace and good stories; friend and emotional support editor, Suze Kopynec; beta reader and problem solver extraordinaire, Pam Kamphuis; my sweet Mary Anne, who loved everything I ever did; friend, beta reader and rock, Carol Anne Timpson; beta reader and Wonder Twin, Dana Willis; the critique partner who got me from Page One to The End, Lisa Whitaker; critique partner and future co-author, Leah Rex McCracken; Kim Lowrie, fellow creative and bringer of positive vibes; Rick Vergot and Mitch Cord for letting me bounce ideas and for being good sports; every single member of the Back Porch; friends and fellow authors, Laura Kemp and Nola Nash, for all the love; Nelsa Cox, the first person who believed I would write a book; that one English professor at NC State who told the class he was pretty sure none of us would ever write a book; that other English professor at NC State who encouraged me to write a book; my dogs; every reader who bought, borrowed, or checked-out a copy of *Lily Barlow*; all the people who left honest opinions; and anyone who unwittingly gave me inspiration for a scene or a character.

Chapter 1

"Nothin' satisfies the murderous intentions of the human heart like rippin' a weed from the very earth," muttered the elderly woman in the gigantic straw hat.

I'd been standing behind her for a good seven seconds, but so far she gave no indication she'd heard me pull into the driveway or get out of the Jeep. Not wanting to startle her into a medical emergency, I waited and watched while she wrestled with a sturdy green leaf bumping up against a delicate pink flower.

It was unclear if her pronouncement regarding murderous intentions was meant for me or for the wilting weed in her knobby fist. Either way, my inner Stephanie Plum snapped to attention. While I puzzled over her statement, trying to decide between criminal intent or crazy old lady, she turned to size me up.

"Hey," I said, with an artificially bright note in my voice, hoping to disguise the fact that I thought she might be a murderer or a lunatic, one. "I'm L–"

"I know who you are," she cut me off. "The Barlow girl. Lily, is it? Lord, you're a tall drink a water. Carbon copy of your mama." She made a soft cluck that somehow conveyed respect, forcing me to nod my head ever so slightly in acceptance of the praise. "I heard you were comin' home. How's your daddy doin'?"

"He's out of the hospital," I reported, trying to fix how she knew my mama, who, by the way, died when I was six. "He's not great, but he's not dead."

"You takin' over the bakery? Haven't had a decent loaf of bread since your daddy got sick."

"I plan to get it going, yes, ma'am. Then I'll hire someone to run it, so I can get back to school. But first I'm looking for an apartment, you know, for the short time I'm here."

She nodded in sympathy. "Near impossible for the baby bird to fit back in the nest after flyin' down to Charlottesville, eh?"

I didn't realize myself how impossible it would be until I passed the "Welcome to Marshall" sign an hour ago, Jeep Wrangler double stuffed with all my worldly possessions.

I had come back last month when Jack Turner, best friend and all-round go-to guy, called to tell me Dad had the heart attack. I stayed until he was out of Fauquier General and settled in with Uncle Dave and Aunt Millie. Satisfied everything was in order, I bolted back to the University of Virginia with the realistic expectation of a complete recovery and return to business as usual for Poppy's Bakery. It was still mid-summer, but the Admissions Office was in full swing, and I was one of a couple dozen work-study go-getters cranking the hamster wheels that kept it running.

However, the full recovery and return to business never materialized and the bakery stayed closed. You know what that meant—no dough, no *dough*. As in moolah. As in tuition. I figured a resourceful human being like me could hire a reliable manager, train her, and square the books in three weeks' time, a month tops. Then I'd carry myself back down to Charlottesville for the fall semester of my junior year. At which point I'd resume switching majors en route to a career path that would get me out of this small town and far away from commercial-sized sacks of flour.

I watched Miss Crazy start the arduous process of old bones standing up. "I have just what you're lookin' for, honey. It's a fully furnished guest suite. Small kitchen, bath. You'll be in your place, and I'll be in mine. There will be no reason whatsoever for us to bother each other." Was I mistaken, or was the implication that *I* shouldn't bother *her*?

"How much are you asking?" Because at this moment, it all came down to cash money. "And will you accept a week-to-week commitment?" Nothing says I'm-not-moving-home like a short-term lease.

"Don't you want a look-see first?"

I shook my head no. The silver lining, if you wanted to see it, was that I had lived in and near the campus community for the last two years. I had moved my little pile of junk the requisite umpteen number of times, landing in everything from rat trap to Roach Motel, and I was completely and satisfactorily desensitized to substandard housing. My requirements at school were biking distance to campus and a locking door. "If the door locks, it'll be fine, but my budget is kinda tight right now. I may not be able to afford it."

"You can afford it, honey child," she assured me. "I want a person on the property more than money in the bank, as long as it's the right person. You're the sixteenth applicant in eight months and the only one I've bothered to interview."

Smiling at what constituted an interview, my gaze landed on a pair of muddy men's work boots, size huge, sitting on the top step of the porch. Hmmm. Did Miss Crazy Pants have a man around despite what she said? Unless the aforementioned murderous intentions of her human heart put an end to that ol' boy. Was he living on the property or buried under it?

Following my gaze, she offered an explanation, "Best home security system on the market. Four dollars at the thrift store. Mud not included."

I nodded my appreciation. I liked this ol' gal more and more...a little bit of moxie wrapped in a floral print tied with an apron string. "I'll take it."

"Woman who knows her mind. Good. Get yourself settled back in town, and we'll come to a monetary arrangement. For now, feed the chickens and pet my dog when he comes around."

Chickens? Mentally calculating how close I had to be to a chicken in order to feed a chicken, I noticed for the first time a lazy, mostly-black mutt lying under a shrub, guarding her collection of trowels. He honored me with one thump of his dusty tail before drifting back to sleep.

"Name's Cro. Short for Velcro. Wandered into the barn five years ago, thin as a number two pencil. Hasn't left my side since. He's good company, and he don't like many people, so the fact he hasn't barked you up is your stamp of approval. Now come on."

Out of the corner of my eye, I saw she was already halfway to the front porch. Quick for old. I took a few giant steps to catch up.

At the door she said, "Wipe your feet. Not just this time. Every time."

We passed through a tidy foyer to a scrubbed kitchen that smelled of something savory, like onions and garlic. The olfactory memory took me back to a time when I was a little kid in my mama's kitchen, helping her pinch tiny mounds of mashed potatoes and cheddar cheese into pierogi pockets. It was a sweet little video clip but why would I think of her now? Probably Miss Crazy's comment on a resemblance; that had to be the reason.

The clatter of scissors and screw drivers being pushed around a junk drawer drew me back. She rummaged with gusto and eventually fished out a key on a plastic key ring shaped like a starfish. Whatever it advertised had long since rubbed off, so just a translucent orange starfish at this point. Out the back door, we cut across the mowed lawn to a free-standing garage that matched the house.

"These steps get slick in the rain." The exposed wooden staircase climbed diagonally up the outside of the garage to a small deck with two weathered Adirondack chairs and a low table between. I pictured me in one chair, Cro in the other, drinking a beer and enjoying the progress toward Operation Bakery Blast Off. Crossing the threshold, it became clear I would be renting my own little piece of the 1970s. Nothing too fragile or frilly. It was, however, heavy on the avocado section of the color wheel.

"I don't care who you bring up here, but Cro might. The password for the internet is on the fridge. There'll be no cookin' meth. Any questions?"

The devil in me wanted to ask where I was supposed to cook my meth, but I stuck to my actual questions. "Two," I said. "What should I call you? And where's the chicken feed?"

"I'm Miss Delphine Walker, and the scratch is down in the garage. One scoop each mornin'. Throw it on the ground back by the coop."

Without so much as a handshake, I had my apartment. Cleaner and more comfortable than I could have hoped. It didn't take too many trips to bring up my clothes and computer, so in about twenty minutes, I was all moved in. I figured the living arrangements would be the hardest part, which is why I snuck home a day early, giving myself time to find something suitable. But now that I had an address, there was only one thing left to do—marinate my broken dream in a couple shots of tequila. Wait a minute...broken? Was my dream of escaping Yawnsville actually broken? Inconvenienced, yes. Broken, no. This was a speed bump, not a dead end.

It was around six p.m. when I jumped in the Wrangler. I put both windows down because I associate a flying ponytail with freedom. My destination was Cinco Sombreros, a small, turquoise-colored Mexican dive on the edge of town. Usually, the name got morphed to Cinco's, as if some guy named Cinco owned it. Other people referred to the restaurant as Manny's because Manny was the actual guy who owned it. I didn't bother to text Manny's daughter, Mercedes. She'd be there. She was always there.

Mercedes and I shared a lot of similar experiences growing up, including the loss of our mothers when we were young, mine to cancer, hers to immigration.

I was never quite clear why her mama got deported when her daddy didn't. As much as I wanted to sleuth it in high school, I managed to refrain. It seemed like Mercedes didn't want to know, and you gotta respect a friend's right to believe a better story. By virtue of missing mothers, we

5

were both raised primarily by fathers, sometimes each other's. Fathers who ran small food service businesses where we were required to help out. A lot of similarities. A few differences. Like the fact that she loved her family's business while I hated mine.

Mercedes made her way to me before I was all the way through the door. Her long, dark hair was in a thick braid down her back. Brown eyes shining. Low-cut tank. Gorgeous wasn't too strong a word. Not quite dinner time, there were only a few customers scattered around. She pulled me by the arm over to the bar where her dad, Manny, came around for a hug. No words. Just a welcome worth coming home for. There is something about being around people who know and love you; it fills a hole.

Mercedes poured me a shot of ice-cold tequila and put a basket of chips and a bowl of guacamole in front of me. "You old enough to drink at my bar?" Manny eyed me seriously.

"Finally." I smiled and tossed the liquor back.

"Go easy," he warned me, like the substitute dad he was. There were plenty of times I wasn't old enough, but I drank at this bar anyway. Mercedes and I spent a lot of time conjuring ever-evolving ways to drink, and no time at all considering what it would mean if her dad lost his liquor license. The self-centered stupidity of youth. We thought because we were drinking beer and smoking pot instead of shooting heroine or dropping acid like some of our peers, we weren't part of the problem and couldn't be classified as troublemakers.

Mercedes pulled a stool to the other side of the bar and started slicing limes. She agreed with my plan to get buzzed and joined me for two beers and two more shots. At one point, Manny raised his eyebrows with an unspoken criticism, but she said, "What? I'm off now." Before long, I was knee deep in the poor-me syndrome, rattling off all the reasons why this current situation wasn't fair.

"What are you going to do?" she asked.

"If drinking is an option, I think I'll just do that."

"Here's my advice," she began, and because she was a sage old soul, I paid attention. "Go home, google 'dough,' and start researching. Learn everything you can about it. Get intimate with it. Embrace it. Maybe you hate the bakery so much because it's always been an adversary."

She pointed to the matching scars on the insides of my forearms. Souvenirs of the second-degree burns I got in the seventh grade, carelessly pulling a rack of cherry turnovers from the oven. Burned my arms and burned the turnovers.

"Learn to love it?" I couldn't have sounded more incredulous.

"No," she shook her head. "That's not what I'm saying." She started again, "You know that *chiquita* in the books you like so much? Stacy Prune?"

"Stephanie Plum," I corrected, tartly.

"Yeah, yeah. *P* fruit. Prune, pear, peach, pomegranate," she said and smiled her wicked smile. "Pull a Plum. Do that detective thing. Get all undercover with dough. Find its weaknesses and exploit them. Maybe, on your terms, you'll decide you could have a relationship with the bakery after all. If there's no bakery, *Lilita*, how will you pay for college? Don't say no. Just give yourself a month to decide."

I didn't have time to respond. From my stool, I watched Wayne Davis and Joe Turner meander into the restaurant. Oh, for the love of a tie-dyed tumbleweed.

The place was mostly empty, but they made their way to the one table that was annoyingly close to our spot at the bar. Joe circled around and pulled me off my perch. "Lily Barlow. Mmh, girl." He leaned in for a hug. "When'd you get home?" Hugging was kind of a standard greeting in these parts, so after Joe, I stepped over and gave Wayne a hug.

"Today," I answered, and to underscore just how recently I had arrived, I added, "Haven't even seen Dad and 'em yet."

Wayne and Joe were friends of ours who drove boom trucks for Republic Building Supply. It was clear from the day's worth of dirt on their clothes that the boys had just gotten off work and were stopping in for a beer before getting serious about their Friday-night options. Oh, and Joe happened to be Jack's older brother. My Jack. Best friend Jack.

Jack was a firefighter with access to a steady stream of gossip related to the comings and goings of neighbors and tourists, so chances were good he already heard I was back in town. Everyone knew he and I were close, so of course people would give him that news. Most of these busybodies didn't understand the exact nature of our friendship, though. They were always trying to make it into something it never was.

Bottom line, Jack would be okay that I didn't text him the minute I got home. He knew how this turn of events with Dad's heart attack was making me bonkers. Sure, I was worried about my dad, but once I got assurances from the doctors that he wouldn't die, my fears took flight and started circling like buzzards around the second most important thing—college.

On the slim chance Jack didn't know I was home, I gave it about fifteen seconds before he heard it from Joe. I watched a waitress drop two bottles at their table, and in my peripheral vision I saw Joe punching something into his phone.

Didn't matter. I was fixin' to leave anyway. I got up to hug Mercedes, which, like any alcohol-laced goodbye, took longer than necessary. During the process, I was surprised when a strong arm came from behind and pulled me into a broad, hard chest. I felt a kiss land on the side of my head.

"Lily of the Valley," Jack tightened his embrace. "When'd you get back, girl?"

I knew Joe had texted him, but I didn't think he'd get here that fast. He probably told Wayne and Joe to run interference. Jeez, how long had Mercedes and I been saying goodbye?

Mercedes rolled her eyes, leaned over and whispered, "Dough," in my ear before she shoved Jack's shoulder and loaded our chip basket and beer bottles onto a tray. They had the familiarity of having dated. She was precisely his type—naturally beautiful, good with makeup, the kind of figure guys find appealing. It didn't last long, though. I made her swear she wouldn't create any weirdness that would impact my friendship with Jack.

He was special to me, and I wasn't willing to give that up in high school. They hadn't dated long before she broke it off, explaining to me that she didn't see it going anywhere, so having sex would be pointless.

Disengaging from the awkward backwards embrace, I turned around to face him. "Hey, Jack-a-lope," I drew out my greeting, taking him in. His short black hair was messy, which meant he had taken off a baseball cap when he came inside and jammed it in his back pocket. His blue eyes were intense, and as always, he looked happy to see me. He wore a t-shirt, trail pants and boots.

After I gave him the once over, I asked, "You here for tacos?"

"Nope. I'm here for you. Joe texted to say you had a few shots. I'll drive you home. I'm on later tonight, and I don't like working single car accidents, especially when they involve people I care about."

I considered just how much I had to drink. It'd been over the course of a couple three hours, and it wasn't like I slammed shots the whole time. "I haven't had that much."

"Listen, it's been my experience that you never know exactly how much you've had. So since I'm here..." He gently nudged me to where I faced the door.

Deciding it wasn't that important, I patted my back pockets for license, credit card, and phone, front pocket for keys and lip gloss. Satisfied, I tossed a mildly sarcastic wave to Joe and Wayne who both smiled back. Jack lifted his chin as he passed their table, and they responded in kind.

Outside, Jack held the door as I climbed into his truck. He didn't speak. Probably considering safe, available topics. As he pulled out of the gravel lot, he decided on one. "Lucy had her puppies."

"Lucy had the puppies?" the squeakiness of my voice was kind of shocking.

"Four. They're hysterical. Mom has her hands full."

I knew the dog was pregnant, but I had sort of forgotten about it. "Hey," I said, "I thought Lucy was fixed."

9

"Yeah, so did my parents." From there we drifted on a low tide of easy conversation, the mark of an old and good friendship. It didn't occur to me to tell Jack where I was staying until he pulled up to the house on Main, next to Poppy's.

"Oh, wait. Not here."

"No?" he asked, sounding confused.

"I'm renting an apartment on Rock Ridge. It's kind of a statement. So no one thinks I'm coming home for good."

"Miss Delphine Walker? How'd you find that place?"

"You know Miss Delphine? She had an ad in the paper. Is she a crackpot? I think she may have killed someone."

"I doubt that, but she's a good ways on the eccentric side. She calls in every so often because she smells smoke. Trouble with a burn barrel. The chimney. Nothing serious so far. You're renting her garage?"

For some reason, I was a little disappointed that Miss Delphine was apparently a known citizen. But I let it go and relaxed into the comfortable, tequila-induced fuzziness that encouraged me to close my eyes.

All too soon, Jack opened his door, triggering the obnoxious dinging noise that brought me out of my half sleep. Now I felt every ounce of the alcohol. I let him walk around the front of the truck, because he always opened doors for women. I remembered when we were kids, his daddy used to fuss at me constantly. "Lily Linn Barlow, how can I teach my boys to open doors for ladies if you never let them do it?"

By now, it was as much second nature for me as it was for him, and it occurred to me that none of my guy friends at school, or anyone I've dated, ever once opened a single door for me. I thanked the good Lord for my own independence, otherwise I'd never get in to or out of any place, ever.

He helped me out, and I dug for the orange starfish in my pocket. The stairs looked a little steeper than they had this afternoon, and I leaned on him, enjoying his clean soapy smell. Then I asked him a question which showed I definitely had too much to drink. "We've been friends for a long time," I started. It looked like he was adding it up in his head.

"Sixteen years, right?" He filled in the number.

"If we've been friends for sixteen years, why haven't we ever slept together?"

He made a soft, hum sound, waited a beat and whispered close to my ear, "Here's the thing, Lily. We just haven't slept together *yet.*"

I stumbled on the next step, but I didn't know if it was from the buzz or this new information.

"Tonight?" I suggested, surprising myself.

"Not tonight."

"Why not tonight?"

"Two reasons. First, you're stressed, which likely accounts for reason number two, you're drunk." Checking to see that I was listening, he said, "When we do, it'll be awesome, and you'll wanna remember it."

He took the key, unlocked the door, and maneuvered me toward the bathroom. The place was small, so there were only two doors it could be.

"Can you stand?"

"Yes," I insisted, holding the doorknob tight.

"Can you pee?"

"Yes."

"Good. I'll wait here."

When I was done, he was right where I left him, only with a glass of water and two Tylenol. I had no idea where the Tylenol came from. For never having been a Boy Scout, Jack was always prepared so he probably brought the pills with him. I drank about half, handed the glass back, moved to the couch and plopped down. Looking up, I smiled. "Thank you."

"You're welcome. Do you need anything?" Tipping my head to think, I decided I didn't need anything. He reached down for my hand and hoisted me up off the couch. "I'll come by tomorrow around ten and take you for the Jeep. Lock the door when I leave."

I followed him to the door, where he gave me a long hug that felt like a warm blanket. He pulled his hands down my bare arms, stopping to grab hold of my wrists.

11

"I'm serious about what I said."

I blinked, "About locking the door?"

"No, Lily. About sleeping together." He let himself out before I could process the comment, let alone formulate a reply. I was still thinking about it five seconds later when he rapped on the other side of the door.

"Lock it."

Clicking the deadbolt, I heard his heavy boots disappear down the stairs, but I side-stepped to the little window and moved the curtain an inch to spy. Jack stopped by his truck. I saw him tip his Washington Nationals ball cap, something he did when greeting women. Was he talking to somebody in the yard? Miss Delphine? I could make out a shadow at the dark end of the porch and a slow, rhythmic movement. Was she in the rocking chair? He nodded in that direction, got in the truck and left.

Back on the couch, I finished the glass of water, wished I had another beer, and tried to remember something from the bar. Something Mercedes told me to do. Google something? What was it? Something to eat? *P* fruits? No...No...Dough! Yes, google dough. Embrace the dough. Be the dough.

I flipped open the Mac, stumbled over to the fridge for the Wi-Fi code, checked the fridge in case the last tenant left a bottle of beer in there, cursed the last tenant for drinking all the beer, and headed back to the living room.

A notoriously bad speller, my hazy mind and slow fingers were not helpful, so the first thing that made it into the search window was the wrong kind of dough. I typed the letters d-o-e and hit enter.

↘ 🐔 ↙

It was a chicken noise that roused me from the hypnotic Doe stupor at five thirty a.m. I hadn't been to bed. In fact, I hadn't moved more than a few inches within the burrow of macramé pillows on the couch. Remembering my commitment to feed Miss Delphine's chickens, I slipped on a pair of lime green flip flops and took the stairs nice and slow 'cause of the hangover.

At the bottom, I encountered one of them blocking my way. We stared each other down for about thirty seconds.

"C'mon, McNugget, get outta the way."

She scratched a weird little foot across the dirt, pecked at something invisible on the ground and stepped toward me. One of life's mysteries was finally put to rest—this is how the game Chicken got its name.

I considered my options, which were a) yell at it, or b) kick at it. Alone, neither offered an especially strong line of defense, so I did a combo.

"Scat!" I shouted while throwing my foot out in front of me. The kick by itself had no effect, but the flying flip flop nearly landed on top of the bird. She squawked which made me squawk. When she took off flapping her wings, I grabbed my shoe and ran toward the garage door which thankfully was unlocked. Breathing hard, I pulled the door closed behind me.

The food was clearly marked, and the scooper was in place. I filled it to what I thought would be an appropriate level and peeked back out the door. No chickens in sight. Motivated by fear, I double-timed it toward the coop where I dumped the grain on the ground in one thick pile. Feeling successful, I checked behind in case McNugget tried to outflank me. No chicken there, so I ran back to the garage.

↘ 🐔 ↙

From the kitchen window, Delphine watched the series of events and shook her head. "Cro, I swear that girl is a walkin' mess."

↘ 🐔 ↙

It was ten-o-five when I heard the knock and yelled, "Come in!"

"Why isn't the door locked?"

"What?" I said from the couch.

13

"The deadbolt. Remember? You locked it last night when I left."

It took me a few seconds to think it through, but I got there.

"Oh, right," I nodded. "I forgot to lock it back after I fed the chickens."

Jack retrieved two large cups of coffee wedged carefully into opposite corners of the box he set on the kitchen table. I knew one was black and one had plenty of cream and sugar. Handing me the cream and sugar, he repeated, shaking his head in obvious confusion, "Wait. You fed the chickens?"

"Not by choice, believe me. It's a little arrangement I have with Miss Delphine."

"Well, how did that go?"

"I'll tell you exactly how it went. I would have dialed 911, except my freakin' phone was up here on the freakin' coffee table." To underscore my point, I gestured toward the offending phone with my bare foot.

He laughed. I guessed he was trying to imagine me running from a single chicken, and then chickens plural. Couldn't blame him. I didn't possess one chicken-related skill, not so much as a partial skill. And the picture in his head must have been right funny.

I watched him take in my messy brown ponytail and overall rumpled appearance. He seemed to notice I was still wearing the shorts and Abercrombie tee I had on yesterday.

"Did you shower?"

"No," I said sheepishly.

"Did you sleep?"

In mid coffee-sip, I shook my head no, avoiding his blue eyes.

"Why not?" he asked, genuinely confounded.

"Jack, you don't want to know," I said on a sigh.

"Literally more than anything." He grinned.

"I kinda got sucked into something on the computer."

"Can you tell me about it while I check the batteries in your smoke detectors?" He moved over to the box he brought with him and unloaded

14

several new smoke alarms and an unopened Costco-sized sleeve of nine-volt batteries. After a quick walk-through, which he could have done standing in one spot and turning in a circle, he asked, "How's your head this morning?"

I groaned for emphasis. "I could use an aspirin. You got any in that box?"

"Down in the truck. Cover your ears while I test this one." He was standing on a kitchen chair, which didn't look safe at all.

The smoke alarm only made a few sickly chirps. He popped the cover and replaced the battery. With that one in good working order, he pulled the chair into the bedroom and got to work screwing one to the ceiling in there.

"Is that for when I'm in here burning up the sheets with my latest conquest?" I smirked from the doorway.

"For when *we're* in here burning up the sheets." Over his shoulder he gave me one of his trademark winks. Was that a reference left over from something we talked about last night? Did we... Did we kiss or something? Impossible. But there was an idea nagging me. I just couldn't pull it out of the dark, drunk corner of my mind.

Expertly changing the subject, I said, "So last night I found this website called the Doe Network. Have you ever heard of it?"

"Dough, like in bread?"

"That's what I was looking for! Mercedes told me to study up on dough, make my peace with the bakery, blah, blah, blah. Well, I don't know if you noticed, but I had a little bit to drink down at Manny's."

"No," he said. The sarcasm oozed like sap from a pine tree on a hot summer day. "You hid it so well." When he smiled, his lip was a little lop-sided from a fist fight in middle school. I remembered that fight. It was over me. Some guy on the baseball team apparently made an unflattering comment about me, and Jack punched him in the locker room after practice. He walked away with a busted lip and missed the chance to pitch in a really big game on account of it, but he always said it was worth it. He never would tell me the comment. Kyle, the offender, apologized to me the next day and treated me a lot nicer after that.

Bringing myself back to my story, I said, "Instead of typing d-o-u-g-h, I accidentally typed d-o-e. I saw the Doe Network and thought—cool, a bunch of people who bake."

"That kept you on the computer all night?"

"Yes! But wait," I said, excitedly. "It's not about baking at all. It's a clearing house for records of all the bodies the cops haven't been able to identify, dating back to the early 1900s. Doe as in John Doe. Or Jane. There are postmortem photos, reconstructed heads, clothing and jewelry the victims wore at the time, dental work, gold teeth. They list any unusual marks, like tattoos, scars. How the person died if they know."

"You spent all night looking at dead bodies?" he asked, stepping down off the chair. "Maybe we should have had sex after all." He smiled. "Way better use of time."

It came crashing back that I invited him to have sex and he took a rain check. This was not and never had been part of our relationship, and I suddenly felt uncomfortable. Shifting my weight from one foot to another while I tried to appear in control, I directed his attention back to the Doe Network.

"Lily, you can change the subject all you want, but we will have this discussion before you head back to school." He squeezed his 6'4 frame past my 5'8 frame, going slow on purpose.

Borderline shocked by the sexually charged repartee, I couldn't decide if something was going on or if he was just messin' with me. Regardless, I was unnerved and didn't know what to do next. In another weak attempt to divert, I said, "By the way, I have a problem."

"Perfect," he said, as he dropped the screwdriver back in the box with the remaining smoke detectors. "I've been looking for an opportunity to solve a problem all morning."

"I can't take a shower because there's a spider in the bathtub."

Chapter 2

The spider issue was resolved without incident. One shower, a second cup of coffee and two more Tylenol later, I was reasonably put together and pretty sure I could pull off a visit with my family. On autopilot, my mind wandered. What was I thinking with that stupid invitation of sex last night? And more to the point, why had Jack taken me seriously? The notion of us engaging in a physical interlude was so far beyond the scope of reality, it'd be like, like, having an interlude with an alien. Not that I was a hundred percent anti-extra-terrestrial. I mean, has Area 51 ever been adequately explained? There was some compelling evidence there, if you asked me.

The point, however, was simple: sex with Jack equaled bad idea. I knew it; he had to know it. The only thing to do was grab the worm and cram it back in the can. I flinched at the idea, not one to bait hooks or grab worms for any other reason. Regardless. The whole thing would evaporate as soon as he found himself in the shadow of the next thirty-six D, so, basically before dinner time tonight. Convinced it wouldn't come up again, I shelved it.

What I couldn't shake, though, were the images of all those unidentified bodies on the Doe Network. The boy, four to six years old, found in California on September 26, 1974 near a golf course (Case File 626UMCA). No signs of abuse or malnutrition and no obvious cause of death. He wore a green windbreaker and a green and white striped shirt. There was a ladybug stick pin on his jacket. Somebody cared enough about this kid to bother with the whimsy of pinning a ladybug to his jacket. Six years old, he would have gone to school. He would have had friends. Teachers would have known him. A neighbor. Somebody. Didn't anyone wonder where he was?

Or the woman in her late twenties to early thirties found in Nevada on July 17, 1982 (Case File 156UFNV). Hikers stumbled across her body slumped on a log, as if she had bent to tie her shoe. The autopsy showed she may have given birth. Her dental work looked European. She had a white lace bathing suit underneath Lee Rider blue jeans and a t-shirt. She had planned to go swimming that day. Her hair was in a bun, and she wore pale yellow sneakers, size 6. She was shot less than 24 hours before they found her. That's pretty specific information. If she was a mother, where was the kid? Who knew them? Was anyone looking?

Or the young woman's headless, handless body found in Florida on February 13, 2018. Probably in her early twenties (Case File 187UFFL). My age. She was wearing jeans from Old Navy. I have Old Navy blue jeans. She was wearing Keds. When it gets too cold for flip flops, I bring out my ratty Keds. There was no indication that she had been sexually abused. She was wrapped in an old blanket, secured with duct tape, and dumped near a swamp. The blanket was woven from coarse pink and purple wool and should have decorated a little girl's bed instead of a dead body. She had a tattoo on her left ankle. The crime scene photographer was no Ansel Adams, and there was some degradation due to decomposition, but the tattoo appeared to be a sweet purple flower growing on a green vine. The violence of decapitating a woman and chopping off her hands made my stomach turn even more than the thought of the murder itself, and I whispered, "I'm sorry," to the tortured spirit who lost her life. "I'm sorry," I repeated, pulling into the driveway at Dave and Millie's.

From outside the big bay window on the front porch, I could see Dad sitting in the rocker-recliner monstrosity that dominated the family room. Even asleep he looked tired. I came in quietly. When Millie heard the door squeak, she peered out from the kitchen. Grabbing a dish towel, she mopped her hands on her way through the kitchen and flipped it onto her shoulder. She met me halfway, arms outstretched. "Welcome home, baby."

"You know I'm not here for good, right?" For some reason I felt compelled to make this statement to everyone.

"We all know." Her words were kind and sincere. "Still, you didn't have to rent Miss Walker's garage. You could'a stayed with me and your Uncle Davy. There's room even with your daddy."

"I didn't want to be in the way." Mentally, I scolded myself for sounding like a little kid instead of an accomplished career-minded third-year college student. The fact that she knew my whereabouts, when I had been where-abouting there for fewer than 24 hours, only reiterated that this town was too small for my own good.

"Go say 'hey' to your daddy," she encouraged, gently. "He's just dozin'."

I eased over to him and leaned in for a hug. He opened his eyes and smiled. Deciding there was plenty of room for my not-so-trim butt on the arm of the Lazy Boy, I half perched there.

"Hey, Snickerdoodle." I watched a weird combination of relief and anxiety wash across his face. "I'm really sorry about this, Darlin'."

"Dad, relax. The main thing is that you're okay." Pulling back six inches to look him in the face, I asked,

"You are okay, aren't you?"

Disgusted with the question, he snorted. "I could unload the flour delivery myself."

"Dad," I laughed, "you couldn't unload the flour before the heart attack."

"Didn't have to," he reminded me. "Every job needs a supervisor."

"Then, why don't you consider me the supervisor for the next three weeks."

"What are you talkin' about, Lily?" At this point Millie brought out some sweet tea and oatmeal cookies.

I took a glass, still on the arm of the chair. "Where's Uncle Dave? I thought we could have a family meeting."

"He's putzin' around with somethin' in the shed. I have no idea what."

Putting my tea on the end table, I got up to fetch him, but from the back door I heard him bellow, "LILY?" Clearly, the loudest of the Barlows, he stomped into the family room, grabbed me up in a bear hug, twirled me once around, and deposited me back beside my dad.

"Excellent timing," I noted.

"That's how the good Lord made me. I'm the only one who doesn't need to set a timer. Never burned a batch of biscotti, and I never will," he said proudly.

Millie snatched her dish towel from its resting place on her shoulder and swatted him with it. "Lily has called a family meetin'. Stop your braggin' and drink your tea."

She handed him a glass, and he kissed her hand when he took it.

"Georgie Boy, these women will be the death of us."

"I will have survived the heart attack, only to succumb to the nagging of the womenfolk," Dad agreed.

"What's on your mind, Lilybug?" Uncle Dave asked.

"Same thing that's on everybody's mind," I sighed. "How we gonna get Poppy's back on track? Here's my idea. Let me find someone to manage it. Someone reliable who can take care of the day-to-day. We'll get the regular crew back to the ovens, so the new person doesn't really even need to know about baking. Just managing. Scheduling deliveries, money in, money out, the basics."

"Well," Millie looked over her glasses at the two she always referred to as "the boys." Clearly, the three of them had a pre-meeting meeting before I got here.

"Lily," Dave took over. "We've been thinking about selling Poppy's."

Now, this brilliant idea had not once occurred to me, and just as I was about to throw my weight behind it, I saw the slightest sag settle on Dad's face. A stab of guilt donkey-kicked my family loyalty, and I said, "Let's try my idea first. For one thing, if we decide to sell—and I'm not saying that's a terrible idea—seems like it would be more lucrative to sell an operational bakery than a shuttered one." Believe me, no one was more surprised at this line of thinking than yours truly.

We went over a few logistical issues, like where I would find this so-called manager, but basically the family meeting was adjourned. Millie and I made our way to the kitchen where she could shower me with motherly love, unobstructed by "the boys." After dinner, she packed me a week's supply of fried chicken and potato salad loaded into a small loaner Igloo cooler. Whether she planned this menu on purpose or not, I appreciated that these were foods I could eat cold. Less time in the kitchen meant more time devoted to the tasks at hand. I didn't mention it to these three, but one of those tasks would be getting back on the Doe Network later tonight.

In addition to the cooler, there was a tote bag full of perishable and non-perishable provisions, including coffee, sugar, home-baked bread, peanut butter, cheese, apples, cookies, Cap'n Crunch, and a big bag of Route 11 potato chips. I could only think of five things that would round out the larder: coffee creamer, milk, Popsicles and beer, all available at the Cumquat, a local mini grocery store conveniently located on the way to Miss Delphine's. The fifth and possibly most important item was tequila, which I could get at the liquor store across the street from the Cumquat.

↘ 🐓 ↙

Easing the Jeep up to the house, I noticed movement on my little deck. Ah, it was Jack and Cro. I waved from the driver's side when I saw him, and he was down the stairs before I had the door opened. "How's she running?" he asked.

"Who?" I teased.

"The Jeep," he replied. I had a feeling he knew where this was going.

"Call her by her name," I said, the sing-songy lilt of my words dripping with honey.

"Sandi," he sighed. "How's Sandi running?"

"Say the whole thing," I simply could not resist.

"Sandi-with-an-i," he got it out. Grudgingly.

"She's running like a master mechanic checks under the hood every chance he gets." Which was true. Jack sold the sand-colored Jeep to my dad two years ago. His was the only family dad would consider buying a used car from because they took care of their vehicles. You could see for yourself down at Turner's Auto Repair where at least one of the two brothers and/or Mr. Turner would be wrenching on their own cars or trucks after hours any day of the week. Jack still worked part-time at the garage to compensate for the teensy-weensy salary the township of Marshall offered its public servants down at the firehouse.

Taking the heaviest things to carry, Jack grabbed the cooler and the tote. I collected the smaller bags from Cumquat's Grocery and the liquor store. "My Popsicles are melting," I said in a panic that was only half joking. "Like my porch?" I asked, dashing up the stairs.

"May be one of my all-time favorite porches," he said. "Definitely in my top ten."

I smiled and asked, "What are you doing here? This is date night if you're not on duty." I was happy to get back to what I considered a more normal ebb and flow with him.

"You said you wanted to show me that creepy website," he reminded me.

"Seriously? You want to see it?" I couldn't disguise my enthusiasm. "I've been itching to go back on for the last two hours. I wonder if there's an app for my phone so I could pull it up when I'm away from the computer, like tonight."

"You told Millie about it?" He sounded shocked.

"Are you crazy? Those three have enough to worry about. They don't need to be psychoanalyzing my morbid hobby." Plopping my bag on the vintage chrome dinette, I took the Popsicles and the tequila and made a beeline for the freezer. While I was in there, I noticed the ice trays. Absently, I dumped the cubes into the sink and filled the trays from the spigot. Nobody likes stale ice, especially me. Ice cubes handled, I threw the creamer, milk and beer in the fridge. "Can you put that chicken and potato salad in here while I get my computer?"

"Chicken?"

"Have it. Millie's. You know it's good."

I carried my computer and two beers to the porch, where Cro was still stretched out. Jack followed with three pieces of chicken and a mound of potato salad. He was a fast eater. He said it was a rite of passage for all firefighters—you only had to miss one meal because of an alarm, and you'd never do that again. He missed his first meal his first day on the job. Jack is nothing if not a quick study. The pile of food was consumed by the time I pulled up the site. He held the laptop while I scooted my chair directly beside his. Pushed together, the wide armrests of the Adirondack chairs made a nice little platform for the Mac. Cro wasn't pleased with the ruckus, but he managed to adjust.

Ordinarily I'd ask Jack what happened today at the garage. It was usually a circus down there. If any of the mechanics cared to post videos of the mishaps, I'm sure they would go viral. I skipped the pleasantries today, though, because the Doe Network had my undivided attention.

"Okay. Where would you like to start?"

"What are my choices?"

"Do you want to see unidentified murder victims in chronological order or in geographical order?"

"What would you recommend, Miss Plum?" He teased, knowing how much I loved the Janet Evanovich series. Over the years he had given me at least half a dozen of the books for various gift-giving occasions.

"I like geographical. It's interesting to see how some states have dozens of unidentified victims while others have none. Want to start with the good ol' Commonwealth?"

"I can't think of a state whose unidentified dead bodies I'd rather see more than those of our own citizens."

In my element, his sarcasm was lost on me. "You realize that not all these bodies are from the states in which they were found," I advised, seriously.

"No," he said, faking sincerity, "I did not realize that. Good thing I have you as a tour guide for this gruesome experience. Otherwise, how would I figure it out?"

I gave him a sour look. "I just fed you, and now I'm about to entertain you. So, you could say this is dinner and a show. A little gratitude would be nice."

"You're right." He put a hand on my forearm. I gave the hand a secret, sideways glance but it was completely innocuous. "So next time, the food and entertainment are on me. And since you're picking the entertainment tonight, I'll be in charge for round two."

That sounded like a minefield, so I skirted around it. "Whatever," I said, twisting the computer so he could clearly see the screen. I scrolled down row after row of profile pictures—black silhouettes where no image was available, artist renditions, pieces of distinctive clothing and tattoos—finally stopping at the heading *Virginia*. "Here they are. These are all the males found in Virginia. The females are on a different tab." Jack looked at the computer, narrowed his eyes and let his head go half an inch closer to the screen. I could see he was taking it in, and he had a hard time making sense of it. He stopped on a picture of the reconstructed head of an Asian victim who was discovered on September 19, 1984, (Case File 252UMVA). "Click on the picture to see the stats," I suggested.

He read off things that struck him, "Fruit-of-the-Loom briefs, tattoos on his fingers, blood type A positive, good quality dentistry. What does that mean? He brushed his teeth?"

"Exactly. And got checkups. The dental records are one of the ways you can identify a body," I said, stating the obvious.

"What do the numbers mean?"

"His Case File is 252UMVA. He is the 252nd man, UM means unidentified male, and VA means located in Virginia."

Jack clicked on the profile picture of a tattoo, Case File 1824UMVA. There was no artist's rendition or reconstructed facial features for this guy, just a heavy, black tattoo of a Doberman Pinscher with the inscription *Capone 2-14-92.*

"Lily, I gotta say, this is weird even for you."

"Oh, Jack. Do you really wanna tug at that thread?" I'd be the first to admit I have a dark side. While some women hid vibrators or stashed erotica, I had a hidden copy of a crime scene text book from the 80s used in training police officers. *Practical Homicide Investigation, Tactics, Procedures, and Forensic Techniques, Third Edition.* It depicted graphic photos of actual human remains, not post-medical-examiner, doctored-up ones like this website.

"I admire how you own your crazy."

"Do you want to see the women?" I asked.

"I always want to see the women," he leered. I told myself not to pick every statement to pieces. Jack and I had always had a kind of mildly raunchy, give-and-take, probably because there were never any intimacy complications. In my mind, we were like two guy friends. This was just normal banter, but after the comments last night and this morning, I still worried a little.

I switched over to the unidentified females and jumped down to *Florida.* I wanted to show him the woman with the flower tattoo. Clicking on the picture of her tattoo, I said, "I call her Misty."

"You named her?"

"She deserves a name, even if it's the wrong one for now."

He tilted his head, and said, simply, "Okay." There was a note of genuine acceptance, maybe respect, as he said it. Respect for Misty.

I wanted to continue exploring the site, learning their stories or at least the endings to their stories, but I could see Jack was saturated. Not everyone had my capacity for these kinds of things. I clicked the computer screen closed and took a swallow of beer.

"I've been watching you watching me since you got home."

Stephanie to Lily—improve upon subterfuge.

"I know what's on your mind, Lily," he continued. "So let's talk about it."

"I don't want to," I said honestly.

"I understand that."

Waiting me out, he sat there. It was a game he played. The first person to speak, lost. I wasn't as comfortable in the no-man's land of long awkward pauses as he was. I always lost. This time, I predicted, would be no exception.

I uncrossed and recrossed my legs. Jack ran a thumb back and forth over an upturned corner of the label on his beer bottle. I pulled my ponytail loose and twisted my brown hair into a knot. Jack took a drink from the bottle. I flicked a blade of grass off the toe of my flip flop. Jack stared out at the horizon. I swatted at a mosquito on my calf. Jack kept staring at the horizon. I knew how this little performance looked—he was over there, still as Mount Rushmore, and I was over here, doing calisthenics. I lasted a full two minutes before cracking under the pressure.

With a barely audible huff, I conceded. "What is it you want to say?"

He smiled as I smacked another mosquito. "Let's go inside. The mosquitoes don't get to dictate the pace of our discussion."

I rolled my eyes, privately, so he couldn't see. From his statement, it was clear *he* wanted to dictate the pace of our conversation, which didn't bode well for me. At least it would be a physical relief to leave the mosquitoes outside.

I put our beer bottles on the kitchen sink since I hadn't yet identified a recycling receptacle and got two more from the fridge. He reached for one, screwed off the top, bent the cap in half, and sent it flying with a snap of his fingers. I could tell without looking that it hit the garbage can. Moving over to the little living area, I was drawn to the far end of the couch, which is where I landed after pushing the macramé pillows to the floor.

Jack came into the living room and sat smack-dab in the middle of the couch. Without saying anything, I made a show of looking around him at the other comfortable chair across from the coffee table, the less comfortable one in the corner, the far end of the couch, and finally back at him, hoping my body language would do the trick. He smiled his lopsided grin but didn't move.

"You're kinda crowding me."

"I know," he assured me.

"Why?"

"This discussion is already making you uncomfortable, and we haven't even started talking yet. When you're uncomfortable, you tend to take flight. I'm sitting close to keep you in one place, so we can actually finish the conversation."

I traded my unopened beer for his opened one. Why rip up my own palm twisting off a bottle cap when there's somebody willing to do it for me? Don't get me wrong, if there was no one else around, I'd make it happen. Sinking back into the smoosh of the couch, I caught myself judging the space between the coffee table and the wall. "See what I mean?" he said, quietly. "You're looking for an escape route already." He loosely held onto my wrist as he talked.

"I'm sitting down. I'm sitting still," I said, maybe a little too defensively. "What would you like to talk about?"

"Our relationship."

"So, a status report?"

"No," he said. "More like a to-do list."

Thinking I could expedite this by cutting to the chase, I said, "Is sex on the list of things to do?"

"That's one of the things I'd like to talk about." *One?* Oh, for the love of the donkey in the manger.

"There's more than one thing you want to talk about?"

"Lily, I want to date."

I nearly choked on my beer. "You want to date *who*?" I asked, thinking he must have someone else in mind.

"You," he said flatly.

A prickle of panic started to pinch my stomach. "I thought we were talking about sex."

"We are. But that's a little further down on the to-do list."

I waited. He waited.

"Jack, that's a terrible idea. Sex itself is a terrible idea, but dating? *Dating*?"

I bounced up, surprising both of us at the microburst of speed that allowed my wrist to slip through his grip before he could tighten his fingers. Exactly why I always identified an escape route, thankyouverymuch. Darting between the wall and the coffee table, I stood behind the big chair opposite him. Feeling more protected now that I had something between us, I repeated, "It's a terrible idea."

Not known for speed or grace, I was acutely aware he could have easily gotten around my blockade and hauled me back to the couch, but for some reason he decided not to make any sudden moves. Maybe he was afraid I'd do something drastic, like take a flying leap out the window, just to put an end to the conversation.

"Tell me," he said very calmly from the couch, "why you think it's a terrible idea."

"There are so many reasons," I said, fully exasperated at this point. "How much time do you have."

He looked at his watch, pretended to do a calculation in his head, then said, "I've got thirty-six hours. Plenty of time."

I shook my head, and just as I was about to break out some of my most colorful language, he said, "Ok, give me just one reason why it's a bad idea. Let's start with one reason."

I took a deep breath, trying to decide which of the three dozen immediately obvious reasons would be the worst. "You're my best friend, Jack. I don't want to ruin that."

"I don't either," he said. He sounded sincere, like he realized what was at stake. He was moving toward me, which was odd, since it didn't register that he had gotten off the couch. I stayed behind the chair. He kept the chair between us but came a little closer. "I know you trust me, Lily. We have a long history of trusting each other with big and little things, don't we?"

I didn't have to delve too deep into the recent past to come up with a couple of examples. Like the time I thought I might be pregnant. I came home for a weekend visit to talk to Jack about it. He always solved things logically, and I knew he would approach this the same way. At his place, after I revealed the scary prospect, he hugged me while I cried, and he didn't let go until I let go first. Then he drove me all the way to Haymarket to pick up a home pregnancy test at the Walgreens. When I couldn't bring myself to go in, he left me in the truck and returned minutes later with an EPT and a bag of plain M&Ms. It turned out I wasn't prego, but Jack was the person I trusted in that moment.

"Until about ninety seconds ago, which is apparently when you lost your ever-lovin' mind, I trusted you with my life."

He smiled. "You can still trust me with your life. That hasn't changed. And I know I can trust you. That's what will make this work."

"That'll make what work?"

"Dating." He paused, as if he wanted to add something but didn't.

One thing became crystal clear. I had to stop the momentum of this conversation and quick-like if I had any hope of regaining control of this runaway train. Perfect time for a pee break. I was known far and wide as having the smallest bladder this side of the Mississippi, so even if I didn't actually have to go, it still would have been believable.

"I have to pee." I tried to make myself sound poised. As poised as was possible given the topic of bathroom necessities.

Jack stepped to the side to let me pass. He didn't say a word.

When I came out of the bathroom, he was still standing near the chair. I caught myself moving toward the couch. *Whoa, baby,* I thought, *don't wanna make that mistake again.* Instead, I twirled and plopped in the chair, feeling pleased that I bought myself a buffer zone. That didn't last long. He foiled my plan with a kitchen chair, put it too close to my knees and sat down in front of me. He was a worthy adversary, this one.

"We've established that we trust each other, and that neither of us will let anything damage our friendship." So much for stopping the train.

"Jack," I started.

"Lily," he cut me off, "let me just explain what will happen, so you know what to expect. Then, fear of the unknown won't be one of the reasons you're afraid."

I listened in disbelief, still amazed that we were on this road at all.

"First, you know how we touch—hold hands, hug, stuff like that?" To illustrate his point, he picked up my left hand with his right hand. And, true to his word, it was the touch of my old friend. "I'll still touch you like this. I love these touches." It made me smile, because I loved them, too. Involuntarily I squeezed his hand in response. "Some of the touches will feel different though, more intense. They'll have a different meaning behind them."

Again, he illustrated his point. Keeping my hand in his, he moved his thumb under my bracelet and lightly traced a squiggly line across the delicate skin of my inner wrist. Following his thumb with my eyes, I wondered how my skin could feel on fire when he had barely touched me. I turned my head to look at him and realized he had been watching me instead of my hand. Suddenly self-conscious, I pulled my arm away, and he let me.

"How did that feel?" he asked.

"I have to pee again," I said helplessly.

"Okay." He stood up and reached down for my hand. I narrowed my eyes, trying to determine what kind of touch would follow, but he read my mind. "This is the old way, not the new way."

He pulled me up but stayed in front of me, pinning me between the chair and his chest. "I'd stay all night, but I know you need some space. Will you come over for dinner tomorrow?"

Cooking me dinner was the least he could do after inflicting all this trauma. "Yes," I said, a little too weakly.

"Now," he said in a low voice, "this will be the new kind of touch." Before I could get a word out, he laid a hand on the side of my neck, resting his thumb in that little pocket at the base of my throat, and moved his lips inches from mine. My eyes were huge and I was afraid to take a breath, so I stayed frozen.

"This is uncomfortable because it's new and unexpected, so let's just take our time figuring it out. I'd never give you up as a friend, Lily. Now, lock the door when I leave, okay?" I nodded the tiniest bit. He didn't kiss me, which was a huge relief. And, simultaneously, a surprising disappointment.

Chapter 3

No matter what I did for the rest of the night, I couldn't get comfortable. I didn't want to sit down, so I paced. I got tired of pacing, so I ate. It was too hot to eat, so I cranked up the window unit. When it got cold, I pulled out a multi-colored afghan.

This annoying restlessness bothered me the way putting on a wet bathing suit bothers me. I hate dragging up that swath of cold, clammy, clingy lycra which doesn't sit right until you can submerge again in a big body of water. I sat there, feeling squirmy in this imaginary wet bathing suit and tried to figure it all out.

What was the problem? Was I really so opposed to a physical relationship? I'd been in plenty up until now. I wouldn't call myself easy, but I'd had my fair share of boyfriends. Was it because I didn't want to date Jack? Or, for the love of chocolate chip ice cream, did I secretly *want* to date Jack?

I wracked my brain trying to think of a time when I might have had a crush on him. Or even a time when I was jealous of any of his beauty-contestant girlfriends. I honestly couldn't lay a finger on one single time. He had been in the brother-zone for so long. Plus, the more he dated, the more beautiful the women got, putting me in a very different category this past year.

Interestingly, the guys I dated were opposite him as well. Most of them talked endlessly about their accomplishments—swinging a hammer on a Habitat for Humanity job site, landing a trophy bonefish in the Keys, dragging a knee in a motorcycle race. Coincidentally, these big talkers were mostly big drinkers. More drinking than doing, if you wanted to get right down to it. Was that the way with all college boys? In comparison, Jack worked on all manner of fixer-upper construction projects; he fished, and as much as I hated it, hunted. Odd how little he actually talked about any of those activities. More doing than bragging, in his case.

This was a futile exercise, like kneading imaginary dough—pushing a single thought back and forth across a flour-dusted countertop without so much as the promise of biscuits at the end. Why not abandon the dough in favor of the *doe*? Smiling at my clever segue, I opened my computer on the kitchen table and went directly to the last site visited. First stop was Misty's profile. I read over the stats again and spent a moment with the sorrow. "What happened to you, Misty?" I waited, but she didn't answer.

Needing a little positive energy, I moved to the "updates" tab. Whenever my optimism went to battle with my realism, the realist stepped on her sister's rose-colored glasses every time. Which is why I knew I wouldn't see Misty's case had been one that got solved. Besides, if it had been solved, there would be a bold purple banner across her picture declaring that the victim had been identified. I really just wanted to see that somebody had actually been identified.

One somebody was Case File 725UFCA. Found on June 8, 1968, the slight woman in her twenties had brown eyes and bleached blond hair like Marilyn Monroe. She died sitting at a picnic table in a park wearing a red and white polka dot bikini, a trench coat, and sandals. Her fingernails were manicured, and she wore a wedding band with an inscription "C.B. to E.J. 9-4-20." As a twenty-something in the 60s, the date on the wedding band probably meant it had belonged to the victim's grandma or someone of that generation, great aunt maybe. Almost fifty years later, a woman named Rita Hood used the Ancestry website to sift through marriage certificates of people with the initials on the ring, discovering that Edna Lydia Jay married Charles J. Bush in Detroit on Sept. 4, 1920. This information led her to positively identify the Jane Doe as Cheryl Ann McMillan.

Holy roly poly! How does that happen? How does a middle-aged accountant and mother of two, with apparently no background in forensic science and no police training, solve a cold case from that long ago? She described herself as an amateur genealogist who researched the initials in her spare time, when her kids were in bed. It took her four weeks to find a marriage record that matched the initials in the ring, then she started tracking down relatives from there. I momentarily considered changing the name of my alter-ego from Stephanie Plum to Rita Hood.

Still tired from slogging through profile after profile the night before, I yawned, stretched, and decided it was time to spend a night in the actual bed. After my short bedtime routine, I padded into the kitchen for a drink of water. Taking a glass from the cabinet, I ran my thumb over the engraved *T* and wondered whose name started with *T*. Not Delphine Walker. Unless Walker was her married name. Maybe she was Delphine Tate before she married Stanley Walker. Still thinking it through, my eyes landed on the shelf of other glasses. There was a *C*, a *Q*, a *B*, an *R* and an *F*. What in the name of the Wiffle Ball Championship was Miss Delphine up to? My mind flashed back to the flower bed and her reference to the murderous intentions of the human heart. Was she killing the tenants and inscribing a glass with each one's initial? Carlton, Quincy, Buster, Ruby, and Felix? Was there a glass down at Things Remembered in the mall with my initial on it, waiting for pick up?

My phone *cha-chinged*, and I glanced to see a text message from Jack. "Go to bed."

"Maybe you just woke me up."

Cha-ching: "I know you. And I know what you're doing."

It was hard to refute that. So I didn't try. "See you tomorrow for dinner."

I connected the phone to the charger, laid it on the nightstand, and fell into the bed, which registered "Marshmallow" on the firmness chart. While I didn't need "Hardwood Floor," something in the "Chaise Lounge" range would have been nice. It must not have bothered me though, because the next thing I knew, the chickens were making their morning ruckus. How many roosters does one flock need?

Rolling out of bed in a t-shirt and pink pajama pants, I found my flip flops, armed myself with a beat-up broom from the kitchen and headed out. As expected, McNugget was parked at the bottom of the stairs. With each step, I let the broom handle bang on the wood, thinking the clatter would be enough of a nuisance to rattle a tiny chicken brain. When it wasn't, I switched over to Kendo-mode and swung the broom over my head. Losing track of the top-heavy sweeping end, it crashed against the siding, slipped out of my fingers, and clattered to the ground. Mission accomplished. McNugget half-ran-half-flew fifteen yards away, and I made a break for the garage door. Since I had left the broom where it fell, I was now without a weapon, so I scanned the garage for another Shinai-style stick. Everything seemed overkill, but I finally settled on a rusty hoe. At the very least, I could decapitate my opponent should the necessity arise. Sticking with the dump-and-run method of spreading the scratch, I got myself away from the gathering gang of feathered freaks as quick as a pimple on prom night.

ↄ 🐔 ↄ

Delphine stopped pouring coffee from the pot in her hand and stared out the kitchen window. "I believe her medication needs to be adjusted," she said aloud, as much to herself as to Cro. The dog responded with a low *harrumph* sound.

After logging onto some sites that offered up qualified prospective employees suited to any job imaginable, I had a list of people who might work as bakery managers. I didn't reach out via email yet because I liked to chew on stuff before committing. Speaking of chewing, it felt like lunch time. Before I rummaged in the fridge for my leftovers, I thought I'd pay Miss Delphine a quick visit to ask about laundry privileges.

I saw a head bopping back and forth by the kitchen window, so I knocked on the door and pushed it open six inches. "Miss Delphine?" I hollered, still not sure how well she could hear. Judging from the metallic clatter, it sounded like silverware being sorted into the silverware drawer.

"Lily, child, you hungry?" she asked. "I'm fixin' to make myself a peanut butter sandwich." I closed the door behind me, happy to be back in the air conditioning. How fortuitous. I was hungry and she was making lunch.

"The glasses are in the cabinet to the left of the sink. Tea's in the fridge." I set about my task, dropping ice cubes into two tall glasses decorated with colorful cartoon fish. For the record, there were no monogrammed drinking glasses on the shelf. Meanwhile, she collected the implements for lunch—bread, peanut butter, jam, two plates and a butter knife.

Sitting down at the wooden table, she unscrewed the plastic top on the Jif, revealing an untouched freshness seal. When she plunged the knife into the foil covering, she smiled and looked up. "I imagine that's the closest thing to stabbin' flesh, don't you?"

I was shocked, and incredibly justified in my assessment that this bat was prone to murder and/or prone to crazy. I did a quick risk analysis to assess any immediate danger to myself. She was old and in possession of a fairly dull butter knife. However, she was sitting between me and the back door. If she lunged, I'd have to dart toward the foyer, and who knew if the front door was unlocked. For now, I cautioned myself to stay alert.

She either didn't notice my alarm, or, and this was way less likely, I did an excellent job of disguising it. Regardless, she didn't skip a beat. Bread on plates, a smear of pb followed by a blob of j, and I had my sandwich. Wowed by the jam, I forgot all about the coming attempt on my life.

"Did you make this jam?" I asked, my mouth a little slow from the peanut butter.

"Of course I did. And it's not jam; it's jelly," she corrected.

"Isn't it strawberry?" I asked.

"Well, it's good to know your taste buds aren't dumb." The not-so-complimentary compliment took a second to register, probably because other aspects of me were, in fact, dumb. "Yes," she confirmed. "It's strawberry."

"I've never had strawberry jelly before."

"That's because it's too much work. And no one for three generations has been willin' to assert that kind of hot, sticky, time-consumin', jelly-makin' initiative. You have to strain every single seed out of the berry mush. Strawberry seeds are the tiniest of the seeds. Near impossible to get 'em all." She pushed the jar over to me. "I dare you to find one seed."

I held the Ball jar up to the light. The sun coming in the kitchen window hit the glass, creating a magical pink glow. It washed over the half-eaten sandwiches and bounced off the ice tea. I was enchanted until a cloud shifted outside, disrupting the sunbeam. The glow vanished from sight. And she was right, not a seed in the jar.

"Miss Delphine, this is the most magnificent, seedless jelly I've ever had."

She smiled and nodded her acceptance. "Take a jar with you."

And so it would appear that any prospective murderer could buy me off if the jelly was good. I've heard everyone has a price, and I guessed mine was strawberry jelly.

As we enjoyed our sandwiches, I told her a little about my attempt to locate a bakery manager. She asked about the qualifications of the prospects and gave me some not-so-bad ideas.

I walked the dishes to the sink and started washing. I never minded washing dishes. I remember my mama used to tell me it was because I was part mermaid, and mermaids liked anything to do with water. Why, I wondered, was my mama always showing up in this kitchen? I stayed on that thought for a minute more, then I asked her about the washing machine.

"The washer and dryer are right through there," she said, pointing to a door off the kitchen. "Use it whenever you need it. Don't let the soap run out. And don't bother my delicates."

I spent the hot part of the afternoon washing a load of laundry, sending emails out to people I wanted to interview for the bakery position, changing my toenails from Bohemian Blue to Lady of the Night Red and looking at profiles on the Doe Network. Around four, I started feeling bored and texted Jack. Regardless of the big pink pachyderm between us, I still loved hanging out with him.

"Whatcha doin?"

Cha-ching: "Cooking your dinner."

"Can I come now?"

Cha-ching: "Yep."

"Did you fix that pothole yet?"

Cha-ching: "Nope. Not my pothole anymore."

"What are you talking about?"

Cha-ching: "I sold the trailer."

"Where do you live?"

Cha-ching: "1212 Wisteria Lane"

"The Candy Lady's house?!?!?!? It's haunted!"

Cha-ching: "It's not haunted. Come on over."

A life that included this man in any way, shape or form, was clearly becoming more and more arduous. Dating a guy I may or may not want to date was one thing. Dating a guy who lived in a haunted house was pushing the outer limits of what could be considered reasonable and acceptable.

We were nine or ten when I encountered the Candy Lady face-to-face. The neighborhood lore among the elementary-aged kids wove a tale of a sweet, old woman who never married or had children. To fill her void, she kept a bowl of candy by the door, and any child who knocked for any reason was given a treat. As the story went, the candy was the good stuff. One evening, I convinced Jack to walk up to the house with me and ring the bell. The cottage sat back from the street in a part of the neighborhood where houses were much farther apart. It was hidden behind big evergreen trees, giving it a spooky feel.

The bell chimed, and we waited. I was getting more and more nervous, but Jack was cool as a grape Popsicle. When the door creaked opened, we were greeted by the oldest, scariest-looking woman I'd ever seen.

So startled by her appearance, I screamed, jumped off the porch, ran to the street and took off for the creek. Jack found me at our rock-skipping place about fifteen minutes later, having stayed to explain why we were disturbing her and what we wanted. He had two cookies in his hand.

"Where'd the cookies come from?" I asked.

"Miss Brown. I told her the story. She said she had no idea people called her the Candy Lady and that no one had ever come to her door asking for candy before. She gave me these cookies to make up for not having any candy." He handed me one of the oatmeal butterscotch cookies.

No matter how nice he said she was, I was convinced that A) she was a witch, and B) the place was haunted. Funny how an inaccurate piece of childhood history could stick with you to adulthood and threaten to ruin a free meal. Hateful ghosts. I grabbed my keys and the jar of strawberry jelly and headed to Wisteria.

The place looked as creepy as I remembered it, and a non-creepy Jack looked so out of place on the front porch. I pulled into the driveway, and, as always, he was there to open my door.

"Where'd you get jam?" He asked, smiling.

"It's not jam," I said, prepared to dazzle him with my new knowledge. "It's strawberry jelly. Miss Delphine strains out every single strawberry seed. You're gonna love this stuff." As I faced the house, I faltered.

He draped a friendly arm around me. "It's not haunted. I promise."

"It feels haunted."

"You mean it felt haunted when you were ten."

"Didn't it feel haunted to you, too? Tell me why, in the name of the ill-fated Susan B. Anthony coin, did you buy it?" I turned toward him, looking expectantly.

"Well, I didn't exactly buy this property."

"What?"

"I inherited it."

"What are you talking about? This was the Candy Lady's house, who, I'm pretty sure, if memory serves, was a witch."

"Remember when we went up to her door that day to ask for candy?"

"Vividly," I said with renewed emphasis.

"After you ran, I stayed to talk with her. She gave me the cookies, remember?"

"That was the first time you ever met her, right? You didn't know her. She wasn't related to you."

"You're right on all three counts," he said. I noticed he was kind of herding me toward the porch, so I dug my heels in a little harder, waiting for the full explanation.

"That was the first time I ever met her, but not the last. She asked if I'd cut her grass. My dad wouldn't let me charge her because she was old and didn't have anyone. He paid me twenty bucks every week to do it, so I wouldn't lose out on the deal, and I added her yard to my weekly rotation."

"She was one of your yards?"

"For years. Until the day she died. Come to find out, she left the house to me in her will." Sorry, but I had to cut in at this point.

"A *witch*…left her *haunted house*…to you…in her *will*." I emphasized the important words so he could hear how bizarre this all sounded.

"If you replace 'witch' with 'sweet old lady' and 'haunted house' with 'house,' then yes, your sentence rings true. It's been tied up in probate for almost two years. I tried to give it to my parents. Didn't feel right taking it on false pretenses. I didn't have a generous bone in my body when I was a kid."

I could, without thinking too hard about it, name a dozen times Jack had done something generous for me as kids. That wasn't the thing to focus on right now, though. He kept talking, "Dad said he didn't have the energy for a project like this. Joe said he didn't have the patience for it. So here I am. You gotta admit, it's better than the trailer."

Jack bought a grubby, old, worn-out fishing trailer when he was in high school with the money he saved apparently cutting the grass of local haunted houses. Anything had to be better than that cricket-infested trailer. "Let me just give you a tour before you decide. This house has great bones."

"Humph," I said. "Bones? Sounds more like skeletal remains to me."

"Speaking of which, how are things on the Doe Network?"

He knew how to wear me down. "Things are good. I looked today at an old case that was solved by an accountant who farts around on one of those genealogy websites. The sequence of events that led to the positive identification was unbelievable."

And that's how he got me on the porch and through the front door, a distraction about as discreet as the "Hot Now" sign on any Krispy Kreme store. Stephanie would have been so ashamed.

Chapter 4

Standing in the foyer of a house whose haunting had not been thoroughly debunked, I reached back for him. He took my hand exactly the way I needed him to—his grip was strong and supportive, without the shenanigans of tracing little lines and circles on my wrist like the last time.

"Do you have a flashlight?"

"There's electricity," he assured me.

"Yeah, until the polter-people disrupt the power. And you know they will."

"Polter-people?"

"It's an all-inclusive term for the poltergeist community. You know. Spirits. Entities. Demons. Devils. What have you," I explained, then redirected, "Um. The flashlight?"

"Lily, I have a flashlight in the kitchen. Do you need it now, in broad daylight, or do you just want it ready for later?"

"Ready for later is fine, as long as you know where it is."

We continued with the walking tour of the house, and I consciously did not let go of his hand. It was the old way of touching, and it was comfortable. I wouldn't admit it out loud, but the place had a certain charm. He had apparently inherited all the furnishings, so in its current state, it looked like a gram still lived here.

"I like your decorating style," I joked, as we surveyed the living room. "The doilies suit you." I smiled and pointed to a series of crocheted pink and white doilies draped across the mantle like bunting.

"Easy, scaredy-cat, or I'll drop this hand, and you'll have to fend off the goblins all by yourself." I didn't think he would, but I tightened my grip two degrees anyway.

There was a beautiful old sleigh bed in the master bedroom with a white chenille spread. Jack was never one to make a bed or pick up blue jeans off the floor, so I wondered if he was sleeping in this bedroom. Since I was a little sensitive to bed-related topics at the moment, I didn't draw attention to it.

The kitchen was dated and looked a lot like Miss Delphine's. Pale yellow Formica countertops matched the pale-yellow linoleum floor. The staircase in the foyer had a beautiful, polished banister and was wide enough to walk two abreast with room on each side. I hesitated at the foot, but he didn't. The first step creaked, and I froze.

He stepped back to where I stood on the hardwood floor. "It's not haunted, Lily." His quiet voice was patient.

"What kind of energy do you feel here?"

"I feel electric air conditioning and gas heat," he said, with just a shade of sarcasm.

"I mean…do you ever feel upset for no reason? Do you feel angry? That could be related to spirits roaming the property. And not just the Candy Lady. There could be spirits that predate her."

"I feel like I'm home when I'm here," he said.

"For real? More like home than the trailer?"

"Much more than the trailer. And you know how much I loved that place."

"More home than your actual home?"

"Almost as much."

That was just the right amount. No house should feel more like home than the place a person grew up. That would be a red flag where hauntings were concerned, as if the spirits were trying to lull you into a state of complacency before they scared you to within an inch of your life. Plus, any undead entity who had anger issues wouldn't waste a lot of time making a place feel too comfortable.

His answer about the homey feeling gave me fortitude. I took the creaky steps with improved confidence. Nothing out of place upstairs, so I didn't think Jack was staying in the spare bedroom or using that bath. That meant he went to the trouble of making the downstairs bed for my benefit. I needed to read something into that, I just didn't know what.

Together we walked back to the kitchen.

"What's for dinner?" I asked, suddenly feeling half-starved and smelling something delicious in the oven.

"Last time I checked the calendar, it was still August."

That meant one of two options if Jack was cooking: KFC and coleslaw or burgers on the grill and homemade baked beans. I didn't see evidence of a red and white bucket, so burgers then.

"I'm guessing we still have to cook the hamburgers?"

"We do. Unless the polter-person took care of it like I asked."

"Jerk." I punched in the direction of his arm, but he dodged, and I swung into the air.

"Kidding. And don't worry, I have cheese and crackers to tide you over. The beans will be done in an hour."

Jack got busy putting together cheese and crackers, and I went to the sink for a glass of water. Noticing a few dirty dishes in the basin, I soaped the sponge and started to do them.

Suddenly he was behind me and way too close. He took a sudsy mug from my hand, set it in the sink, and pushed my hands under the spigot to rinse the soap. My breath was dangerously shallow. When he turned the tap off, he produced a dish rag so I could dry my hands. Then, still standing behind me, he tossed it on the counter. Even though I was facing forward, I knew there wasn't a lot of space between our bodies. He wasn't touching me, but I felt his heat. He laid his hands on my shoulders, on each side of my neck. After a few seconds, he rubbed his thumbs lightly back and forth across the nape. My palms were stuck to the edge of the sink, and I'm pretty sure I stopped breathing altogether.

"You okay?" He asked.

I moved my head in a poor attempt to nod.

"Give me an audible," he whispered in my ear.

It required a small intake of air, but I croaked, "I'm okay."

"Tell me if you stop being okay," he said.

Since I didn't say I had stopped being okay, he moved his hands to cup the round part of my shoulders then slowly worked his way down my upper arms before dropping to my hips where they remained. Not wanting to move for fear of making the situation even more intimate, I stayed still as a lizard trying to decide which way to dart.

"Jack," I said.

"Yeah," he replied.

"I need two things, and you're not going to like either one."

"Is one of them a flashlight?" The comedy relief broke the tension and made me smile.

"No, but just so I know, where is the flashlight?"

He took half a step to the left, pulled out what I assumed was the junk drawer and pointed to a medium sized MagLite. That gave me just enough wiggle room to move half a step to the right and face him.

"Thanks. Good to know where the flashlight is. Now, the first thing I need is a shot of tequila to get me ready for the second thing—a full accounting of what in the name of Armageddon is going on here."

I could see him think, but he didn't speak. Instead, he went to the freezer, pulled out a bottle, and picked up a shot glass from the dish drainer. He carried both into the living room. I followed and sat on a round pink pleather ottoman opposite the polished coffee table. He poured a shot and put it on the table in front of me. Tossing it back, I contemplated a refill but decided against it. One would settle my nerves, two would get me yammering like a magpie.

"Thanks," I said. "Ok. It seems like you have something in mind here, which puts me at a serious disadvantage since I have no idea what it is or where it came from. Can you fill me in? What's with all the sensual crap?"

"It's a fair question." He thought for a bit. "I'm just not sure how much to tell you."

"How 'bout…oh…everything?" I said it with more self-confidence than I actually felt.

"Everything is a lot, Lily, and I don't know if you really want all that."

I waited, although patience had never been my best quality.

"Okay," I agreed. "Break 'everything' into two halves and start with the first half."

I saw an internal struggle behind those searing blue eyes. I saw him glance at the bottle between us, so I leaned forward and inched it toward him. He considered it but then shook his head no. Ah, brave Jack Turner. He always did have more natural courage than me. Probably why he became a firefighter.

Without any wishy-washy build up, he plunged into the deep like he was wearing waders. "Lily, I want to make love to you, and I've been fantasizing about it ever since you came home for fall break last year." Suddenly, I was there in the deep with him, only my waders were filling up with water, and I was flailing helplessly and sinking fast. He didn't stop to pull me out, though. "The fantasies have grown in number and intensity, until I've literally lost track of them. But it all starts with me undressing you. Slowly. It would take a good forty-five minutes to get you outta your clothes."

He kept his eyes riveted on me. Hard as I tried not to, I squirmed on the stool. I couldn't tell if I was embarrassed for myself, embarrassed for him, or completely turned on. He didn't bother to analyze it, though. "Then, with you completely naked, I'd spend another hour memorizing every inch of your body, even the things I already know by heart, like your scars and freckles."

My saliva felt like glue, and swallowing was hard at this point, but he didn't seem to notice. "At that point," his eyes narrowed a hair and took on an almost sinister glow, "using only my hands, I would conjure an orgasm the magnitude of which you never thought possible."

I looked toward him but not at him, hoping to appear bolder than I felt. "Are you still in the first half of 'everything,' or have you jumped ahead?" I asked.

"Darlin', I'm not even one tenth of the way through the first half of everything. It gets a whole lot dirtier from here." He stood slowly and held his hands up, palms out, the way you might if you were trying to show someone you were unarmed and therefore not a threat. The low footstool combined with my natural lack of athleticism put me in an awkward position with no option to retreat. He held out a hand, and when I didn't take it, he reached down and gently levered me up.

I tried to formulate a coherent protest, but he stopped me. "This is not the new touching; this is the old touching. I promise not to remove one article of clothing," he smiled and more quietly added, "until this is hashed out."

He led me to the couch and let me sit. Then he joined me, near but not too close, and he waited. I had a feeling we were in another one of his games to see who would move or speak first. Which, of course, I lost in about six seconds flat. "Where did this come from? What changed?"

"Remember when you came back last October? You were different. There was a quality I'd never seen before—you were free. Confident. It was smokin' hot. You picked up a pound or two and started wearing clothes that showed off your shape. That's when I started looking at your shape more closely. I was totally into the new you, but I didn't want to freak you out, so I sat on it. Suddenly, the women I had been drawn to weren't enough. I couldn't run my hands through their hair because it took them too long to fix it in the first place. I couldn't kiss them passionately because it would smear their lipstick. At any given moment, I was dating a cardboard cutout of a beautiful, sexy woman. I started to realize the picture wasn't enough anymore. I wanted a flesh and blood, beautiful, sexy woman. I wanted you."

In my mind, I scrambled back to last fall break, a little less than a year ago. What was going on at that time in my life?

"From that point forward, every time you came home, the feelings got more intense for me, but I could tell you didn't notice, which meant you didn't feel the same way. It was a very thin line."

Still dredging up the months leading to this so-called transformation, a realization started to crystalize in the way back of my brain. At the end of last August there was an annual music festival called Backroads out in Nelson County. I was already on campus for my work-study job, and friends decided we should make a weekend of it, camp, drink, smoke some pot, listen to the music. Never much of a camper, the alcohol, pot and music were reasons enough to tolerate the tent sleeping. I made some quick money helping a wedding photographer on a couple gigs so I could afford the heavy price tag of the three-day ticket then started amassing a collection of borrowed camping gear that would have put any Army surplus store to shame.

The festival landed in my favorite part of the hot summer. Minus the bugs and spiders, it was the perfect setting. An easy fellowship flowed through the tent community. Friendships were forged between complete strangers from all walks.

That first night sitting around a campfire, I saw a woman across from me. Over the course of an hour, an inexplicable force pulled us toward each other. She called it sideways gravity. Her name was Storie Sanders. She was a hiker, drifter, hippie, gypsy with long blond hair in two thick braids. She wore a thin, moss green knit hat. The ties that held her braids were decorated with tiny silver charms that made the purist, softest sound when she moved. She wore bracelets. Lots of bracelets. Leather, silver, beaded, string. Her eyes glowed like the picture of that Afghan girl from the cover of *National Geographic*. She wore a flimsy skirt down to her ankles and a gauzy tank top without a bra.

There was some kind of cosmic energy between us, and we spent that night, the next day, the next night and half of Sunday together. I'd never been interested in or even curious about a physical relationship with a woman, but we did everything I never knew I wanted to try, knowing it wouldn't last longer than the music festival. She was hiking the Appalachian Trail with a few companions, and when the festival broke up on Sunday, we kissed goodbye. She hiked south, and I went back to school with a new interpretation of myself as a sexual being.

Jack's hand on my knee couldn't have startled me more than if he'd stuck a pin in a balloon right next to my ear. I tried hard to remember the last thing he'd said, but I couldn't. Did he ask me a question? He was looking at me like he was waiting on an answer.

"I don't know where you went just now," he said, "but it seems like you enjoyed it."

"I might know what caused the change you noticed."

"I'm listening."

"Remember when you said you didn't think I was ready for everything you had to tell me? Well, I'm not sure you're ready for this."

"Oh, I've never been more ready for anything."

I licked my lips, cleared my throat, and took a step off what felt like a very high cliff. "I had sex...with...it was...well...a woman." By way of trying to offer some sort of meaningful explanation, I added, "Who was a complete stranger I met at Backroads. The music festival."

Jack looked like he just suffered a blow to the head, resulting in a concussion. I'm not sure I could have manufactured a sentence that would have culminated in more stars and birds circling his head than the truth I just revealed. The only thing that broke through the stunned silence was a tiny curve on his lips.

"Jack?" I said.

He didn't answer, just continued to hold me in a locked gaze that started to feel uncomfortable.

"So," I stammered, "that may have been the reason for the change you noticed."

"Oh, I guarantee it," he said. The tiny curve had developed into a full-fledged smile, but he still seemed stuck in the initial image.

"Well," I said, desperate for anything to move the conversation forward, "mystery solved, I guess."

"Not so fast," he stopped me. "I'm gonna need some details. I'm having a hard time putting these pieces together."

I'm not sure if he was seeking full disclosure in order to fill in the blanks or to create his own Playboy TV mini-series to revisit at a later date.

"What do you want to know?"

He handed me my own words from earlier in the conversation, "How 'bout…oh…everything?" Even mimicking the tone of voice I had used when I said it, which, I realized, was annoying.

I thought I could satisfy him and, at the same time, stick a wad of bubble gum into the crack that was quickly forming in this dam. My solution was a simple compromise. I made my offer. "I'll answer three questions. Shoot."

"Make it ten," he counter offered.

"Five," I negotiated.

"Nine."

"Six," I said.

"Eight."

"Seven," I offered.

"Eight." He smiled the smile of a man who felt confident his offer would be accepted.

But I wasn't ready to concede. "Seven," I said, more firmly. In response to my firm offer of seven questions, he moved his hand, which was still on my knee, ever so slightly, alluding to the fact there was a lot of territory he could cover beyond where his hand was currently stationed.

"Eight," I said, pushing away. "Okay. Eight questions. I'll answer eight."

He chuckled, and I made a mental note to handle this new Jack like a snake. "Ask your questions," I said, making no attempt to disguise the testiness in my voice. First, he reached across the table and poured himself a shot of tequila.

"So, now you're ready for a drink?"

"To steady my nerves for what I'm about to hear," he winked.

Knowing I wasn't going to make it through this without another shot myself, I reached for the bottle, but Jack poured it for me.

"Number one. What's the most erotic thing you did with her?"

I focused on the liquor burning my throat on the way down. After a little bit, I finally said, "It was all pretty erotic. That first night we took a walk, found a quiet place by the river and went skinny dippin'. I hadn't done it before, either alone or with another person."

"Lily, I can't tell you how turned on I am right now."

"You know, you're making this difficult."

"Yes, I do know that." He moved a tiny bit closer to underscore his point.

"So," I observed, "it's intentional."

He smiled, and his resemblance to a cartoon shark was uncanny. I narrowed my eyes, having no other response at the ready.

"Number two. How long did y'all stay in the water and did it turn into anything else while you were in the water?"

I was beginning to wonder what I was thinking when I agreed to answer his questions. I wasn't sure I had the guts to follow this through now that I had started. "That's two questions."

"Okay. Make it two and three, then."

"Sharing these details is a lot harder than I thought it would be." I was hoping he'd show me some mercy without me having to ask for it.

I saw his rodent brain working and knew he was cobbling together some kind of deal. "Care to renegotiate?"

"What are your terms?"

"Simple game of truth or dare. You can either answer the question I ask, or you can take a dare as your way out."

"What's an example of a dare?"

"I'm sorry. I'm not at liberty to discuss it unless you're actually selecting the dare."

"I'll agree, as long as I can reverse course if I don't like the dare."

"Reverse course? You mean go back and answer the question if you don't like the dare?"

"Yes."

"You know that's basically cheating."

"Be that as it may."

"Interesting. Tell you what I'm gonna do," he said in a cheeseball-used-car-salesman kind of way. "I'll give you an opportunity to reverse course one time. If you agree, I suggest you think carefully before using your reversal. Chances are, the dares will get tougher as we go along."

I really wanted another shot of tequila at this point, but I could see the whole scenario devolving into a warped version of strip poker if I wasn't careful. I licked my lips again, "I'll answer question number two."

"Excellent choice."

"We were in the water for about twenty minutes, maybe thirty."

"Nice," Jack mumbled under his breath, nodding his head, completely lost in the lesbian daydream.

I shot him a warning look but obviously had no way to back it up.

"You know question number three. Would you like to answer it or take the dare?"

I swallowed. "After we splashed around in the water for a bit, I reached for...her..." Unable to supply anything even remotely graphic, I summed it up with, "The water was...cold...and...she was...cold."

Jack was silent, probably because his head was about to explode. I privately acknowledged that his imagination was pretty good if he could fill in all those blanks, and I thanked the boogie-woogie blues that he didn't ask me to elaborate further.

"Question four. What happened next?"

I calculated my options. If I asked for the dare and didn't like it, I could answer this question. But that meant I would have four more tough questions or four more tough dares. I didn't think he would come up with dares that were over the top, given the fact that we were in uncharted territory, but I couldn't be sure. I was realizing I had no idea who this guy was.

"I'll take the dare."

He looked surprised and pleased. "I dare you to let me kiss you."

I sucked some air in through my nose and said, "I'll accept that dare, and since you didn't specify, you can kiss my cheek, neck or hand." Beyond pleased with my skills to ferret out a loophole, I was smug.

Jack nodded approvingly, picked up my hand and played with my fingers then leaned in to put his rough cheek against mine. Here he took a deep breath, smelling my hair or skin, one. I couldn't tell which. He grazed my neck with his lips until he found a spot he liked and lingered. It lasted too long and caused too much confusion. So, clearly the dare was a slippery slope.

"Number five, I'm sticking with the last question. Y'all splashed around." By way of letting me know that the holes in my sketchy description did not slip by unnoticed, he added, "Then…touched." Leering, he asked, "What happened next?"

Still reeling from the first dare, I opted for the question. "While I was…um…she, you know." Hoping I could end the answer there, I stopped.

Hanging on every word, he tipped his head expectantly. I didn't say anything.

"The rest of the answer?" he inquired.

"Is that the next question?" I asked.

"No. That's the rest of the current question."

I wasn't getting enough oxygen, so I took a breath and held it for a second. "She touched me."

The following question came quickly.

"Number six. What did she do next?"

I closed my eyes and asked for the dare.

"I dare you to let me kiss you on the mouth." To be honest, I knew it was coming. He wouldn't repeat the mistake of not specifying the target like he did the first time. I also knew after the neck thing I didn't have a lot left in the tank to manage much more than that.

"I'd like to use my option to reverse course on this dare."

"Completely within your rights. I feel obligated to remind you that this will be your one and only reversal. Question is the same—What did she do next?"

He didn't seem too upset that he wasn't going to kiss me. I guessed because there was a very real probability that the lip kiss would work its way back into the rotation. This stupid game still had two more levels.

"She…made it more intimate." I swallowed hard and closed my eyes mainly to avoid his eyes.

He let that sentence hang between us before presenting the next.

"Question seven. How did she make it more intimate?"

"I'll take the dare."

"Ahh. The shelf life of the last dare has expired. Now I dare you to kiss *me* on the lips."

"Wait. What?"

"I'll stay still. You have to kiss me. In fairness to you, I'll keep my mouth closed, so lips only."

This was playing dirty if you asked me. I acted like I needed a minute to collect myself, but I was really searching for another loophole. There was none to be found. I kind of had to twist around in order to reach his lips. By way of taking up more time, I rearranged myself completely until I was basically sitting cross-legged facing the back of the couch. He watched, and I'm certain I saw amusement in his eyes, but he didn't say anything. To assist, he scooted toward the edge of the couch so our faces were closer together. I leaned in, hesitated, and lightly touched my lips to his. There was a low moan, like someone just tasted a bite of the most delicious pecan pie, but I don't know if it came from him or from me. His hand reached up through my hair to hold my head in place for a few seconds, but true to his word, he didn't open his mouth or press back. My whole body reacted; it felt like when you're in the shower and you squeeze the washcloth so a long trail of soap bubbles slides down your skin. Now I was the one suffering the brain injury.

"Jack, I don't think I can finish this game."

"You can, slugger. You're doing great." He tucked a strand of hair behind my ear. "Last question. What did her body look like, from head to toe?"

That seemed easy. Was that a pity question? Who cared? Thank the sugar plum fairies for pity questions.

My vision blurred as I thought about Storie. "She had long blond hair in braids. Silver earrings. She was almost my same height, maybe an inch or two shorter. Her eyes were the kind of green that seemed lit from behind. Her skin was tan. She was lean and muscular. It was obvious she had done a lot of hiking. She had a pierced belly button. Her legs were beautiful. Strong. Graceful like a dancer. She had a tattoo on her left ankle. It was a flower."

She had a tattoo on her left ankle. It was a flower. In my mind, I was stuck on the tattoo. What was it about the tattoo? It was a purple flower. Wait. Oh! She had a tattoo of a purple flower on her left ankle. I nearly fell backwards off the couch and threw my arms out wildly trying to catch myself. Jack did the catching, steadied me, and said, "That's exactly how I feel."

"Jack." I was sure my voice sounded a little panicky. "Can I use your computer?"

"That's a weird transition. Usually when you're uncomfortable and feel like you gotta get out of something you use the bathroom." He wasn't wrong about that. And, come to think of it, I did have to pee. But this was way more important.

"I have to see Misty's profile on the Doe Network. I have to see the tattoo of the purple flower."

Chapter 5

"Am I hearing you right? You think the woman you had a fling with is the same person you saw on the Doe Network? The one who was decapitated in Florida?"

I was a little surprised he remembered that, but my panic was building to a crescendo, and I really didn't have time to reflect on it. "I don't know for sure. I gotta see that tattoo again."

Becoming aware that I was straining unnaturally, his rescue instincts kicked in. He took my shaking hands in his steady ones and said quietly, "It's okay. We'll take a look at it together. I'll get the computer." He waited until I made eye contact, then he followed with, "You're okay, Lily. Do you hear me?" I did. I nodded.

"Now do me a favor; take a slow, deep breath, hold it and exhale. Make it last for ten seconds."

I drew in the breath, the deepest one I'd taken in the last sixty minutes. Jack counted to ten, watching me. "I'll be right back."

Everything that had been building up to this minute was in the distant past. Just then, the timer on the oven dinged, signaling baked beans, and I remembered I had been hungry, but not anymore.

Could Storie Sanders possibly be the unidentified murder victim in Florida? Wrapped in a dirty old blanket and bound with duct tape? My Storie Sanders? Hiking Storie? Soulful Storie? Skinny dippin' Storie? Passionate Storie?

Computer in hand, Jack detoured through the kitchen to take the beans out of the oven. He was back on the couch in less than a minute. "You doin' okay?" he asked.

"Not exactly."

"You're alright," he reassured. "I got you, Lily."

The computer took forever to ramp up, then two times forever to connect. I put the blame for that squarely on the shoulders of the resident spirit. As a group, they were known to disrupt power sources. I didn't mention it to Jack, though, since I was already swimming in the shallow end of mental illness with this little episode.

He had pulled the coffee table closer to the couch so we could both see the computer screen. His screen saver caught my attention. It used to be a picture of him and a bunch of firefighters who did a 9/11 Memorial Stair Climb event. They traveled to NYC and climbed flights of stairs in full gear, remembering their brothers and sisters who perished in the Trade Towers that day. Now the screen saver was a picture of me, earlier this summer, hanging onto the rope swing down by the lake. I was out over the water, but I was clinging to the rope with a death grip, hair flying, eyes closed, look of sheer mortification on my face. We were with a bunch of friends, but I don't know who snapped the picture. I remembered Jack caught the rope when it swung back to land. I tried it three different times that day, but I never could let go over the water.

The memory faded as the internet connection came online, and I pulled up the website. It was obvious I had visited Misty's profile a lot. Within a few keystrokes, I was there. I clicked on the picture of the tattoo to enlarge it. Then I enlarged it again, but that only made the resolution wash out.

Jack waited, bouncing his gaze back and forth between my face and the screen. Finally, he asked, "Is that the tattoo?"

"I don't know. I don't know. It was a purple flower. There was some green in the background. I was aware of it, but, you know, I was in the middle of having sex with another woman. To be honest, the tattoo wasn't the focal point."

It seemed like he was picking his way carefully from one question to the next. He nodded then asked, "What was her name?"

"Her name is Storie Sanders." I consciously used the present tense to battle the bad vibes that were crashing in on me. "She was hiking the Appalachian Trail back then. I don't know who she was with or where she was from. She was traveling. She could have been from anywhere."

"Okay," he said. "Let's think this through. First of all, there's a chance that Storie is the woman on the website, but it's a pretty slim chance. There are thousands, probably tens of thousands of purple flower tattoos out there. You said she had a belly button ring, but there's no mention of that in the profile."

"Sometimes critical information is overlooked or inadvertently omitted. She may have taken it out. Maybe it was lost in the course of a stab wound." There was urgency in my voice even I could hear. It sounded like I was barreling toward a break down.

"Okay," he agreed and put his hand on my back. "Was there anyone else with y'all that weekend who might have talked to Storie's hiking friends? Would they remember a name or a place?"

"I'm not sure. Everyone was pretty drunk or high. A lot of people were both."

He thought. "Here's my suggestion. This is an intense development. Very different from the intense development we were experiencing a few minutes ago. I think we need to deal with one development at a time, and I can guess where your head is."

I must have been staring blankly, because he said, "You with me?"

I nodded, but I was most definitely not with him. I was with Storie.

"I also know you're not completely comfortable in this house, yet. I have the feeling we'll need to perform some kind of Ouija-centered cleansing ritual to exorcise any lingering ghosts before you'll relax enough to spend the night. So, let me take you back to Miss Delphine's. I'll stay over there with you. No foolin' around. I promise."

"You don't have to, Jack."

"I'd feel better. You've already had a few shots on an empty stomach, so I'll be driving you anyway. And call it a hunch, but I think you'd feel better with company, too."

Puzzled by the weight of this change in the stars, I was quick to cave on this one and sighed, "Ok."

For some reason, the universe felt it necessary that our paths should cross. Yet, I could tell you very little about Storie's life leading up to our encounter. She was an important part of my sexual revolution, but I hadn't spent more than a handful of days in the year since, thinking about her. Certainly none in the last six months. If she was the unidentified victim of a violent murder, I felt I owed it to her to tell someone. I was obligated. Surely there was a family member who was wondering where she was and why she hadn't checked in. A friend. A lover.

Jack grabbed his backpack. Without looking or asking, I could tell you what was in it—clean Buck Naked underwear, clean socks, clean t-shirt, ball cap, toothbrush and paste, Old Spice deodorant, compass, orange Leatherman Skeletool I had given him for his sixteenth birthday. He had the same backpack, filled with the same items, since he was a junior in high school. He usually carried it in his vehicle, making impromptu overnights away from his own house very easy.

He put the beans in the fridge, and I grabbed the strawberry jelly from the kitchen table. I still wanted him to try it. Heading out to his truck, I wondered if Sandi-with-an-i would be safe in the haunted driveway. What if she picked up a spirit I'd have to deal with later? Reminding myself that wasn't my biggest problem at the moment, I let it go. Besides, she was a Wrangler, built to handle difficult situations, hopefully that included the unseen along with the seen.

Jack's phone contacts were split fairly evenly into three groups—personal friends, beautiful women, and take-out restaurants. He hit the number for Giovanni's as he backed out of the drive. Without asking me, he ordered a large pepperoni and mushroom pizza for pick up. That's probably what I would have ordered, too, but it would've been nice to be consulted. Gio was fast, and the pizza would likely be ready before we drove the ten minutes it took to get there.

When Jack popped in to grab the pizza, I closed my eyes. The last couple hours had been exhausting with Jack's revelation, my revelation, dipping a toe in this muddy new water, then the Misty-Storie shocker. I dozed off in the few minutes he was gone and woke to the smell of pizza filling the cab. Ravenous was an understatement.

When we got back to Miss Delphine's, I had the pizza and the jelly. Jack had his backpack and the poker chips. Poker chips?

"What's with the poker chips?"

"I thought this would be a good distraction. Get my mind off kissing you and your mind off whatever the f-." He paused, letting the pending obscenity fizzle out. I knew Jack was on a mission to dial back his use of profanity, and I appreciated his attempt here. I didn't acknowledge it, though, because he was obviously regrouping.

"Get your mind off whatever it is you're thinking about," he finished. "Can we agree to a hiatus for the night?"

While I had originally planned to get back online after devouring my half of the pizza, I thought this wasn't a terrible idea. I could see the value in letting the dust settle but felt the need to protest nonetheless. "You're asking me to ignore my natural inclination to perseverate?"

"It touches me that you're still so focused on our first kiss," he teased. "But yes, that's what I'm asking you to do. Ignore your inclination to perseverate. For tonight anyway."

I wanted to mumble something not too flattering about the sneakiness of how said kiss was obtained, pointing out its sophomoric, spin-the-bottle characteristics, but truth be told, I *was* still contemplating said kiss and preferred to do it in the privacy of my own head. So, I let that dog lie and instead dropped the pizza box on the table with a flourish. It was now the center of our solar system. No need for plates or really even napkins. But there was a need for a cold beer.

Reading my mind, Jack was at the fridge and had two bottles opened before I was halfway through my first slice. For the next fifteen minutes, it was all eating and no talking, until my phone *cha-chinged* with a text message from my dad: "You want dinner?"

"Eating pizza with Jack."

Cha-ching: "Tomorrow?"

"Yes. I'll call you."

I took another bite of pizza, washed it down, and said, "Dinner with Dad and 'em tomorrow. Want to come?"

"I'm on tomorrow afternoon. But tell your Pop I said 'Hey' and hope he's feeling okay."

With the pizza gone, I stood up to wash my hands but had a vivid flashback of what happened the last time I stood at a sink with Jack in the room. I rerouted toward the bathroom. Seemed he was on to me, though.

"I promised you no funny business tonight, Lily. You're safe."

"I know," I lied. "Just gotta pee," I lied again.

⌐ 🐓 ¬

Poker was a lot of fun. When I thought I had it, I did not. We played for a couple hours until the yawns became too pronounced. We were both tired. Finally, he tossed the cards down, pushed the chips aside, and took my hand. I was wary.

"Let's talk about sleeping arrangements."

"We never had to have this conversation before," I mused.

"I know. But we started something tonight that we will revisit soon, and it kind of changes things, don't you think?"

"There's a hiatus in place. As such, there are rules governing changes to long-standing friendships under a hiatus."

"I imagine there's a statute, but it's not something I'm familiar with. Can you pull it up online?" He played along.

"Don't need to," I informed him. "I know it by heart. Article Seventeen, Clause five-point-three clearly states that under a hiatus, the dominant form of a previous relationship shall remain intact, ipso facto, requiring both parties to abide by all previously agreed upon logarithms heretofore established and shared thusly."

"So you want to share the bed?"

"We've done it before. A lot of times. It never used to be weird. And, I don't know, I'd kinda like you closer than the couch. We can do it without funny business, right?"

He put his arm around my neck. "We can. It'll be a funny-free zone. Tonight. Just want to be clear, though, eventually the funny business will get off the ground, and when it does, I have a feeling business will be good." I nodded, because to me that was less committal than speaking words.

Laying down beside him was the first thing that felt normal all night. I wore my pjs but he stayed in his t-shirt and gym shorts. I was asleep in minutes and didn't wake up until Jack came back to bed from somewhere out of bed. "What are you doing?" I asked through the fog of sleep.

"I fed the chickens."

All I heard was "chickens" and bolted upright. "I gotta feed the chickens!"

"No, crackpot, I just fed the chickens."

"Ah, Jack," I breathed, sinking back down to the pillow, "I could kiss you." It was out before I realized what I'd said. My eyes flew open, but he couldn't see me in the dark.

"In that case, I'll be over this time every morning."

When I finally got up around eight a.m., he was at the kitchen table, drinking coffee and eating donuts he had procured off-site. He was engrossed in something on his phone. It looked like he had showered and was wearing the clean t-shirt from his backpack.

Reaching for my coffee, I said, "Thanks for feeding the chickens. Did the rooster wake you up?"

"What rooster?"

"Whichever rooster that makes all that freakin' noise in the morning. I think there's more than one."

"There aren't any roosters down there, Lily. I don't think Miss Delphine wants any chicks."

"Well, who's out yonder making all that noise?"

"It's called an egg song. After a hen lays her egg, she's apparently so proud she makes a world-class hullabaloo to tell the rest of the flock."

I sat in silence, wondering how he knew anything about chickens, roosters and egg songs, and wondering if egg songs were real or made up. Then, I spied the strawberry jelly. "Did you have some?" I nodded my head toward the jar. "It'd go great on your jelly donut."

"No, I didn't." He smiled.

"I'll get you a spoon."

"Don't need one." Leveraging his forearm against my shoulder, he gave a little push and I plunked back into the chair as he unscrewed the lid and stuck his finger in the jar. Before the jelly made it to his mouth, he appeared to waver. Holding his finger out to me, he said, "Ladies first."

"I don't think the laws governing the hiatus allow strawberry jelly to be shared in this format."

"Had you gotten your sleepy self outta bed, you could've enjoyed the protection of the laws governing the hiatus. Since you chose to stay in bed—and for the record, I'm in favor of that decision in nine of every ten situations—however," he checked his watch, "time has run out on the hiatus."

His jelly-covered finger stayed in the air between us. "Nobody loves sugar more than me," I acknowledged, "but you know in the mornings I like my sugar in a bowl. With milk."

Before I could stand, he had my wrist. "Then I'll need you to sit still for just a sec while I imagine some creative ways to use this jelly that don't involve toast."

I grabbed his hand, and in the least sexual but quickest way possible, I ate the jelly. He sat there, smiling like the village idiot, and said, "Now, my turn to try it." He passed the jar to me.

"So try it," I said, passing the jar back to him.

"I want you to feed it to me on your finger."

Was he kidding? I had to figure out a way to regain control of the situation. Fast. So I stuck my finger in the jelly, waited a second while a blob dropped back in the jar, looked at him sweetly and ate it. "Get your own jelly," I said, pushing the jar back to him.

It had an effect, but not the desired one. From the look on his face, I just added a scene to his porn episode. He did, in fact, get his own jelly. With a dark, smoldering look that was way too much for a wholesome jar of homemade jelly, and just like in the poker game last night, I was out. Breaking eye contact, I stood up to get my cereal and a bowl.

I made a lot of noise as a way to sterilize the scene. When I came back, he was still half laughing, but he moved on.

Pouring the Cap'n Crunch and two percent, I went about eating the cereal in the usual way—saving all the Church Berries for last. They're like the dessert part of the cereal.

We tottered around what each of us had going on. I told him about the bakery manager interviews I had set up for the day; he said he was pulling a couple hours at the garage this morning and on duty the rest of the day.

"Can I borrow your Jeep this weekend?"

"What's her name?" I asked cheerfully.

He sighed a heavy and disturbed sigh. "Sandi-with-an-i. Can I borrow Sandi-with-an-i this weekend?"

I laughed on the inside. That'll teach him to have me lick jelly off his finger the second a mutually agreed upon hiatus cancels out.

"Sure," I said, smiling on the outside. "What are you doing?"

"Rick and Mitch are wheeling this weekend. The Hindsight Crawlers have an event out there at Buckshot Junction. Wanna come?"

Ugh. Rick Vergot and Mitch Cord were two yahoos who worked at Republic Building Supply with Jack's brother, Joe. They had big Jeeps on mechanical steroids and liked to drive them over things that God designed as scenery, not roadways.

"I'd love to," I said, mustering my best fake sincerity, "but I'm scheduled for a medically-unnecessary frontal lobotomy on Saturday, and I really hate to miss it."

"Come on, they're decent guys."

"I didn't say they weren't decent human beings. But they do take up a lot of the planet's limited air supply talking about their own Jeeps, each other's Jeeps, other people's Jeeps, what you can do in a Jeep, how you can make a Jeep better…don't let them talk you into doing anything to Sandi."

"What is it you think they might want to do to her?"

"I don't know," I shook my head. "Fix her up so she could keep up with theirs?"

"Even stock, your Rubicon is very capable. With the right driver behind the wheel, she can already keep up with them. Do you even know what she can do?" He started to rattle off a list of foreign words like "skid plates" and "lockers." It was no secret—I was into the Wrangler strictly for the Jeep waves. Complete strangers being friendly toward each other on the road, what's not to love about that philosophy? The other details tended to bore me, so I let my chin drop to my chest and snored to show exactly how interested I was. Undeterred, he kept talking.

"The only thing she really needs is a lift to give her a little more clearance."

My head snapped up, "Do not, under any circumstances, let those boys make my perfect Jeep any taller." I took a shot in the dark. I didn't really know what a "lift" was, but it sounded tall.

"Tell you what," he said, and I knew by the way he squared his shoulders he was about to offer me the bargain of a lifetime. "I won't let Rick and Mitch make your perfect Jeep any taller, if you agree not to leave the county today in search of Storie Sanders or her family."

"Jack Turner," I breathed out hard, "everything is *not* a negotiation."

Rubbing his thumb over the knuckles on my hand, he looked me in the eye and said, "Oh, I can assure you, Lily Barlow, everything most certainly is."

"Are you actually telling me not to leave the county? I can't believe you're trying to prohibit me from leaving the county."

"No. Not at all. Leave the county for any other reason, except to look for Storie. If there is an unidentified body involved, you gotta be smart about this. And I don't mean Stephanie Plum smart."

I gazed toward the heavens and sighed, but he wasn't done. "And don't look for any of your asinine loopholes." He waited. "Deal?"

"Don't you have to go to work?"

Pausing after each word as he spoke, he drew it out—"Do...we... have...a...deal?" The staccato rhythm gave the sentence an added layer of seriousness.

The fastest way to get beyond this sticking point was to agree. "I won't physically look for Storie or her family today."

"Okay. Do you want a ride to get the Jeep?"

"Yes, but I guess I should put some clothes on."

A goofy grin spread across his face. I rolled my eyes and left him at the table.

As we clomped down the outside stairs together, I spied Miss Delphine in her floral print glory out past the chicken coop. Garden hose in hand, she was watering a patch of brown earth on the edge of the yard. I scanned the area for McNugget but saw no threat.

"Mornin', Jack. Lily," she said loud enough for us to hear. Not a person prone to smirking, I'm not sure how to classify the smile she gave us.

Jack tipped his ball cap. "Morning, Miss Delphine."

"Nice job with the chickens, Jack."

"Thank you, ma'am."

It crossed my mind to wonder how she knew Jack fed the chickens instead of me, but I whispered, "Did the crazy one try to attack you?"

"Who? Miss Delphine?" He whispered back.

"No, wing nut, the chicken."

"Um…No. Does a crazy one try to attack you?"

"So far, every morning."

Shielding my eyes from the sun, I waved at Miss Delphine as I waited for Jack to open my door. What had she planted over there? It was a weird spot for flowers. Back toward the tree line on the edge of the yard, not great light. I guess some shade-loving plants would work there, but there was no real bed to speak of. More like a plot. Oh, sweet maple sugar candy.

Chapter 6

At the bakery, I unlocked the back door and encountered my entire life summed up in a bank of cold ovens. Would I ever escape Poppy's? The cast of characters in that nursery rhyme joined me there in the dim light—the butcher, the baker, the candlestick maker. Together we discussed the merits of each career path. I guessed a butcher shop would have been worse than a bakery, but what if this was a candle store? Ignoring the fact that the shop would still be in the town I was trying desperately to vacate, I could see myself melting beeswax in a big copper kettle. I would add essential oils I procured from traveling apothecaries who boiled and pressed the thin leaves or the chubby roots to produce drops of fragrant potions that would cure anything from road rage to butter fingers. The vendors would call in the early morning, and I'd offer them chamomile tea. Sometimes I would pay money for their oils, other times I would barter with some of my candles. They would save all their most precious and exotic oils for Poppy's Candle Works, because, well, it was my daydream, and I didn't need a better reason than that.

I started scrolling through the fragrances I'd heard of. Cedarwood. Smelled like Millie's old cedar chest more than likely. Ylang Ylang. Was that the aphrodisiac? Helichrysum. It smelled like, like a hint of honey. It smelled like. Wait. It smelled like Storie's skin. Storie's skin smelled like honey! She used helichrysum in a natural sunscreen she wore all the time. There was a clue there somewhere. Did she do something with essential oils? Was that how she funded her travels?

I glanced at my watch and realized I only had thirty minutes until my first appointment. The smell of Storie's skin disappeared once reality stomped her foot on the hardwood floor. That delicate fragrance was replaced with the smell of yeast. Funny how the good baking smells never stuck around for long, but the smell of yeast could cling forever.

No getting around the fact that the place had been buttoned up for a while, but I had time to make at least one corner feel cheerful. I could pick up a few daisies next door at the florist. Ginny, the owner, had a little case over there where customers could mix and match their own bouquets. A couple blooms would go a long way in brightening up the table where I planned to conduct the interviews.

It was always daisies on the tables. You'd think a bakery named Poppy's, with a big red poppy on the sign, would put poppies on the tables. Nope. Daisies. They had been my mama's favorite, and Dad refused to use anything else. On the rare occasion when daisies were hard to come by, we'd use a look-alike chrysanthemum—white petals and yellow center. Maybe someone from the NC State School of Horticulture would know the difference, but the casual customer saw a simple, lovely daisy. More evidence upholding the speculation that people generally see what they want to see.

Next door, I picked out two daisies and something purple, because it reminded me of the purple flower tattoo, and let's face it, that was definitely on my mind. Ginny refused to let me pay. "How's your daddy these days?"

"Ornery as ever and stronger by the minute," I said.

"Can't wait to see his smiling face back next door. Miss that George Barlow."

Ginny was a widow from my dad's generation, but she looked so much younger. Her rich, mahogany-colored skin showed no flaws and barely a wrinkle. Her dark eyes always glowed with the warmth of true friendship. Over the years, she had grown into much more than just a fellow merchant; she was part of my extended family.

We chatted for a bit longer, then I headed out with my flowers. Passing the plate glass window, I thought I saw a shadow in the store, which was weird, because that meant someone had come in the back door since I hadn't unlocked the front. It was obviously dark. What in the name of dangling participles was going on here?

I thought about Stephanie, wondered what she would do in a situation like this and decided I should consider carrying mace.

I stepped through the delivery door. "Hello," I hollered. No answer. I walked through the kitchen to the customer section of the store and saw a lanky man standing in the back by the coffee cart. He wore a collared golf shirt, but his baseball cap was pulled down over his eyes. I knew that trick well; it's what you do when you don't want to make eye contact. "Hey," I greeted him.

"Hello," he said back, a little too flatly.

"Are you here for an interview?"

He didn't answer right away, then said, "Yes, I am."

"Are you Carl Middleton?"

Another pause, "Yes, I am."

My Spidey senses started to tingle, and I said, "Can you give me just a minute, Carl? I'm in the middle of a text conversation with another applicant."

I texted Jack. "You busy?"

Cha-ching: "What's up?"

"Applicant making me feel weird."

Cha-ching: "Two minutes."

I knew it wasn't an exaggeration. Everything was close in a town this size, but Turner's Auto Repair was literally at the end of the street. I invited Carl to have a seat, mainly so I could keep an eye on him. As a way to keep the counter between me and Mr. Weirdo, I put on a pot of coffee and stuck my flowers in a little cobalt-colored vase. Just as I was about to ask him how he took his coffee, Jack busted through the back door.

"Ah, great, you're just in time." Turning to Carl, I said, "Carl, this is Jack. He's helping me with the interviews."

Carl looked disappointed, as if he wasn't expecting a second interviewer, and male to boot. He hemmed and hawed and asked if the job required much manual labor, to which Jack clarified that it was about eighty percent manual labor. Not exactly true. "I'm afraid this is not the right position for me. I'm recovering from back surgery."

Jack stuck out his hand to shake Carl's. He stood there waiting until Carl finally took hold, and I wondered how hard Jack was squeezing. "Sorry for your back trouble, man, but you're right, this is not the job for you." There seemed to be another message wrapped up in the first one. Some kind of guy code, maybe, but Carl broke the connection and headed toward the back door before I could decipher it. Jack flipped the bolt on the front door and swung it open. "Here you go," he said, in a polite but pointed way.

The place felt better with Carl gone, and I smiled. "Thanks. Sorry to interrupt your workday. He probably wasn't a serious threat."

"No problem," he said, making light of it. "I wasn't in the middle of anything, just poking around online to see what kind of lift kits are available for two-door JKs." He said it with such a straight face, it was possible he was serious.

"As you can see," I spread my arms wide for emphasis, "I'm trapped here with back-to-back interviews. When would I have time to drive anywhere to search for anyone? And, furthermore, where exactly would I drive?"

"Just making sure our deal is still in place."

"It's in place," I said, then called him a freak under my breath. "Do you want a cup of coffee before you go back?"

"I do. I'm gonna sit here for a few minutes to make sure Carl the Creeper doesn't try to reapply."

I poured his black coffee and one for me before realizing that the use-by date on any creamer in the cooler would have long since passed. Feeling a tiny bit cheated, I spooned some extra sugar into my cup. This is how Mercedes drank her coffee. She called it "hot as hell, black as night, and sweet as sin." Not to mention bitter as hemlock. I made a show of just how bitter I thought it tasted.

"Drink it black for one week, and you'll never go back."

"Is one of the reasons people don't go back at the end of the week because they've died of black coffee poisoning?"

"I'm pretty sure there's never been a documented case of black coffee poisoning, but I'd have to double check with the paramedics on that."

Jack studied my face, then asked, "How you feeling today?"

"In general terms? I'm good."

"How 'bout the more specific terms of reliving a long-buried lesbian romance, or thinking your one-time lesbian lover may have been murdered, or kissing your platonic best friend of almost twenty years, or dealing with your dad's recent heart attack, or hanging around a bakery when you'd rather take a sharp stick to the eye, or worrying about how and when you'll get back to UVA?"

"Viewed in those terms, this may not be my best day ever."

"I know you don't have the time or the inclination to dissect any of this right now," he said. "We'll take our thing slow, and as for the rest of it, I'll help you figure it out."

All I could really say to that was, "Okay," because Ethel Baxter made her grand entrance. Oh, Miss Ethel. Points for timing.

Jack excused himself, put his mug in the plastic bin at the end of the counter where all the dirty plates went, and fished his ball cap out of his back pocket.

"Ma'am," he said as he passed her on the way to the door. Then to me, "Call me if you need me, Lily." He paused. "I'm off on Wednesday. We can look for her then." And he was out the door.

Leave it to Jack to formulate a plan of action that conveniently involved him. Okay. The real issue at stake was time. And time was a tickin', sista. I had a log jam of things to do ahead of the fall semester. Speed was the key. What did Mario Andretti say? If everything seems under control, you're not going fast enough? Well, I must be going fast enough, because nothing, not one single thing, was under control. So would it be so terrible to accept Jack's help as a means to an end?

I pasted a cheery smile on my lips and greeted Miss Ethel Baxter, who was about a hundred and three. Through the course of our conversation, it became apparent that Miss Ethel's greatest qualification to manage a bakery was her secret chocolate chip cookie recipe. The cookie had won first place at the Fauquier County Fair for nineteen of the last twenty years, and the one year it didn't take first, it was second.

I knew it wasn't a smart business move to hire someone who could barely lift a spatula. Even though the manager wasn't responsible for the commercial baking, it just didn't make sense. But that cookie recipe was very tempting. "So, Miss Ethel, would you be willing to share your recipe if I give you the job?" The look on her face was white hot indignation. Gathering up her suitcase-sized purse, she made her way to the door.

"Good day," was all she said on her way out.

My third candidate, Harold Callahan, was a middle-aged man, not at all creepy, but highly allergic to apparently everything. He sneezed from the time he walked into the building. "Is there a cat in here?"

"No," I said. "I don't know if resident cats are considered hygienic in a business that prepares food."

He *achooed* another robust sneeze. "No? Perhaps something else with fur? A rabbit?"

"No," I said.

"A ferret?"

If this guy made it down the list of fur-covered animals to rat, I couldn't be held responsible for the bodily harm that would be inflicted. "So, tell me, Harold, are you only sensitive to animals or do you have other allergies?"

That question launched a laundry list of allergens that would have impressed the American College of Allergy, Asthma & Immunology. "Leaf mold, tree pollen, goldenrod, mildew, latex, cigarette smoke, diesel exhaust, dander, fire ants, bees, wasps, three food dyes—carmine, annatto, and FD&C yellow #5, casein, gluten and dust."

I found the last three culprits on his long list particularly interesting. "You're allergic to casein, gluten and dust?"

"Dust is possibly the biggest offender."

"Isn't casein in milk?" I asked.

"Yes. It's the protein in milk."

"Isn't gluten in flour?"

"Yes, a naturally occurring component in flour and sometimes an additive."

"And dust," I said, getting my facts straight.

"Yes. Dust. It may be my biggest offender," he repeated.

"Harold, you're aware that we use a lot of milk and flour in the bakery business, aren't you? And I don't know if this would align with the hard and fast definition, but couldn't flour also be considered a form of dust? You would be working around flour all day long. This would be a flour-coated, dust-covered environment. Would that be a pleasant workplace for you? Or is this just a suicide mission?"

"I was hoping to manage the bakery from the hermetically sealed back office."

"I'm sorry, Harold. There's a back office, but it's as dusty if not dustier than the kitchen. Every time you walk in the door you'd be risking anaphylactic shock. And to be honest, that wouldn't be great for business."

The fourth applicant was maybe eighteen. Online, he had described "years of experience with bread." In person, however, that amounted to years of *eating* it. I gave him credit for writing a convincing resume and suggested he try his hand at fiction instead of baking.

The fifth applicant had managed a commercial bakery for thirty-seven years, until the workforce was downsized and his position eliminated. He was looking for a six-figure salary. The sixth applicant was Carl Middleton, but he vanished as soon as I yelled for an imaginary Jack.

Exhausted, discouraged and borderline depressed, I decided to call it a day. I read a text from Mercedes.

"Find a manager?"

"No. Not one qualified candidate."

Cha-ching: "Just your first round."

"I know."

Cha-ching: "Chin up, Lilita."

"You busy later? Lots to tell."

Cha-ching: "Come on by."

"After dinner with the Barlows."

※ 🐔 ※

The family time was nice, and the stories of the interviews kept Dave, Millie, and Dad entertained. I watered down Carl *Middleton*. Best not to draw the unwanted attention of the older generation where this was concerned. No need to incite a riot about my personal safety, especially when I was contemplating a sortie to positively identify a murdered lesbian lover. Talk about choking on a chicken bone.

Big hugs and noisy kisses all around, and I was out the door and on my way to Cinco's. Mercedes was in the parking lot when I pulled up, enjoying a break with a gentleman customer she may or may not have been sleeping with. The guy was vaguely familiar. As I walked up, he leaned in and whispered something that made my friend bestow her most radiant smile on him. Whatever he said, the boy just moved his checker to the "King Me" spot on the back row.

I parked myself on the stump next to hers. Manny used the stumps to mark off the front part of the parking spaces, but they made nice seats in good weather and it was not uncommon to see people, both employees and customers alike, perched on the stumps like chipmunks. There were a couple groupings in particular that were almost never blocked by cars—the two spots near the dumpster and a few at the very back of the lot. The rest were up for grabs depending on the flow of customers.

I waved my thumb in the air, pointing in the direction of the dude, and she offered a demure shrug, meaning he was a plaything that she hadn't played with yet. "I hope you don't have a rendezvous with that guy tonight. I need to talk."

"You want a beer?" She tipped her head in the direction of the restaurant.

"Yes. But I'd better have it at home. Jack is on me like pink on a flamingo right now. I'm not sure how he does it. I know he has a network of spies feeding him intel. On top of that, it wouldn't surprise me if he planted a bug somewhere on my person." I patted my pockets, checking. "I can't so much as pop a bottle cap without him knowing about it. The last thing I need is him showing up to give me a ride home after one little ol' beer."

"I can come by later. Mondays are slow. Say eight o'clock?"

"Great. I have tequila. Plan to stay over."

↘ 🐓 ↙

Waiting on Mercedes, I sipped a cold beer from the bottle while I perused the Doe Network. Case File 33UFTX caught my attention. The woman, or girl, was somewhere between fifteen and thirty years old. She was strangled on October 31, 1979. Her ears were pierced, her fingernails were painted, she wore an abalone ring and orange socks. In the story I wrote in my mind, she picked out those socks that morning because it was Halloween. Something I would do if I owned a pair of orange

77

socks. Had she been hanging out with friends, drinking beer, talking about spooky things? Did she eat any Halloween candy? Milk Duds in those tiny boxes? Banana Laffy Taffy? I thought back to Halloweens past when I was fourteen, fifteen, sixteen, seventeen, eighteen. I spent those nights with friends. I always felt safe. Jack was always there. Was that the reason? For the last two years, I was with a different group of friends at school on Halloween night. Was I still as safe without Jack there? Was I exposed to the danger this woman encountered wearing her orange socks on Halloween?

Her body was found in a ditch near a highway in Texas. A serial killer named Henry Lee Lucas took credit for her murder, calling her Judy or Joanie, but he later denied killing her. Authorities nicknamed the girl Orange Socks, and the grave where she's buried is marked, simply, "Unidentified Woman."

I looked at the artist renderings of Miss Orange Socks. I looked at her ring, wondering where she got it. Something of her mama's? Christmas gift? Flea market? Bubble gum machine? "I'll call you Suzy, for now," I said to her. "I like your orange socks, girl, but that shouldn't be your name."

Without warning I heard Cro start barking his fool head off, and it brought me from my swamp of glum thoughts. A car had pulled up, and I assumed it was Mercedes. Leaving Suzy on the screen, I stepped out on the little porch. Mercedes was stuck in her car, pinned in by Cro on the driver side and McNugget on the passenger side. The dog I could deal with, but wasn't that crazy chicken supposed to be in bed for the night?

I whistled, and Cro turned toward me, wagging. He put his front paws on the bottom step and looked up as if he couldn't believe his great good luck finding me on the porch. "Cro, let her come up," I admonished him gently. He wagged his answer, then moseyed back toward his own porch, stopping to sniff at McNugget. I cursed the stars that the dog wasn't more prey driven where that chicken was concerned. That would solve a big, recurring problem for me.

Seeing her opportunity, Mercedes jumped out and dashed up the stairs, right past me and into the apartment. "Cute, *Lilita*," she said, twirling around to take it all in. "I could do without the welcome committee, though." She put a bag of what I could only assume were chips and guac on the table. "For snacking," she confirmed.

She grabbed the bottle from the freezer and the *C* and the *F* glasses from the cabinet shelf and sashayed to the living room. One thing about Mercedes, she could pour a standard shot of liquor into any unmarked container and get it to within a drop of 1.5 ounces. I considered it genetic wiring and wondered why, if she could do it with whiskey at a bar, I couldn't do it with a dry ingredient like cream of tartar. Add that little detail to the pile of munitions fortifying my personal standoff with the bakery.

Handing me the *C* glass, she said, "Cheers!" and we clinked. Then she sat back, dark eyes shining, and said, "Start with Jack."

"How do you know I have anything to report about Jack?"

"Because you said he's been all over you, so I figured something's going on."

"Yeah, you're not going to believe it. He decided he wants the two of us to date. And you'll love this—eventually sleep together." I rolled my eyes.

"Well thank the Virgin Mary!" Making the sign of the cross, she said, "It's about time you two got naked."

"You're kidding me."

"No. No, I'm not," she said with a surprising degree of genuine enthusiasm.

Trying to cope with the sudden loss of what I had considered a guaranteed source of support on this issue, I stammered. "Well, uh, it would never work. In case you haven't noticed, he has a raging character flaw. He's an overbearing know-it-all. Acceptable in a friend because I can ignore it like eighty percent of the time. Completely unacceptable in a boyfriend."

"You never know what you can tolerate in someone until you test your limits. Besides," she continued, "things look different depending on where you're standing. Right now you're at Friendship Fork. Try driving over to Lover's Lane. See how things look from there." She smiled at herself. That made one of us.

"Why are you taking his side in this? Did he talk to you?"

"Don't you think I would have said something if Jack talked to me about this? But if you want the truth, everyone has been waiting for y'all to get there on your own."

"Get where?"

"You know. A romantic relationship. Funny, I always thought you would figure it out before he did."

She went to the table for the bag of chips. Lifting the flimsy lid on the Styrofoam container of guacamole, she put it on the coffee table and folded down the sides of the paper bag, engineering a makeshift bowl for the chips. Then she went for a couple beers. I stayed parked on the couch and let her treat my apartment like her restaurant.

"Alright, what else you got?" Ticking off my really important things to talk about, she had already moved on from Jack.

"Well, I was hoping we could spend a little more time on Problem Number One, but since you've glossed right over that pending disaster… let's address Problem Number Two."

It took about an hour and another shot of tequila to get her through the gory details of the Doe Network. She was no coward by any stretch, but Mercedes had a pronounced superstitious streak that regularly got tangled up with her pronounced Catholic streak. Each time I tried to show her a dead body, she invoked by name one or another of a hundred or so saints, muttered a prayer in Spanish, and again made the sign of the cross over her chest. It was a painstakingly slow process to get through it. And, now that I thought about it, kind of ironic since I was following her advice to google "dough" when I stumbled on the Doe Network in the first place.

I contemplated full disclosure but decided to hold back the fact that I might have known one of these unidentified murder victims in the Biblical sense. It was, after all, truthful to say I met Storie at the music festival and that she might be the woman with the purple flower tattoo. Mercedes took another shot of tequila and sat in stunned silence. When she could finally talk, "Poor soul," was all she could say, over and over. I took a shot and nodded my agreement.

When I felt we could move forward, I asked, "What should we do?"

"Oh, Lily, we have to find her family. It's so terrible, but they should know. They need to know."

"Jack is against me doing anything that he considers directly or indirectly dangerous. So, I gotta keep that in mind. He can be a real pain in the posterior when he wants to be."

"What does he think is dangerous?"

"Sitting. Standing. Walking."

"No, not day-to-day danger, I mean in terms of this problem only."

"So far, he doesn't want me to leave the county looking for Storie or her family."

"Okay. There's plenty we can do without leaving the county. Let's list off the things we could do from the comfort of this couch. Then we can talk about the usefulness of each."

Thinking this was a pretty solid way to begin, I pulled up a blank Pages doc on the computer and started recording our list.

Call the number for the detective in charge of the case listed on the web page.

Google "Storie Sanders" to see who comes up.

Write down every detail and google those things as a way to cross reference.

Hire a private investigator.

Contact friends who were at the music festival to see if they remember anything.

We drank beer, ate chips, and fleshed out the ideas on our list. "As for number one, I'm not sure I want to call the detective in charge of the case in Florida," I said. "My goal is to honor her memory by letting her family know. Then, they can get their closure by notifying the police and moving the investigation forward."

"That seems reasonable," she agreed. "If for some reason they were estranged, and the family shows no interest in contacting the police, then you would obviously have to do it. We can take it off the list for now."

"Let's also hold off on number four—private investigator. That costs money."

We skipped to the easiest thing on the list. Upon googling "Storie Sanders," we got a lot of hits for *stories* about Bernie *Sanders*, some stuff about Colonel *Sanders*, something about an antique computer game called Pong, author George *Saunders* who wrote short *stories*, and some people with the last name *Storie*. "Maybe Storie was a nickname," Mercedes suggested. I hadn't considered that. It so perfectly suited her, and I always assumed it was a given name generated by two hippie parents who were probably high at the time.

"Okay, on to number three," Mercedes prodded. "Let's think about what you can remember."

"I don't really remember a lot of specific details," I confessed.

"That's okay. Let's just start with anything you can think of."

So I began rattling things off, "Silver jewelry, bracelets, helichrysum oil, hiking the Appalachian Trail with a small group, tattoo on her ankle." It made me sad that I could only list five things.

"She was a hiker. Did she have equipment?" Mercedes asked.

"I remember she had good hiking boots. Apollo? Astollo? I thought the name looked funny." She took over on the computer and searched "Expensive hiking boots Apollo and Astollo" and quickly found the European Asolo brand. REI stores carried them, along with some others. We were both exuberant, as if that fact alone conclusively solved the mystery. Until we realized what it actually meant.

"That seems like a lot of stores. And what would we do? Visit each one and ask if they sold a pair of boots to a woman a year ago?"

"Talk about leaving the county," Mercedes mused. "Seems like a long shot to boot." I giggled at the pun.

"Get it?" I asked. "To boot? Like, hiking boot." And she let out a peel of laughter.

I was happy to be getting drunk with my good friend. It gave this whole situation a more manageable feeling. Right on cue, Jack texted.

Cha-ching: "Where you at?"

"How does he know I'm drinking?" I asked, annoyed. "It's like he has telestepy."

I thought Mercedes was going to bust a gut laughing. "No, it's tethlepothy."

We were both laughing so hard at this point, neither of us knew the word we were trying to say.

I typed my answer, "Jack-a-lope!"

Cha-ching: "You only call me Jack-a-lope when you're drunk."

"Shhhhh," I hissed, apparently afraid he would overhear us. "He knows I'm drunk." That sent us into another tizzy of laughter. Then I sent my response.

"I'm safe. At Miss Delphine's. With Mercedes."

Cha-ching: "Two drunk hot chicks. Sounds like fun."

"You're not invited."

Cha-ching: "Bring y'all breakfast and aspirin tomorrow morning?"

Who knew breakfast and aspirin were so hilarious. Again, we were rolling.

"Yes please. Love you."

I sent it before I saw it, but once I saw it, I repeatedly punched the backspace key in a desperate attempt to call it back from the ether. "Mercedes, I just typed 'Love you'."

It wasn't as funny when she was laughing at my panic.

Cha-ching: "Love you too, baby."

"I didn't mean that literally."

Cha-ching: "I did."

I handed her the phone, so she could assess the damage. "He's messing with you," she tried to assure me. "He knows you're drunk. Just don't answer back."

"I did the same thing the other night when he stayed over," I started to relay the story.

Mercedes interrupted me, "Stayed over how?"

"The traditional way," I said. "We were crashed in the bed," but she interrupted me with a kissing noise reminiscent of a fourth grader.

"It was esplicketly stated, 'No Funny Business'," I informed her.

"Esplicketly," she repeated, then we both howled. "Okay, okay, what did you do when he stayed over the traditional way?" By then I had forgotten what I started to say. Mercedes supplied, "Did you tell him you loved him then, too?"

"No, I told him I could kiss him after he fed the chickens. Which reminds me, we have to feed the chickens in the morning."

"Oh, no no," she was emphatic. "There's a lot of things I will do to a chicken—pluck it, spatchcock it, fry it—but I will not feed it."

"It's really not a big deal," but the lie made me laugh so hard I thought I was going to pee. "Please," I begged her. "Please do it with me."

"I will, but you'll owe me something so big, you'll probably never be able to pay me back."

"Thank you, thank you, thank shoe." And we were off and laughing again. Once I came up for air, I set my phone alarm for too-freakin'-early, so we wouldn't sleep through the egg songs.

We bounced around a bit longer before realizing it was bedtime. The main thing we decided was that we were far too snookered to keep working on the mystery at hand. Mercedes said she could get away from Cinco's on Saturday, and maybe we should do some recon down in C'ville. Jack wouldn't love it, but he'd be occupied driving my Jeep over boulders up at Buckshot Junction. Kismet.

I woke up to the phone alarm, head pounding, thirsty, confused. Slowly, I tuned into a chicken singing an egg song outside, and it all came together. Mercedes was only pretending to be asleep, trying to get out of her commitment. "You promised," I prodded. Her response was in Spanish, and I'm pretty sure, not very polite.

We both decided it would be a good idea to pee first. Then I grabbed the broom from the corner and told her to arm herself. She picked up a pot and a wooden spoon, looked at it, gauged the noise-to-hangover ratio, and thankfully decided against it. She settled on a much quieter plastic fly swatter, which in my mind offered as much protection as a finger gun. Half pushing each other down the stairs, it looked like the coast was clear until McNugget stepped out from a shadow.

Mercedes screamed, I laughed, she pushed me forward, and I swung the broom out in front of me. McNugget took the opportunity to fly up, landing on the outside railing very near Mercedes, who ran back up the stairs. From the safety of the porch, she frantically waved the fly swatter at the chicken. I was already down the steps, just ahead of the threat, so I ran for the safety of the garage. Broom in hand, I dumped the scratch in the spot where I always dumped it, which drew my nemesis off the railing and toward me. I swung wide and ran around the chicken coop, only to realize I was standing on top of Miss Delphine's makeshift grave. I screamed again and took a straight line back to the garage, dropping the scooper in the process.

"The disease is catching, Cro. Now appears two are infected." Delphine stood at the sink, looking out the window, sipping her first cup of coffee. Cro took a sloppy drink from his water bowl.

After the chaotic chicken-feeding experience, Mercedes and I fell back onto the bed and didn't budge until Jack hollered from the kitchen. I peeled open one eye and saw him standing in the bedroom doorway with a look of stupid boy-joy on his face. I launched from my side of the bed, crashed into him, and successfully pushed him out of the room. "She does not know the whole story," I hissed, and thumped my fist on his chest for emphasis.

Delighted with the close proximity, he grabbed me up in a big hug and teased, "So you love me, eh? That'll make dating so much easier from the get-go, don't you think?"

"Jack, focus." My voice was quiet but urgent. "I didn't tell Mercedes everything about Storie."

"Relax, girl. Your secret's safe with me." His smile was downright salacious. "As long as I can ask a few more questions. And by a few, I mean twenty or thirty."

"Whatever. Don't breathe a word. To anyone. Ever."

"Done." Then over my shoulder he said, "Morning, sunshine."

Catching us in the hug, Mercedes asked, "Do y'all need a room? So soon?" She made a little swivel gesture with her shoulders that somehow implied sex. "I'll be outta here as soon as I drink this coffee and take that aspirin you brought."

"Thanks, Mercedes," Jack played into it. "That'd be so great."

I levered myself out of the embrace. Jack had already worn out his welcome, and my other friend's welcome was wearing mighty thin.

"Can everyone please stop talking?" I implored them. Trying hard to get myself off the radar as the butt of this new joke, I pretended the hangover was worse than it was and asked for the aspirin. Jack pulled a bottle out of his pocket, then handed us each our preferred form of hydration— citrus Gatorade for me and red Gatorade for Mercedes. Clearly not his first time tending our pounding heads.

Mercedes hugged me bye and told me we were on for Saturday.

Chapter 7

"What are y'all up to on Saturday?" The way he asked the question, he sounded like he was only half interested.

"Well, since we're not going Jeeping with you and those other wing nuts, we figured we'd hang out."

"Girl stuff?" he asked. "Paint your toes?"

I gave him a patronizing bobble-head nod and kept nodding as he listed the usual stereotypical bologna.

"Have a pillow fight? Shop for shoes? Look for Storie?"

Unbelievable. Who did he think he was? *Steven* Plum?

Realizing he might be onto me, I said as nonchalantly as I could, "I have to get by the bookstore on campus to pick up a book I ordered for a popular psych class. Maybe we'll drive down."

I took a drink of coffee (he got it right every time) and rummaged in the paper bag to see what he brought for breakfast. Mmm. Breakfast burrito. I saw one for Mercedes who was gone, but I figured it wouldn't go to waste with JT around. When he hadn't said anything for a while, I turned to see him observing me.

"What?"

"I just think it's interesting that you need to pick up a book you ordered new, when as far as I know, every other book for every other class since the beginning has been bought used at some co-op off campus. Cheaper that way, is what you always said."

"Well, this is the first semester this course is being offered, so there aren't any used books available." I smiled because it felt like I was beating him at his own game.

"A new course that's already so popular the books are selling out. Again, interesting."

I heard the voice of my alter-ego in my head, encouraging me to stick with the lie.

"It is interesting," I said boldly.

"The timing is also interesting; don't you think? That you're going down to Charlottesville the same weekend I'll be rock crawling with Mitch and Rick. Charlottesville," he said again, "which is not far from the last known whereabouts of one Storie Sanders. This trip wouldn't have anything to do with that, would it?"

"Since when do you let your imagination run away with you?"

"Since a year ago October," he said matter-of-factly. "My imagination runs away with me every single day. Like now. I'm imagining what it would be like to put my lips on your lips."

Oh for the love of a Yeti in a yodeling contest. Could this man not pick a lane and stay in it? One minute it's Storie, the next minute it's me. Talk about attention deficit disorder.

I stood there, chomping on a mouthful of burrito, buying myself some time. First, I swallowed the food; then I spoke. "Jack…" It was all I could manage to get out because he was invading my personal space again.

"Ma'am?"

"Can I please eat this burrito in peace?"

"Define peace."

"Without you bothering me."

"Define bothering."

"Touching, hovering, needlessly moving around, staring at or doing anything else to put me off-camber."

He smiled. "You said 'off-camber.'"

It was a Jeeping term. In all honesty, I didn't know exactly what it meant, but it seemed to apply. The few times I'd been with Jack, Rick and Mitch doing unimaginably dangerous things on rock formations, they would try to lessen my terror by saying I just wasn't used to being off camber. I think it had to do with the concept of being in a Jeep that was about to tip over. In my defense, I'd like to know how a human being, who is designed to be upright in a normal, non-tipped position, gets used to the feeling of nearly tipping over. It seemed like Jack's new experiment regarding our relationship was nothing but an exercise in tipping me over. Mentally. Emotionally. And worst of all, physically.

"Okay. In honor of your spontaneous use of wheeling terminology, I will not," he cleared his throat to indicate that he disagreed with my word choice, "*bother* you while you eat your breakfast. Can I at least talk to you?"

"Only about non-bothersome subjects. I'll give you a list of approved topics—flu shots, dogs, recycling initiatives in the town of Marshall, anything that happened at the firehouse last night." Throwing him a bone, I added, "And baseball."

He nodded his head and picked his topic. "You gotta come see Lucy's puppies. I'm thinking of taking one."

"You're getting a puppy?" It was all I could do to keep a full-blown squeal out of my voice. This was exactly the kind of morning conversation I could get on board with. We talked about the challenges of puppy parenthood. The hardest part would be Jack's schedule. He was counting on his parents and brother to pitch in, and he had a lot of dog-loving friends he could call on as well. I guessed, actually hoped, it could work out because who doesn't love a puppy?

"Do you have one picked out?"

"They're all great. I thought you could help me decide."

"Yes! I will help you pick out the puppy!"

"Let's do it on Wednesday," he said. "We can work it around anything you've got going on at the bakery."

"Speaking of the bakery, what time is it? I have interviews starting at eleven."

"It's nine-thirty. And by the way, how'd it go feeding the chickens this morning?"

"I bribed Mercedes to help, but as it turned out, she was a colossal liability. Between the two of us, we're up for the Presidential Medal of Are You Kidding Me?"

"Do you want a lesson?"

"A chicken lesson?" I was taken aback by the mere concept.

"Yeah. I could walk you through it, help you climb one or two rungs back toward the top of the food chain."

I didn't know what kind of experience he was drawing on. I had known Jack for a long time, and his family had never tended chickens. I couldn't place a single chicken at his grandparents' house, an aunt or uncle, even a neighbor. However, I also didn't know he mowed the lawn of a haunted house every week growing up. Maybe this was one of those cases where the guy had multiple personalities. Which would explain all this sudden relationship crap. It wasn't actually Jack wanting to date, it was Jacque wanting to date. But if he had a split personality, wouldn't Jacque have different mannerisms than Jack? Hmm. So maybe not a split personality, but maybe a whole other secret life?

"Okay. You can teach me about chickens," I conceded. What was the point holding out on account of pride? I clearly had none left where those dirt yard denizens were concerned. Then it dawned on me. Was he just angling to spend another night over here? "When is chicken school in session?" I asked.

"It makes the most sense to do it first thing in the morning, since that's kind of the root of the problem."

"Are you staying over or coming over?"

"Which do you prefer?"

Slick. Putting it back on me. "I'd say stay over, 'cause I like the company, but I feel like it might not be worth the risk. Let's face it, you're kind of a loose cannon right now with all these deranged ideas about dating and sleeping together."

"I know I've been coming on a little strong, Lily. I've had a year to come to my conclusions and you've only been chewing on it for a few days. Here's the thing. I want to be with you. And the first step to achieving that is talking about being with you. And when we're close enough to talk, well, we're close enough to touch."

He stopped. It seemed like he wanted to say something else. I didn't try to pry it out of him. Long years of friendship told me Jack didn't need encouragement to say what was on his mind. If he didn't say something, he wasn't ready or he wasn't going to.

What exactly could I say to that? Sitting there, trying to decide if I should take a left or a right, I opted to stay straight and sank my teeth into the burrito.

Finally, because it was clear he had stopped talking, I asked, "What are the chances we could invoke another hiatus if you stayed over tonight?"

"Not especially strong," he leaned closer, "but I'd be willing to listen to your case."

I agreed to let him stay over, feeling sure I could build a respectable case today between interviews and have something airtight to present by tonight.

Before we left, he decided he needed to change the oil in Sandi-with-an-i. He wanted to drive me to the bakery so he could take the Jeep to the shop. I wrestled with the logistics in my head—that meant his truck was still here, so we'd be riding back home together at some point. "You at the garage all day?"

"I am."

I wasn't sure how that made me feel. Hemmed in, because without a vehicle my independence was in jeopardy, or secure, in case there was another Carl Middleton on my list of applicants today. I hauled my backpack over my shoulder, checking to see I remembered the plug for the computer, and we started out.

He opened the door on the passenger side and said,

"Throw your pack in, and let's walk over to the coop."

"The coop? Why would we?"

"Lesson number one."

"I thought the chicken lessons started tomorrow morning?"

"Officially, yes. But right now, let me introduce you to the principle of proximity." I cocked my head and half closed one eye at him. He explained further, "You know, tug on the edges of your comfort zone by forcing you to get closer to the thing you don't want to get close to—the principle of proximity. Ultimately, it's how you expand your comfort zone."

I had the vague impression we were talking about something else here, but with McNugget unaccounted for, I couldn't take the time to think it through more carefully.

"Do we have time for this?"

"Five minutes," he assured me as he hooked my arm and escorted me to the coop. Chickens were everywhere, and they were going about what appeared to be their natural chicken business. The fact that they pretended to ignore us didn't fool me for a second, and I dialed it up to DEFCON 3, which, if I'm not mistaken, is when the Air Force is prepared to launch fighter jets within fifteen minutes.

"They're really not that interested in you," he pointed out as we stood amongst them. "Have you ever seen one up close?"

"Yes. Every morning I come face to face with a rabid killer chicken."

Then, Jack did the most horrifying thing. He snatched a chicken right up off the ground. He was lightening quick, and the chicken didn't even try to defy him. There he was, holding a chicken. I made an inexplicable noise, ran for the Jeep, and opened the driver side door to use as a shield. Standing behind it, I watched Jack approach with his feathered friend. I held out my hand, traffic-cop style, to reiterate that I didn't want him to come any closer.

"Lily, I promise this chicken will not hurt you."

"You have it tight?"

"Yes. Just look at it through the window." Still standing with the Jeep door between us, I took a step back on my side. Jack held the chicken on his side, framed in the glass of the window. Its tiny little head never stopped moving, and it sized me up with those beady little orange eyes. Overall, it appeared to be a very untrustworthy bird.

"You know," Jack pointed out calmly, "You could bend down and get a little closer. She can't get to you through the glass."

"You have it tight?" I asked again, apparently not believing the first answer.

"She's not going anywhere."

I bent down and watched her through the safety of the window. When she was compressed against him, all the fluff of her feathers disappeared, and she seemed smaller by a third. I watched her watch me. She was a very curious thing. Her head twitched and suddenly she reached out and tested the glass with her beak. I nearly jumped out of my skin. Jack laughed, and that was the end of Chicken 101 for me.

"I'm sorry," he said through his laughter. "I can't help it. You're cute when you're off-camber."

"I'm glad this amuses you, moron."

"Okay, okay. You did great. I'll take her back to the coop. Do you want to get in before I put her down?" That was the first considerate thing he had said in the last five minutes, and I definitely wanted to get safely in Sandi before he released the chicken. I backed up around the tailgate of the Jeep, jumped in the passenger side, and reached over to pull the driver's door closed. Jack waited for me to nod before he put the chicken back on the ground. She stood there, looking up at the man who could have easily served her on a platter with dumplings, showing no animosity whatsoever, like they had been friends since she hatched.

At one point in his life, Jack wanted to be a veterinarian. This little display of animal know-how shouldn't have surprised me at all, but again, I couldn't get off the fact that it was a chicken and where in the name of ice cubes and onion rings did he learn to wrangle chickens?

Sliding in behind the wheel, he gave me a huge grin, reached over, and grabbed my whole knee in his hand. "You lived to tell about it."

"If that's the way you plan to teach the morning class, then I'm gonna skip."

"*Co-ed Plays Hooky on a Chicken Farm*? That's one of my favorite porn titles." It was so stupid I laughed out loud. Boy humor wasn't sophisticated and had little redeeming value, but every once in a while, it came across as particularly funny. It loosened me up, and we joked the rest of the way to the bakery.

⅄ 🐓 ⅃

Round two of the interviews kicked off with a lovely woman named Lydia Baker. In her early thirties, she had already tested and rejected a list of career choices, including receptionist at a dentist office, secretary at an elementary school, interior designer, appointment scheduler at a massage and acupuncture studio, telephone medium, assistant manager at the Pump-N-Go gas station, and beauty consultant with a direct sales company. Lydia explained that she had attended a retreat on how to pick a fulfilling job by aligning the path historically, using the surname as the guide.

"That's why you want to manage a bakery, because your last name is Baker?"

"Yes."

"So, if your name was Lydia Fisher, you'd be applying in the aquatic department at a pet store?"

"Yes, something fish-related."

"The person at a big box store who gives out little bite-sized samples of fish sticks on toothpicks for people to try?"

"Exactly!"

"Who sponsored this retreat?"

"WISSP."

"And what does WISSP stand for?"

"The World Institute of Sensory and Spiritual Projection."

"Um. I'm not familiar with that organization."

"They were founded in the 1990s by a group of disenfranchised mediums and non-native Native American spirit guides."

"Do you have any interest in baking whatsoever?"

"None. But the exercises provided in the retreat will retrain my senses and force me to enjoy something that was inherently passed to me through my name possibly hundreds of years back."

"Lydia," I started, but quickly realized I didn't know where to go with it. "Well, okay. I have your contact information. We're still interviewing, so it may be a while before I select a final candidate."

The next applicant was Bob Patterson, a military cook in a past life who loved the challenge of turning meat marked "fit for human consumption" into lunch or dinner. After Bob, came Desert Rose. I had no idea what kind of bakery or managerial experience she had because I couldn't get around her name. Was Rose her last name? Ms. Rose? Did that mean her first name was Desert? Who names a baby Desert? I didn't want to offend her by asking, but the interview stalled out pretty quickly because of it. After Desert, there was a woman who reminded me way too much of the Candy Lady. A set of twins showed up wanting to job share the position, which wasn't a bad idea, but by themselves, neither one could identify the writing end of an ink pen. The last applicant of the day was a pregnant woman, Darby Rose, who cautioned me that she was already one day past her due date. We talked about baby names, and I suggested Desert. You know, for a girl.

It was about fifteen minutes after five when I finished not hiring a bakery manager. Jack wouldn't be done at the garage until six or so. Forty-five undisturbed minutes to peruse the Doe Network. Funny that even though I already had one unsolved mystery to deal with, I still wanted to know about the others. Completely engrossed in the bodies from New York, I never heard the door or the footsteps. The presence of a human form startled me, and I knocked an open water bottle onto the floor.

"Wow," Jack said. "Good thing I wasn't Carl Middleton."

"Who?" I felt disoriented as I pulled myself away from Case File 151UFNY.

"The Creeper."

"Oh, yeah. Him."

I took one last look at the picture of her tattoo. It was a peach, shaped like a heart with a bite taken out. The woman was missing her arms, legs and head.

Her torso was found in a plastic bin with a towel and a pillowcase. The cops didn't have much to go on, so they published a photo of the tattoo in a trade journal for the tattoo industry. An artist claimed it was his work. He thought the woman was about 18 or so, and she came in with two other women, an aunt and a cousin, possibly. Weren't they looking for her now?

Jack peered over my shoulder, and quickly sized it up. "Another tattoo?" He could have easily made a joke about me sleeping with this woman, too, but it didn't cross his mind or else he thought it was in poor taste.

"Did you name her?"

"Wendy," I said.

"Wendy," he breathed it softly. Then quietly waited a minute before continuing, I'm sure out of respect, and I appreciated it. "Any more thoughts about Storie and Misty?" He asked.

"A few. If you want to know, I can tell you over take-out Chinese." I tipped my chin and tried to look like a cute hungry person.

"Take-out Chinese it is." Jack put his hand on my shoulder and slid his index finger under the neck of my shirt about half an inch. Smiling, he grabbed his phone to dial. This time he asked me what I wanted. And where Chinese was concerned, that was a must, because I had a varied palate for this style of cuisine and liked to mix it up. I ignored his finger and focused on my order.

"I'd like an egg roll, Szechuan spicy beef with extra broccoli, and fried rice no broccoli."

"You know, it would be a lot easier for the cooks if you just ordered each dish with the normal amount of broccoli. You order it this way, and some guy is back there picking out the broccoli from the fried rice and tossing it into the Szechuan beef."

I shrugged. "I like it the way I like it."

Back at Miss Delphine's, we unpacked the bag and spread the contents out on the table—the white cardboard containers with red pagodas; the fortune cookies; and the rainbow of yellow, orange and brown sauce packets that appeared to leach toxins even through the plastic. I grabbed two forks and two glasses with the initials *B* and *R*. Jack filled them with ice and water, and we bellied up to the trough.

"So, remember, I'm off tomorrow," he eased into the next topic.

"Yeah. Are we picking out your new dog?"

"Among other things." He hid his smile with a forkful of crispy beef.

"Such as…" I pressed.

"You want me to give you a list or would you rather help generate the list?"

Thinking this was a trap of some kind, I hesitated.

"While you think about it," he continued, "I have a couple things in mind. First, I think we should do something to look for Storie."

I waited, trying to figure out where this was going and how it could come back around to bite me in the butt. He marched on, ignorant of or unconcerned by my lack of participation. "I know you and Mercedes are cooking up some half-baked scheme to find Storie on Saturday when I'm at the Junction with Mitch and Rick."

I gave the fried rice my full attention, teasing out a wayward piece of broccoli that somehow got overlooked in the "no broccoli" request.

"Well?" he asked.

"The purpose of the trip is to pick up my textbook at the bookstore." I hoped I sounded definitive.

"Oh, okay. So down and back. No other stops."

I kept poking around in the fried rice, but after ninety seconds, I cracked. "Okay. Okay. What are you, the Gestapo? I thought, while we were down there picking up my book, I might ask a few friends what they remembered about that weekend."

"Gestapo my a——." He snorted over the obscenity, sticking to his goal of cursing less. "I have way better ways of making you talk, and I'm saving those for later." He winked. "But this is good. See, not so hard to tell me what y'all want to do."

I told myself to wait for it. Wait...for...it.... "I think I can be of service." There it was.

"Jack," I started to strongly disagree.

"Lily, just hear me out."

In my experience, "just hear me out" was Jack-speak for "just do it my way." He had pretty well perfected his reasoning skills at a young age, and you had to be sharp to identify even a narrow little chink where you could drive a wedge. I braced for the challenge.

"Let me take you down to C'ville tomorrow to get your...book, is it?" He flashed me a snarky smile which I didn't care for at all. "Then, let me

98

drive you around town looking for any possible witnesses who attended the Backroads Music Festival."

I was flummoxed by his congeniality, but I had to be careful. All I knew, that was his tactic. "What's in it for you?"

"Peace of mind," he said simply.

"Peace of mind?"

"Yeah. It'll give me peace of mind knowing someone is there."

"The way it's set up now, Mercedes will be there."

"Someone who can throw a punch," he clarified. "So in other words, me. I want to be there. I want to make sure you're safe. I understand the importance of this whole thing. I promise I'll lay low. I won't micromanage how your investigation unfolds. I just want to be there to help you read any potentially dangerous situations and respond accordingly."

I chewed on that for a second and hit on something that was borderline genius. "How much is this peace of mind worth to you?"

"A lot. I'd be willing to trade getting you naked tonight for driving you to UVA and around Charlottesville tomorrow."

I played that all wrong. There were a lot of things between eating Chinese and getting naked that I may not want to do, tonight anyway. "How 'bout you reinstate the hiatus for tonight, and I'll let you drive me to Charlottesville tomorrow."

"Nope."

"Why not?"

"Because I'm not interested in the hiatus tonight."

"Well, then I'm not interested in letting you come to Charlottesville with me tomorrow."

"Fine. Just so you know, we'll be getting naked tonight. Plan accordingly."

"Oh, really?" I said it with about as much confidence as I felt, which was on the low end of the one-to-ten scale.

"Mm hmm," he swallowed a big bite of egg roll. "I got the skills, babe. I know it. You know it. We can start now if you like." The challenge was extended, and this fool loved him some eye contact. So there we were, in a stare down, my least favorite way to be face-to-face with another human being. I sat there, forkful of Szechuan beef poised precariously. My options were limited. He cocked his head, conveying an unspoken question. I tilted my head, mirroring him, but I had absolutely no idea why. Just felt like the thing to do.

"Okay," I said, after what felt like fifteen minutes but was probably only one.

"Okay to what?"

I wondered what he would do if I said okay to getting naked. Fall out of the kitchen chair? Maybe hit his head? A trip to the ER would certainly change the direction of the evening in my favor. Here's the thing about Jack Turner. Do not bluff. Under any circumstances. Unless you're willing to follow through. Since I wasn't willing to follow through on this particular bluff, I said, "We don't get naked, and you can drive me to school tomorrow."

"Nice try," he shook his head no. "Designing a loophole to execute at a later date?"

I narrowed my eyes. Out loud I asked, "What are you talking about?" In my head I finished with, *you gigantic turd*. Because I was, in fact, giving myself a loophole.

"The statement reads, 'We don't get naked TONIGHT, and you can drive me to school AND AROUND CHARLOTTESVILLE tomorrow.'"

I hoped the look on my face conveyed the appropriate level of disgust. "I agree already."

"Do I need to make you repeat it verbatim, or can I take your word?"

"You probably need to make me repeat it," I admitted, somewhat ashamed of my own shiftiness, and although I found it distasteful, I repeated the statement. "So," he said, and he couldn't keep the amusement out of his voice as he said it, "what do you want to do after dinner?"

"Oh, I don't know," I said. "I've never been waterboarded."

He busted out laughing, "Seriously, Lily, you gotta get it outta your head this will automatically be bad, or hard, or painful. I know it's scary. It scares me, too. But if we go slow…" he trailed off.

"How slow?" I wanted to know.

He thought for a second. "Remember that turtle you entered in The Great Cacciatore Turtle Race? Remember how slow he was?"

I smiled at the memory of Taekwondo the Turtle. I entered him in the big race in third grade. The race had nothing to do with a recipe for chicken, but we wanted it to sound important, and Mavis Bennet had chicken cacciatore for dinner the night before, so we went with cacciatore. Four syllables, Italian, exotic, seemed like it conveyed just the right level of importance for a turtle race.

My turtle…and by "my," I mean the turtle Jack caught and carried around for me because I wouldn't touch it…moved at the speed of a glacier. He came in last place, a good twenty minutes after all the other turtles crossed the finish line. The owners had taken their contestants to the celebration which consisted of juice boxes and Lance crackers and, of course, lettuce for the racers. But Jack sat with me until Taekwondo finished the race because I couldn't give up on him. Still smiling, I nodded that I remembered how slow he was.

Jack stood up, walked behind me, and put his hands on my shoulders. He bent down and kissed the top of my head. "That's how slow we'll take this."

Since I was comfortable with that rate of speed, there was really not another way to stall. "I don't know how to go about it," was all I could say.

"I do," he said, his mouth still near the top of my head. "Let me take that part off your hands."

Chapter 8

Once we finished eating, Jack, grimy from the garage, jumped in the shower. I toyed with the idea of going on the Doe Network. And then, big surprise, I went on the Doe Network. I wanted a quick peek at the peach heart and the purple flower tattoos. My urge satisfied, I closed the computer and gathered up the dinner dishes. Since we ate directly from the cartons, all I had were glasses and forks, which I deposited in the sink. With Wendy and Misty-Storie on my mind, I was on autopilot. First, I shoved all the leftovers in the fridge. Then I tossed a few older and more questionable food items in the garbage and put those dishes in the sink, too. My mind wandered to Storie. Would I be prepared to confirm that the decapitated body was her body? The body I explored in what could only be described as the most radical encounter of my life. How would I deal with it? Therapy? Maybe I could do something in her memory. Make a donation in her name. Sponsor a marker on the Appalachian Trail. Do they have markers on the Appalachian Trail? I knew when a cyclist got killed on the road, people erected a ghost bike—an old bike painted white—on the spot where the cyclist died. Was there something like that for hikers? A pair of boots sprayed white, tied together by white laces and tossed over a tree branch to mark the spot, maybe?

Sudsing up the dish sponge with a squirt of pink Palmolive, I looked out the kitchen window at the yard below where I noticed Miss Delphine with a shovel and a plastic garbage bag in a wheelbarrow. Too far away to make out the details of the bag, I briefly considered what Stephanie would do and then abandoned that in favor of pole vaulting straight to my own unfounded conclusion.

For the second time in one day, Jack snuck up on me, sending me right into another full-blown episode of tachycardia. Standing too close, he asked, "What are you looking at?"

I jerked at the unexpectedness of his voice, the fork slipped from my fingers and clattered into the sink. I grabbed at it, knocking over the *B* glass, but thankfully no damage was done. The same could not be said for my spastic heart.

I took a breath, trying to steady myself. What was it with this guy and the kitchen sink? Perhaps I needed to stop doing dishes altogether. He closed the already narrow space between us and any progress I had made toward slowing my heart rate was out the window. Taking a page from the possum's playbook, I froze, pretending not to notice he was there.

"You're stiff," he observed.

Since it wasn't in the form of a question, I didn't feel compelled to answer.

"Want to tell me what's going through your head?"

"No."

"At least you're honest." Again, not a question.

He persisted. "Would you like to know what's going through my head?"

"Is it that dirty dishes make you horny?"

He laughed, sincerely but softly. "Everything you do makes me horny, but that's not it."

"Is it that I'm easy prey when my back is turned to you?"

"No, girl, nothing about you is easy."

"All right, I give."

"The principle of proximity is what's going through my head. Remember that from Chicken 101 this morning? Just like with the chicken, my objective is to put you in a slightly uncomfortable position by forcing you to get close to the exact thing you obviously don't want close to you."

"If you think this is 'slightly' uncomfortable for me, then the fire chief needs to seriously re-evaluate your judgement."

"How uncomfortable is it?"

"If the range goes from fuzzy pink slippers to a branding iron, the heat coming off the iron is already singeing my skin."

"Wow. That's pretty clear."

"Clear enough for you to take a step back?"

"Nope."

"Jack," I started but stopped.

"You're okay," he whispered. "I promise I won't do anything. I just want to stand here until I feel your muscles relax. That's all. Promise."

Oh, that was all? Was he serious? He may as well have asked Lady Liberty to relax, set her torch down on the grass, pull up a lawn chair and stay for a glass of sweet tea.

Apparently in his world, not doing anything involved slowly moving his hands to my shoulders and massaging the spot where my neck connected to my body. It actually felt good. I dropped my head forward and closed my eyes, focusing on the neck massage while trying to ignore the presence of the masseur. To my own astonishment, I felt my muscles unclench in spite of myself. He noticed, too.

"Ah," he said quietly, "there it is." He massaged for a few more minutes. When he stopped, he laid an arm across the front of my shoulders and pulled me into him. He put his lips to my ear and said, "Thanks for trusting me to do that." Dropping his arm, he stepped away and sat down at the kitchen table. I could feel him watching me, but I took the opportunity to finish the dishes in order to regain my composure. When I finally turned around, he was smiling his lopsided smile, blue eyes charming as ever. That's the smile that got him dates with some of the most beautiful women I'd ever seen. That's the smile that made their clothes just fall off their bodies. Oh, no no. He wasn't using that smile on *me*. Was he trying to use that smile on *me*? Unbelievable.

Before I could call him on it, he said, "Want to take a walk?" The idea temporarily bamboozled me, until I remembered I did want to take a walk to the backyard to see what Miss Delphine was burying out there, or who, as the case may have been.

The walk didn't yield any useful evidence that would indicate a crime had taken place. There was a newly dug patch of dirt next to the last one she dug. But that was all I could deduce without exhuming the remains, and Jack for some reason was adamantly against that idea. We strolled a little farther. The thin summer light of late evening was pretty, and neither of us turned back. We ended up walking the property line, as best as we could, since I wasn't interested in following it through the wooded sections. It was a nice piece of land that took us about thirty minutes to circumvent. Eventually we found ourselves in the chairs on my little porch. When we lost all the light and the skeeters came out, we headed inside.

He closed the door behind us and took my hand. There was a weird look on his face, which could only spell trouble for me. Pulling me toward him, he said, "I want to smell your neck."

"My neck?"

"Your neck," he repeated, smiling.

"What?"

"Remember the Night of Eight Questions?"

"Like I remember not to put tin foil in the microwave."

"Remember when you let me kiss you, but only on the hand, cheek or neck?"

"Vaguely," I said, with obvious sarcasm, waving my hand to dispel an imaginary thought bubble, which, by the way, was filled with some very spicy expletives.

"I know you didn't mean it to be, but that little loophole of yours was crazy hot. Your neck smelled like oranges, and it made me dizzy."

"You just took a shower with my soap. Smell your arm," I told him. "Your skin smells the same as mine."

He shook his head. "It's not the same. It's not even close," he persisted.

"Sorry, honey. This skin smells like a day of mediocre interviews, stale bakery air and summer sweat."

"So go take a shower," he suggested.

Liking the idea, but not necessarily the outcome, I was indecisive. No worries. Jack to the rescue with a reasonable rationale that benefited him, of course. "Take a shower. You'll feel great, and I'll get to smell your neck. Everybody wins."

"Can you limit yourself to my neck only?"

"Swear."

I took a little longer in the shower than usual. Blatant stall tactic. Ordinarily, I would have jumped into my comfortable summer jammie pants and a t-shirt but decided that might not be the message I wanted to send. He needed very little encouragement these days. Instead, I slipped into the bedroom and put on clean shorts and a tee, with a bra and panties. And then, since it seemed like part of the freshly showered/clean clothes package, I slipped back in the bathroom and brushed my teeth. Before exiting, I smelled my arm to see what all the fuss was about. It did smell like oranges. But that's why I paid $9.50 for the soap.

Jack was sitting on the couch, looking at something on his phone. Deciding not to make this easy, I plopped into the big chair opposite him. "Feel good?" he asked.

I nodded.

"Can I smell your neck?" he asked.

I thought it was nice of him to ask again, and I nodded. He was off the couch, over the coffee table, and standing in front of my chair before my nodding head came to rest. He hoisted me up by the hand so we were both standing there in the small space, but that didn't last long, because in one smooth motion he dropped into the chair and pulled me onto his lap. He slipped the elastic band from my ponytail, and my messy brown hair fell around my shoulders, which seemed to enhance the game for him. Moving my hair aside like a curtain, he leaned in and drew a slow deep breath. I think I heard him whisper something, but I couldn't make it out. His voice was thick, and I was a little dizzy, probably still from the flash of vertigo when he spun me onto his lap.

"Can I kiss your neck?"

I heard very loud warning bells going off in my head, and the only sound I could make was, "Um."

After another deep intake of my orangey skin, I felt him trace a line down the length of my neck with his thumb. It was light, and it tickled. He didn't seem to be in any sort of a hurry.

"Can I kiss your neck?" he asked again.

I coughed, still unable to get a word out. He pulled his face back enough to look at me, and I did the only thing I could, I turned my face away.

There was a hint of amazement in his voice when he asked, "Did you like it when I kissed your neck the last time?"

He waited, twirling a piece of my hair around his index finger.

I wasn't good at not speaking first, especially when the stakes were high, so I resurrected a phrase I learned from a sailor I once dated, something they were taught to say to avoid admission. "I can neither confirm nor deny the presence or absence" (and here's where I filled in the blank) "of any feelings, positive or negative, about that kiss."

"You liked it," Jack said, almost to himself. "Look at me, Lily."

As if that was going to happen. Not voluntarily, anyway. He shifted under me so he could twist my face toward him, but I kept my eyes closed, not wanting to answer this line of questioning. "Look at me," he said with a little more urgency, then added, "Please."

Oh for the lost art of hacky sack. I opened my eyes and lifted my chin in the best display of defiance I could manage. "Did you like it when I kissed your neck the other night?"

This was embarrassing on a level that approached incapacitation, and I didn't know why. I wrestled with myself for a few seconds. I could have lied and said no, but I had a feeling that would result in an even more intrusive line of questioning. Glancing down, I breathed a very soft, "yes." He said nothing, but when I finally looked back at him, his eyes were shining like Christmas morning.

Holding my gaze, he said, "Can I kiss your neck again?" Wow. He really wanted me to sign off on this. Which coincided with the fact that I really wanted to sign off on it. Why couldn't I?

"Just your neck," he assured me. "I won't kiss or touch anything else, and I'll stop if you start to panic." Now, that's something I would not have believed from any other guy I ever dated. But I believed Jack.

"Okay. You can kiss my neck." And to my utter surprise, he didn't. He stayed right where he was, looking at me with his blue eyes that were two or three shades darker than usual.

"What?" I asked, defensively.

"Just giving you a chance to think it through and change your mind."

I smiled at him. "I don't want to change my mind," I said. "But thank you for checking."

We engaged in this neck play for well over an hour. There was smelling of skin, touching, and kissing, but it was all confined to my neck. I'll be honest; it was sensual. And at one point, I even contemplated busting out with a lip kiss but decided I didn't want to deal with those repercussions at this point.

When we got tired, we talked about bed, going back and forth about sleeping arrangements. I offered to crash on the couch. All this neck kissing had one very obvious result, he was turned on, and I guessed he knew I was, too. Sharing the bed in the traditional way seemed fraught with potential hazards, and I think he agreed. He ended up taking the couch, and I laid in the bed for what felt like an average summer solstice, eyes wide open, wondering how we got here and what in the name of the elf on the shelf I was doing.

This was such a bad idea. When this ridiculous plan of his went south, and he got bored with the idea of it, where did that leave our friendship? Where did that leave my already confused feelings? Through the closed bedroom door, I heard him get a beer, and in my mind I saw him bend the bottle cap and send it flying into the trash can. He was probably coming to the same conclusions. We could still safely end this before it got out of hand.

It felt like I had just closed my eyes when I heard Jack calling me from the doorway. He got no response, so he came into the room and sat on the bed. "Hey," he said. "You ready for chicken school?"

I rolled over so I could look at him, but I couldn't get my foggy brain to generate a word strong enough to tell him exactly what I thought of those chickens. The idea occurred to me that he would probably go feed them himself if I asked nicely, but that would further ingratiate him and deepen my dependence, two things that would work against me in the long run. I forced myself out of the bed and into my flip flops. Passing through the kitchen, I grabbed the broom.

"What are you doing with that?"

"Defending myself."

"Lily," he started but then cut off whatever sermonette he was about to deliver. "Leave the broom." I complied, making it clear that I thought advancing unarmed was an extremely poor decision.

On the porch, he asked, "So what usually happens?"

I scanned the ground near the bottom step. "What usually happens is that the ringleader, McNugget, blocks my way, forcing me to create a distraction so I can get by."

Jack looked for McNugget, who may have been off amassing reinforcements. We moved down three steps and waited. No chicken. We were halfway down when she popped out from under the stairs. So that's where she staged her ambush.

"There she is!" I hissed.

"I see her. Have you tried walking past her?"

"Jack, I thought you were here to provide useful suggestions!" Again, it came out as a hiss.

"Stay here and watch what I do. I'll show you how to walk right past her." He took the last half of the steps in what I would consider a very normal fashion, stepped to the left of the chicken who was stationed dead center, and passed without so much as a cluck of disapproval.

"Now you come down," he directed from the ground.

"Hard no."

I guessed he knew that my trench was already dug because he passed by the chicken again and came back up the stairs. "Let's go down together." Facing forward, he reached his left hand back to me and waited until I took it. Slowly and a little awkwardly we moved down the rest of the steps. McNugget hadn't moved, and Jack retraced the same route he used the first time, not giving me a chance to falter. The chicken looked up at me, scratched her creepy little stick foot, and turned away. I didn't stop to savor the victory, because I wanted to get into the garage before she changed her mind.

"Do you see how easy it is to walk right past her?"

"Well, this time it was easy. She's afraid of you. You won't be here every time, though."

"We'll keep practicing," he offered. "You'll get it." Turning to the garbage can of chicken scratch, he asked me if I knew how to throw it on the ground.

"What do you mean? I just dump it out."

"Okay. That gets the job done. But the thing about chickens is, they like to find their own food. If you spread it out, they get to hunt for it."

"Spread it out?" I tried to visualize how this would look but came up blank.

"Yeah. Broadcast it. Take some in your hand, and kind of toss it." My look of mystification must have given me away, because he said, "I'll show you what I mean." Scooper in hand, he opened the door for me to go first. I shook my head adamantly, like a pitcher shaking off a catcher, until he stepped out first, and I followed.

He closed the door to the garage, explaining that chickens are curious by nature and love to explore new places. An open garage door was as good as an evite in the inbox. Now this I found useful. What would happen if I ran back to the garage one morning only to find that McNugget had camped out by the chicken feed planning a surprise attack? I'll tell you exactly what would happen, Miss Delphine would be digging another shallow grave to bury my cold dead body, that's what.

I was on Jack like syrup on a pancake, which he probably loved. Right now, I didn't care what kind of lewd thoughts I may have been provoking. I would undo them after this miserable chicken class was over.

Out by the coop section of the yard, we stopped. Most of the birds were still inside. But one or two of McNugget's recruits were out and about. I stood behind Jack as best I could. He took some scratch in his hand. Moving his arm in a semi-circle, he spread the small amount on the ground. He did it twice more before he held the scoop out to me and said, "You try it."

I noticed that the chickens were already pecking in the area where he tossed the grain. And since he threw it pretty far, they were actually moving away from us, McNugget included. Lacking his ball-player's grace, my throw was wildly unchecked. When Jack didn't laugh or comment I disposed of the remaining scratch. Once the job was finished, I felt an insanely overinflated sense of pride in my work.

We walked back to the garage, him casually, me still on alert for rogue bombers. But once I deposited the scooper in the bin, I threw my head back and laughed. He held his hand up so I could slap him a high five to complete my celebration. "Nice job, Barlow."

"Thanks."

"Think you can do it by yourself?"

"Nope."

"Okay then."

Delphine stood at the kitchen window, pouring herself a second cup of coffee from the pot, watching Jack going down and up the garage steps. "That boy's got his work cut out for him," she told Cro, who came to stand beside her. "Seems like he's not afraid to take it on, though."

Back upstairs, we washed the corn dust off our hands. I let him use the kitchen sink while I opted for the bathroom. This girl ain't dumb. Hands clean, he met me coming out of the bathroom and corralled me into the bedroom. "Let's lay down for another hour," he suggested. "I missed you last night."

The bed looked comfortable, and it was still really early, but I wasn't sure what he meant by lay down.

"What do you mean by lay down?"

"I mean take your body from a vertical position to a horizontal position."

"No skin smelling or neck kissing?"

"No."

"Alright then."

He stretched out on top of the bedspread, shoes off. I climbed under the covers, which provided an added barrier of protection, and without any further complicated discussions, we both fell asleep.

Rolling into Charlottesville in Jack's truck, I remembered how much I loved the town. Full of different opinions and ideas. Full of people treading water between youth and adulthood, wanting desperately to be taken seriously but still screwing up every chance they got.

Our first stop was the campus bookstore. The store and the campus in general were dead. The official start of the fall semester was still a couple weeks away, and the last summer session was already finished. The handful of people were probably locals, a few professors, and some work-study folks like me. Jack came in with me and walked around. I noticed a particularly attractive woman trying hard to get his attention, but he was completely oblivious. Jack Turner not zeroing in on a beautiful woman? Hello, Devil? I hear it finally froze over. Can I get a bucket of ice up here?

The price tag on the new textbook could have paid the bakery manager's salary for the first week. I sucked it up and hauled it to the checkout. Jack grabbed his wallet, but I gave him a do-not-start-with-me stare that chilled the air between us. He felt my message loud and clear, and I think he decided to pick a different battle later in the day.

With the legitimate obligation concluded, I was ready to put Charlottesville under the microscope. We decided to make a plan over lunch. Jack picked the local bagel joint because he thought they made the best bagels in the world. Literally. The world. I found this funny since he'd never been off the East Coast. I knew it was unlikely that South America would have a better tasting bagel, but still, if you had never tasted it, how would you know?

The only reason he was allowed to extend such high praise to a competing bakery was if the bread or bread-like product concerned was not on Poppy's menu board. Since Dad and Uncle Dave had never been in the bagel business, Jack was free to pick another favorite bakery for his bagels. Interestingly, even though NYC was regarded as the gold standard for this particular item, he stuck by Gordo's, having tried and rejected the famous New York bagel when he was there for the firefighters' 9/11 Stair Climb event a few years ago.

You could get just about any kind of sandwich at Gordo's. It was good and cheap. So cheap that during the semester, I usually ordered two extra sandwiches, a turkey and cheese and a peanut butter and jelly, to give to a homeless woman I regularly passed on the edge of campus. Since the PB&J didn't need to be refrigerated, I always suggested she save that one for later and eat the turkey first, but I don't know if she ever took my advice.

Pulling out a chair for me at a corner table, Jack took the seat beside instead of the seat across, and as always, we were facing toward the restaurant instead of looking out the window. I never asked him about this preference, just kind of took it for granted, but I had a suspicion it was so he could stay alert to potential problems, you know, choking, armed robbery, what not.

In no time, I was working on my egg salad bagel and he was almost finished with his first ham and Swiss. He ordered two. To keep his strength up, I think is how he explained it. No explanation necessary, really. Jack burned calories like the Qin Dynasty burned books. Probably all the muscle. He wasn't bodybuilder bulky, but he was densely packed. In other words, a lifeguard would struggle with the rescue stroke because the boy would sink like a bag of bricks. Me on the other hand, I had just enough pudge to make me buoyant. I'd be the easy one to save, and frankly, I saw that as a check mark in the plus column.

Unwrapping his second sandwich, he said, "Okay, Detective. What's the plan?"

"Well, I made a list of all the people I remember being at Backroads last year. There were 23 people I knew well or fairly well." I transferred a smudge of egg salad from my fingers to my shorts before unbuttoning the side pocket. That was a predisposition from growing up in a bakery. An apron made it easy to wipe your hands on your clothes, even when you weren't wearing one. I saw a really perky, redheaded girly-girl at an adjacent table use a paper napkin like a delicate lace hanky to wipe her hands. Her watermelon nail polish made it look like a commercial for, well, a commercial for napkins. Or maybe nail polish. I decided to rethink my slovenly habit of wiping my hands on my clothes at some point, just not this second. At the present moment, I was too busy fishing for the piece of paper crammed in my pocket. Once retrieved, I passed it to Jack.

On it, I had listed the names categorized by reliability. There were three categories—Expert Witness (the most reliable), Kinda-Sorta (50-50 on the reliability spectrum), and Snowball's Chance (meaning these people probably didn't even remember they were at the festival).

"I like your categories. Very descriptive."

Of the twenty-three people, six were considered Expert Witnesses, nine were Kinda-Sortas, and eight were Snowballs. I left the Snowballs on the list for no other reason than the fact that it seemed like good police work to me.

"So," I continued, "of the twenty-three people, I have contact information for twelve—one Expert Witness, three Kinda-Sortas, and all of the Snowballs." Watching the expression on his face, I waited for him to comment.

"Go ahead."

"Go ahead, what?" He asked, innocently.

"Go ahead and make a crack about the people I know."

"I have permission to make a crack?" He sucked in a noisy breath and blew it out. "Just to be clear, the people you know well enough to have their phone numbers are the people who were so drunk or high they may not even remember the festival?"

I nodded, but he paused, I assumed to bypass the preferred profanity he would ordinarily use in a situation like this one. Notwithstanding his commitment to clean up his language, I proceeded to taunt him with a half-smile and an eyebrow raise, waiting expectantly.

He tossed a sideways glance at nothing in particular and clucked his tongue. When he re-engaged, he simply said, "Raise your standards a foot or two, will ya?"

"What can I say?" I shrugged. "I'm an ambassador of the people."

With physical effort, Jack refrained from further comment. I thought it best to just move along with the plan. "From this list, I took the liberty of contacting the four people I know from the first two categories." And here's where I simply could not keep my mouth shut. "Thanks to the magic of text messaging, you'll notice this was done without leaving the county." I sweetened up the acrimonious intent of the last sentence with a sugary smile.

"I noticed," he said, cocking his chair at an angle so he could see me better. Under the guise of aiming for a crumb, he reached his hand toward my face and moved his knuckles lightly down my cheek and past the corner of my mouth. The action accomplished exactly what he intended it to accomplish—it shut me right up.

"Now, where were we?" he asked, more to himself. "Oh, yeah. You honored my request not to leave the county. Instead, you magically texted four people. Right." He smiled with tight lips, like he was in charge. "What'd you get?"

"I got stuff," I said, "but after that stunt, I'm not all that excited about sharing it."

He leaned in and said, "Remember when you called me the Gestapo? I told you then, I have ways of making you talk." The statement was followed by his trademark wink, but it felt sinister, not flirty.

Oh for the sake of the Prime Meridian. I had to stop giving this man opportunities. By way of deflecting, I covertly gestured toward the redhead a few tables away. Her tight tank and super short skirt would surely get his mind back in his own arena. He glanced over and back. "Pretty," he acknowledged. "But I told you, I found something better."

That left me with one option—fall back on bodily function. "I have to use the bathroom."

"Oh, I'm sure of it," he said.

I hoped the time-out would ice the kicker before he tried for a field goal. When I got back, Jack was appropriately distracted, but not by Ginger, who had changed seats at her table so Jack could more easily see all the gifts the good Lord gave her. To her consternation, his eyes were glued to his phone.

"Are you ready for the results of the text messages?"

"Yes, I am," he said, and it seemed like the steamy moment was behind us.

"Here's what I got. The Eye Witness said that one of Storie's hiking friends told her Storie really liked a band at the music festival. In fact, according to the Eye Witness, they timed the hike to get to the music festival just so Storie could see that band."

"Wow, that's actually good information," Jack admitted.

"Wait," I told him. "It gets better. The Eye Witness said a guy on the Kinda-Sorta list could probably tell me more since he was hanging out with the hiking friends most of the weekend. That guy's name is Frank. I don't have his contact info, but the Eye Witness said he waits tables at a bar across from campus, The Rathskeller."

Chapter 9

Sitting at an outside table on The Rathskeller's shady patio, we ordered two Coronas. The server asked for ID and studied mine but barely glanced at Jack's. It didn't matter, we were both legit, but still. When she brought the beers, Jack tossed his lime on the table. I pushed mine down into the bottle, plugged it with my thumb, and turned it upside down in a move that took me years and more than a couple sprayed beers to master.

We asked the server if she knew Frank. "Frankie? Sure. Be right back," she said with a huge smile and a pierced tongue.

Frankie, as it turned out, was a girl, but by happy coincidence she knew Frank, the boy. "He doesn't work here anymore. Got canned. The manager didn't like him taking leftovers off people's plates for his own personal doggie bag at the end of each shift."

"Well," I said, giving poor Frank the benefit of the doubt, "A guy's gotta eat."

"Whatever," Frankie said, not taking her eyes off Jack, who used his baby blues to ply her for information.

"You know where he's working now?"

"Yeah," she said coyly, wanting the flirtation to continue.

"Well?" I said flatly, wanting the flirtation to end. Believe me, no one had to point out the hypocrisy here. Don't want to date him…don't want anyone else to date him…when did I become jealous of Jack?

She looked at me, gave the thinnest little huff, and said, "He's tending bar over at The Purple Lampshade." The accompanying look said, why don't you go find Frank while I take Blue Eyes here back to my place. She left to make a circuit of the tables she was waiting, but apparently she had claimed us, or at least one of us, as hers also, because eventually she wound her way back. When she did, she made no secret of writing her number on a napkin and sliding it over to him. I appreciated her femme fatale persona, even though I obviously hated her, and wondered if I could take her in cat fight. I wasn't known for my cat-fighting abilities, but I felt like I had it in me this once.

Jack kept his eyes on me. My guess was he wanted to see how I would play this hand. For some reason, I was fuming inside. I knew if I made a big deal out of it, my best friend would use it to secure his boyfriend status. I chanted in my head—let-it-go, let-it-go, let-it-go.

Coming through it, I turned the tables as Frankie slithered away. "I dare you to call the number," hoping my expression was more of a smile and less of a sneer.

Jack may have been onto my jealousy, and he seemed just a hair disappointed that I didn't give in to it. "I know what you're waitin' on, Lily. You've been waitin' on it all day—the chick in the bookstore, the ginger at Gordo's, this little hottie—you want me to take the bait." He took a drink of beer. "Here's the thing. The same old bait isn't working anymore." He tossed some bills on the table then tossed back the last of his beer. "The new bait," he smiled a lecherous smile, "smells like oranges." He took a pretend whiff of the air in my direction and acted like the very fragrance was more than he could humanly take. To further underscore his point, he rolled the napkin with Frankie's number into a long fake joint and dropped it into his empty beer bottle.

119

The gesture was an overt demonstration purposefully devised to clear up any doubts about what might have happened to the napkin with the number. By doing it, he put to rest every single question that could nag at me later. My guess was, he knew I remembered an old Jack who would have slipped the napkin into his back pocket when all heads were turned.

He held my eyes for a few seconds, and I tried hard to be a blank page. Then he stood up, pushed his chair under, and held out his hand. "To The Purple Lampshade?"

I willingly accepted this offer of a graceful exit. "The Purple Lampshade."

I had never heard of The Lampshade before, so he put the name in his phone and found a street, which I had also never heard of. Jack google mapped it, and we were within walking distance, so we left the truck parked. The establishment was a dive, and it looked to be closed, but we found a beer truck around back and approached the driver. "Hey man, you know a bartender named Frank?" asked Jack.

The tall, sweaty driver never raised his eyes from his clipboard, tipped his head toward the door, and half-spoke-half-grunted, "Inside."

We took it as an invitation to enter. The place was every shade of purple. Little stage, sticky floor, and more purple. It was a relief to see the color scheme included the lampshades. I imagined that anytime they needed or wanted to paint something, they just went down to the Home Depot and picked a can of purple paint from the deeply discounted shelf of mixed colors that had come out wrong. I visited this shelf on occasion, when one or another of my college rooms was too gross or, one time, too orange. I even knew a person who once had the paint guy mix a particular shade of green, left the store without taking the paint, and came back the next day to find her color on the shelf. Seventy-five percent off. I had never stooped to that level of working the system and hoped I never would.

The bar was long and covered with a pretty magnificent mosaic that looked a little like Vincent van Gogh's *The Starry Night*, only in a purple-centric palette. I ran a finger across the tiny bits of glass. Sticky. I rubbed the now-sticky finger on my shorts to clean it off, not even considering my resolution from earlier in the day to abandon this objectionable habit.

From the far end of the building, and somewhere near the floor, we heard a voice yell, "Closed!"

Jack took over. "You Frank?"

"Nope."

"You know Frank?"

"Dude, who *are* you?"

"Just a couple people who want to say 'hey' to Frank."

The guy stood, holding a bottle of vodka in each hand. "I don't know y'all."

Jack smiled and nodded, "So you are Frank."

"I don't have time for this, dude. I gotta count inventory."

"We're not here to get all up in your shtick, dude. Just trying to track down a friend you might know."

Frank said alright but squished the sounds together so it came out "aw-ite." He found a place behind the bar for the vodka and walked toward us. It seemed to make sense for me to take over since I did sort of know the guy, so I said, "I'm Lily. I was at Backroads Music Festival last year with some friends, and I think you were there." Recognition spread across his face.

"I remember you," he smiled, finally sure we weren't from some collection agency or, you know, rival drug dealer.

"We had an econ class together," I added.

"That was the bomb. Backroads, not econ. Don't have the cash to go again this year, but it was a good time. Who y'all lookin' for?"

"There were a few people hiking the Appalachian Trail. Do you remember them?"

"Oh yeah. Those boys could party."

"Do you remember a woman named Storie Sanders?"

"Naw. There was a Stella, though," he smiled.

"Storie was hanging out with some other people, not the hiking crew. She had long blond hair in braids."

"Wait, I remember that girl. Her name was Storie? Hot."

I could feel Jack's enthusiasm surging. "I met her at the festival, and we kinda lost track. I'd like to find her again. Do you know where she lives? Anything else about her? Do you remember anything about her friends?"

"Let's see," Frank stretched his memory back to a year ago. "I remember a couple of guys she was with saying they were there for the band Gravel in the Whiskey because your girl was Jonesin' for the bass player. They had seen the band somewhere in Maryland, and those two hooked up." He thought a few more seconds and added, "That chick Stella was from Georgia. I remember because we got to talking about the greatest name ever for a sports team."

Jack cut in and supplied the team name, "The Macon Whoopee."

"Dude," Frank was smiling and nodding at his new best bud.

"Dude," Jack smiled back.

"What kind of baseball team calls themselves Makin' Whoopee?" I asked.

"Ice hockey," Jack corrected. "Not M-a-k-i-n'. M-a-c-o-n, like the town of. The team folded but classic name."

I gave myself an invisible shake and tried to gingerly pull my feet out of the growing pile of dude manure. "Is Stella from Macon?" I asked Frank.

"Yep," he had a far-away look in his eyes and was possibly reliving a session of making whoopee with the woman in question. I really couldn't blame him, but I needed more information.

"Do you know her last name?"

"Last name? For real? I wasn't planning to marry her. I wanted to get it on with both of them, Stella and Storie, but Storie was off with some other chick, gettin' a little girl-on-girl action."

At this juncture, I snuck a peek at Jack who looked like his brain was a can of Coke left too long in the freezer, the top was busted, and the slushy mess was oozing out. Still, he didn't give me away. Thanking my lucky Aurora Borealis, I anticipated there'd be some sort of fee for this service, due upon receipt. Add that to the existing debt I owed him for not blabbing to Mercedes, and it was getting kinda steep. Maybe he'd settle for smelling my neck. That seemed to be worth something to him.

"You want to find Storie? Find the band. They play all over. They've even been here in C'ville."

"Thanks for your time." Jack stuck out his hand and they performed some sort of brief male closing ceremony. As if seeing me for the first time, Frank said, "Lil-ly. Girl. Whachoo takin' this semester? I'll get in the class."

Jack cut him off and staked his territory, "Dude."

Frank backed down. "Sorry, dude. My bad." Then he added, "Y'all stickin' 'round? Come back tonight, and I'll buy you a beer."

"Thanks, man. If we're around, we'll stop by."

Stepping out of the monochromatic establishment, it was nice to see the full spectrum of color the world had to offer. I gave my girl, Stephanie Plum, a virtual hug, not at all disturbed by the fact that I was seeking the approval of a fictional character. Jack stepped out behind me and grabbed me up in a real hug. "You did it!" He twirled me in a circle. "You tracked down some very useful information. We're on our way to solving this mystery."

The joy started leaking out of the moment when I realized what his compliment implied. We were on our way to proving the identity of a murder victim. It landed on him at the same time, and he tried to recover, but there was really nothing to say. He pulled me to him again, and this time the hug was less celebratory and more supportive. It also lasted longer.

It was about three in the afternoon, and Marshall was around a two-hour drive home. We decided to head back so we could go look at the Turner puppies. The day's events, those surrounding Misty-Storie and those surrounding Lily-Jack had been exhausting. The conversation on the way home was on the quiet side, and mostly we just listened to the radio. With Jack driving, I even fell asleep at one point.

Jack, ever safe behind the wheel, had his phone connected to Bluetooth so he could do stuff handsfree. When his mama texted, he hit the button to hear the text. "Dinner at six?"

Looking over at me, he said, "You feel like dinner with my folks?"

"No."

"That's fine. I'll get it to go," he smiled. The unspoken meaning was that we would be eating together at Miss Delphine's. I ciphered an even deeper meaning that he planned to spend the night again.

"Are you staying over?"

"Yes, I am. Unless you want to stay at my house. Lady's choice."

I didn't respond, which he correctly interpreted as hesitation regarding our relationship. "I won't ask to smell your neck." He reached for my hand and squeezed it. "Just want to be your friend tonight, not your lover, not tonight."

That came as a relief. "Okay," I said, closing my eyes. "We can't stay at your house, because I have to feed the chickens."

Testing this hypothesis, he asked, "Would you stay at my house if you didn't have to feed the chickens?"

I answered him, still with my eyes closed, "I don't see how that's a relevant question."

My eyes snapped opened when I heard him say to his phone, "Call Delphine Walker."

"Jack, what are you doing?"

But before he could tell me, Miss Delphine was on the line.

"Hello?"

"Hey Miss Delphine, it's Jack Turner."

"Jack, honey. So nice to hear from you."

"I have Lily with me."

"Hey, child. You doin' okay?"

"Hey Miss Delphine. I'm fine. Hope you are."

Back to Jack, "Miss Delphine, could Lily get a pass on feeding the chickens in the morning? She may be over my house."

"Well, of course, that'd be fine. It'd give Lily a break and more importantly it'd give my chickens a break. Y'all be careful and watch for deer if you're drivin'."

"Yes 'um, we will. And thank you."

"Bye now." Miss Delphine ended the call.

I had a few questions vying to be asked first but the one that fought its way to the top of the heap was—Why in the name of the hyphenated zip code did he have Miss Delphine's number set up as a contact?

When I asked it, he answered without so much as a shred of chagrin. "I want to make sure I can get hold of you if I need to."

"That's why you have *my* number in your phone," I said it with an enhanced sense of upsetment.

"What if you aren't able to get to your phone? Like, you're doing laundry at Miss Delphine's and you leave your phone upstairs. It's a good idea for me to have the numbers of people you may be with or who may be near to you." He waited for a response, and he got one—my stony silence. "Don't you have other numbers for me?"

I thought about it, and unfortunately I did. His parents and his brother, Joe. Not people I would call ordinarily unless I had been trying unsuccessfully to get hold of Jack or possibly if I was planning a surprise party for him. "So I guess I should also have Rick and Mitch's numbers for when y'all are four-wheelin' this weekend? In case you roll my Jeep into a deep crevasse, losing your phone and breaking your leg in the process."

"That's a ridiculous scenario, but you got the right idea. I'll text you their numbers later."

I quietly withdrew my unspoken quit-spying-on-me accusation since he had satisfactorily explained the contact situation. Besides, it was possible that I really didn't care that much, just being cantankerous.

When we pulled into the Turner drive, Jack's mama came onto the porch. I hadn't seen her since I'd been home this time, and the shot of pure, sweet affection did me good. Of course, she didn't know anything about the Misty-Storie mystery. Her attention to me was based on Dad's heart attack and the temporary closing of the bakery. She knew we weren't staying for dinner and didn't make a federal case out of it. Refreshingly unlike my own family. Once I had a chance to hug Mr. Turner, who was still greasy from the garage but knew I didn't care, we turned our collective gaze to the real stars of the Turner household—four crazy-cute puppies with absolutely nothing in common. After interacting with each one individually, my decision was for Jack to take them all.

"No," was his response. "One dog or no dogs."

"Is there still time to pick one, or are y'all ready to give them away?"

"There's time, darlin'," Mrs. Turner assured me. "They can't leave Lucy yet, and the boys have first dibs. Joe hasn't decided on his either."

"You didn't tell me Joe was taking a puppy." I looked up at Jack who was holding a puppy in each arm.

"I didn't know he was."

"Yeah," Mr. Turner chimed in, "your mama's after him to pick one."

"A boy needs a dog," she said, sweetly. Joe was twenty-seven and Jack was twenty-two, but in her mind probably still fourteen and nine. "Joe says he can take his to the yard and leave her in a back office once she's trained."

Before we put all the puppies back in the large pen with the mama dog, I learned there were three girls and one boy.

"Do you want a boy or a girl?" I asked Jack.

Playing the proud new parent, he joked, "It doesn't matter to me, as long as the baby is healthy."

I decided not to ask which were the girls and which was the boy. If it didn't matter to him, then I wanted to pick the one with the right personality. I would definitely need a little more time to get to know them better.

On the way out, Jack asked if I wanted to stop by Miss Delphine's for anything. I knew I could borrow a clean t-shirt, and I knew he kept a supply of toothbrushes on hand, in case any of his dates went long (all of them, in other words). "I guess not. I used up the last of my Ghost-Off spray the other night. I don't suppose you have a spare can?"

"Fresh out. But I have some WD-40. Will that work?"

"Probably not, but I'll give it a try."

When we turned onto Wisteria Lane, the protective layer of puppy love, achieved while playing with the puppies, started to peel away, and I noticed myself clenching a little. Wow. Ghosts and their associated ghostly avocations really weighed on me. Did that mean I was clairvoyant or just a superstitious, crazy college student? Maybe I should try a little harder to embrace the supernatural. But that would be like, like embracing Poppy's. Whoa. Really? Did I seriously equate a friendly family bakery with the tortured souls of people who were stuck between the living and the dead, forced to roam the planet while trying to resolve their unsettled business? That was a bit of a stretch, even for me. Lost in my own thoughts, I was still sitting there when Jack turned off the ignition.

"It's not haunted." He said it carefully, as if he thought I was really close to a dangerous ledge maybe twenty-five to thirty stories up, and good firefighter that he was, he wanted to talk me down.

"What are the sleeping arrangements for tonight?" I suddenly needed to know.

"Well, given the pending issues of the perceived haunting," he smiled, "my money says you'd prefer to sleep in close proximity. But if not, you got options."

"If you think for a second that we'll be in different parts of this haunted house tonight, then you're jousting with a chopstick, son. So you can either stay in the same bed, no funny business, or you can back this truck out of this haunted driveway and take me home."

He listened to me rant. "I told you, Lily, I'm your friend tonight, not your lover." He leaned over and pushed a piece of hair behind my ear. "I can't wait to show you that those two people are not mutually exclusive, but tonight is not the night."

After we ate the meatloaf and mashed potatoes his mama packed for us, I did the dishes, peacefully unaccosted. Then, I made Jack accompany me to all the possible sleep spots in the house. I was deciding which would be the least obvious portal to the otherworld. No, really. That's what I was doing. Good sport that he always was, he kept his comments mostly to himself. To be honest, the living room had the best energy, but I ruled it out. If I took the couch, he'd have to sleep on the floor, which he would do in a second without a single complaint, but I would feel bad for at least a few minutes immediately before I fell asleep.

"I think we should sleep in your bedroom," I said.

Jack scrunched his eyebrows into a semi-scowl. "I vote for the upstairs bedroom," he said.

"Why? Have you seen a ghost in your room? Oh for the long way home, you have seen a ghost!" I said emphatically. "Male or female?" I asked, but I had no idea why that mattered.

He stepped toward me, put an arm around my neck and brought me into his chest. "No ghosts. If I had seen, heard or felt the presence of a ghost, I wouldn't be here and I sure as shark sh—." He pulled up hard to avoid the cuss word, and I decided to mess with him.

"Sure as what? Shark sh...iitake?"

I laughed; he smiled. "The point, Lily, is I wouldn't risk bringing you to a haunted house."

"Then why don't you want to sleep in the main bedroom?" I pushed back from his chest so I could see his face. He looked stuck, which was surprising. I couldn't remember the last time I saw Jack Turner at a loss for how to express himself.

"What's going on with you?" And to help matters along, I started to process all the reasons he may not want to sleep in that room, supplying the first one that came to mind. "You were sleeping with someone else in that bed and you haven't changed the sheets yet!"

"No," he ground out the word and followed it with "Lily." The exasperation was real, not fake. "I'm not sleeping with anyone else period. I haven't slept with anyone else since the beginning of the summer. Tonight I made a commitment to you that I would be your friend. To fulfill that commitment, I swore to myself not to bring up anything that would make you feel even a little uncomfortable."

It was becoming apparent that this issue was strangely important to him. I could push it for the sake of my own inquiring mind. And I'll be honest, as far as the human capacity for selfishness, I am the reigning champion—acutely aware of my own needs and desires, to the point that I can, without a speck of guilt, put myself first ninety-eight percent of the time. Staring at his face, the curiosity was practically scorching my innards. By acquiescing, I'd probably lose my selfish person crown but would surely still hold on to runner up. What would be the harm? Other than the fact that this would work its way into my brain like a parasite in a pig's belly and probably cause an aneurysm before the light of day. Oh well. Die of an aneurysm or die as a result of some violent paranormal attack. Either way, you're dead, right?

"You can hang on to whatever dirty little secret you're protecting," I said. "We'll sleep upstairs tonight."

The look of relief that flooded his blue eyes was remarkable. Hmm. And I did that. Maybe I should, on occasion, put someone else's needs before mine. "Thank you," was all he said, but he said it with a degree of sincerity that made me a little ashamed I had thought about forcing him to do something he really didn't want to do. I was even more ashamed when it occurred to me that he wouldn't have done that to me. I hit a third, higher level of shame, when I flew by the first two levels and caught myself wondering how I could get the information out of him even though I had, seconds earlier, agreed not to. Admittedly, there is no real way to disguise the fact that I'm a terrible person.

The queen bed in the guest room was plenty big enough for us both, and the temperature in the room was comfortable for an old house. Sometimes second floors got the shoddy end of the AC, but this one was all good in regards to climate control. For PJs, Jack loaned me a t-shirt and a too-big pair of gym shorts. I had to max out the drawstrings in order to keep them up, but they worked fine. There were no disturbances to speak of, as far as apparitions went, which was good, because I had plenty else to think about, like the intrigue surrounding the master bedroom.

Wrestling with a serious case of monkey-mind, I flopped around like a flounder fish trying to settle into the sand, but I couldn't quite get there. Eventually, I was thoroughly tangled in the blanket and the extra fabric of the loose shorts. I thought Jack was sleeping through my bed sheet ballet until he asked if I was okay. I could tell from the quality of his voice that I didn't just wake him up, even though it was one in the morning. He wasn't sleeping either.

"I'm okay. Just restless."

"Me too. Let's have ice cream."

The only thing that slowed me down was the white sheet with the yellow rosebuds still twisted around my left leg. And since no sheet stands between me and my good friends, Ben, Jerry, and Mr. Breyers, I kicked my way free and headed toward the door with Jack on my heels.

When it came to ice cream, I gave myself a pretty wide berth. Jack, on the other hand, was a lot more selective. His go-to was anything home-made using whatever fruit was in season. Strawberry in May. Blueberry in June. Blackberry in July. Peach in August. Chocolate the rest of the year.

When the Turner boys were young, they picked the fruit, but when they grew up and had jobs and lives, Mrs. Turner started getting it from a fruit guy out of Pennsylvania. He had a stand at the Leesburg Farmer's Market, and she made the trip to town almost every Saturday until she finally got Dad and Uncle Dave interested. They thought the fruit was exceptional and the price was fair, so they started sourcing from the fruit guy, also known as Clem at Birchwood Fruit. When the bakery was operating, there was a weekly fruit delivery. At that point, Mrs. Turner started shopping in the bakery's parking lot. I supposed she was back schlepping to Leesburg while the Marshall deliveries were indefinitely suspended.

Jack made his ice cream using an antique churn that belonged to his granddaddy. He didn't mind cranking the handle and never relied on anyone else's sweat equity to start, assist or finish the process. Sure, he was happy to let other people take a turn, knowing the good Samaritans would get bored or tired in short order, and he never held that against them, against me in other words. He saw the ice cream as its own delicious reward for the effort it took.

Now the question was, did he have any already saved in the freezer or did we have to start from scratch? Not knowing his kitchen, I randomly opened cabinets and drawers, looking for spoons and bowls. He gave directions like "next one over" and "go left." Meanwhile, he went to the freezer and pulled out a half gallon container of what I knew had to be peach. Winner, winner, chicken dinner.

He scooped out two huge bowls. And all I could think was *manna*. As in manna from heaven, but that wasn't the word I was actually trying to find. "There's a word for 'food of the gods,' do you know what it is?"

"Ice cream."

"No, banana brain. It's from Greek mythology."

"Oh, right. Let me dust off my vast knowledge of mythology. Wait. Can't help you. My expertise lies in the area of Roman mythology, not Greek."

"Just google it, jerk."

Phone always close at hand, he did. "Ambrosia. It's delivered by a dove or a nymph and brings immortality if you eat it. Nope. The nymph was turned into a grapevine by a rival. So, I guess just the dove now."

I lifted a spoon of the creamy frozen ambrosia and held it out to him. "Food of the gods," I said.

"And goddesses," he added. "To immortality." Touching his spoon to mine in a makeshift toast, he smiled and asked, "How you feeling?"

"Ice cream makes me feel great," I tipped my head and shoved another spoonful into my mouth.

I heard a voice in my head, possibly belonging to Ms. Reason, repeating the phrase, "Don't do it. Don't do it. Don't do it." But I flat out ignored the voice of Reason and just went for it.

"So good, in fact, maybe we could have a conversation."

Jack took a bite. "Late night kitchen conversations. My favorite. What do you wanna talk about?"

"Us."

I think he wanted to snap his head up but realized he might give himself whiplash in the process. It must have been by sheer force of will that he kept his eyes on his ice cream. "You sure you're up for that?"

"I am. Are you?"

"Does a leprechaun poop Lucky Charms?"

Smiling at his choice of words, I said "Okay. Let's talk."

"Oh, no, no. You brought it up; you tell me what's on your mind, and I'll weigh in."

I stirred my spoon around in the last little bit of ice cream soup, picking my words carefully. What I really wanted to ask was why we didn't sleep in the downstairs bedroom. I have a difficult time letting things go. I like to think of it as charming, not obsessive. I could be wrong, though.

He waited, loving the long pause. I was sure he would literally stand there until his next shift at the firehouse before he broke the silence. So what were my options? I could ask him my question, the one he implored me not to ask, reiterating that I'm a narcissistic human being who thinks only of myself. Or—I could apologize for being that selfish person and confess I still wanted to know. Is there any measure of growth in the latter? Because I'd really hate to set a precedent.

I finally pulled my gaze away from the soup in the bottom of my bowl. He was, of course, studying me. I lifted the bowl, offering him the soup.

He nodded and then moved from where he was standing opposite me to lean against the counter beside me. Putting his empty bowl in the sink, he took mine. There was a sliver of relief not having to face him. Maybe he did it to make this a little easier, but he still didn't speak. He just stood there and finished the last of my melted ice cream.

"Okay," I said, weakly.

Turned out, all he needed was for me to say something first. Didn't matter what I said, because that one word was enough.

"I have a suggestion."

"Oh, thank the mighty Mississippi," I said under my breath.

"We each get to ask the other person one question." I waited and eventually pointed out the obvious.

"You know what I want to ask you."

"I do," he said.

"You begged me not to pursue it."

"I did."

"Well, you don't have to answer it, Jack."

"Then ask a different question, Lily."

Okay, that sounded like permission to me. "Before we get started, what are the rules of engagement?" I thought it would be a good idea to get these ironed out in advance, not to mention, it would help me scope out any loophole I might want to use later.

"You ask me a question. I answer it. I ask you a question. You answer it."

"Do we talk about the answers or just move on?"

"I propose we table discussion for the time being. We can circle back around at a later date. Can you live with that?"

"Yes. At what point does a reply go from an answer to a discussion?" I was only protecting myself by nailing down the specifics. The less I could get away with saying, in the form of my answer, the better off I'd be.

"Basic, complete answer. So, if you ask a yes-or-no question and you get a yes-or-no response," he explained, "the question has been fairly answered. Pick your phrasing carefully." He turned so he was facing me again, "You can't buy your way out with a dare this time if you think the question is too tough."

Suddenly, it occurred to me to consider what *he* might plan to ask *me*. I was so consumed with the question I wanted to ask, it didn't resonate that he got to ask one, too. Mention of the dares brought all the neck sniffing and kissing to the front of my brain. What could he possibly be up to? I knew it would likely be something I couldn't skirt. To buy myself a little more time, I said, "I need to pee before we start."

"Good idea."

When I got back, he was sitting at the kitchen table in his usual spot with his back to the wall. I automatically picked the seat to his left, putting him on my right side. Nothing advantageous about it, I just always liked having the other person on my right side.

Chapter 10

"Do you want to go first?" I offered, generously I hoped.

"Nope."

Of course not. What did Lady Macbeth say about courage? Screw it to the sticking place? Lady Macbeth? Seriously? She was my paragon for pointers on courage? Regardless. I relaxed my shoulders and asked my question. "Why didn't you want to spend the night in the downstairs bedroom?"

Without so much as a stutter, stammer, or even a blink, he laid it out. "I'm saving that room for the first time I make love to you in this house." Since he had answered the question completely, he was technically done, but he added two details for my benefit. "No one else has been in that bed with me. I haven't brought any other women to Wisteria Lane."

Well, talk about your run-of-the-mill show stopper. Luckily, no discussion, so I swallowed hard and kept my big mouth shut. He let it sink in like rain on dry dirt, and when I looked up, he was grinning. Since becoming invisible was something I had yet to master, I decided the best way to deflect was to get away from my question and let him ask his, although frankly, I didn't know if that would be better or worse. There were frying pans and fires every direction I turned. "Your go," I finally said.

No hesitation. It was almost as if he had practiced this question ahead of time. "What are two things I could do right now, before I kiss you, that would help put you at ease?"

And there it was. So I satisfied my morbid curiosity regarding his bedroom secret, but at what cost? I doubted this would have come up if I hadn't picked at the scab. I only had myself to blame here. "Well, for starters, we could stay out of your bedroom."

He laughed, "Okay. Downstairs bedroom is off limits tonight. Number two?"

What else could I really say that would help me out in any way? Tell him to keep his clothes on? Tell him to keep my clothes on? I sat there, mentally drumming my fingers, wondering how to get out of this one. Risking a discussion that was expressly banned when the rules of engagement were established, I asked, "Is this your interpretation of Taekwon-do-the-Turtle slow?"

It seemed like he contemplated calling me on the discussion point but reconsidered. "Remember when I gave you your first off-road lesson in Sandi-with-an-i?"

Ha. Was he willingly using her full name without me forcing him to say it? Slick. And suspicious. "Yes." My tone was dry on purpose.

"Do you remember the first thing I taught you?"

I did remember it but not because it was an especially practical nugget of driving wisdom. Maybe, just maybe, it would be useful if I ever took Sandi off-road. For a mall crawler like me, though, it was only a funny-sounding phrase with very little real-world application. "Go as slow as possible but as fast as necessary," I recited.

"Exactly. Same thing applies here. We're going as slow as possible. If we weren't, I would have slept with you the first night you were back in town. You propositioned me, after all. Remember?"

No way, no how, was I taking that bait. Once he realized I was committed to maintaining radio silence, he proceeded. "Think of this kiss as a rock or an obstacle you would encounter in the Jeep. All I'm gonna do is give it a little gas. Just enough to bump it. That's it. For all intents and purposes, we're still going Taekwondo slow."

If Stephanie found herself in a similar situation, I'm sure she'd figure out a way to use it to her advantage. Now there was an idea. Use it to my advantage. But how? For number two, I should focus on the long term vs. the short term. You know, ask for something that might be helpful somewhere down the road. Suddenly, it came to me, and it was as obvious as the first cannonball splash of the summer swim season.

"The second thing you could do to put me at ease is don't freak out when I tell you that Mercedes and I are going to see Gravel in the Whiskey on Saturday when y'all are Jeeping up at Buckshot Junction. They're playing in Winchester. At a place called The Switchback." Rarely, in our many years of friendship, have I gotten to out-shock Jack Turner, and this moment had big historic longevity.

His admiration of my trick was authentic. He chuckled and shook his head. "I see what you did there, girl. You're good." Then he stood up and reached for my hand.

"What are you doing?"

As he pulled me to my feet, he said matter-of-factly, "I'm sticking to the rules and tabling the follow-up discussion for the time being. I've done my best to increase your comfort level by honoring your two requests—not taking you to my bedroom and not freaking out. Now, we kiss."

"Let the record show that I formally oppose the idea of kissing, and I disavow any outcomes of this kiss and its associated risks."

"Noted. While we're at it, I want the record to reflect that I disagree with you and Mercedes going to the concert without support."

I guess I had that coming, so I nodded. "Also noted."

I stood there, trying to stall. He had me by the hand and was inching his way backwards, out of the bright kitchen toward the dim foyer. "Why don't you just kiss me here and get it over with?"

"Get it over with? Are you crazy?" He stopped moving, and it looked as if he was sizing up the heretic before him. "Lily, this is not the kind of thing you do just to get it over with. This is the kind of kiss that orbits the planet a couple of times before the two people involved fall through the stratosphere back down to Mother Earth. It's hard for you to understand, because you've closed yourself off to the possibility, but you'll get it in a minute." Then, he resumed his backwards baby steps toward the foyer.

My stomach felt weird. It was like looking at twenty feet of tangled Christmas lights. There was a certain dread associated with the snarl, but when you plugged the cord into the outlet, it was also kind of thrilling to see the big ball of blinking bulbs. I had a hard time separating the dread, or panic if you will, from the other inexplicable sensation of excitement. Jack seemed to be having a hard time getting wherever he was trying to go, because he stopped in the foyer, dropped my hand and moved toward me. There was only so far I could step back before I found myself sandwiched between the wall and his body.

"You okay?" he asked.

"I don't want this to go too far," I said.

"Kissing on the mouth. That's as far as we go tonight," he assured me, and he waited.

"Just on the mouth," I reiterated.

Before the last syllable had escaped my lips, his face was near mine. He took a deep breath in, pulled my ponytail loose, dropped the elastic band on the floor, pushed one hand through my hair and put the other on my waist. I felt off balance, like when you miss the bottom step coming down the front porch. To steady myself, I laid my hands on his chest, but it was awkward, too intimate. So I lifted them half an inch, and they floated there. This subtle shift caught his attention. He moved his hands to cover mine and exerted just enough pressure so my palms reconnected with his shirt. "I like your hands here," he whispered. "It feels good." After a few seconds, he let go and smiled when my hands stayed put.

His mouth hovered close to mine for hours, or was that the space-time continuum playing games with the minutes? Finally, our lips touched. A small hum came from somewhere below my lungs, and I think it signaled the disintegration of the last particle of resistance I could muster against this kiss. When he took the kiss from lip to tongue, all my concerns got crammed into a Tupperware container and shoved to the back of the fridge where they were promptly forgotten.

He was breathing hard, but I was breathing harder. I hoped it was an indication of our levels of fitness and not our levels of excitement. My right hand moved up to rest lightly on the back of his neck. Without taking his mouth from mine, he leaned his head back, pushing his neck more completely into the palm of my hand. Then it was his turn to make a sound that moved through me like fingers trailing in the water over the side of a canoe.

I don't know how long we stood there. I let myself lose track of time, fear, and consequences, knowing it would all be waiting for me on the other side. When we finally pulled apart, he whispered, "Don't say anything. Let's just sleep on it."

Without a word, I followed him through the foyer, up the stairs and into the guest bedroom, where I meant to lay down, but instead where I backed him against the wall and started the kiss again, surprising us both. When we stopped, I laid a finger on his lips and searched his features for some iota of what he was thinking, but I was too confused or too tired to piece anything together. I think I saw the eyes of my friend, though. That meant the friendship was still intact, at least for the time being, which was a colossal relief. A more imminent concern was the fact that I had been totally and paradoxically swept away by the kiss, to the point where I was finding it hard to generate an appropriate boundary. Was it really such a great idea that we were about to lay down together in the same bed?

"Is it really a great idea to sleep in the same bed tonight?"

"I like where your head is," he said, nodding. "But we're definitely sleeping in the same bed tonight. No clothing will be removed. No body parts will be explored. I'll lasso my libido; swear it." He raised his right hand, to show he was, in fact, swearing, then lowered his tone to add, "I want the smell of oranges to be the last thing I notice before I fall asleep." He lost himself momentarily in a fog of orange fragrance, then added, "And one more thing…"

I waited for the one more thing, but it turned out to be another long kiss. Not a bad last thing at all.

When we finally got in the bed, I had no idea what time it was. Fatigue gushed in like a big wave swamping one of those milk carton boats kids make when they're in the second grade. The plastic-straw mast and the paper sail were completely destroyed in the process. I wanted to think about what just happened and prepare any necessary rebuttal I might need in the morning, but my eyes were closing against my will. I stayed quiet.

"Hey," he said, "Sweet dreams." Reaching across the imaginary line down the center of the bed that delineated the two separate sides, he squeezed my fingers.

"You, too," I said softly.

"Nah," he whispered. "I don't need a sweet dream tonight. No dream could top what just happened." And we were both asleep in minutes.

I slept like a dead person and woke up holding Jack's hand. He was on his side, I was on mine, just our hands violating the line of demarcation. He felt me stir and opened his eyes, which weren't sleepy looking at all.

That made me think he had been awake for a while. "Hey," he greeted me.

"Hey." Before I could start backpedaling, he laid out his argument.

"Lily, don't pick it to pieces. Something awesome happened last night. We're still going slow."

Wow. It was like he knew I was preparing to erect a good old-fash-ioned rampart, complete with parapet, which, of course, I was. Harder now after I fell for the whole lip-lock thing, and, regrettably, liked it.

That'll hurt me. But I was a professional backer-outer of uncomfortable situations. I just had to rally to the purpose and stay the course.

"Here's the thing, Jack," I started, but he interrupted me.

"No," he said a little more forcefully, "*here's* the thing, Lily. I refuse to accept your refusal to accept the possibility that our friendship has relationship potential. Don't try to dilute what happened last night. Just enjoy the feeling. I am. And I'm looking forward to the next experience, whatever and whenever that is."

I blinked a couple times. No wonder his eyes weren't sleepy looking. He had been up a while formulating that little dissertation.

"Can I ask a question?"

"You just did," he teased.

I smiled in spite of myself and carefully made the next request in the form of a sentence. "I'd like to ask another."

"Sure."

"Now that we've kissed, is it your assumption that kissing will be the new status quo?"

I wasn't looking at Jack. My head was on the pillow and my eyes were glued to the ceiling, which had a simple but elegant crown molding I hadn't noticed before. Jack's head was also on his pillow, but he had turned toward the center of the bed, facing me.

"I get it," he said. "Just because we kissed last night, doesn't mean we've moved to a place where kissing is the norm. My assumption is that we'll find a time and a place to kiss again, when we're both ready." The unspoken translation read—*when you're ready, Lily.*

I nodded acceptance of this understanding.

"My turn to ask you a question."

"Okay."

"Did you like it?"

I knew there was virtually no point in denying it. He had been there the whole time, after all, collecting the hard evidence of my reactions. Any moron with a Y chromosome could have figured out that I was turned on last night. Still, it embarrassed me for some reason. Keeping my eyes on the molding, I said as emotionlessly as possible, "Yes."

I didn't have to look at his face to know he was smiling. "I thought so," he said, running his thumb lightly up and down the hand he still held.

After a few minutes of silence, he said, "Ask me."

"Ask you what?"

"Ask me if I liked it."

Oh for the love of all-night laundromats. Was this guy serious? By way of declining this invitation to stir the pot, I stayed quiet.

"Come on," he needled, sounding more like a spoiled brat than a grown adult. "Ask me."

"Jack," I said, trying to sound disinterested, "did you like it?" I didn't actually think he would say he didn't like it. It may have been a little tame for him, given the women who made up the magnum opus of *Jack Turner's Dating Life*, twelve volume encyclopedia set.

He didn't kiss and tell; that wasn't it at all, but any amateur could recognize a common thread among the women he dated. Let's see, most couldn't make toast, so he wasn't stopping by for their fried chicken. Most couldn't talk about anything besides hairspray or high heels, so it wasn't for their titillating conversations. Most didn't know that water was wet, so it wasn't for their intellect. Nope. It was pretty basic—they all had tiny waists, curvy hips, spectacular bosoms and slinky bodies. So, since this was a departure, I was the tiniest bit curious about his reaction to our kiss. Although, I'd never admit it.

He pushed himself up on one elbow, leaned across the line to my side, and gently tilted my face toward him. His need to make eye contact was enough to provoke a temple full of Buddhist monks, revered for their ability to suppress annoyance. Once he had my eyes, he said, "It will go down in history as the best I-want-to-kiss-you of my life."

So this was how the shy dwarf felt. What was that guy's name? Blushy? Bashful? I opted to ignore it and pitched him a no-brainer he couldn't resist. "What's for breakfast?"

"What do you want?"

"Cereal."

"Got it."

"Sweet cereal?"

"Nope. But there's sugar." He let go of my hand and proceeded to climb over me to get out of the bed on my side instead of exiting from the appropriate side.

"What are you? Ten?"

By way of answering, he slapped me on the gluteus maximus and ran down the stairs to the kitchen. So, yes. He was a ten-year old.

Breakfast chitchat intentionally steered clear of any reference to the last time we were in the kitchen a few hours earlier. The one glaring clue—ice cream bowls in the sink—was easy enough to ignore, and I washed those as soon as Jack headed to the shower.

On the way over to Miss Delphine's, we talked about our schedules. We wouldn't see each other at all since he was working at the garage all day and the fire station tonight. I asked if we could hang out on Friday evening, and he snatched that up like he was grabbing an EpiPen for a bee sting.

"Want to go down to the lake? Mitch and Rick are camping there so we can leave early on Saturday."

"If you're suggesting we camp, then, I'm gonna have to say...no."

"I'm not suggesting we camp. Just hang out for a couple hours, maybe swim, cook out, come home."

"Well then, yes, the lake sounds great."

The lake was one of the destinations our group of peers used for meeting up and socializing. There were some good places to pitch a tent if you were so inclined. There was a well-used fire circle surrounded with logs for sitting, but most people brought folding chairs. There was that stupid rope swing. I doubted anyone even knew who owned the property. We started hanging there in high school, and no one ever accused us of trespassing, so we just kept going back. The classes behind us didn't seem as interested in the lake, probably because it was a dead spot. No cell signal for miles.

I was still thinking about the lake, but Jack had moved on to a different, more prickly subject. Gravel in the Whiskey. "When did y'all track down the band?" he asked, using a decidedly nonchalant tone.

Last night, any bookie would have given great odds that the first thing out of Jack's mouth this morning would have been a tirade about us going to the concert. After tabling the discussion in favor of the kiss, he had to be dying to get into it. It was uncharacteristic of him to sit on something like that for so long. Maybe the kiss was more of a narcotic than I realized.

"I texted the name to Mercedes, and she found where they were playing." Then, to help push the conversation in a direction that favored me, I added, "Lucky they're right around the corner, isn't it?"

"Lucky," he said, but I doubted his sincerity.

I didn't offer anything else in the way of specifics. Generally speaking, I tended to create a hassle where one didn't exist just by running my mouth, although keeping it closed was harder than it sounded. Problem was, he didn't expand on his points of discussion either.

"Wishing you could come hear the band?" I asked.

"The band would be cool, sure, but that's not what this is about."

I knew exactly what this was about; I just wasn't feeling all that charitable and wanted him to say it out loud. I figured I could use it to support my case against dating: the fact that I didn't think he could handle me having a separate life outside his sphere of influence.

"Then what's it about?" I prompted.

"It's about you and Mercedes not being clear on where a fun adventure stops and something more dangerous starts."

"Or is it about you not being in control of a situation?"

"Me? Needing to be in control?" He blustered with false bewilderment, like he was having an epiphany. Or a brain hemorrhage.

"Face it, JT, you're a control monger."

"Hey, I'm Jack," he said, taking his right hand off the wheel and offering to shake mine while his left hand took over the driving. Then he followed the fake introduction with something he might be expected to say at a meeting for a twelve-step program, "and I'd like to be in charge. Right now. Of this meeting." I laughed because it was stupid, but it was also true, and since he had taken the first step of admitting it, I wanted to leverage that.

"So, I'd like to enter into State's evidence your admission of needing to be in control, which clearly supports my assertion that you could not date me without bossing me."

"Well constructed litigation, counselor," he said. "How can I prove it to you? Give me a test that doesn't involve you identifying a murder victim." Was I mistaken, or did he put a little extra emphasis on the word *murder* to underscore the danger? Was that supposed to be a subliminal message or something?

"Well, I can't generate a test off the top of my head. Who am I? Horace Mann?"

"Who?"

"Horace Mann."

"Who?"

"You know, the father of standardized testing. It's funny. Horace Mann"

"Yeah, it's funny."

"You're not laughing."

"Because it not ha-ha funny. It's oh-yeah funny. Hence, no laughing." Then, he added, "I'll tell you what else is not ha-ha funny—y'all going to the concert by yourselves."

"Jack," I started to defend myself, but as usual, he shanghaied the conversation.

"Lily, I have two very explicit concerns. If you can make me feel okay about both of them, I'll back off. Swear it." He raised his right hand to show how serious he was, but for emphasis, he repeated, "Both of them."

"Shoot," I challenged, feeling supremely confident in my ability to parry his worries. "What are your concerns?" In my head, I made the dumb animated gesture of putting the word *concerns* in air quotes. I realized it was a jerk thing to do, that's why I did it in my head. And yes, it made me feel better. And yes, I knew that was pathetic.

"First off, which one of y'all will be able to listen to a band in a bar and not have anything to drink?"

Well, now, that was a thorny one. Neither of us was known for our desire, let alone ability, to abstain, and I knew he wouldn't settle for the one-beer-only argument. So, since I didn't have a ready response for that one, I simply said, "And secondly?"

"And secondly, what's your plan if the bass player turns out to be the killer who murdered Storie?"

Hmm. Another exceptionally valid point. I hated to acknowledge that his air-quote concerns were valid, but did I have another choice? While I was gung-ho, I was not an idiot.

"Okay," I said, trying to give him credit without losing face. "I can see where these two points may be of interest to you."

"Of greater interest is your response to these two points." And he waited.

"Well, I may need a few minutes to think it through."

"I've already thought it through."

Of course he had. Anybody want to wager he also had a proposition in mind?

"Joe and Luis can serve as designated drivers slash bodyguards. Side benefit, Mercedes has the hots for Luis."

Luis Mendoza worked with Jack's brother at Republic driving a forklift. They were definitely not the worst two babysitters Jack could appoint. Rick and Mitch would have been way bigger stink bugs up under the lampshade. Those two bucket heads would have driven us in their ridiculous Jeeps across every rock formation on the side of every back road

146

between here and Winchester. Happily, they would be occupied doing just that, up at the Junction with Jack.

"Mercedes has the hots for Luis?" Funny how this unknown tidbit was way more noteworthy than the fact that I might have a face-to-face encounter with Storie's killer on Saturday night. And it suddenly clicked that Luis was the guy I saw with Mercedes on Monday evening in the parking lot over at Manny's. Ahhh. That's where I knew that guy from. So, she was into Luis? Why didn't she say anything to me about it? Maybe because I've had a monopoly on all big news since I got home. Wow. Self-centered? I told myself to text her a cheerful, how's-it-going message after I got rid of Jack.

"Well?" He asked.

"Well, what?"

"Can Joe and Luis drive y'all to see Gravel in the Whiskey on Saturday?"

"Don't you think you oughta ask them first?" As soon as I said it, I realized he probably already had. The grin on his face verified my assumption. I shook my head. "Dude," I said, "you have a problem."

"I most definitely have a problem. Her name is Lily," he smiled and took my hand. "I'm protecting my own interests here. Just want you to be safe, so I can get that next kiss." Did he think the memory of the kiss was enough in the way of smoke and mirrors to distract me from the fact that he was micromanaging my life again? I considered it briefly before mentally giving in. He was right. The memory of the kiss was definitely distracting.

He pulled into Miss Delphine's driveway and put the truck in park. Great. The conversation obviously wasn't finished.

"I'm serious about what I said. Give me a test so I can prove that I know how to step back and let you live your life. Your free spirit is one of the things I love about you, girl. I don't wanna change it or be in charge of it."

"For all our lives you've made sure I was always okay. I like that you do that. Which is why it'll be hard to switch from friends to, to…" I stammered because I almost said lovers. Yikes. Wrong word to use at this juncture. So I started again, "From friends to anything else."

"I know it seems like it will be hard. But I think the switch from one to the other will be so natural, it'll surprise you."

"You're gonna have to prove it to me."

"I'm up for it."

He had a strange look on his face, like he wanted to kiss me. I waited, deciding this would be a good first part of a multiple-part test. He seemed to get he was being judged and settled for squeezing my hand.

He jumped out, came around, and opened my door. When I got out, I looked up at him and said, more seriously than I intended, "Be careful tonight."

"It's always my first rule." I hugged him, the good old you're-my-best-friend hug.

It was still fairly early in the morning, and I didn't have to get to the bakery interviews until around noon, so I decided to shower and wash my hair. Afterward, I picked a new polish for my toes, a dark iridescent plum called Drama Mama. Seemed to suit my current situation perfectly. With a whole Jack-free day to myself, I felt like I could catch my breath. Sure, I had interviews, but those sort of ran themselves at this point, and since I was being a lot more selective in contacting prospects, I only had three today.

With a couple hours 'til I needed to leave, I opened my computer, popped onto the Doe Network and scrolled down to look at the Misty-Storie tattoo. Then I went on to the great state of Illinois where I clicked on Case File 276UFIL. The artist's rendition was of a woman 18-22 years old, but in the postmortem photograph, she was beautiful. Race—black, height—five-one, weight—one hundred twenty, found on May 24, 1994. She tied her ponytail with a black ribbon. She wore a pink bodysuit and a black bra. She had pierced ears but no earrings or other jewelry. She had a six-inch scar on her belly. According to the person charged with her murder, she was a prostitute.

I thought about the black ribbon in her hair. I thought about the similarities in our lives—both women and both early twenties. That was it. She may have been pregnant at one time, even given birth. The closest I ever came to being pregnant was that EPT test I took when I was a few days late. She was probably never safe; I almost never felt unsafe. If she was a prostitute, she had few opportunities. I had so many. I thought about the man who killed her. I wondered about the family who loved her. I called her Charlotte. Under my breath I said a prayer that she was at peace, that the fear she felt during her murder lasted only seconds and she was free of it now.

Now that I was good and depressed about another unidentified murder victim, I clicked the screen on the computer closed and sat there thinking about the next step. I ran through a mental dress rehearsal of meeting the bass player. To give myself a visual, I popped the screen up again and googled Gravel in the Whiskey. They had a website, complete with concert dates, venues and pictures. The guy with the bass was Ditch Miller. Wavy brown hair, a little long and a little messy. Green eyes. Tattoos for days.

On the website, each band member and a couple roadies all had their own tabs. I found myself drawn into Ditch's photo gallery, which showed him mostly without a shirt, in blue jeans, cowboy boots, and a cowboy hat. Not a bad look at all. Ditch was hot. I scanned his tattoos. There was a set of dog tags, but it was hard to see the inscription. In a different tattoo, Semper Fi. Was he a Marine? Another one showed the outline of what looked like a bear, chopped into geometric pieces, almost with a native American flair. Inside the pieces was a landscape of sky, mountains, river. It seemed like something a hiker would identify with. There was a skull on the card symbol for a spade. There was a classic pin up calendar girl. Then I saw the deal breaker—a 3D black widow spider on his shoulder that looked like every bit of a real spider. For a normal person like me, who had a normal hatred of spiders, the idea of this tattoo was menacing,

149

times ten. Still, I couldn't take my eyes off it. How did the artist get it to look so real? And why would anyone want that? Danger quotient?

Okay, hot Ditch with the spider tattoo. I sat there looking at his green eyes and wondered how I should handle our meeting. Toying first with the ideas of flirting, playing dumb, and playing drunk, I ultimately decided to regurgitate the same line we used with Frank down at The Purple Lampshade—tell him Storie was a friend, we lost track, and I was trying to find her. An acquaintance mentioned he might know how to get hold of her. Probably good not to say anything about the fact that she was possibly a groupie or that maybe they were sleeping together. In the true crime shows I'd seen, the cops always held something back. I didn't think a musician would be too concerned about protecting anyone's privacy, so I didn't anticipate much resistance, unless, of course, he was the killer and was worried I might finger him. What if he thought I was onto him and decided to kill and decapitate me, too. You know, to shut me up. Jack's air-quote concerns started to coagulate.

Maybe I should do something in the way of a disguise to make myself look different in case he tried to track me down later. Apply makeup? Fix my hair? Wear a skirt? I should also probably keep Joe and Luis close by while I interviewed him. It would be too chaotic to try talking before the band went on, or even between sets. We'd have to get to the bar early enough that the band members would still be milling around.

How would we get in? I'd leave that detail to the sexy Mercedes. That girl had seriously special talents in the bewitching department. It didn't matter what a guy liked, she had it covered—risqué outfits, provocative body language, seductive dark eyes, full pouty lips. Seriously, the works. I think she could talk a security guard into letting her hold the Hope Diamond without too much hemming and hawing on his part.

Satisfied that I had put enough thought into Operation Ditch Miller, I checked my phone and saw I had a little over an hour to get to the bakery. Why not pop down to see Miss Delphine? Pump her for info on those shallow graves out back. While I was solving mysteries, might as well take a crack at that one, too.

She was snapping beans in the kitchen and invited me in for a glass of ice tea. Having snapped a garbage barge of green beans in my lifetime, I washed my hands and offered to help.

"I got lots of beans to put up," she gestured to the crate on the counter. "Get a bowl."

"Yes 'um." Funny how she assumed I would know where to get this bowl in a kitchen I'd only been in twice before. Without asking, I turned around and spied one in the dish drainer. Gotcha.

"You get anybody for that bakery, yet?"

"No, ma'am. Hasn't been as easy as I thought it would be. But I have three more interviews today."

"Well, who's been applyin'?"

I ran down what I was now calling the Long List of Losers, in reverse order, omitting Carl Middleton, and ending with Ethel Baxter.

"That biddy, Ethel Baxter, applied to run your bakery? She brag about her chocolate chip cookies?"

"As a matter of fact, she did," I said emphatically.

"Don't believe that lyin' old bat. She never baked an original cookie in her life. Gets the recipe right off the bag of chocolate chips. She's been riggin' that contest for goin' on two decades now. That's serious business in the bakin' world. Mark my words, that woman's gonna turn up missin' or dead, one. And she'll have nobody to blame but her cheatin' self."

Based on the ominous note in her voice, I felt compelled to check on Miss Ethel. Maybe a call later in the day? I knew we didn't part on the best of terms, but I certainly didn't want her dead. And incidentally, could a rigged county fair lead to a crime of passion? Were those black trash bags the body parts of judges that voted in favor of Miss Ethel's cookie?

Thinking I could establish the motive I'd been looking for, I asked, "Did you ever enter your cookies in the fair?"

"Oh, Lord no. Cookies are for greenhorns, child. Professionals bake pies. Now, your daddy can bake a pie. Your mama could, too."

This reference caught me completely off guard. "I don't think I ever heard anyone talk about my mama baking anything," I mused. The sudden change in direction made me forget about working my way back around to those plots she was digging in the backyard.

"Oh, child, Connie did an especially good job with blackberry pies. And I never tasted anything like that woman's pineapple upside-down cake. She used to make it for the cakewalk at the church bazaar every spring. I do believe it was the most coveted cake on the walk, year in and year out."

I looked at Miss Delphine through a haze of amazement. I'd never heard anything about this pineapple upside-down cake before. And I found it interesting that Poppy's never included it on the menu board. She must have read my mind, because she said softly, "Don't let it eat at you, Lily. Your daddy loved that woman so much, relivin' some of those memories would have killed him for sure."

We continued snapping beans in silence until we got through the crate on the counter. Then I headed to the bakery, and she started the hard work of canning.

Chapter 11

Unlocking the back door, I sagged as I stepped into the dark hallway. This whole turn-Poppy's-around initiative wasn't coming together as perfectly as I believed it would. What if I couldn't get the bakery open in time for the start of the fall semester? Was there any kind of dispensation for a family crisis that would allow me a late start, or would I be looking at forced drops across my schedule? Then what? Pick up whatever dregs that couldn't get a minimum number of students enrolled? Ultimate Frisbee and some anthropological linguistics course focusing on the last decade of words added to the Merriam-Webster dictionary under the Slang and Informal Language category? My major wasn't set, so for the time being, it really didn't matter what courses I took since I wasn't working toward the completion of a specific program. However, taking classes just to take them was kind of a wasted attempt at a college degree. Sure, there were people doing it who fancied themselves professional students. How they paid for a never-ending college career was a mystery the magnitude of crop circles.

The concept of putting the bakery up for sale reemerged as a tempting possibility, but then I remembered the look on Dad's face. I had to keep trying. If we sold the bakery, I envisioned a very short decline until he turned off his oven for good. Then, both my parents would be dead, and I would be an orphan. Were you considered an orphan at twenty-one years old, or just a parentless adult? My thoughts went down this weedy path as I put coffee on for the interviews. The daisies on the corner table still looked, well, fresh as a you-know-what. Mama's daisies. Mama's pineapple upside-down cake. Connie Barlow. A whisper of sadness blew across my soul. What made me sad was not that my mama had died, I was sad that I never even knew her. The memories saved up by a six-year-old are an odd collection of junk that makes sense only to the six-year-old heart, like a little girl's purse that holds a spoon, three different kinds of string, and an expired plastic rewards card. There's meaning, but you have to be six to understand it.

A knock on the front door brought me back to the present. When I unlocked and pulled it open, I encountered what was easily the most magnificently perfect woman I had ever met in real life. Too bad Jack had turned over this weird new leaf of his, because she was right in his wheelhouse.

Her auburn hair was half up, half down, and there were these wispy strands that curled around her face. How come my loose pieces never looked wispy like that? Self-consciously, I pushed one annoying culprit behind an ear while I continued my survey. The top of her off-white sundress hugged every inch of what was simultaneously a slender and curvy body. I shook an imaginary fist at the universe and screamed *Unfair!* in my head. The spaghetti straps grazed flawless shoulders that had no tan lines or freckles. The skirt part of the dress swirled like when cream hits coffee. I stepped back, and she swished into the bakery carrying a large leather portfolio. Her strappy blue heels matched a small blue purse. Red lips. Red toenails.

"Are you Sue Jennings?" I asked.

154

"No, I'm Laurie-Anne McCoy," she said. "Sue is my agent."

"Your agent? Are you here for the bakery manager position?"

"No, I'm here for the magazine spread."

"What magazine spread?" I asked, wondering if I myself was in the wrong place.

"The magazine spread for Poppy's Bakery," she explained as if she was talking to someone with a developmental delay.

The fact that we were both supposed to be at Poppy's was only slightly reassuring.

She continued. "I brought my portfolio, but I understand if you want to take a few test shots." She glanced around, and I assumed she was looking for the photographer.

"Laurie-Anne," I started, "the only spread we're doing right now is butter on bread. If I needed a spokesmodel, for absolutely anything, I'd hire you without so much as a single test shot. But right now, I need someone who can run this bakery, so unless you moonlight as a manager, I don't think I have anything for you."

She was sure I was mistaken and offered a persuasive argument, making me think she might be right after all. I had to catch myself before I agreed to produce the magazine spread in question. "Do you have a résumé you could leave with me, so when we're ready to start our ad campaign, I can call you?"

She dug around her portfolio, sifting through an array of loose photos that made me wonder exactly which magazine she thought she would be in. She finally pulled out the one and only G-rated picture of herself complete with the contact info for an agency called Jennings Talent Plus on the back, along with some statistics like her height, weight, measurements, etc. She pushed the others back in the portfolio and tugged the zipper with more force than was required. Under her breath I was pretty sure I heard her cursing Sue. I put the head shot on a table and showed my future spokesmodel to the door.

After I poured a cup of coffee, congratulating myself for remembering to pick up a carton of half and half on my way in, I checked email, downloaded a song by Gravel in the Whiskey, and listened to it while I visited Misty-Storie's profile.

Donna Listerfell was my next applicant. When she arrived, fifteen minutes late, I shut the laptop and asked if she'd like a cup of coffee.

"Can you make it Irish coffee?" she kind of slurred and then laughed.

"Donna," I looked her over carefully, "are you drunk?"

"Well lubricated," she corrected.

"So…drunk." I reverted to the original phrasing.

"Yes, then," she pulled out a chair and nearly missed the seat as she tried to land on it, "if that's the term you prefer."

"Let me get this straight. You came to a job interview drunk?"

"Correct."

"Drunk," I said again because I just couldn't believe it.

"Yes."

"Will you be drinking on the job?"

"I do my best baking after I've had a few," she smiled. "Rum cakes are my specialty."

"Of course they are. Well, I admire your honesty, Donna. The problem is, I need a sober honest person, not a drunk honest person."

"It was lovely to meet you," she said, in a way that sounded too moist.

"Please do not get behind the wheel." I begged.

"Oh, for goodness sake. I never drunk and drive." With that she staggered out the door and started weaving down the sidewalk. When I saw her nearly stumble off the curb halfway between Poppy's and Turner's garage, I ran after her.

"Donna, why don't you let me drive you home?"

She agreed just as my phone *cha-chinged*. Text message from Jack.

"What's going on?"

I couldn't really accuse him of spying on me, being in a public space with a slightly unwieldy drunk lady, right in direct line of sight from the first bay at the garage.

"Applicant drunk. Driving her home."

Cha-ching: "Need a hand?"

"Can you take her? Next interview in 15."

Looking up the road, I saw him come out of the garage bay, walking toward us with long strides. When he got there, I said, "Donna, this is Jack. He's a fireman. Can he drive you home?"

Jack tipped his ball cap, "Ma'am."

"Yes," she said happily. "That would be fine."

Donna grabbed hold of Jack's arm, grateful for something sturdy to lean on. Having shared that same gratitude more times than I could count, I understood completely. I moved to Jack's other side, kissed him on the cheek and whispered, "Thanks." He reached a hand up to where my lips had been and then clutched his heart.

"Moron," I hissed, and he winked.

I headed back to the bakery to await my final applicant, wondering how anyone could top those who had thus far applied. A mime. A mime could top the list, I guessed. The candidate turned out not to be a mime, but a person with profound body odor. The odor was beyond the ability of my nostrils to cope, and my gag reflex was working against me. His name was Sam Jones, mid-thirties. His clothes looked clean, and he seemed normal in every other regard, but I'm not sure he ever met a bar of soap. Ever.

Sam, who appeared to be nose blind to his own odor, answered my questions and described his qualifications and experience. When I couldn't take it any longer, I looked around with fake confusion and asked if he noticed a strong smell.

"That's me," he said without even a pinch of embarrassment. "I haven't taken a shower in two and a half years."

I said the only thing that came to mind. "Why?"

"Sodium lauryl sulfate."

"What?"

"It's a chemical in thousands of personal products linked to carcinogens. It's like rolling out the red carpet for cancer cells to invade our bodies."

"Cancer?"

"Cancer."

"What about an all-natural soap?"

"They exist, sure, and I used them for a while. It's really hard to find a certifying body that you can trust when it comes to the word 'organic.' Back when I was using all-natural soap, I only used products certified organic by the Soil Association in the UK. Bottom line, though, mammals aren't designed to bathe. So, I finally made the hard decision to go back to what mammals are supposed to do. I call it the paleo-hygiene movement. PHM."

"Sam, I'm just not sure Poppy's is ready for PHM. The kinds of smells you generally want coming from a kitchen are good ones, smells that encourage the mouth to water. Body odor goes in the opposite direction. Plus, all employees are required to wash their hands, with soap, when they start work and after every trip to the restroom."

"I didn't consider that."

"Maybe you'd be better suited for something outdoors? Lawn service?" In my head, I added, sewage treatment plant.

He thanked me for giving him the chance to interview, and I poured him a cup of coffee to go. Once he was gone, I opened every door and jimmied every window, trying to air out the Sam funk.

Cha-ching: "Donna home safe."

"Thanks, dude."

Cha-ching: "Lunch?"

"Starving."

Cha-ching: "Come on down. We got pizza."

I left the windows open, turned on a couple fans, turned off the AC, locked the doors and walked up the block. Pizza would help put everything into perspective. I knew the pizza would either be in the break room or the back lot, so I waved to Lucinda at the counter and headed back like I owned the joint. Mr. Turner loved the seventies and always had the radio tuned to a seventies station. Spending time in this garage growing up influenced the emergence of my musical tastes, and I knew a lot of these sappy old songs by heart.

I figured Jack would be out back on the picnic table, but I peeked in the lounge on my way past, just to be sure. Empty. Too hot to sit inside a closed-up room. The picnic table was on the shady side of the back lot, near the basketball hoop. Three large pizza boxes were spread out, offering different combinations of toppings, all of which included pepperoni, a Turner boy food group.

"There she is!" Mr. Turner greeted me as I sidled up to the table.

"Thanks for the pizza," I said. "I'm starving."

Jack was deep into what may have been his fourth piece. "Mom brought it by."

I grabbed a slice and turned toward his dad. "What's the latest on the puppies, Mr. T?"

"Well, that raggedy white and brown one has learned how to get out of the pen. I had to chase him around the yard last night for thirty minutes."

"A troublemaker." I tipped my head at Jack and said, "That might be your dog."

The look he shot me hinted at a dark secret between us, I just didn't know which one. "Isn't one troublemaker in my life plenty?"

His dad came to my defense. "Don't you dare insinuate that this lovely girl is anything but sunshine with a ponytail."

I smiled a huge, bratty grin in support of my new best friend, Mr. Turner.

"She's got you fooled, old man."

"Ignore him, Lily." He gave me a side squeeze before heading back into the bay, leaving Jack and me by ourselves.

"How'd the interviews go? I mean the ones where the candidates were sober?"

"Isn't that crazy? Showing up to an interview drunk?"

"That gal was a real hoot. She had a lot to say on her way home. Thanks for not letting her drive."

His gratitude was super sincere. "You're welcome. I generally try to make good decisions where alcohol is concerned." Knowing my decisions were usually better before I had anything to drink, I decided to get off this topic altogether. "The first applicant from today thought she was auditioning for a modeling gig. According to her agent, it was an ad campaign for some magazine. She was drop-your-pizza gorgeous."

"Hmm. Did she have brown eyes and a messy brown ponytail? Did she wear ratty shorts that had something spilled on them?" He let his eyes fall to just such a questionable stain on my own shorts.

I rolled my eyes.

"What?" he asked with a degree of innocence that was annoying. "I'm just describing what drop-your-pizza gorgeous would look like." Then he pretended to bobble his pizza, as if he was about to drop it.

When I didn't bite, he took the innocent thing up a notch with a smile reserved for a cherub on an ice-cream truck. Ignoring him as best I could, I kept the conversation moving. "And the last applicant was promoting an anti-bathing lifestyle he called the Paleo Hygiene Movement."

"He didn't shower?"

"Ever. He's worried about chemicals in the soap."

"How'd he smell?"

"I may not be able to go back in today."

"Wow. Gutsy."

"No. Stinky."

We chatted for a bit longer while I ate one more greasy slice of pizza, then I headed up the street. It wasn't lost on me that I had already seen Jack twice on a day we weren't supposed to see each other at all, but I chalked it up to life in a painfully small town.

Once I got to Poppy's, I took several deep breaths like I was preparing to swim through an underwater cavern. Inside, I quickly closed the bakery windows but my lungs were about to explode before I could get my computer packed up. I ran to the front door, exhaled, sucked another big breath with slightly more drama than was necessary and tried to get out of there as fast as I could. Outside, I stopped short of the Jeep, annoyed that I had forgotten about the air conditioner. There was no choice but to run back in. Climate control was crucial. I didn't need the humidity wreaking havoc with the flour.

On the way home, I decided to swing by Manny's. Not that I was hungry, having just snorked down the pizza, but I wanted to touch base with Mercedes. I'm sure she didn't know Luis would be chauffeuring us on Saturday, and given her feelings about him, at least according to Jack, I thought it was only fair she got a heads-up. Plus, revealing this information in person as opposed to a text message would give me a chance to dig a little deeper, with the facial expressions and the body language. At the very least, I anticipated this news would touch off a radical departure in the wardrobe department for Saturday night. Heels would be higher. Skirt would be shorter. Bra and panties would be skimpier.

This mission to get close to Gravel in the Whiskey threatened to be an unwieldy balancing act. I didn't want to alarm Mercedes with Jack's idea that Ditch Miller might be Storie's killer. Judging from how she handled her half of the chicken-feeding responsibilities the other morning, this had all the makings of an even bigger and sloppier soup sandwich.

The lot was empty when I pulled in, but that didn't necessarily mean the restaurant was. The place was close enough to Republic Building Supply and a couple other businesses that sometimes people just walked over to grab a bite. Still, at two p.m. on a Thursday, I didn't expect to see many folks.

When I stepped inside, Manny lit up. People in small towns, like people in college dorms, share a love of the drop-in visitor. No phone call or text message was necessary to alert the target audience that you're coming by for a spell. The unspoken assumption was that the person would want to see you, no matter what. You'd think cities would offer even more opportunities and a similar affection for drop-ins given the denser populations, closer proximities, and all. I learned, though, that it's really the opposite. People in busier places seem more isolated the closer they live to one another. When I stayed on campus freshman year, my roommate, Jeannette Peters, was from Philadelphia. She didn't even know her neighbors at home. It took her awhile to adjust to the drop-in vibe living on campus.

"Hey, Manny." I leaned in for a hug, which he proffered, giving me two thumps on my shoulder as an extra shot of affection.

"How's Poppy's?"

I shrugged. "You know," I said, "it's not so easy finding good people."

"Aye, *Lilita*." He nodded in agreement, then reiterated, "Not easy." His eyes got bright as he said, "You need a strong person who knows business."

"Right. Sounds simple when you say it."

"I have the perfect one for you."

"What? You know someone? Manny, who? Who is it?"

In a loud voice, he hollered for his daughter. "Mercedes!"

"*Qué?*" She hollered back from the kitchen, then strolled into the main dining room, nursing a cup of something hot. I couldn't imagine Mercedes had any big ideas for a bakery manager. She would have shared them before now. She leaned into me, close enough to touch her cheek to mine, but carefully so the drink wouldn't spill.

"Mercedes has a cousin in Mexico…Tatiana. She is coming here and will need a job."

"What? When?" Mercedes seemed surprised by this revelation. Meanwhile, I was trying to figure out how to tell Manny that I wasn't sure a person new to the country would be the best bakery manager before we got too far down this wrong turn.

"I just got this news, Mercedes. My sister wants Tatiana out of the town. There's some trouble. I don't have all the details yet."

"Does she have any experience in business?" I asked.

"No. She's only seventeen. All her experience is with the wrong boys right now."

"Papa, are you suggesting Tatiana should manage the bakery for Lily?"

"No. I am suggesting that Tatiana work here, while she learns a little more English and finishes high school."

"I don't understand," Mercedes said, shaking her head.

"*She* will work here; *you* will manage the bakery for Lily." He said it as a matter of fact, as if he was stating the color of orange juice. Orange juice is orange. No room for discussion.

"*Qué?*" Mercedes slipped into Spanish, something she did when she was with family or when she was thinking faster than she could talk.

"*Qué?*" I said. Not known for my Spanish, it came out more like "Kcy?"

Facing me, he said, "Lily, you need a reliable employee who knows something about business. Someone you can trust. Someone who won't cheat or steal from your family." Turning toward Mercedes, he said, "Mercedes, you need a chance to use your experience and spread your wings, something to challenge and inspire you." Then, to both of us, he said, "Tatiana needs a safe place where she can finish growing up, the same chance you both had. If Mercedes moves over to the bakery, that frees up a safe place here where I can keep an eye on her."

I was bowled over by the sheer artistry of this plan, but I tried not to give myself away, not knowing how Mercedes felt about it. She rattled off something in Spanish, but of course I had no idea what it was. The intonation sounded the same to me, whether it was conveying anger or enthusiasm. I waited. Manny listened. Mercedes kept going in shotgun-babble mode.

Eventually, she slowed to a rate where Manny could interject, also in Spanish. The conversation continued that way for a few minutes. If I had to guess what was unfolding, I'd say Mercedes was telling him that she needed to be here to look after her dad. It's probably what I would have been saying to my own dad, you know, if I liked the business I was helping my family run. How was a kid, who didn't know anything, new to the country, new to the culture, going to fill Mercedes' espadrilles?

When the chatter wound down, Mercedes looked at me. I knew her well, and I could read that expression like I could read a sign for the ladies' restroom. She loved the idea. Why all the wing flappin' and feather fluffin', I had no idea. She wanted to do it.

"Well, *Lilita*?" She asked me.

"Are you freakin' kidding me? *Si*," I said. "*Si! Si! Si!*"

She smiled wide, her dark eyes sparkling. Manny smiled the same way.

"You gotta know I'm not sure how much the bakery can pay you right now."

"I know," she acknowledged. "We can't pay out what doesn't come in, so let's start with a very small base salary until we show a profit again. I'll outline a business plan."

I loved the way she immediately implied shared ownership by saying "we" when referring to the bakery. People said not to go into business with friends, but sidewinders in a sawmill, this was an answer to a very sticky problem. My mind went wild with the possibilities, and I found it hard to rein myself in. Me and Mercedes, business partners.

Her mind seemed to be racing, too. She happily studied the brew in her fuchsia-colored cup, swirled it once and took a sip. I smelled a hint of chocolate, and I believed it to be what she called Mexican mocha—cayenne pepper and cocoa powder plus some other ingredients in coffee. An actual product of Mexico? Who knew? She followed the recipe her mama put in the small, lacquered box she left for Mercedes upon her alleged deportation.

I knew the contents of the box by heart because Mercedes and I sorted through it every week growing up. The recipe, a rosary whose wooden beads were shiny with prayer, a notecard with an unknown address in

Mexico that her dad either didn't recognize or didn't admit to recognizing, a hair comb of polished mahogany and inlaid mother of pearl, a medal of Our Lady of Guadalupe, and an alligator refrigerator magnet whose legs were attached to the body by tiny springs so they jiggled hysterically every time someone opened the fridge. To this day, the alligator was the only thing Mercedes had removed from the box. It was on the fridge in her house. In middle school, I wanted her to wear the comb, and while she would put it in her hair when we were in her bedroom, she never wore it outside the house. I think she was afraid of completely losing the idea of her mama if she lost anything from the box.

We both came out of our reverie at about the same time. "You want some?" She held the bright pink cup out so I knew what she was talking about.

"Yes, please." I followed her back to the kitchen where she grabbed another bright cup, as yellow as the center line on the road out front. She started adding different spices from memory. She did it perfectly every time. The idea occurred to me that her innate sense of measurement would be one more asset to the bakery.

She filled my cup and topped hers off, then we walked back to the restaurant area and took the back corner booth. It's where we sat together whenever there was important business to discuss growing up, business that included a slew of various crushes, teachers we loved or hated over the years, the death of a classmate to a drug overdose, plans for our lives after high school…

Manny considered it our booth. He even let us decide on the design for that booth when he installed hand-carved wood furnishings years ago. Mercedes picked a beautiful woman walking a horse along a path toward a church. I picked a woman carrying a tray of cakes through a market square. Without going too deep into the psychoanalysis of it, I'm pretty sure we each picked our own mama. That gesture of letting us decide kept us connected to the restaurant in a very real way, which was probably exactly what he wanted when we were growing up. He gave us a place to be that was our own where he could keep us safe. I always respected Manny, but coming to this new and amazing realization about what he did for us, my respect bloomed a little bit more just now. I wondered how he would manufacture this connection for his niece, Tatiana, when she got here. And, of equal importance, how could I give Mercedes a connection to the bakery?

An idea laid itself out in front of me, clear as footprints in snow. "Hey, do you want to put your mama's coffee on the menu at Poppy's?"

Mercedes stared at me. Her dark eyes looked a little too misty in the dim light of the back corner. She nodded her head.

"What do you want to call it?" I asked.

"Mexican Coffee?" She shrugged when she said it.

"You could call it Ana Sofia's Mexican Coffee if you want. It's your mama's recipe, after all."

She put down her heavy cup, and the moisture in her eyes finally collected into a single tear that spilled down her cheek.

"Can I call it that?" She asked.

"You're the bakery manager. You can call it whatever you want. I think Ana Sofia's Mexican Coffee sounds so much prettier than weird-hot-pepper-nutmeg-cinnamon-with-a-little-cocoa-and-some-coffee mixture." I smiled. "It also takes up less room on the menu board."

Mercedes hollered for her dad, who delivered us each a churro to eat with our coffee. When she told him about the addition to the menu at Poppy's, he nodded deeply and opened his mouth to speak, but nothing came out. He put his hand on my shoulder, then left us alone. I felt like the Grinch must have felt when his heart grew three sizes that day. Watching the reactions of Mercedes and her daddy, mine grew at least one. Maybe one and a half.

We finished our coffees as we talked about action steps for the bakery. She had her order pad on the table and made notes as we listed things. She seemed serious about the business plan, and it amazed me that she knew how to put one together. "I took a class online back in eleventh grade. Mr.

Blankenship suggested it when he didn't think I was getting enough out of Business Tech."

I wasn't just hiring my friend; I was hiring a trained businessperson. Nice. Dad would love that. "Write down that we need to introduce the new bakery manager to the owners."

She wrote her names for them on the list, *Tio* George and *Tio* Dave.

"Do you think they will mind?"

"Are you kidding me? They'll only be sorry they weren't the first ones to think of you for the job."

Once we had six or seven action steps listed, I asked, "Can you still get off for the band Saturday night?" I already knew the answer, but it was a good way to push the conversation from legitimate business concerns to the quasi-business concerns of a detective-wanna-be.

"Yeah, yeah," she said. "I already arranged it with Martina."

"You know how Jack likes to stick his nose in my business, right? Well, he arranged for us to have a designated driver. Drivers, plural, actually."

"Who? Please don't say Rick and Mitch."

"Luckily no. Those blockheads will be Jeeping with Jack. He's sending Joe and Luis."

She froze for a split second. Then she deliberately placed the pen on the table, and slowly said, "Luis who?"

"Mendoza," I confirmed. "Luis Mendoza."

"Luis Mendoza is coming with us on Saturday night?"

I was having a hard time deciding if this was good news to her or bad. Jack told me she had the hots for Luis, but maybe the two of them had already burned through the hots. I watched her for a bit then said, "Is that alright?"

"*Lilita*," she said in a husky voice that conveyed all I needed to know. "He's fine, that one."

"So you like him?" I probed.

"*Si*." She said it with a little wiggle in her torso.

"Why didn't you tell me?"

"Ah," she said. "There was so much to talk about. Luis wasn't that important. But Jack's over-protective thing is finally paying off, yes?"

"For you, maybe." I gave it a little more pout than it required, but it didn't catch. I could see her mentally sifting through her clothes closet, picking out and rejecting a number of outfits.

"What are you wearing?" She asked, completely oblivious to my pout. "Not shorts and a t-shirt."

"I was thinking shorts and a t-shirt."

"No, no. Let's go look. I have something for you." She yelled something in Spanish as we moved toward the side entrance.

Mercedes and Manny lived in a beautiful expansion Manny built onto the restaurant. The interior was awash in all the same bright colors found next door in the bar and restaurant, but it was a quiet haven in comparison. There was a bedroom for Manny, an even bigger bedroom for Mercedes, and a nice-sized office. Not surprisingly, the center of the house was a huge kitchen. There was a computer, but no television. A fireplace and two comfortable chairs just off the kitchen made the living room.

"Where will Tatiana sleep?" I wondered out loud.

"Maybe in the office?" She suggested. "Maybe she'll share my room."

Then we turned our full attention to the clothes closet, forgetting all about Tatiana for the moment.

"What do you like?" She gestured to the deep, roomy walk-in closet that seemed so out of character given the architecture of the addition. Manny sure knew his daughter when he laid out this place.

I was acutely aware that this endeavor could go one of two ways. It could take a long time, meaning I would go through a futile exercise of pulling choice after choice from the endless options, only to have each one rejected by my fashion-forward friend. Or it could go quick, if I just let her pick out what she had already decided I would wear. Ordinarily, I would relish torturing her with my choices. Today, however, I opted for the shorter version, hoping it would also be less painful for me. "I'll wear whatever you think looks good."

I was taller than Mercedes, but otherwise we were about the same size. The big difference was her curves. In other words, her tops would be loose on me, but I'd let her figure that out. It only took about fifteen minutes to complete the transformation, and that was without jewelry, hair and make-up. I checked the mirror, amazed. Mercedes laughed, and I wondered what Jack would think. Wait a skinny minute. Why would I care what Jack Turner thought? I never cared what Jack thought about my clothes before. I shook my head, to myself, trying to dislodge whatever twisted voodoo sorcery that had descended on me.

This super-sexy, low-cut and mostly see-through top over a tight, sheer cami that barely covered anything together with a short skirt that made sitting down wishful thinking, had one purpose and one purpose only—turn the head of Ditch Miller long enough to figure out if he could tell me how to find Storie Sanders. If he wanted to flirt me up because of the outfit, that wouldn't be the worst thing in the world. In his pictures on the band's website, the dude was sexy with a capital S-E-X. If he wanted to decapitate me, however, that's where I'd have to draw a line.

"Something's missing," Mercedes said as she tipped her head and studied me closely. Then a slow, and in my opinion evil, grin spread across her face. She pushed some bins out of the way toward the back of the closet and fished around on the floor, eventually pulling out a pair of black cowboy boots with pink stitching.

"Seriously?" I didn't think I could pull them off.

"They're perfect. For three reasons."

"I'm listening."

"One, it's a cowboy bar. Two, they go with this outfit. And three, you don't like very high heels."

I surrendered, based on reason number three alone. Since the skirt was too short and too tight to sit in, I didn't want to be standing around in a pair of her ultrahigh heels all night.

Once I got them on and stood up straight, she nodded enthusiastically. "Now this, this is a start!"

I turned around, and she said, "Walk." I stepped into the short hallway that connected the two bedrooms. "Not like a boy, *Lilita*. Move your hips a little. *Si!*"

I exaggerated the movement, sure as a shot put on a sugar high that I'd never walk around that way in public, but it made her happy and moved the process forward. Standing there in Mercedes' cowboy boots, I had to admit I was pretty happy with everything I accomplished today—hired a bakery manager, got the Luis topic on the table, found an outfit that would make Jack snap a vertebra. I meant Ditch! It would make *Ditch* snap a vertebra. Why was Jack constantly invading my thoughts?

My phone *cha-chinged.* Of course. Who else but Jack? This was happening way too frequently. Think about Jack, get a text message from Jack. Solution? Stop thinking about Jack.

"You at Manny's?"

"Mercedes is picking out my clothes for Saturday night."

Cha-ching: "I like it. She'll put you in something sleazy."

"Too bad you'll never know."

Cha-ching: "Joe will send me a picture."

I felt a flash of excitement that he'd see this outfit after all, followed by a wave of something uncomfortable. Embarrassment that I wanted him to see me looking sexy? Time to sidestep.

"Aren't you at work?"

Cha-ching: "Changing the subject?"

"Don't answer a question with a question."

Cha-ching: "Just passed Manny's. Saw Sandi in the lot."

That meant he was on his way to the firehouse.

"Be careful tonight."

Cha-ching: "You too."

When I put the phone down, Mercedes asked, "What's Jack have to say?"

"Nothing useful, that's for sure. He likes that you're picking out my clothes for Saturday."

"Of course he does. All men want to see a little…" She raised her hands above her head and circled her hips like she was twirling a hula hoop in slow motion.

"Listen, I know you're a fan, but you don't have to shamelessly promote it. I'm still undecided on this whole date-Jack dilemma."

"Okay," she nodded, but it seemed like she was humoring me.

Ten minutes later, she had her outfit. It was tight and red, and did I mention tight? Luis would be pleased. And if that didn't work out, she could always pick up a few extra bucks on any street corner.

Chapter 12

"Now that we're all set to steal the show on Saturday night, do you have time to go talk with Dad and Uncle Dave? We can run by real quick." I was anxious to get the bakery thing moving so I could tie it with a bow and be done with it. I figured I would still need a couple weeks to find Storie's family and break the sad news of her murder before heading back down to Charlottesville. It seemed logical, in my mind anyway, to put Dad and Uncle Dave in charge of showing Mercedes the bakery biz, freeing me up for the next phase of my investigation. Hopefully Ditch Miller would give me something to go on, otherwise, I was back to my original but only semi-pragmatic plan of looking at matters through my Stephanie Plum lens.

"Let's go now," Mercedes suggested.

"After we change, you mean." I didn't think that's what she meant, but these outfits would not win the day with my dad or my uncle.

"No?" she asked, smiling and turning a risqué little *pirouette*-like spin to emphasize her dress. Or was it supposed to emphasize how the dress fit her body? Either way, that girl had the balance and grace of a Chinese acrobat. In sharp contrast, I had the grace of a blindfolded crossing guard swinging a spatula at a badminton shuttlecock. Or possibly the grace of the shuttlecock itself. Whichever demonstrated the least amount of grace.

In the midst of his recovery-forced retirement, I didn't think Dad would be too busy to talk to us, so we headed over. Turned out, we actually were interrupting but only a game of Golf. The card game Golf, that is. The Barlows were card-playing folk from way back, favoring quirky or antiquated games over games with more mass appeal like poker. The true mark of a card-playing family was that they wouldn't pause the game just because someone walked into the room, even if it was the only daughter and the daughter's good friend.

Mercedes knew the routine. "Who's winning?" she asked.

"Your *tía*," said Uncle Dave, trying but failing to keep his cut-throat side at least partially under a bushel.

Dad stayed quiet, concentrating. This was his game. Millie liked Canasta, a game for four players. Dave liked Gin Rummy, a game for two players. But Dad's favorite was Golf, a game for two, three or four people. Since the three of them were under one roof for the time being, I guessed Golf was getting a lot of play.

"Ha!" Dad took the round, or the hole as it was called, and Millie recorded the scores. Only then did he look up to verify who had entered. "Lily Linn! Mercedes Manuela! You girls give me a hug," he demanded.

We smiled and hugged, me then her. I could tell by the way he chuckled he enjoyed the outpouring of our attention. He looked a little better than even a few days ago when I saw him last. I suspected the announcement that I had hired a qualified bakery manager for Poppy's would be more good medicine, giving him another boost in the right direction.

"Y'all get yourselves a glass of tea," Millie instructed as she dealt the next round. "Your daddy's about to win this game." Checking the scorecard as I went to the fridge, I saw she was ahead, but only by a point. They were on hole seventeen of eighteen. The game went fast, so just a few more minutes. I fixed a glass of tea for Mercedes and one for me, and we crowded two more chairs around the kitchen table to watch.

Dave lost another hand and tossed his cards down with insolence. "This game's more luck than skill," he complained. "Give me a robust round of rummy," he challenged. "That's a game with a strategy."

"Oh, quit your blusterin' and deal those cards," Millie scolded as she tallied the points. She was right, Dad had pulled ahead by two points.

"You girls wanna bet on a winner?" Dad asked as he positioned his six cards. "I'll double your money."

"Nobody's taking that bet," Dave grumbled and then glared at us. "Keep your money in your pockets."

As predicted, the last hole went fast. Millie calculated the final scores. "I got you, Georgie," she said, laughing.

Dad demanded a rematch and blamed his narrow loss on the sudden appearance of the two prettiest girls in town. Uncle Dave mumbled something under his breath, probably a curse he wouldn't dare say loud enough for Aunt Millie's ears. Turning to me, he boomed, "Lilybug!"

It made me feel good that my mere presence in the room was enough to take my uncle's competitive mind off losing the card game.

"Uncle Dave," I said, standing up to greet him.

He wrapped me in the usual big hug, then did the same to Mercedes. "What brings you girls over?"

"I have big news," I said, measuring out just enough build-up to milk this moment without belaboring it. Waiting for the obligatory oohs and aahs to taper off, I said, "Poppy's has a new bakery manager."

That announcement amped up the oohing and aahing big time.

"Her name is Ms. Cabrera." It was a common surname, and I was banking on the fact that they wouldn't catch onto my little joke, so I kept going. "She has years of experience in food service and has managed a successful restaurant." I saw the slightest smile bend the corners of Aunt Millie's mouth, but I didn't stop. "Experience aside, she's a people person.

In fact, her best qualification may be her ability to relate to customers." Here I stopped to let them process it.

"*Mercedes* Cabrera?" Millie asked, breaking into a full-blown smile. Dad and Dave whipped their heads around to look at Millie.

"*Our* Mercedes Cabrera?" Uncle Dave asked, turning toward the Mercedes in question.

"*Si*," she replied happily.

"You want to run the bakery?" Dad asked. "What about Cinco Sombreros?"

"Dad, there are a lot of moving parts in this story, but basically Manny's bringing his niece up from Mexico to work in the restaurant."

Mercedes chimed in, "We'll have more help than we need, so I could make room for Tatiana if I move over to the bakery."

"She's qualified," I added.

"Oh, of course she is," Dave agreed, then looking at Mercedes, "of course you are, Darlin', but how do you feel about it? I mean, we have a certain way of doing things over there. Are you okay with that? George and I can be hard to work for."

"Just like my dad," Mercedes assured them, nodding. "I will not do anything against your wishes or anything that will hurt the bakery." Her sincerity was deep.

"Oh, I think it's an answer to a prayer," Millie moved over to give Mercedes a side squeeze. "We really need the help. Otherwise, we'll have to sell the place, and the boys would be brokenhearted if that happens." She looked over at Dave and my dad. They didn't say anything, either of them, as if they thought speaking the words would turn Millie's sentence into a self-fulfilling prophecy. The looks on their faces implied she was right, though.

"Mercedes, we want to treat you fair, but we've never budgeted for a manager's salary before, and cash flow is tight," Dad pointed out.

"Oh, I know, *Tio*," she said, nodding her head enthusiastically. "I don't have any expenses living at home, so before I draw a paycheck, I'll make sure we turn a profit."

"Don't be silly, girl," Dad admonished. "Working for free is a fool's errand and a bad business plan to boot."

"We'll get a loan from the bank," Dave offered. "Poppy's has good credit. That'll pay Mercedes a starting salary."

My head bobbed from person to person like I was watching a weird, outer space version of a ping pong match being played from four different tables. In my mind, a bug-eyed cartoon version of myself rubbed big hands together, relishing the glee of seeing the solution unfolding in front of me. It was easy from here. My family loved Mercedes. Mercedes loved my family. Uncle Dave was known to very clearly spell out agreements in writing so there would never be a misunderstanding between the two families.

As far as I was concerned this was the highest degree of luck, the kind you could expect only when you found an Indian on the Tootsie Pop wrapper. Political incorrectness notwithstanding, the Indian was the clearest sign of good luck when I was growing up, out-lucking a ladybug holding the big side of a wishbone, sitting on a four-leaf clover, looking down on a penny that was heads up.

Even while I was splashing around in this sacred pool of special Tootsie Pop luck, I couldn't resist shining a light on one minor detail which threatened to thwart the forward motion. "So, can y'all train her on your methods?" I gave the word "methods" a little extra attention when I said it. Both Dad and Uncle Dave had certain ways of doing things. Their methods were based on conventions I believed to be popular back in the pioneer days, if not earlier.

The tiniest bit of technological awareness would make those obsolete ideas completely unnecessary, but I didn't think either of them was prepared to let go. I called it the Rand McNally Syndrome. No Global Positioning System would ever, in their opinions, be any match for a good ol' paper atlas, and the more times you suggested it the more tightly they clung to their beat up, outdated map.

"Yes," Dad assured me. His word was sprinkled with a stingy bit of sugar that did absolutely nothing to disguise the cynicism. "We'll teach her all the systems." Then turning to his new bakery manager he said, way more amicably, "When can you start, Mercedes?"

"I can spend a few hours a day with you, going over the books and learning the systems," she smiled in my direction, and I gave her a thumbs-up shielded by my glass of tea that only she could see. She was no dummy, this one. "I won't be able to start full-time until my cousin arrives from Mexico, though, because otherwise Cinco's would be shorthanded." She turned toward me, "Did Dad say when Tatiana would be here?"

"No, he didn't. I think the details are still coming together."

"That's fine," Uncle Dave and Dad said, simultaneously.

"We can start going over things here first before we take you to the bakery," Dad suggested. "Can you come on over this Monday?"

"Yes," she sounded enthusiastic.

Not wanting to remain involved but feeling some kind of indentured relationship with the bakery, I asked, "Do you want me to get in touch with the employees? Let them know that we'll be opening again? If any of them can't come back, or don't want to, I could start looking for replacements."

"I'll do it, Lily," Mercedes said with a smile. "Managing the employees will fall under my job responsibilities."

I swear I would have laid a golden oven mitt at her feet if I'd had one.

We probably spent another twenty minutes on a few more bakery-related topics before Mercedes and I were dismissed. Dad and Uncle Dave wanted to call Mr. Wilkerson at the bank and maybe get by there before close of business to start the process of applying for a loan. They hadn't owed money to the bank in years, and I knew this was a big thing for them. It made sense, though, if the Barlows wanted to continue in the bakery business.

When we got ready to go, Millie handed us each a reusable shopping bag. Inside there was a small, homemade lasagna and a loaf of bread. I imagined both were originally for me, until I showed up with a friend, but I didn't mind sharing this time. In fact, I should probably give my lasagna to Mercedes as a down payment on this debt I owed her, but have you tasted Millie's lasagna?

After dropping Mercedes back at Cinco's, I headed home. It was just about dinner time, and even though I had pizza for lunch, I didn't mind more Italian. Who was I kidding? Even if I didn't have a taste for it, I'd still eat it. The simplicity of sticking a prepared meal in the oven for forty-five minutes spoke to me. Way better than starting something from scratch. Or, more likely, opening a bag of chips.

The chickens were clumped around the coop, pecking earnestly, when I pulled into the drive. Miss Delphine was rocking on the porch. I waved cheerfully, mainly to throw her off, but then automatically checked the area for anything that looked unusual or out of place, anything to support my theory that she was up to something diabolical. She must have done a decent job of covering her tracks, though, because my Stephanie sense stayed dead quiet.

When I hopped out of the Jeep, I hollered, "Hey, Miss Delphine!"

"Hey there, honey," she said, and waved back.

I had been looking forward to a quiet, Jack-free evening where I could eat at least two heaping helpings of lasagna and cruise the Doe Network in peace, but for some inexplicable reason, I said, "You eat yet?"

"Not yet, child. Too hot to cook."

"I got a lasagna from my Aunt Millie." I held up the bag as best I could, as if to prove I wasn't lying. In the process, it went zigzagging wildly, catching the eye of one McNugget. Upon regaining control, I tried to ignore the bird, and said, "It'll take forty-five minutes, but you're welcome to come up for dinner."

"I can't hardly say no to the likes of that invitation," she said. "Forty-five minutes?"

"Yes, ma'am."

"You have wine for that lasagna?"

Wine for the lasagna? What a great idea. A great idea that I did indeed not have.

"No, ma'am. But I have beer," I offered, then as an afterthought I added, "and sweet tea." I didn't bother to mention the tequila. I figured that'd be like hanging a mirror for a vampire. Pointless.

"I'll bring a bottle."

Miss Delphine with a bottle of wine? I never would have gone there. "Thank you! That'll be nice."

From the corner of my eye, I saw McNugget disengage from the group and mosey in my direction so I headed toward the stairs. "See you soon," I said over my shoulder, making a break for safe base. I beat the chicken but banged the lasagna into the handrail along the steps, nearly dropping the bag for the second time.

Fifty minutes later, Miss Delphine appeared at the door with her bottle of wine, wearing what appeared to be a fresh blouse. I couldn't remember the last time, or anytime for that matter, that it occurred to me to change for dinner. I was thoroughly charmed that my landlady represented a bygone generation of genteel customs lost in today's chaos.

"Come in," I invited, genuinely happy to have the company.

"This is a nice treat, Lily," she said. "Thank you for havin' me." She handed me the bottle of wine. "There's a corkscrew in the drawer by the fridge."

Wine had never been my buzz of choice, and most of the little bit I had consumed over the years came in a bottle with a screw top or, in some cases, a carton with a plastic spout. Wine with a cork was uptown.

"It's the least I could do," I told her, "especially since you've been so sweet about letting me live here. By the way, we need to talk about my rent. We never settled on an amount."

"I don't generally like to talk business when I'm enjoyin' company, but we'll make it quick," she said.

"Yes ma'am. I just don't want to take advantage of your hospitality."

"I won't be chargin' you any rent, girl," she said with certainty. "Having reliable people comin' and goin' is worth any amount I'd ask."

"That seems like I'm taking advantage," I said, circling back around to what I was afraid of doing in the first place.

"Not a wit. You'd be takin' advantage if you tried to talk me down, or worse, didn't pay at all. Now, what can I do to help with dinner?"

I had the distinct feeling that Miss Delphine had, in under fifteen seconds, concluded the rent conversation. She didn't just put it on the shelf to take down and ponder at a later date. No. She chained it to a cinder block and pushed it off the starboard deck into the deep part of the Chesapeake Bay. I'd have to come up with another way to pay her back, aside from my questionable chicken tending, which wasn't worth much. I couldn't bake her anything that she couldn't bake better herself, that's assuming I cared to try. Maybe I could help with some yard work. Maybe I could help her in those mystery beds she was digging out back.

As I considered my options, I raked through the odd collection of serving utensils, measuring spoons and an unusual number of potato peelers in the drawer by the fridge. The corkscrew was hiding in the back, jammed into the business end of potato peeler number four.

Now…wine glasses. One of the benefits of being a college student was the ability to accept an alcoholic beverage in any receptacle. Solo cups were always very popular, but I'd gotten drunk from Dixie cups, paper snow cone holders, jelly jars, and plastic coconuts for a luau-themed party at a frat house. One time a boyfriend emptied the pills from a prescription medicine bottle, and we used that for shots. Which begs the question, when you have to work that hard to find a shot glass, why not just drink the booze straight from the bottle? However, Miss Delphine brought cork wine, and she may be expecting an appropriate glass. Although, it was her efficiency apartment, and she surely knew how the kitchen was equipped.

My mind on the glasses, I worked at the heavy foil covering the cork. The foil and I argued for a second, then the foil won that argument, slicing my finger like the edge of a sticky note with a switchblade. As I ran it under some cold water in the sink, Miss Delphine went to the cabinet and pulled down two of the monogrammed glasses—the *C* and the *R*. I couldn't be sure, because I was bleeding, but it seemed like she spent a little too long looking at each letter. Remembering the kills, maybe? Enjoying the trophies? I didn't exactly know how to delicately mine her for information, so I did it indelicately.

"I like the glasses you put up in here," I started, turning off the spigot. "It's interesting that they all have different monograms."

I opted not to dry my hands on my shorts and reached instead for a paper towel. Stickiness from a honey bun was one thing, blood from an open wound was a whole nother kind of yuck. As I tore a towel from the roll, I saw her trace her finger over the *C*. "The letters are for names of people who were special to me," she said, without a drop of anything that could be classified as nefarious. "I scour yard sales and thrift shops for the right initials."

I stopped dabbing at my wound and looked up. "People you knew?" I dug a little deeper. "People who died?" Or perhaps people you *killed*, I wanted to add but didn't.

"Yes. People who died."

The oven timer cleared its throat and started a prolonged and annoying bleat. I turned it off and grabbed my favorite oven mitts, the ones with the NASA emblems, simulating an astronaut's gloves. These didn't come with the apartment but from my own stash of special kitchen stuff. They hardly ever got used because, let's face it, who needs a potholder when you're fixing a bowl of cereal?

When the lasagna came out, the bread went in, already sliced, slathered with butter, and sprinkled with garlic powder. Meanwhile, Miss Delphine didn't offer any additional information on the initials, and I didn't exactly know where to go with it. As I stood there looking for a way across this creek, she expertly popped the cork and poured the wine, handing me the glass with the *C*. The transfer happened in what felt like slow motion, with both of us holding onto the glass and looking each other in the eye for a frozen moment. When she released and picked up her glass, she raised it to mine and we clinked. "To people who are special to us," she toasted.

"To people who are special," I said softly.

I had a feeling we were each thinking about one particular person, special in each of our own lives. I had no idea who she was thinking about, or whether she had killed that person. I also had no idea why I was thinking about Jack.

I wanted to clear his image from the tableau, but I didn't know how. Words from a yogi in a meditation class I took last semester came spiraling back to me on a cloud of peaceful lavender yoga mist—when a thought intrudes on your meditation, acknowledge it, then politely ask it to leave. I nodded to Jack, then invited him to leave. In typical Jack fashion, he winked, pulled out a chair and sat down at the table.

The taste of the wine managed to do what the yogi could not. Jack? Jack who? "Wow," I said, and I'm sure the note of surprise in my voice was as obvious as a dingo at a daycare. "This tastes good."

"California," was all she said.

"What?"

"The wine tastes good because it's from California."

"This is California wine?"

"There's a big push 'round these parts to sing the praises of East Coast vineyards; you know they're springin' up everywhere in Loudon and points west."

"Believe it or not, I think that's one of the reasons Poppy's has gotten so much traffic the last couple of years. Folks stop in first thing in the morning on Saturday and Sunday to fuel up for a day of wine tasting."

"Makes sense," she agreed. "It's swill, though."

This proclamation made me snort, but I covered it with a fake cough.

"The East Coast doesn't allow grapes the hang time they need to develop the more complex flavors of really good wine. You might get a decent Viognier, down Charlottesville way, bein' the Commonwealth's signature white grape. If you ask me that's more hogwash pushed by the tourism industry than good wine makin'."

I stood there holding my *C* glass, speechless. She had secret wine knowledge? Like Jack had secret chicken knowledge? Like Mercedes has secret entrepreneurial knowledge? What in the name of misfit menswear was going on around here? Could I really be so far out of touch with my community?

"Enough of that nonsense," Miss Delphine declared. "Looks like dinner's on."

Dinner was definitely on. I had an interesting companion, a gold-star lasagna, and a great glass of wine. What more could I want?

Cha-ching.

Because I had conjured him during the toast, I knew it was Jack. The message was a simple "*Hey.*"

I looked up from the phone, feeling a little embarrassed that I had interrupted the dinner party to check it at all. "It's Jack," I said.

"Ah, Jack." She smiled and seemed pleased to be included. "I like that boy. He treats you right."

"Oh, I don't know," I confided, "he's a little Tyrannosaurus Rex at times. I've learned to ignore it over the years."

"Lily, it's good to have someone in your life who reminds you to keep your hood up and your life jacket on."

The line struck me as particularly funny, and I let myself laugh. "Where'd you get that little gem?"

"When I was a girl, a neighbor would take us kids out on his boat every once in a while. Before we were allowed to step foot on that old rust bucket, he'd line us up on the dock and say, 'Now y'all keep your hood up and your life jacket on at all times.' It came to be a term I associated with somebody carin' 'bout you. Like somebody tellin' you to be careful."

"Ah." I considered that, imagining a nine-year-old Delphine wanting to go on a boat ride. "When I was learning to drive, Dad would tell me to 'watch out for the other guy' every time I got behind the wheel."

"Same kind a thing."

"You're right," I conceded. "Jack does that." In the midst of the conversation, I almost forgot about the text.

Holding my phone up, I said, "Should we text him back?"

"Tell him I said 'Hey.'" So, I texted exactly that.

Cha-ching: "Miss Delphine?"

"Yep. Having her up for dinner. Millie's lasagna."

Cha-ching: "Save me some."

"I always do."

And then I sent another text, "Jack, keep your hood up and your life jacket on at all times tonight."

Cha-ching: "What?"

"It's Miss Delphine's way of telling somebody to be careful."

Cha-ching: "I like it."

I had the feeling that it wasn't the funny phrase he liked as much as the fact that I wanted to look out for him, which made me smile. When I took my eyes off the screen, I realized Miss Delphine was watching me with a lovely, tender expression in her eyes. It felt like she was onto what was happening between Jack and me. Did she think I was caving? And the more important question—Was I?

I brought the meal and the wine to the table, peeling the tinfoil back from the garlic bread, which was lightly toasted. All the aromas together made me realize I was half starved. Completely ignoring the Jack conundrum, we ate and talked and drank the rest of the wine.

We covered everything from low voter turnout and using a canning jar ring as a makeshift biscuit cutter to honor killings in the name of religion. At around nine, Miss Delphine figured she'd better get down to Cro, so she stood to do the dishes, but I insisted she leave them. We said good night, and I gave her a short hug before walking her to the door. Peeking through the curtain, I waited until she was down the stairs and on her own porch before I flipped the deadbolt. I didn't want to do it when she was in earshot for fear she might think I was eager to get rid of her.

At the sink a few minutes later, my mind and my nerve endings drifted back to one of the times Jack snuck up behind me while I was doing dishes. I noticed the faintest scattering of goose bumps, confirming that my physical response was still the same. And that was just from the memory alone. Wow.

How could we move that piece forward without doing permanent or even long-lasting damage to our friendship? It'd be an interesting experiment, without a doubt. Now that it was on the table, I had to admit, the idea was intriguing. It'd be fun to see what kind of moves that boy had under the sheets.

Maybe, just maybe, my curiosity was rooted in the fact that I wasn't actively seeing anyone at the moment, and any kiss would be a fun kiss at this point. Could I risk it? What would happen if we alienated each other through the course of this weird little research project? It always worked when we weren't intimate. What made him so sure it would also work the other way?

My limited knowledge of osmosis came tumbling to the front part of my mind. Didn't the molecules push across a membrane to equalize the concentration on both sides? Our friendship was balanced because our friendship molecules had been equalizing for so many years. If the intimacy molecules started piling up on one side or the other, what would that do to the overall concentration? After I muddled through this analogy for a bit, two things became clear. The dishes were done, and I should definitely not major in chemistry, biology, or any other science that included the fundamentals of osmosis.

Pulling the Mac out of my backpack, I pushed some pillows around on the couch until I found a comfortable arrangement. That was just the starting point. It would take three to four rearrangements to really bond with the couch, but that was simply how I worked. Visiting the Doe Network was like…like dessert after that great dinner. I was looking forward to making a new discovery, and I wanted to be completely comfortable when I did it.

As always, I stopped first at the Misty-Storie profile, looked at the purple flower tattoo and closed my eyes to say a little prayer for her family. It was hard to imagine how her parents would react to the news of her murder. Losing a loved one in a car crash was bad enough, but decapitation was outside almost anyone's realm of possibility. I wondered if I'd even be able to find her parents, and my thoughts turned toward hot Ditch Miller. Did he know her well enough to have useful information on her hometown? Did he kill her? Did I have a plan if I could prove that he killed her?

Wracking my brain, I decided I did not have a plan to catch a killer. Should I just take my information to the local authorities? Should I call the contact listed on Misty-Storie's Doe Network profile? Should I ask Jack for advice?

There was really no way to get all these details worked out before Saturday night when I would come face to face with Ditch. I would stick to the plan to pump Hottie Miller for info on Storie. That's it. My dad always said ninety percent of the stuff we worry about never comes to pass, so why was I worrying about any of this now? I needed to stick to the plan, and I thought Stephanie would agree.

After recommitting to the plan with one firm nod of my head, I studied the tattoo. Maybe I should get a tribute tattoo in Storie's memory. A tribute tattoo? The idea struck with such energy, I jerked. Not only could I honor Storie, but what if I showed up to meet Ditch Miller sporting the same purple flower tattoo on my left ankle? Would that get his attention? Would his reaction give him away? Did I have time to get a tattoo before Saturday night? Was there even a tattoo parlor in Marshall?

Liking this idea a lot, I decided to sleep on it and ask Jack about tattoo parlors when I saw him tomorrow. For now, I skipped over to unidentified males and skimmed down. I hadn't spent much time on the men, and there were so many more. Not only that, they were a lot less detailed. Slowly paging down, something drew me to Washington State.

Near the bottom, right before the profiles for Washington, D.C. started, was Case File 233UMWA, a white, native or maybe Hispanic man probably in his twenties. His hair and nails were neatly groomed. His teeth were nearly perfect, probably because of braces. He had his appendix out and had recently lost a lot of weight. His eyes were hazel; his earlobes were attached.

At the hotel in Amanda Park, Washington, he may have spoken with a Canadian accent. He registered using the name Lyle Stevik, a character from a book titled *You Must Remember This*. He paid for one night but said he intended to stay longer. Lyle switched rooms because the first one was too noisy. At some point after that, he hanged himself from a coat rack with his leather belt. He was wearing blue jeans, Timberland boots, and a blue plaid shirt with long sleeves. He left money for the room. His body was discovered by the maid on September 17, 2001. The police think he died the day before.

I whispered his name, "Lyle. Lyle. Lyle." I pictured his boots. I pictured his attached earlobes. I wondered why he identified with the character from that book, so I googled the book. *You Must Remember This* was published in 1987 by Joyce Carol Oates. From the blurb, I gathered the story was set in the fifties. Lyle is a used furniture salesman. There's some illicit stuff between his daughter and his brother, a boxer, which may or may not involve incest.

How does a person so closely identify with a character in a book that he assumes the character's name before dying from depression? Wait a skinny minute. People making bizarrely strong connections to fictional characters...don't I do that with Stephanie Plum? Doesn't she come to mind a couple times a day? More if I'm knee deep in a good true crime story? Don't I even have conversations with her in my head?

What's the difference between Lyle and me? Am I on his one-way track to complete and total isolation? I compared our clothing, nondescript but in good condition. I compared our straight teeth and noted a shared familial belief in braces. I compared our love of literature. As a memorial to the man who took his life, I promised to read the book.

Staring into space, I pictured the hotel room. The profile said he had no luggage, but there was a toothbrush and toothpaste. Abstractly, I wondered why no deodorant. If hygiene was important, and he went to the trouble of brushing his teeth, why not use deodorant? Maybe he didn't shower but wanted fresh breath for the afterlife?

Having never entertained a suicidal tendency myself, it put me in the very peculiar position of considering the circumstances of taking my own life. I was pretty sure I'd shower and use deodorant. I'd want a fresh shirt, too. I would also floss before brushing my teeth. Yes, I was pretty sure I would incorporate a ritualistic cleansing in preparation for the act. Did Lyle do a version of that?

"I'm sorry you were without a friend, Lyle. Maybe that would have made the difference. I hope you're at peace now."

Lyle's story had exhausted me. I glanced at the clock in the kitchen, compared it to the time on my phone, cross-referenced that with the time in the corner of the computer screen, and decided it was roughly ten thirty-five, a good time to crawl in the bed. Logging off, I closed the computer. As I went about my evening routine, I wondered for the umpteenth time how all these lives went unnoticed, untouched, and unremembered. So many cold cases. Who were they? What happened to them? I drifted off with that thought in my head.

Chapter 13

I woke up to the sound of someone pounding on the apartment door. The last thought when I fell asleep was the first thought when I woke up. I immediately assumed a crime had been, or was currently being, committed. The door didn't have a peep hole, so I looked for a heavy object to thwart this home invasion,

I hollered, "Who is it?"

"Jack," came a low husky voice from the other side.

Throwing the door open, I gasped, "What's wrong?" First, I scanned him from head to toe, thinking he must have been stabbed. Detecting no obvious blood on his clothes or on the porch, I looked down the stairs to make sure he wasn't being followed. No one in pursuit.

I imagined Stephanie would shake her head and say something like, "Way to panic, Barlow," but I couldn't dwell on her imaginary disappointment at the moment. "Relax." Jack put a hand on my shoulder. "I'm fine," he said. "Sorry I didn't call first."

"What are you doing here?" I tried to piece it together through the fog of my still slumbering brain. "You're supposed to be down at the firehouse," I said, stepping back so he could come inside.

"Too many people showed up. They took volunteers to go home early. If anything big happens in the next couple hours, I'm on call." He dropped his backpack on the floor by the door.

"So you came here?"

"I wanted to see you."

"You wanted to see me?" Nothing about this was making sense.

There was something in the quality of his nod that put me on guard.

"*See* me or *kiss* me?" I asked, highly suspicious of his motives.

"See" he reiterated. "Unless you're inclined to be giving out kisses. If that's the case, I'd like to change my answer."

"Jack, it's…" I started to declare the ungodly hour, but not knowing exactly what time it was, I finished, "it's something o'clock in the freakin' morning!"

"Five," he said. "It's five o'clock in the freakin' morning. And I have a surprise for you." He leaned against the door and crossed his arms over his chest.

"A surprise at five in the morning?"

He tipped his head sideways and smiled. "I fed the chickens."

"You fed McNugget?" Until now I was having a hard time keeping up with the action associated with this unexpected visit. That got my attention, though. "I don't have to face her?"

"Not this morning." I could tell he was basking in his hero moment, and I had no problem with that. It wasn't like I wanted to set the women's movement back, but I was a damsel, and those birds absolutely distressed me.

"For that, I will kiss you!"

Still leaning against the door, he snatched my wrist and yanked me into his chest.

"Wait," I stammered, pushing back. In my weakened sleep state, which was not all that different from my weakened fully awake state, I was no match for Mr. Muscles. He circled his arms around me as I tried to explain. "That's not what I meant."

"Are you sure? Because that's what you said."

"I meant the generic on-the-cheek variety. You know. The commonly acceptable and benign way to thank another person."

"Okay. I'll take the benign version." He was smug, and he wasn't budging. I was kind of locked in place until this was resolved.

The eye contact at this close range was too much for me, and the only way I could think to break the intensity was to move my head toward his cheek. I hated giving him what he wanted, but in the name of self-preservation, I swallowed my pride. Kiss the cheek and duck outta Dodge. In my mind I saw myself giving a thumbs up to Wyatt Earp and Bat Masterson, well known deputies of Dodge City, Kansas, back in the day.

Meanwhile, JT waited patiently, even turning his face slightly so I had better access to his cheek. I didn't waste time thinking about it. It was just a friendly peck, and I'd done it a million times before. My error was momentarily forgetting that Jack had assumed the role of antagonist.

In the time it took my lips to move toward his cheek, he twisted his head back so we were again face-to-face. The motion was so smooth and so quick I didn't realize it happened until I found my lips grazing his. For a reason known only to Aphrodite or possibly her Roman counterpart Venus, I did not pull away. He released his arms, moving one hand to the back of my head and resting one hand lightly on my hip, so technically I didn't have anything holding me there. Regardless, I stayed rooted to the spot, with our lips barely touching.

To a casual observer, it would have appeared that I made the next move, parting my lips about an eighth of an inch. If questioned later, I planned to deny it. In the moment, however, I suspected the gesture was as clear as an embossed invitation on the really good card stock. And Jack RSVPed by elevating the wayward cheek kiss to a full-on tongue kiss that went deeper and burned hotter than our last round a couple days ago. I was badly out of breath when he finally let me up for air. Out of breath, and a little dizzy. Out of breath, a little dizzy, and suddenly wobbly in the knees.

I leaned into Jack for support, and it became evident that he was delighted to oblige. When I realized how turned on he was getting, I did the only thing I knew how. I lost my nerve and subsequently started to hyperventilate.

"Easy, now," he murmured. "I know you're not ready for this. Nothing happens 'til you're ready. Remember?"

I nodded, unconvinced, trying to get my lungs to accept even a small amount of air.

"Slow down," he said. "Deep breaths."

"Jack, I'm having this, this, this physical re-re-reaction," I struggled to talk before I could breathe, "but it doesn't ma-ma-match up…"

"You can tell me about it when you catch your breath."

"I, I, I…"

"Shhhhhh." His voice sounded soft and low in my ear. "Deep breaths. In." He waited as I inhaled, then said, "Out."

We stood there, me leaning on him, him leaning on the door, for what seemed like most of the early morning, but it was likely just a few minutes. Eventually, he guided me toward the couch. I sank down, and he positioned himself beside me, an arm around my shoulder. I dragged in another ragged breath, and the noisy gasp struck me as incredibly stupid-sounding. While I had faith Jack wouldn't take advantage of my oxygen-deprived predicament, I still felt uncomfortably vulnerable.

He didn't say anything, and I surely wasn't saying anything. You know, for three or four minutes anyway. The time it took me to get my bearings at the very minimum. We both knew eventually I'd sing like a traveling salesman after three beers at a karaoke bar.

"Jack."

"Lily."

"What's going on with me?" I sucked in another rough breath. "It's not like I'm a virgin. Why is this turning me into a raging idiot?"

"You're thinking about trying something that scares you."

"I never try things that scare me. It's a known fact. I never let go of the rope swing at the lake. I never touch reptiles. I never go in the ocean because of sharks."

Sitting there, side by side, he took my hand. The old way. "You're right," he said. "Those things scare you. But there are other times when you're afraid, and you try it anyway. You were scared when you got accepted to UVA. Remember? But you rolled down there like you were Thomas Jefferson's direct descendent. You're scared of telling Storie's family that she was murdered, but you've managed to put that paralyzing fear aside so you can see this thing through."

He waited as I chewed on those thoughts for a minute. "Lily, I feel like I know what's going on."

I released his hand and twisted sideways so my back was against the arm of the couch, and I was facing him. Crossing my legs meditation style, I plopped a large, crocheted throw pillow on my lap. This sequence surely looked like I was constructing a blockade to fortify my area. Well, I was. I wanted something between me and the source of potential discomfort—aka, Jack. Playing with the tassel on the corner of the pillow, I glanced up and saw amusement on his face, then dropped my eyes back to the pillow.

"Go ahead," I sighed, unable to keep the exasperation from my voice. "Tell me what you think is going on here."

He gently pulled my hand from the yarn tassel, which was a sneaky way of forcing me to look up again. Holding my hand, he said, "I think your courage is tied to a sense of control. When you feel you have some control over an outcome, you take charge of your fears, and you become fearless. I've always loved that about you."

I tripped over his use of the word "love," thinking he was pushing this bad idea from kissing to dating to sex to love in under a week. As I scanned his face, though, he clearly meant the platonic love of a good friend. Wow. Was I doomed to overanalyze every single thing he did or said from this point forward? For the love of the sweet, four-part harmony. If this was my new reality, I might as well check myself into the local psych ward now because Crazy Town was just up the road a piece.

"You with me?" I nodded yes.

"You want to say something?" I shook my head no.

"Mind if I keep going?"

"There's more?" I sputtered.

"Well, I haven't really gotten to the core of what I think is going on, so yes, there's more."

"By all means." With my free hand I made a flamboyant gesture for him to continue.

"Those things where you don't have any control over the outcome—letting go of the rope swing, touching a reptile, dating me, swimming with a shark," he paused.

It amused me that dating him came between reptile and shark, and I cracked a smile in spite of myself. I think he knew why I was smiling, but he didn't bite.

"The things you don't have control over make you doubt yourself, doubt your ability to survive a situation."

I stopped him. "No," I said emphatically. "That doesn't make sense. I know people don't die from touching frogs."

"First of all, frogs aren't reptiles." I rolled my eyes, but he continued. "And secondly, most fears don't make any sense. That's what gives fear its power."

I digested this revelation. "Why doesn't fear have any power over you?"

"It does."

"I've never seen even a shadow of a fear cross your face. Not one time."

"I'm afraid of screwing this up with you."

"What?"

"I'm afraid that I won't do it right, in a way that makes you feel safe enough to try what scares you. I'm afraid you'll be disappointed in me for that."

Jack Turner afraid of something? And not something credited with a universally high fear factor, like drowning or perishing in a plane crash. Afraid of my disappointment? Was my disappointment scarier than bodily harm in a four-alarm blaze?

"Let me get this straight. You're not afraid to run into a burning building, but you're afraid to disappoint me?"

"Yes." Jack was very articulate when it came to answering questions. Unlike me, who worshiped at the altar of circumbendibus. After delivering a clear, direct response, he would generally elaborate. Knowing this, I waited.

"I constantly train to fight fires," he said. "Sure, there's always a risk, but I know what I'm doing, and I trust that the people around me know what they're doing. When it comes to repositioning my relationship with you, I don't know what I'm doing. It scares me somethin' fierce. The only thing that keeps me moving forward is the rush I get whenever I think about being with you."

I realized he just shared a deep secret. He didn't like to admit to any type of weakness. I also wondered if he could be onto something with his assessment of the control issue. If we moved forward, I may not be able to control my feelings and I definitely couldn't control Jack's. Was that the part holding me back? What if my bobber went under and his stayed on top? What if I was the mudslide and he was the one house that remained untouched in its wake?

"Tell me what you're thinking," he begged.

Out of nowhere, I blurted, "I can't bear the thought of unequal feelings, where one person wants more and the other wants less. Right now, you're required by the laws of friendship to accept all of me, and I am required to reciprocate. If we divest from the friendship, the laws change, and there is nothing, *nothing*, to bind us to each other the way there is now."

"You're afraid you won't be into me."

"No," I said quietly. "The opposite."

"You're worried you'll like this idea more than I will?" I detected a note of disbelief in his voice. "That you'll be into it and I won't?" When I heard him say it out loud, I was supremely embarrassed by what I was being forced to admit.

I looked for the stepping stones I had used to get myself onto to this sandbar, but the tide was rolling into this estuary pretty fast. Replaying his sentence in my head, there had to be a way to flip his words in my favor.

Jack smiled, leaned in, and said, "There's no loophole."

Nodding my head absently, I replied, "There's almost always a loophole. I just need more time to find it."

"Take all the time you want," he said, using a deceptively generous tone. Then he stood up and pulled me to my feet.

"What are you doing?"

"Giving you time to find your loophole." And he pushed his hand into my hair, closed the space between us, and kissed me but good.

When we pulled apart, he asked, "You still thinking?"

"I forgot the…" I started to say, but he cut me off, closing his mouth on mine again.

A minute later, he offered, "The question is—once we start dating, are you worried you'll like the idea more than I will?"

I nodded, closed my eyes, and leaned in for another. This accomplished two things. One, I got back to the good part, and two, I couldn't give a more complete answer to his question because my mouth was, you know, full.

His hand on my waist found a sliver of skin between my t-shirt and pajama bottoms and the heat from his fingers lit me up like the key on Ben Franklin's kite string. My eyes flew open; breaking the kiss, I stumbled backwards.

Jack's expression approached one of rapture. "Me, too," he breathed.

He took a step toward me, and I responded with an equidistant step back, bumping into the ottoman. He reached for my hand, but I moved my arm behind me. "I won't put my fingers under your shirt, Lily. As nice as that felt. I just want to iron out the part that's got you worked up."

This time when he reached for my hand, I let him, and I allowed myself to be drawn to the couch. He sat down first, in the middle, pulling me down beside him. We were arranged on the couch very much the way we had started out, except his arm wasn't around my shoulder. Then he changed things up by turning sideways, like I had done earlier, minus the criss-crossed legs. His knee effectively pinned me between the arm of the couch and his body, giving me absolutely no buffer or barrier of any kind. The mere position forced me to turn my head toward him, because it seemed ridiculous to look straight ahead while he was staring at my left ear.

It occurred to me that one downside of entering into a relationship with someone who knew me was exactly that—he knew all my moves. I silently congratulated him for effectively restricting my movements so he could have his conversation without my histrionics interrupting every three minutes.

I think he was waiting for me to explain how I was feeling, however, I couldn't get started. When he reached his hand over to my face and drew his thumb across my lower lip, that did the trick.

"I'm not your type. Let's be honest. I'm not fit, fashionable, poised, or coiffed. I don't wear enough makeup, and I don't have the right bra size. I know what you said when we were at the bar in Charlottesville the other day, but I think this appetite you've developed for something different may be short lived. And on the flip side, you're not the kind of guy I usually date either."

Jack listened to the rush of sentences tumbling from my mouth. When I was done, he said, "Yeah. Remind me of the guys you like to date again?"

I hesitated, sure I was about to trigger a booby trap.

"Well," he said not waiting for me, "let's start with the guy who wanted you to try cocaine. Filipe? And how 'bout the guy who put his fist through your friend's wall? Roger? And there was Bernie, who treated you like a human teller machine."

I started to feel the need to defend my recent dating history. "There were some nice ones, too. Like Judd."

"Judd the Dud?"

"He was nice," I repeated, lamely.

"Okay, I'll give him nice. But did he inspire you? Did he challenge you? Did he drive you crazy in bed?" Judd did none of those things, but he was nice.

"No," I said, slightly defeated.

"Lily, I'm not interested in any of those guys. If you're interested in any of the women I've dated, then ask me. I'll tell you whatever you want to know. But this comes down to you and me, at this point in time, and the possibility of taking a really great friendship to a crazy new level."

I did what I never do. I made eye contact. And I held it. I was trying to verify what he was saying by the look in his eye.

"I know you're not all in," he said. "Just don't say no. Give me time to make you feel comfortable enough to try this. And then let's see what happens."

I kept looking in his eyes. Wow, they were blue.

"Will you give me time?"

"I will."

He waited, expectantly. I raised my eyebrows in return, pretending I had no idea what he was waiting on. When he narrowed his eyes, I felt we were at an impasse, so I caved and repeated the entire sentence. "I will give you time." I didn't like being bound by oral contracts, but oh well.

"Thank you. We can shake on it or seal it with a kiss, lady's choice," and he smiled that lopsided grin of his.

The handshake would have been the safe bet and also would have helped reiterate the issue of pacing. But the kiss was hard to resist. I leaned in.

� ☙ ☚

It was a slow start to the actual day. After the kiss-a-thon on the couch, we moved to the bedroom so he could catch up from the night shift. I laid in bed with him but never really found my way back to anything that could be considered restful sleep. Left on my own to poke holes in his theories, my mind took tiny doubt saplings and nurtured them into a huge banyan-like network of mature interlocking doubts. On that bleak note, it seemed like a good time to get up.

I started the coffee, fixed myself a bowl of cereal, poured some OJ in the Q glass, and googled Ditch Miller to see what else I could find out about him. The internet was rich with morsels. He was a decorated veteran of the Marines, hence the Semper Fi tattoo. Completely engrossed in Ditch's battlefield exploits, the hand on my shoulder delivered a thousand volts. My arm jerked back involuntarily, and I slammed my funny bone into the chrome part of the kitchen chair.

A lackluster wail slipped from my throat, followed by several standard curse words. "What are you doing up, besides causing mayhem in the breakfast area?"

"The bed felt lonely."

I let that one go. "Aren't you tired?"

"I'll be okay." Walking toward the coffee pot, he asked, "What'd you find out about Ditch?"

So that sneak-up maneuver was all about surveillance, pure and simple. He wanted a peek at the screen so he could keep tabs on my activities. Okay, Turner.

"He's a decorated war hero."

"Did you find his rap sheet?"

"Rap sheet?" I tried not to sound shocked, but I don't know if I pulled it off.

"Yeah. He was charged with domestic violence, but it didn't stick."

I held the cereal bowl, about to scoop up a big spoonful of Crunch Berries. "Domestic violence?" This was huge. If he was prone to domestic violence, if he had a record of it, could he actually be Misty-Storie's killer? "What happened?"

"Something with a girlfriend. She stopped talking, and it got buried mysteriously. There's a hint that ol' Ditch has some pretty powerful relatives."

"How do you know this?"

"I asked Antonio Lopez to run a background check on him."

"Tony Lopez is a police officer?"

"Yep."

"He made it through the police academy?"

"Top of his class. He goes by Antonio now."

I smiled thinking about Tony Lopez. He was a good guy; played baseball with Jack. Not one I would consider especially academic, so it thrilled me he did so well in the police academy. His sense of justice would make him an excellent officer. "Did he find anything else?"

"A couple a things. Name's Beau Miller. Honorably discharged. But I'm more concerned about the domestic violence activity."

Jack stood there leaning on the kitchen chair across from me. I could tell by his stance we were about to disagree on something.

"I have a couple suggestions for when you meet this guy on Saturday."

"If by *suggestions* you mean *commandments*, then we're done here."

"Okay," he said. "You're right."

I did a double take. Having never won a standoff with him so handily, I felt like I just crossed some virtual finish line way ahead of the nearest competitor. It was empowering, and I liked it.

"We should call them what they are," he continued. "Commandments."

The air hissed out of my empowerment balloon. I took two seconds to regroup. Regrouping consisted of sitting up a little straighter in my chair.

"Jack, I know you think you're the boss of literally everything I do, but if you continue to dole out random commandments like some dictator and expect me to follow them, I'll be forced to declare my deep disappointment in you." I knew it was risky, using something so private he had revealed to me during our talk early this morning, but I was angling for some respect.

He took a sip of black coffee before setting his mug on the table. His eyes were gleaming, like he was about to chomp into a big slab of red meat. "Playing dirty, girl?" he asked. His smile was far from the flirty, lop-sided grin he used to get his way with women. This smile was dangerous, almost predatory. "If those are the new rules of engagement, I promise you, darlin', you're outta your league." To drive home his point, he pulled his t-shirt over his head and tossed it in the direction of the living room. Now, basically half naked, he moved like a wolf stalking its prey.

I shook my head, wondering how this thing got away from me so fast. Like any unarmed animal in the wild would do, I held up my hand and gestured for the wolf to stop. He shook his head no. An inch at a time he curved his way around the table toward me.

If I dropped my hand, I was accepting defeat. If I kept my hand in place, it would be on his bare, flat stomach in 4…3…2—

"Okay!" I declared, throwing my arms up in surrender.

"Okay what?" he asked, his jaw set in a hard line.

"I accept defeat. I'll listen to your commandments, but you have to put your shirt on."

"Listen to or abide by?"

I rolled my eyes, "Whatever it takes for you to put your shirt on." He was standing unnecessarily close to me, and I was looking at him the way I would look at a man instead of the way I had always looked at my friend.

"Since I appear to have the edge in this transaction, the stakes just got higher."

"That's…" I started to respond, but I swallowed the rest of my words.

"Playing dirty?" He filled in the blank for me, the predatory smile back on his lips.

"This is blackmail."

"You set the tone."

"What are your demands?" I asked, frustrated with the situation, and frustrated that I found myself mesmerized by his bare chest.

"Abide by the commandments and lay your hand on my chest. Then I'll put my shirt back on."

Not realizing it had dropped, I snapped my jaw closed. "Are you testing my limits?"

"Nope." He smiled. "Expanding your horizons."

"Oh, no. No. No. No. I'm onto you, son. If I agree to that demand, you'll pull some crap about how it's your turn to touch my bare chest since I got to touch yours. Don't think I haven't noticed how you wormed your way into this morning's kissing frenzy almost effortlessly, and how you dragged me down with you. I'm drawing a line. The answer is no."

"Are you sure? Because my next move is to take off the shorts."

I froze in disbelief, reminding myself that Jack doesn't bluff. "You are a colossal disturbance in the atmosphere."

"Remember this next time you want to play dirty," he said, popping the button on his shorts, as if he were preparing to drop them. "I will beat you at this game every single time."

"I want your assurance that, if I put my hand on your chest, you'll put your shirt back on."

"I like that I can fry your nerves just by taking off my shirt." He stood there nodding. "How long has this been going on?"

Ignoring his tease, I asked more vehemently, "Will you put it on if I touch your chest?"

"I'll put it on as long as you uphold your end of the bargain—meaning you listen to and abide by the commandments."

I contemplated using a heavy touch, more like a punch, but decided the likelihood of retaliation was too high. Given the fact that he was already shirtless and I was still wearing my pajamas, there wasn't a lot of fabric standing between me and *SexwithJack*.

There. I said it. In my head anyway. *SexwithJack*. The idea, which had never surfaced until a week ago, seemed to be morphing from "No way."

to "What if?" Next up came "Let's go!" I was dismayed by the realization that, while still on the horizon, *SexwithJack* was stampeding toward me like a herd of buffalo.

Eyeballing the spot on his chest I intended to target, I reached out while turning my head away. I didn't want him to read my face. His chest was as muscular as I expected. What I didn't see coming was the thrill attached to the touch. I could barely suppress the quiver in my palm. After a few seconds, he lifted my hand from his chest to his lips and lightly kissed my fingers. Without turning back around to look, I decided this was a good time for a pee break and shot directly into the bathroom.

When I came out, his t-shirt was back on and he was sitting at the kitchen table, looking at his phone as if nothing had happened.

He watched me pour a cup of coffee and doctor it up with cream and sugar. I took a long time on purpose. When I sat down, he asked, "You ready for my suggestions?"

I clenched my teeth, pursed my lips, and nodded tightly.

"One—Joe is never more than five feet away from you at any time throughout the entire night, including when you use the restroom. That means he waits near the door until you come out."

We exchanged looks. Mine said something like, "You annoy me on the cellular level." His was along the lines of "I dare you."

"And two?" I asked defiantly.

"Are you clear on number one?"

"Crystal."

"Then two—you don't give Ditch your real name or any way to contact you. Address here or at UVA. Phone number. Email. Any social media account. No meeting place."

Jack knew that I didn't use any of the vast social media options other than Facebook, which was really more a way to stay in touch with Dad and 'em. However, by including it here, he effectively prevented me from creating an account in order to connect with Ditch.

Smart. For a weevil.

"Why not give him my name?"

"Lily, you don't know this guy. You don't know his motives. There are accusations that he beats on women. And he may have murdered your friend, Storie. Don't give him a way to find you."

When he laid it out that way, it didn't look like Ditch was up for Guy of the Year. "Alright," I said. "Is there a three?"

"Yeah, there's a three—stay smart. You're not in this to apprehend the guy. Leave him to the cops if it comes to that. You're just looking for Storie's trail so you can find her family." I nodded.

"Any questions?"

"Yes."

"Shoot."

"Where can I get a tattoo?"

Jack let his head drop so his chin almost touched his chest. After so many long years of friendship, I'm sure he was used to erratic jumps in my stream of consciousness. I was hoping this particular jump would allow the Ditch debriefing to die a natural death. "You want a tattoo?" he asked.

Ah, sweet victory. "I'm thinking about it."

He nodded approvingly. "Hot." It looked like he might be picturing me naked, trying to decide where he would find this unexpected and surely exotic piece of artwork. Once he came out of his reverie, he said, "You know they use needles to ink tattoos. It's not like they're kissed onto your skin by Lucy's puppies."

"I know that."

"Has your tolerance for needles improved lately?"

"I think I'll just get good and drunk first."

"Reputable parlors won't let you get a tattoo if you've been drinking. You have to sign a liability waiver which you can't do when you're drunk." He got up to pour himself another cup of coffee then went into the fridge for something to eat. Spying Millie's leftover lasagna, he grabbed that and a fork, eating it cold, right from the casserole dish.

"You can warm that up in the microwave, you know."

He stared straight at me while he took another huge bite.

"Or just eat it cold," I said, but in the thought bubble above my head, I added *like a moron*.

He laughed, as if he could read my thought bubble.

"When did you decide to get a tattoo?"

Not only was I trawling for information about ink. This was also a test probe to see how Jack would respond to my wild hair. Frankly, I thought he would try to talk me out of it, from the point of view of a person with no tattoos. I was half hoping he would so I could draw his attention to his burning need to micromanage me. This acceptance was unexpected.

"I've been thinking about a tribute tattoo in memory of Storie. A purple flower on my left ankle."

"Ah."

Call it a hunch, but it didn't feel like this was the time to bring up my idea of confronting Ditch with a flash from his past, so I didn't elaborate.

"Well, if you want to go through with it, I know a place in Winchester. Super sterile. Amazing artists."

I felt my forehead wrinkle. "You don't have any tattoos. How do you have a tattoo parlor?"

Jack didn't say anything. He didn't have to.

"You slept with the tattoo artist."

He nodded, still eating. "I did. If that makes you uncomfortable, you don't have to see her or even go when she's there. The main thing is that they keep everything clean. You won't get hepatitis at this place."

"Hepatitis? That's a problem with tattoos?" I'll be honest, I didn't really know what hepatitis was. I knew if there were two columns, one for things you wanted and one for things you didn't want, birthday cake would go in the former and hepatitis would go in the later.

"It used to be a bigger problem. Now they use autoclaves to clean everything. But yes, the risk exists."

While I started rethinking my memorial gesture to Storie, something else pinched at my subconscious. Just how many partners did Jack have over the years? I wanted to ask. I mean, he said I could ask anything about his previous relationships. Somehow it felt like an abandoned mine shaft with warning signs posted all over the place. Seeking info about sexual partners implied I was thinking about *SexwithJack*. Sure, I was thinking about it, but I was way safer if he didn't know that for now. I was still recovering from the surge of sexual energy just a little while ago. No need to provoke him further by dipping a toe in this pool. It was on my mind, though.

Chapter 14

Jack finally left my place late in the morning to spend the second half of the day at the garage. He said he'd pick me up around six for the barbecue down at the lake. My job was to get beer and burger stuff and swing by his haunted house for a cooler. I refused his offer of money, so it irritated me when I found fifty bucks tucked under my keys by the door. Trying to give his money back always required a level of duplicity that would make the secret squirrels at the Central Intelligence Agency take notice. Challenge accepted, Turner. I stuck the three bills in my pocket and headed out.

"Hey, Miss Delphine!" She was deadheading the marigolds in the flower bed along the porch, and I waited until she pushed herself back on her heels before throwing her a cheery wave. The size of her straw hat was comical, casting a shadow to make a lunar eclipse jealous. "Oh, hey, honey. Saw Jack this mornin'. Fixed my shutter on his way out. That thing came loose in the storm a few weeks back and nearly woke the dead."

I glanced in the direction she was pointing and saw that the shutter, previously hanging akimbo, was now back in place and parallel to the window. "He's handy like that," I agreed. I wanted to warn her about how he would wheedle his way into your life with these little favors, hanging shutters, feeding chickens, etc., and before you realized it, he had secured himself a spot as indispensable. But I didn't. At her age, she may not have all that much time to really worry about it.

I jumped in Sandi and rolled down the windows. Even though the mercury was on its way up, I figured the breeze would be cool enough for now. Jack and I would eventually swap vehicles so he could take the Jeep for his playdate tomorrow. He surely had a plan worked out, but we hadn't discussed it before he left. If he was picking me up at six, was he dropping me here afterwards so he could go back to the campsite with the boys? Would he stay here with me and leave early in the morning? Would he ask me to stay with him at his house and leave early from there? Um. No. I could tell you right now he wasn't leaving me alone in that haunted house, especially while it was still dark outside.

I made the haunted house my first stop so I could pick up the cooler. Things looked fine standing in the driveway. Jack told me where to get the spare key, but as I headed around back to the patio, an eerie sensation lapped at my feet. I kept walking in spite of it.

The key was easy to find. He should definitely reconsider the home security initiative he had in place. Welcome mat? Really? That's the first place any third string burglar would look. Key in hand, I decided to go in through the front door, because the light was better on that side of the house this time of day. I was operating under the belief that natural light helped fumigate unwanted spirits, but I could have made that up.

Walking through the door, I got a chill in the foyer. It wasn't the resident ghost giving me the creeps but the recollection of Jack kissing me in this space. Slowing just long enough to smile at the memory, I rounded the corner to the kitchen and stopped dead in my tracks. On the counter was a bouquet of zinnias.

Jack Turner with flowers? What in the name of the narwhal tusk was Jack Turner doing with a bouquet of flowers? The arrangement had one of those plastic forks with a tiny card in a tiny envelope. Someone sent him flowers.

This discovery sucked the smile off my face and created a spasm in the pit of my stomach. Maybe it was disappointment, but it felt an awful lot like sadness. Who was sending Jack flowers? It had to be one of his conquests. He was banging some bimbo, and she sent him flowers. And it had to be within the last couple of days because they weren't here before.

This was the proof I had expected to find all along. This was the Jack I knew. What pained me as much as catching him in the lie was the fact that the hussy sent him *zinnias*, my own all-time favorite flower. I was so disturbed I couldn't even enjoy the bright bursts of jubilation. The blooms seemed dim.

Plucking the card from the fork, I didn't think twice about reading it. He should have tossed the flowers if he was so concerned about me snooping. On the card, in vaguely familiar penmanship I read the words: *For you, Lily. Thank you for not saying no. —Jack*

It took three or four re-reads to sink in. The flowers were for me? He left me flowers. I bet he knew I'd jump to the wrong conclusion. He set me up. I should have been mad, but I wasn't. I was relieved. Was that his point? Was he trying to show me I was farther out on this rickety bridge than I was willing to admit?

I looked at the flowers differently this time, appreciating the colors. Some were saturated—deep purples, oranges, reds, yellows, and fuchsias. There were some softer hues, too—peaches, whites, creamy yellows and pale pinks. There was even an unusual bicolored variety combining pink and green, the kind that looked old-fashioned to me. The bouquet was gorgeous. Were the zinnias a coincidence? For the first time, I noticed a note tucked under the vase. It said simply, "Text me when you get these."

I texted, "Thank you for the flowers."

Cha-ching: "How'd you know they were for you?"

"I read the card."

Cha-ching: "I was counting on that." (Smiley emoji)

"Sorry I snooped."

Cha-ching: "Did you jump to the wrong conclusion?"

I paused, not wanting to admit it. "Yes."

Cha-ching: "I want you to trust me."

"I know."

Cha-ching: "Are zinnia's still your favorite?"

So, it wasn't a coincidence after all. That fool knew my favorite flower. "Yes."

Cha-ching: (Another slightly different smiley)

Cha-ching: "Don't forget the cooler."

"Right."

I sat in the kitchen for a few more minutes, looking at the flowers. My dad gave me sixteen yellow roses on my sixteenth birthday, but other than that, I really couldn't remember getting flowers from a guy. My heart was unusually full. I liked the flowers and the feeling they gave me so much, I wanted to take the bouquet with me, but I was afraid they'd wilt in the hot Jeep when I went into the grocery store. Maybe I'd swing back by on my way home.

Hopping up to get the cooler from the laundry room, I bumped my shoulder into the door jamb hard enough to make a thud. It gave me that unpleasant after-sensation of shooting stabs of pain, and I rubbed at it to stop the hurt.

Under my breath I formulated one of those clunky Shakespearean curses based on a pox, directing it first at the door for being there, next at Jack for getting me loopy, and finally at the real source of the problem, my two left feet.

I always figured I would grow into a little grace at some point in my life. Sadly, at twenty-one years of age, I still showed no signs of graduating from the gawky phase. Clumsy was destined to be my thing. Some people can calculate the restaurant tip or read super fast or say something funny every time. Nope, my thing was crashing into stationary objects.

Still rubbing the outside of my upper arm, I wondered if maybe I had some type of disability related to knowing where my body was in space. It wasn't exactly hand-eye coordination, although I didn't have that either. This was more like body-eye coordination.

Bad body-eye coordination didn't seem that serious when you were tripping over furniture or falling down a few steps, but people like me were the ones who misjudged the train platform and fell onto the tracks. We were the ones who stepped into empty elevator shafts or ricocheted off the bumper of a parked car into oncoming traffic. With all the near misses I've survived, I found it amazing I was alive to have this conversation in my head.

Before I left, I had to find a way to leave Jack's fifty bucks somewhere he would see it unexpectedly. Underwear drawer? He'd find it, but maybe that was a little too private. Did I seriously want to draw his attention to underwear—the last thing you take off when you're getting ready to have sex? No...not the underwear drawer. What does Jack always do for sure? Eat. Where could I hide money so he'd find it the next time he went for something to eat? Fridge? Pantry?

I fingered the bills, pondering the idea of an origami swan. I started making random creases when my fingers took over. The finished product was a non-aerodynamic paper airplane instead of a delicate swan. I followed the exact same blueprint with the remaining two bills and dropped the three planes in his favorite coffee cup.

It was a chipped, beat-up old mug advertising a defunct company called Scorpion Welding. I refused to use it or even touch it myself because of the life-sized scorpion image emblazoned across it. I regularly lobbied for him to retire the mug to coffee cup heaven, but he said it was the perfect size and had a handle that fit his grip, so no. As much as I wanted that thing to fall and break, I didn't want to be held responsible for the wreckage. Just to be on the safe side, I used a wooden spoon to push it back one inch, so it wasn't too close to the edge of the shelf.

Then, to counter my act of charity, I tapped the rim sharply and said, "Take that, Scorpion Welding," as if for some bizarre reason I thought I had one-upped the hated cup.

Dropping the wooden spoon back in the canister of assorted wooden spoons, I noticed a black cat clock on the wall, the kind whose tail swings back and forth. Must have been the Candy Lady's clock, and I mused at that connection—witch, black cat. It was so obvious! Regardless, according to the cat, I needed to get moving. Besides the grocery store, I planned to spend a little time with the puppies over at the Turner place. If I wanted new nail polish, I needed to swing by the drug store because Cumquat's only carried three colors—the same three colors they carried since the 1950s. Oh, and I was definitely coming back for the flowers.

⅄ 🐦 ⅄

Returning to Miss Delphine's, I was relieved she was nowhere in sight. Not even worried about what crime she was busy covering up, I wanted to get the zinnias up to the apartment before she spied me. If I could avoid giving her one more reason to like Jack, that was the way to go.

I had just enough time to polish my toes. An orange color called Crush. Yeah, I got the hypocrisy. Then I changed into my bathing suit and pulled shorts and a tank over top. I was sitting on my little porch, drinking a beer, when Jack got there. He looked at me for a long moment from the driver's seat before he shut the truck off. Hard to read his face with the sun on the window like that, so I didn't have a clue what was going through his feeble little brain.

Bringing his backpack with him, he easily took the steps two at a time. When he got to the porch, the first thing he noticed was the bruise blooming on my upper arm. His smile faded. Tracing the edge lightly with his index finger, he said, "What happened here?"

"Fell into the doorway of your laundry room."

"Ow. Does it hurt?"

"No more than usual." He knew I bruised frequently and spectacularly, mostly due to my own ineptitude.

"You want me to kiss it?"

"In your dreams."

"I can do that." He laughed low. "I kiss a different part of you in my dreams every single night."

He reached for my beer bottle and took a big swig. This would likely be the extent of his drinking for the night. He tended to appoint himself lifeguard at the lake because he didn't like the combination of swimming and alcohol. The designated sober-person responsibilities were definitely distributed unequally between us.

He passed the beer back to me. "Mind if I take a shower?"

"Nope." I truly didn't. Jack could shower in under three minutes.

"Want to join me?"

I looked down at an imaginary watch, "Aw, darn. We don't have that much time." I sneered.

A look crossed his face like he was about to change our plans for the evening. "Okay. For now, I'll do that in my dreams, too."

After he showered and changed, he grabbed the cooler off the kitchen counter and my canvas bag of beach towels. Coming out he rested the load on the arm of my Adirondack chair and held out his hand. "Key."

"Wait," I said, remembering my empty beer bottle. "Let me put this inside." It was more for Miss Delphine than me. I didn't want her to be disappointed in her choice of a tenant, especially since I was living here rent free.

Jack waited as I set the bottle on the table, but I didn't like the way it detracted from my bouquet, so I moved it to the designated recycle bin where it should have gone in the first place.

After he locked up, he loaded the cooler in the back of the Jeep and walked around to open my door. On the ride to the lake, I stayed a hundred yards away from any subject linked to emotions, relationships, or *SexwithJack*. Given Jack's knack for making anything dirty, not so easy to do. I talked about the puppies the entire way. Since he was still committed to having a dog, I drew him in like a librarian to a used book sale, giving him my thoughts about which dog would suit him best.

Twenty minutes flew by and we pulled up to the lake having never mentioned anything that would make me uncomfortable. The rest would be easy. Just say the word "Jeep" around Rick and Mitch, and they were good for an hour of mind-numbing non-stop Jeep babble. Drop a phrase like "bead locks" or "onboard air" and that was the rest of the night.

The group had pretty much already gathered, and people were milling around and cutting up. A lot of traffic meant that the bugs and spiders would be trampled. Good for me. It wasn't the biggest crowd I'd ever seen down here, only about a dozen or so friends from high school. Some were a year or two older, some a year or two younger. By the number of tents, it looked like most people would be camping out. I turned to Jack, "Are you sleeping here tonight?"

"I'm sleeping at your house tonight." He smiled and looped an arm around my neck. Then, because he just had to get it in, he said, "Does that make you nervous?"

Before I could shut him down, Rick grabbed me from behind. He gave big, happy hugs, and I smiled at his enthusiasm. "Lily B. You crawlin' with us tomorrow? I'd pay money to watch you show Jack how to drive a Jeep."

"Rick, I'd love to give you boys a lesson. Fact is, I don't like y'all that much."

He had a deep, booming laugh that was a pleasure to hear.

Mitch came up with a hug and a beer, "Wow," he said with fake disappointment, "I don't think she likes us."

"You know what that means?" Rick asked.

"Yeah." Mitch nodded his head solemnly. "She must not know us very well, otherwise she'd hate us."

I took the beer and the hug Mitch offered just as he noticed my bruise. It had already doubled in size and gotten a lot more colorful. "Whoa. I'd hate to see what the other guy looks like."

Rick leaned in and asked, "Where'd you get that doozy?"

I shrugged off his concern. "My normal propensity for crashing into things."

"Why don't you hold the beer bottle to your arm for a minute," Rick suggested.

"Rick, if I iced every bruise, I'd use up the polar caps faster than global warming."

Jack chuckled. I imagined he was scrolling through a catalog of my bruises. The four of us walked down to the fire circle. The rusty grill that stayed here was chock full of charcoal, and Joe was about to toss a match.

"Lil-Lee," he said, smiling. "You ready for our big date tomorrow?"

"Joe, it's not a date," I said, a hint of panic tinging the edges of my voice. "It's not even a fake date." Granted he was working with limited information, but still, he had to understand what I was trying to accomplish. "Do you even know what your job is?"

"Yes ma'am. Jack was very clear when he gave me my marching orders. I'm stickin' to you like a tick on a dog."

"Joe, you can't give the impression we're together. I may have to flirt with Ditch a little to get him to confide in me."

"Flirt it up, babe, so long as you do it within a five-foot radius of my fist."

I opened my mouth to huff out a response but decided it was pointless. Maybe I should just lay this out tomorrow, away from all these distractions and curious onlookers. I was sure Luis would need a stern talkin'-to as well.

Luis and Mercedes were not at the barbecue. Mercedes was working and if I had to put money on it, Luis was having dinner where Mercedes was working. I scanned the group of my friends, enjoying the diverse mix of white, black, and Hispanic. Plus Larry, who coined the phrase "reskimo" to describe his redneck Eskimo heritage. That kind of multicul-turalism wasn't something you typically expected in a small Virginia town, but somehow this group had achieved it. It made me happy to see them all. I liked my people at school, but the chemistry here was hard to find in other groups. Over the years, different couples hooked up, changing the dynamic like the phases of the moon. Sometimes it worked, sometimes it didn't. But there was an unwritten rule that governed the group—no breakup would break the group up.

A few of the water lovers had already headed down to the dock. Jack saw me taking my tank top off and whispered in my ear, "Skinny dip-ping?"

I nearly gave myself an injury looking around to see if anyone heard him. No one was in earshot, thankfully, so the secret was safe. I knew he wanted a reaction, so I tried to resist. That lasted, oh, four seconds before I pushed a fist awkwardly in his direction. He easily dodged the assault with a step to the side.

"Careful," he warned. "Remember what happened the last time I retaliated?"

I felt the color drain from my face as I wondered if he really would. Here. In front of all these people.

He read my mind, and answered, "I'd do it in a second, girl." Watch-ing me sputter made him laugh.

The only response I could generate was to snatch my lilac beach towel and turn my back to him as I walked away. It took literally every fiber of my willpower not to look over my shoulder, but I knew his blue eyes were drilling holes in me because I felt that uncomfortable sensation.

The end of the dock was in water almost over your head. There was a strictly respected no-diving rule. I tended to favor the sit-and-push method of entering the water over the run-and-jump method. I made a good-sized splash hitting the surface. The day was still hot and the cool water felt good.

Since Jack planted the seed in my head, I had a flashback to that weekend a year ago when I was skinny dipping with Storie. It made me sad that she wouldn't get to enjoy that again. I decided, instead of a tattoo, I'd find opportunities to skinny dip. That's how I'd honor her memory.

Lost in my thoughts, I didn't notice the raft until it bumped into me. My friend Maureen Parker had paddled up, offering me the other end of her float so I didn't have to tread water. We each draped our arms across the raft, bodies for the most part dangling in the water. We lounged this way, catching up until a couple yahoos came along and dunked us under. The shenanigans went on for twenty more minutes. When it looked like the burgers were close to done, we all started filing out of the water and drifting toward the smell of food.

By the time Jack and I were ready to leave, I'd had probably three beers. After the cathartic swim and the alcohol, I was feeling pretty breezy. A lot of my pent-up resistance to Jack had been washed away in the lake or drowned in the beer. The Jeep was parked well away from the group, and when he walked me to the passenger side, I surprised him with a kiss before he could open my door.

He enthusiastically accepted. "Watching you come out of the water, I was so hot for you, Lily."

"Was it the wet-rat hair or the no makeup face?" I asked him, kind of sarcastically.

"The total package," he said, pulling back so he could see me better. "This is what I've been trying to tell you. I like how you do what you want, not a care in the world about how it looks or who's watching. It's hot."

Not knowing if it was his compliment, the beer or the moonlight, I wanted to kiss him again, so I did.

When we stopped, he said, "I want to be clear about something. As much as I want to, we're not having sex tonight."

"Why?" I asked, and there was a distinct pout to my voice.

"I want you sober, so I can be sure I'm not taking advantage."

"Well, Jack-a-lope," I said, "I can promise you I'm not drunk."

"Mhmmm," he drawled. "You just gave yourself away, girl."

"What?"

"You called me 'Jack-a-lope'. That's your term of endearment when you've been drinking. So, not tonight, but soon." He smiled and kissed my neck before he opened the door. "I like the way your skin smells after you've been in the lake," he added so quietly, I wasn't sure if he was talking to me or to himself.

⅄ 🐓 ⅃

In the morning, I jerked awake and fumbled for my phone on the nightstand to check the time. Impossible. Could it be eight thirty? I slept through the egg songs? The chickens were probably starving half to death out there. Dealing with a chicken was bad enough. Dealing with a starving chicken? No telling what they'd do, peck my eyes out maybe?

I jumped up, made a quick pit stop in the bathroom, then grabbed the broom. Given that the chickens may be starving, I decided eye protection was warranted, so I grabbed my sunglasses off the kitchen counter. In lieu of safety goggles, that was the best I could do against a flurry of angry beaks.

Stopping to put the shades on, I noticed there was a tablet on the kitchen table with a note from Jack. I quit reading after the first line. *Hey, I fed the chickens…* My eyeballs were safe. I could take off the sunglasses. Expelling the breath I had apparently been holding, I plopped into a chair as relief spread through me like the Holy Spirit through a bus full of Baptists.

The rest of Jack's message constituted the fine print. I guessed he figured I wouldn't be as upset about it once he established that the chickens were fed. Clever. *Be careful tonight*, the note went on. *And remember, Joe is my deputy, vested with all the authority I would ordinarily exercise in a situation like this. Don't give him any grief. Please. —Jack*

I crumpled the note and tossed it toward the garbage can, off by a good twelve inches. Ball sports were not my forte. I may have missed the three-point shot, but I happily settled for the consolation prize—a hot cup of coffee. Jack must have put the pot on before he left. He was clearly working every angle to swoop in and save the day, or at least the morning, by feeding the chickens and fixing the coffee.

Speaking of swooping, I gave him plenty of chances to swoop last night and he steadfastly refused. He could have easily had sex with me. In almost every conversation he alluded to it. It would have eliminated virtually all the complications to do it and just be done with it. We could have chalked it up to a couple beers, a stupid decision, and the open window of opportunity. Once it was out of the way, I would activate my standard state of denial and refuse to discuss it. Eventually it would disappear from the topographical map of our friendship. So why didn't he do it? Yeah, yeah, that whole taking advantage song and dance. I gave a nod to his parents for raising him to have principles. He was still an obnoxiously persistent totalitarian, but the boy had principles nonetheless.

I finished my coffee and got up to pour another cup, but coffee could wait. From the kitchen window I saw Miss Delphine out there, rusty wheelbarrow loaded up with black garbage bags. What in the name of magenta-colored sweatpants was she burying out there? Or...who?

I flew down the stairs with my flip flops clapping on the wooden steps and dashed through the chicken yard. McNugget was sipping at the water dispenser, pretending to be uninterested in my sudden, noisy appearance.

As I passed within what I judged to be earshot for a chicken, I said, "Keep it up, and I'll introduce you to a cast iron skillet." I wasn't exactly sure what I meant by that. What was I challenging her to keep up? Drinking water? Ignoring me? Well, she called my bluff and kept doing both of those things. I had no come back for that.

Shaking off my persistent poultry frustration, I plastered on a smile and willed my brown eyes to sparkle with congeniality. When encountering a murder suspect, it worked better if you kept your suspicions under wraps. I didn't have time to check with Stephanie, but I believed that to be the case.

"You digging a hole, Miss Delphine?"

"Well, Lily, I'm not playin' Tiddlywinks," she said dryly.

I pressed my lips together. Admittedly, my opener was lame even for me. "You want some help?"

"Lord, child, I need it done before dinner time."

She had a point. You could pretty much tell by looking at me I was no speed digger. "How 'bout I get Jack to do it for you? That boy lives to be a good Samaritan."

She lifted another spade of dirt, "Does he now?" By her tone, it sounded more like she was indulging a two-year old than giving serious consideration to my offer of assistance.

"What's in the bags?" I knocked the tip of my left flip flop into the rubber wheel, in case she was confused as to which bags I meant. They were the only bags on the scene, but she was pretty old.

"…ounds."

What did she say? She was kind of talking into the hole, and the shovel made a noise as it scraped against the rocks in the soil. Clowns? Hounds? Wait. Was she burying a hound? Did Cro die? Ordinarily that ol' mutt would have been right by her side. I looked back toward the porch, but a movement in the woods caught my eye. On cue, the black dog popped from behind a tree, gave a hearty shake, and flopped down on the other side of the hole. Okay, so she wasn't burying her dog. That was good.

"Worms love 'em," she added.

"Worms love who?" I asked, baffled.

She stopped her digging to study me. I detected a distinct what's-the-matter-with-you expression on her face. "*Grounds*, girl. Worms love *grounds*." I seemed to be taxing her patience.

Grounds? What did she grind up? A body? Oh, sweet molasses. Miss Delphine ground up a dead body, and she was burying the evidence. So stunned by her admission, I completely lost control of the interrogation and repeated my thought out loud. "Worms love ground up bodies?"

She stopped digging. "What on earth are you talkin' about?"

I watched her carefully. Her confusion was convincing, but that could be her modus operandi. I moved quickly to cover my gaffe. Fabricating on the fly was one of my specialties, so I let the story rip. "Oh, that's just a line from a funny movie. 'Worms love ground up bodies.' It's from *Death and Dying in the Parkview Cinema*. Not even a B-movie. It never achieved the cult status the filmmakers were hoping for. But very funny if you like that kind of thing." I learned early on if you pretended to know what you were talking about, delivered whatever made-up fact convincingly, and added a lot of detail, people generally bought it without question.

Miss Delphine shook her head. "Heat got you already?"

"No, ma'am. I'm fine."

"Then grab that bag."

What? Did she expect me to help her dispose of a ground up body? Would that make me an accomplice or an accessory? Coming in direct contact with human remains put me at a crime scene. I'd be hard pressed to convince a cop that I wasn't involved. What if I went right to the police after confirming the contents of the bag? That's what I would do.

Wishing badly for a pair of latex gloves, I lifted a heavy black trash bag from the wheelbarrow.

"Drop it in the hole, and I'll bust it open with the shovel."

I lugged the unwieldy load to the shallow hole where I dumped it with a grunt. As she plunged the shovel down, I screamed involuntarily. Cro jumped up, barking, and Miss Delphine scolded us both.

"Sorry," I said. "I thought…I thought I saw a spider on the bag. I, um, hate spiders."

"Have you lost all the sense the good Lord gave you?"

"No," I assured her, but I could see by her face she didn't believe me. "Well, maybe half. Half the sense the good Lord gave me," I admitted.

She hit the bag one more time with the shovel and a blackish material spilled out. The glare from the sun made it hard to see in the hole. Skipping that second cup of coffee this morning was a mistake; I thought I could smell it now. Probably just a response to the trauma of burying a human slurry.

"Now reach down there and get that plastic out," she instructed.

Contemplating what my tolerance for ground up body parts would be, I bent down. The desire for coffee overwhelmed me now, and I wondered if this was some precursor to a seizure. I'd read once that some people with epilepsy smell a very distinct odor, like gasoline, bleach, or tar, right before they have a convulsion. Granted, I had no history of seizures, but this could be a new thing brought on by the stress of this experience. Either way, I smelled coffee.

I braced myself as best I could in case the seizure struck as I was hovering over the hole. Last thing I wanted was to take a nosedive onto the deceased person in this bag. Strange, other than the coffee smell, there was no other indication that I was about to blackout. I felt fine in every other regard, so I grabbed the edge of the bag and yanked hard.

Tiny bits of matter flew skyward. When gravity kicked in, they rained back down, clinging to me, Miss Delphine, and Cro. The dog was the only one who seemed happy about it. He barked and scratched the ground as if to keep the game going.

"This is coffee," I said, smelling at the stuff that covered my arms.

"Of course it's coffee. What else would it be?"

I didn't really want to accuse her of a grizzly crime based only on the circumstantial evidence I'd collected so far. So I said, as vaguely as possible, "Something other than coffee."

She took her big sun hat off and shook it out. Coffee grounds fell into the hole. Then she gingerly dusted her blouse. "Girl." She apparently couldn't connect another thought to that word, so she left it at that.

Circling back to her earlier statement, I asked,

"Worms drink coffee?"

"Don't be ridiculous. Of course they don't."

"Didn't you say worms like this stuff?"

"They compost kitchen scraps. It's called vermicomposting. They're especially fond of coffee grounds."

"Why are you feeding worms coffee grounds?"

"Worm castins' make good fertilizer." She said this as if it were the most obvious fact ever uttered. "I use it in my flower beds and on the tomatoes out back. It's how I get my blue-ribbon peonies."

"Vermicomposting," I repeated, mesmerized by the word.

"They save me the finished grounds down at the Perk Up Coffee Cup in town. I collect 'em a couple times a week and bury 'em out here. Give this plot a week's time, and it'll be squirmin' with worms. Can you picture that?"

The idea was enough to fuel a month's worth of nightmares, so I tried hard *not* to picture it. Once we finished burying the other three bags, we walked back to the garage together. I pushed the wheelbarrow with the shovel. We parted outside the garage when the tools were stored. She went inside to rinse off the coffee grounds, and I went upstairs to do the same.

As I climbed the stairs, I replayed my investigation. That couldn't have gone worse. Was it possible I was no good at this? Was it possible I didn't know as much as I thought I knew? If my Ditch Miller recon mission went this badly tonight, it could jeopardize the whole Misty-Storie case. If the case stalled, what were my options? Let the mystery go unsolved so I could get back down to UVA?

☙ 🐓 ❧

Mercedes and I had agreed to get ready together. No. Correction. Mercedes demanded that I get ready over her house so she could make sure I "didn't screw it up." Her words. Screw it up. It took more energy to argue with her, and since I wasn't that invested, it wasn't worth the fight. I showered at home and slipped on a transition outfit to go from my place to hers.

The transition outfit looked exactly like every other outfit I owned. Shorts and a t-shirt. Scanning the small apartment, I decided I didn't really need anything besides phone, sunglasses, keys, license, lip gloss, and money. As usual, nothing that necessitated a purse, but I wagered Mercedes would have one lined up regardless.

I glanced at my phone. No new messages. I knew Jack didn't have a signal out in the boondocks where they were wheelin', so why was I disappointed when I didn't see a text from him? The bar would be fun with Jack, and I was kinda missing him. Sure, he'd be a total liability on the mission, but still.

Chapter 15

I couldn't tell if Mercedes was more excited about seeing Luis tonight or seeing me in a skirt. From my point of view in front of the mirror, it should be me in a skirt. Even I was excited about it. I looked so glamorous, I really should consider wearing skirts and make-up more often. Unfortunately, there wasn't a lot of time to stare at my own reflection. I heard Joe's Bronco pull up outside, and seconds later they were banging on the door.

As Mercedes was still putting the finishing touches on her loveliness, I tore myself away from the mirror and let them in.

Standing in the doorway, Joe took his sunglasses off and looked me up and down. Twice. "Girl." He stretched the word to two syllables.

I turned around to give him the three-sixty.

"I'm sorry," he said, pretending to be fazed. "We're looking for Lily Barlow. Tomboy in a t-shirt. You know her?"

"Never heard of her."

"Then who do we have the pleasure of meeting?" Luis asked as he bowed his head and kissed my hand. While I was busy giving Luis a little curtsy, I noticed Joe snap a picture on his phone. I was sure it would make its way to Jack at some point.

"I haven't thought of my stage name, yet. Any ideas?"

The two of them took turns rattling off a rapid-fire list of what I could only assume were the names of their favorite porn stars.

"Chloe."

"Aspen."

"Scarlett."

"Ruby."

"Summer."

"Nikki."

"Skylar."

"Leyla."

"Kylie."

"Lexi."

"Kinsley."

"Roxie."

"Angel."

"Lola."

"Jade."

"Okay. Okay. I get it. Something with a little va-vavoom. Which one?"

In low voices, they simultaneously said, "Nikki."

When I asked Joe why, he said Nikki was just the right amount of dirty. Luis must have enjoyed the right amount of dirty because he nodded his agreement, grinning like a baboon.

Mercedes chose that moment to make her entrance. One of the things I loved about Mercedes was how she never needed to steal the show. Oh, make no mistake, the show would be stolen for sure. By not drawing attention to herself, though, she had perfected a subtlety that made her even sexier. I equated it to the exact opposite of twirling into a room like a 40's film star. Instead, of spinning into the room, she let the room spin around her. For years I wished some of that could rub off on me but gave up the wish as futile in high school.

She played along with my new persona. "This is my friend, Nikki. Did you meet her?" she asked, as she fussed with my hair one last time.

"Mmhmm," Luis murmured, already under a different spell. He handed her the bouquet he had been holding, and as he made the transfer, Joe snapped a pink flower off a stem and gave it to me. He and Jack were so much alike, especially in the flirtation arena.

Mercedes was thrilled with the flowers and went to the kitchen for a vase. She even cut the stems before arranging them, so they'd stay fresh longer. When she leaned over to put the vase on the kitchen table, Luis got a perfect view of her perfect cleavage. I don't think any boy was ever happier to deliver a bouquet of flowers. Ever. She smiled innocently, like the devil she was, and asked who wanted a beer.

Joe abstained. An onlooker would have guessed Jack had a hand in that, but believe it or not, Joe was as responsible as his brother when it came to drinking and driving. Their parents really lucked out. It was a safe guess he'd have one beer at the bar. I didn't know if it would be to enjoy the beer or just so he had a bottle in case a fight broke out. Either way, holding a bottle would help him blend in.

Mercedes brought over three cans and we clinked, or rather made the sound that aluminum makes when the cans come together in a cheers. She gave me a secret look that said, "This is your chance. Give these boys orders." Then she took the flower I was still holding and tucked it in my hair.

"So, y'all know the point of tonight, right?" I started slowly.

"Four friends hanging out, listening to some live music, right?" Joe responded.

"Well," I started, "that's the cover, but not the point."

"We know, Nikki." Luis assured me. "You're looking for an old friend, and this chump in the band knows her. If he gives you any grief, Joe and I will kick his a—."

"More or less," I cut him off. "But if we could keep the, um, bodily harm to a minimum, that would be helpful."

"Seems like that'll be up to Ditch, now," Joe said, and I thought he sounded serious.

I took a long pull off my beer, giving myself time to phrase my next statement. "If and when a physical response is required, I'll be the one to give the signal."

"Lily…I mean, Nikki…if it makes you feel better to think you get to pull the trigger, then okay, you go ahead and think it." Joe tipped his head and kept his expression very flat.

I took a breath, preparing to deliver a strongly worded rebuttal, but I ended up blowing the air out of my mouth in a noisy rush. What was the point when mule-headed ran in the family like black hair and blue eyes?

Mercedes chimed in, trying to give me back control. "This is Nikki's thing. Nikki calls the shots. You hear me, José?" While the Turner boys might be able to railroad me, she was a lot harder to manage.

Joe laughed. He liked when she used the Spanish version of his name, and he responded with his English adaptation of hers, "I hear ya, Sadie." Meanwhile he stared at me, pointing two fingers at his own eyes and then flipping the two fingers toward me. I returned with another hand gesture, using one very specific finger accompanied by a super sugary smile. I had the feeling this was going to be a long night.

Those of us drinking beer finished up, and we all headed out to the Bahama blue Bronco. Anybody who was into cars could tell this was a special one. Back in middle school, Mr. Turner always said a boy without a project became a man without a purpose. He let each of his sons pick a jalopy, and he helped them restore it from the lug nuts up. They had to earn the money for parts, but Mr. Turner provided plenty of sweat equity.

Joe loved the classic Broncos, and Jack picked a Jeep CJ. These projects took them both through high school, scouring online forums and scavenging junk yards and swap meets to get all the parts they needed. Both the Jeep and the Bronco looked amazing and ran great, and they

228

only came out on very rare occasions. I wondered how tonight's event rated as all that special. Ultimately, I didn't care so much about the why, it was just fun to ride in the Bronco and get all the looks.

The gentlemen opened the doors for the ladies as per the Turner protocol. They didn't have much of a back seat, the early Broncos, so guess who got to ride back there? Obviously, the women. The short skirts were either a handicap getting in and out of a classic car or an advantage, depending on whether you were wearing one or watching a person who was wearing one.

Boot raised, pondering the best approach, I wondered if Luis talked Joe into bringing it just so he could watch the sizzling hips of the sultry Mercedes as she worked her way into the back seat.

Standing in the open door of the driver's side, I looked at Joe. "Seriously?"

He tried not to, but he lost it, howling with laughter. "Luis, switch places with Nikki."

No arm-twisting required, Luis hopped back there quicker than cat hair on black slacks. Joe walked me around to the passenger side, gave me an arm to use as leverage, and closed the door once I was settled. Through it all, he looked as if he could easily burst out laughing again.

Winchester was about an hour's drive. The two in the back were having their own exclusive conversation, so Joe and I had to entertain ourselves.

"Are you ever gonna pick Jack's dog so I can finally pick mine?"

"What?"

"Every time I ask about it, mom says the same thing—you get first dibs. Since I can't see you taking a puppy back to school, I assume you're picking Jack's."

"Yeah. And I got one picked out for you, too. The chubby, crabby one. You know, like owner like pet."

Joe wasn't chubby or crabby. While I wouldn't call him jolly, he was definitely easygoing. Nothing ever seemed to ruffle him.

"As long as it's not that yappy, whiny one. That'd be like having you around all the time."

I nodded my approval. That was a pretty good comeback. "Touché."

He gave me a little side knock with his elbow to let me know we were still friends. Once he got the smile he was looking for, he checked the rear view and said,

"Hey, you people in the back hungry? We got time."

"Big Bill's BBQ?" asked Luis.

"You got it."

Beautiful. Barbecue. I was neither a spotless eater nor one to forgo barbecue, hence the pending predicament. I felt a tiny bit obligated not to drip a blob of sauce on this outfit, even though it was a risk Mercedes assumed when she dressed me from her closet. I needed to choose my meal carefully. The fallout would rain down in a spray of Spanish. Funny to witness if you weren't on the receiving end.

Settling on the pulled pork sandwich platter and sweet tea, I knew I had two choices. One, try to pay for my dinner while Joe had an aneurysm, or two, just let him pay. The average citizen would find this hard to believe, but Joe was even more determined than his brother when it came to paying for things. I didn't think chauvinism was the right word, but something along the lines of take-care-of-ism, and it stuck in my craw the same as when Jack did it.

I reminded myself that ameliorating one of Joe's longstanding foibles wasn't on the list of objectives for this evening. If I peacefully went along now at the cash register, that might buy me some flexibility later at the bar. Still, I struggled internally with the assumption that someone else should pay for me. It made me feel beholden.

Pushing the tray forward along the cafeteria-style counter, Big Bill himself handed me my plate. I didn't know him to talk to him, but he greeted everybody as if you and he went way back, and he hadn't seen you in a year.

Joe's plate was heaped with what looked like double helpings of everything. He wedged it onto the tray beside mine, and said in a low voice, "Lily, I got dinner. And just so there's no misunderstanding, I got the cover at the bar, and the beer. If you want ice-cream on the way home, I got that, too."

Concentrating on the unequally distributed load I was carrying, it was obvious this wasn't the perfect time for a spitting contest. I shook my head softly to show I disagreed with him as a whole, but he took it to mean I disagreed with his edict. In response, a large hand landed gently on my shoulder, and stayed there, expectantly.

"Okay, Joe," I replied, agitation simmering. "Pay for everything. In fact, I was thinking about buying that used John Deere," I gestured out the window and across the parking lot. "Can you go ahead and pay for that, too?"

"Love that sass."

"Kiss my…" The third word of my response was spoken so quietly, it almost didn't exist.

I carried the food back outside to the little corral of picnic tables and chose one in the shade. It was kind of amazing I was able to get the food and drinks through the parking lot without dumping the whole thing curbside. To celebrate, I shook a set of pom-poms in my head. A pink one and a purple one, which was a weird color choice for imaginary pom-poms. Who was I pulling for? The Easter Bunny?

Dinner was easy. We talked about nothing in particular, laughed a lot, and enjoyed the barbecue. Amazingly, I came away spatter free. Next stop, hot Ditch Miller.

Call it a hunch, but it felt like Joe had been to this bar before. He never activated an app for directions, and instead of pulling up out front where a line was forming, he wound his way down three narrow alleys and through a bank parking lot to get to the back of the building. He effortlessly parallel parked between a dumpster and a van with the band's logo painted on it.

231

I watched as band members gravitated to Joe's Bronco like yellow jackets to a snow cone. Ah. Could that be why he drove this car instead of his truck? I obviously didn't give the boy enough credit.

The way the car was situated, the passenger side was adjacent to a vacant lot, away from the back of the bar. Joe walked around to open my door and help me out.

Praise and admiration from the onlookers gradually percolated.

"Man."

"This thing's a beast."

"Retro, dude."

"Bruh, your car is sick."

"I like your ride."

As he closed my door, he walked around the front of the vehicle, "Thanks." Small talk about cars ensued, and there was an exchange of information useful only to those who rebuild cars or those who like rebuilt cars. In less than ten minutes, Joe had effectively made friends with the entire band, a few groupies, and a bouncer from the bar.

"You here for the show?" That was tattooed Ditch Miller, wearing a tight white t-shirt, and he was talking to me. He was as hot in person as his pictures promised.

"That depends," I said. "This band any good?"

He nodded and gave me the once over, which was only fair since I just did it to him. Out of the corner of my eye, I saw Joe leaning against the Bronco. I knew his posture well enough to understand he wasn't as relaxed as the casual pose suggested. There was a tautness about him, like he would go Tasmanian Devil on the first person who made the wrong move.

"We are, sweet thing." Ditch smiled at me as he answered my question. "We are good. Why don't y'all join us for a drink before we go on?"

The group had drifted away from the Bronco toward an assembly of folding metal chairs, lawn chairs, wooden crates and one five-gallon bucket, all of which were bunched around the back door of the establishment. The door was propped open with a cinder block, and there was music coming from inside. A couple guitars leaned against the building. One guy sat on a stack of pallets, strumming his guitar, stopping now and then to chug some beer.

Ditch took a bottle of whiskey off the stack of pallets and rummaged for some paper cups in a bag by a cooler. He gave a shot of whiskey to whoever stuck a hand over, including me and Mercedes. I glanced at Joe who had put some distance between me and him but seemed very aware of my every move. He nodded the tiniest bit, and it made me feel like he had everything under control.

I took the cup and tossed back the shot. "Thanks, honey," I cooed to Ditch. He tried to pour me another, but I asked for a beer instead.

When he handed it to me, he noticed the big bruise on my arm from the day before. "Well, now," he said, "you like to play rough, don't ya, girl?"

I saw the line of Joe's jaw tighten ever so slightly and figured the aforementioned fist fight was about to be upon us.

I smiled and said, "I can hold my own." Ditch was standing close, and he grazed my bruised arm in a way that gave me an ominous feeling. Did he really have a history of domestic violence? Just then, Luis bumped lightly into my back.

"Oh, sorry, Nikki," he said and moved on. It didn't seem like an accident, so I thought maybe it was his way of letting me know he was also watching.

I decided to stick with the flirty approach even though it was making me uncomfortable. It seemed like the fastest way to get anywhere with a guy like Ditch. I put my hand on his chest, "Aren't you the bass player?"

"I am," Ditch grinned, obviously pleased to be recognized.

"I saw you play at Backroads last year." I lied. I was way too busy with Storie to remember any of the performances let alone the individual performers, but he wouldn't have any way of knowing that.

"You know what they say about bass players?" He touched my hair in a way that made it seem like he knew me better than he did.

"What do they say about bass players?" I went along with him, making my eyes big and innocent.

"They give the best orgasms in the band." He leaned closer.

At that point, the guy sitting on the stack of pallets nearly fell off laughing. Regaining his balance, he bellowed, "Nobody ever said that, because nobody would believe it." He went back to his strumming, but I took this as my opportunity.

"Well, a friend of mine said it." I smiled and took what I perceived to be a slow, sexy sip from the beer bottle. "Storie Sanders. She slept with you, and she said bass players were the best in the band."

"Who?" he asked, a note of confusion tainting his voice. Was it genuine?

"Storie Sanders," I persevered.

"Never heard of her."

"Are you sure? She used to follow your band around."

"I probably banged her. That sounds like me. But I don't do repeat performances. How do you think I got the name?"

I didn't know how the name came about, so I guessed. "You dig ditches on the side?" I swallowed hard at the inference to shallow graves.

His smile got a little more deviant as he shook his head and said, "Nah. That's not how I got the name."

"I give." A look of domination crossed his face the second I yielded, and I glanced at Joe. He had moved himself into my line of sight, and while he was laughing with a cute groupie, he made eye contact with me to show he still had me.

"I do 'em, and I ditch 'em." He stared at me. "Don't let that scare you, sweet thing. You should take your friend, Stoney's word for it and give me a try."

"Her name is Storie. Are you sure you don't know her?"

"Stoney, Storie, I don't know her, babe."

234

From his responses, I couldn't tell if he did or didn't know her. I also couldn't tell if he did or didn't kill her. My chance to dig deeper, or possibly get myself date raped, was slipping away, because the band started moving around with purpose.

Ditch grabbed his bass, leaned into me and whispered, "Meet me after. We'll have some fun." He wrapped his hand around my upper arm and squeezed the bruise. It hurt. As much as I would have liked to respond with a poker face, I'm sure he saw my grimace.

Just then Joe appeared, beer in hand. He said, "Hey, Nikki, it's getting pretty thick in there."

"Yeah," Ditch said. "We sell this place out." Then without another word to me, he headed through the door with the rest of the band.

Mercedes had been sprinkling her magic dust this whole time and slipped up to Joe and me. "Free cover!" she said. "We're with the band." She smiled, and we followed her through the back door.

In a dingy hallway, Joe pulled me back. "You okay?"

"Yeah."

"Did you find out about your friend?"

"No. He said he never heard of her."

"That sucks."

"Joe?"

"Yeah?"

"I don't want to hang around after the show."

"Lily, we can leave now if you want."

"No. I just want to get out of here before they play their last song." A cape of disappointment lay across my shoulders as a cloud of doom gathered above my head. I didn't like Ditch Miller, and I didn't like that Storie was into him. She was way too good for a jerk like that. So was I, for that matter. The cloud of doom came from the realization that he thought he had a chance with me. That's the kind of guy who would push himself on a woman. Is that what happened to Storie? She thought she wanted to be

235

with him, but when she figured out that she didn't, maybe it was too late. Did he kill her? Cut off her head and hands?

When Luis realized I was no longer right behind him, he stopped to wait for us. He and Joe exchanged some wordless form of communication, which served to get Luis up to speed, or so it appeared. As we entered the main barroom, I scanned the place looking for Storie, Stella, or any of the hikers. The only one I could recall clearly was Storie, and it was disheartening to observe a dozen Stories floating around the bar and crowding the dance floor. None of them were my Storie, though. And, with the exception of Joe and Luis, every guy in the joint looked like he just rolled off the Appalachian Trail.

Luis went to get beers, and Joe found a place by a wall where we could see the band and the room. The music started, and as much as I disliked Ditch at the moment, I couldn't help but get into the song. It was a gritty, bluesy, country sound, and I liked it. The rhythm induced a half-sway-half-dance response from me, Mercedes, and most of the women in the audience. With the camouflage of the crowd, I was pretty sure Ditch couldn't see me, so I relaxed enough to enjoy myself.

Thirty minutes later, every inch of floor space was occupied, and I could only imagine what Jack would have to say about the number of fire code infractions currently on display. Mercedes was beside me, but I periodically checked behind for the boys. They seemed to be having a good time, so it wasn't a complete waste.

Just as I was making that assessment, a woman in front of me lost her balance and stumbled backwards. I got a two-phase beer bath, first my own beer and then hers. My top was soaked, my bra was soaked, and the effect was what guys expected to see in a wet t-shirt contest down at Ocean City. Sticky, and cold, I looked down at my ruined, and now revealing, outfit.

The woman squealed something unintelligible, then blathered, "I'm so sorry. You're dripping wet. I'm so-ooooo sorry!" Watching her overreact, I thought she was more of a klutz than a drunk. Hmm. One of my kind.

I stood there, collecting myself. There was bound to be an alcohol-related mishap at a venue like this. Unavoidable. If you drank enough and went to enough places, you would eventually dump your beer on somebody, and you'd eventually get somebody's beer dumped on you. It was a law of the universe. Like you would eventually lose your luggage on a flight, or you would eventually lock your keys in the car, or you would eventually drop your phone on the sidewalk. It happened. How you chose to respond to it, now that was the only thing you really had any control over.

Having dumped beer on people more times than the universe prescribed for one person, I always appreciated a low-key response. So, it was my turn to give one.

"Hey, it's alright. Don't worry about it."

Joe leaned over, "I have a clean shirt in the Bronco."

"Thanks. I'll change before we head home."

My kindred klutz continued to beg forgiveness, so I tried to give her some relief. "Really, I'm okay. My dad always tells me I'm not made of sugar. Since I don't melt in the rain, I certainly won't melt from a little beer." I smiled, and she laughed. "The band is great," I added, changing the subject.

"I've never heard them before, but they can sure pack 'em in," she yelled. "This place is jam up and jelly tight."

I grabbed her shoulder, and more earnestly than I meant to, I asked, "What did you say?"

Raising her voice even louder, she yelled, "I said this place is packed!"

"No," I insisted, "you said something about jelly."

"Oh, I said this place is jam up and jelly tight. You know, crowded." She gestured toward the throng.

"I knew a person who said that once, but I've never heard anyone else use that phrase." Storie. Storie said it. Did this woman know her?

"Yeah. It's kind of a quirky saying. I heard it at a farmers market. The woman who said it was a total hippie. She was all about peace, love and light."

"Do you know her name?"

"Get this. Her name was Storie, like Storybook, only with an i-e. Enchanting, isn't it? Hard to forget a name like that."

How many people could possibly have the name Storie? I never felt so lucky to have beer splashed on me. What were the odds? "Storie Sanders?"

"Do you know her?" She asked, still yelling, but very surprised.

"I met a woman named Storie Sanders last year, but we lost track. I'd like to get back in touch. Do you know how I can find her?"

"I met her a while back at the Culpeper market. It's been a couple years now. She was raising vegetables on a farm called Sanders' Ridge. I assumed it was her family's farm, since she said her last name was Sanders. Never saw her after that, but she left an impression."

"I met her at a music festival a year ago," I explained to the stranger, "and she left an impression on me, too."

I was buzzing like one of those long fluorescent light bulbs in a community center kitchen. I had the name of a business that may belong to Storie's family. I had a town where the business was located or at least a proximity. The woman didn't know her and probably couldn't give any more info than that, but that was pay dirt.

"Small world," I said and let her get back to the music.

I turned around to Joe only to see that he had been closely scrutinizing the whole scene. "What was that about?"

"The woman who spilled the beer, she met my friend and thinks she might be from Culpeper!"

"Are you serious? You got all that from a spilt beer?" I nodded wildly.

"Leave it to you to go panning for gold and come waltzing out with a doubloon."

I laughed and turned back around. I was giddy, and I wished Jack was here. He was the only one who knew the real value of this information, and I kinda felt like giving him a hug. Or a kiss.

Luis, who went to get me a replacement beer after the mishap, handed it to me.

"Thanks, dude!"

"You're welcome."

I smiled at Mercedes and raised my eyebrows toward Luis to show my approval.

"I know." She said this in a loud whisper directly in my ear, so as not to alert the man in question to the fact that she agreed with me.

Everything made me so happy. I had a fresh beer, there was a dry t-shirt waiting for me, me and Mercedes were falling in love at the same time. Just then the band took a break, and the lights came up. Whoa. Whoa. Whooooa! Falling in love? Where did *that* come from? I could certainly miss Jack and want to kiss Jack without falling in love with Jack.

I must have looked distressed because Joe asked me if I was alright.

"Yeah, yeah," I said, trying to push away the thoughts of Jack.

"You sure? You look like you're about to have an anxiety attack. I know Ditch was gettin' under your skin. You don't have to talk to him again."

He had keyed on the wrong thing, but still, the way he said this made me feel like there was a very high stone wall standing between me and Ditch. The wall was Joe. In that second, I deeply appreciated his concern. It was touching and very reassuring. I regretted that Misty-Storie didn't have these kinds of protective people around her.

"Thanks, Joe. I know I gave Jack a lot of grief about you coming, but I'm glad you and Luis are here tonight."

He smiled a wise, older-than-you smile. "You give Jack grief about everything, girl, but that's alright. He likes it."

I cut my eyes toward the ceiling, then back to Joe. "Right," I agreed, "but let's not discard all the grief he gives me."

"Oh, I don't. You two have always had a weird little relationship. I think it works because y'all give each other such a hard time."

I suddenly wanted to confide in Joe about what had changed with me and Jack, but I held back. He had always been Jack's closest confidant, and I suspected he already had an inkling if not the whole naked truth. Plus, I didn't want him taking anything back to Jack that I wasn't ready to divulge.

After a short break, the band started up again. We listened for another forty minutes before I turned to the group, "Y'all ready to get outta here?"

Luis had his arms around Mercedes, and they both smiled and nodded. Joe asked Luis to go grab the t-shirt from under the front seat so I could change in the bathroom before we left. He was taking this five-foot radius thing to heart. Ordinarily I would have changed in the parking lot without a second thought. Only when Joe mentioned the bathroom did I think about Ditch or a Ditch-like character, lurking, watching. It made my skin crawl. I definitely had to be smarter about how I interacted with the world. Women were abused and killed. It hadn't been my reality, but it was Misty-Storie's reality.

Chapter 16

Joe dropped Mercedes and Luis off at Luis' house and then took me to Miss Delphine's. It was close to midnight, and I was shocked to see my Jeep in the drive.

"Why is Sandi here? Is Jack here?" A surprising level of concern kicked in and was largely unaccounted for.

"Is he okay?"

"Yeah. He's fine." Joe made it sound so run-of-the-mill. "He texted to say he was heading back to your place when he got off the trail today."

"Was that his way of checking up on me without checking up on me?"

Joe shook his head as if he couldn't believe what he was hearing. "You've met Jack, right? He's been checking up on you for the last four or five hours. I guess Rick's phone gets a signal out there in the boonies. I'm just surprised he didn't cut his day short and show up at The Switchback to check on you in person." Then he added with a grin, "He really liked what you were wearing tonight, by the way. Before you took the beer bath." He chuckled.

It is an established fact that the mind of an average guy has all the complexity of four basic Lego pieces—a yellow, a blue, a white and a red. You can change the configuration, but you'll never achieve anything with real depth or dimension. Operating under this principle, it was obvious to me Joe was thinking about the wet t-shirt component of the evening, and I wondered briefly if he sent Jack a picture of that, too.

I let it go, though.

"Why didn't he text me he was here?"

"I don't know. Something about proving he can be in your life without smothering you. He mentioned a test and some guy named Horace." Then he narrowed his eyes at me. "Horace who? Who's this Horace chump?"

Remembering back to the conversation about the little test Jack wanted me to invent, I sighed and said, "Never mind. Want to come up?"

"Nope. I'm off duty now. His turn to put up with your crazy." He smiled, and I smiled back.

"Thanks again, Joe."

"Anytime, Nikki." He walked around to open my door, then we hugged good night.

"I'll wash your shirt and give it back to Jack."

"Don't give it to that joker." He laughed. "I'll never see it again."

Joe got back in the driver's seat. The engine was running, but I knew he was waiting for me to get inside. I clomped up the steps as best I could in the short, tight skirt and cowboy boots. Miss Delphine must have let Jack in, since he wasn't sitting on my porch. As I reached the top step he opened the door, smiling like a sailor who just made port after three months at sea. He grabbed me up in a big hug. Even with my head resting on his shoulder, I knew he was waving bye to Joe with an open palm raised in a silent gesture of gratitude. Completing the ceremony, I felt him tip his chin toward his brother. That's when I heard the Bronco pull away.

"Before I tell you everything that happened, I have something to say, and I don't want you to take it the wrong way."

"Okay." He waited.

Admitting I was wrong didn't come easily to me. I took a deep breath and blurted, "I wish I hadn't given you such a hard time when you were worried about me meeting up with Ditch."

Putting his hands on my shoulders, he pushed me back a few inches so he could see my face. "I appreciate you saying that. Now, what's the wrong way for me to take it?"

"Well, I don't want you to automatically think you get to call all the shots from now on."

"I've dated women who let me call all the shots. It's not as much fun as it sounds."

"It's easy to say that now, when I'm being agreeable," I cautioned. "I'll remind you how much fun you're having the next time you're about to bust a gasket because I won't listen to you, or worse, agree to your demands."

"And I'll remind you that you put yourself in the path of a potentially dangerous predator."

I couldn't argue with that, so I ended it. "Fair enough."

He pulled me inside. "I know this wasn't the outfit you started out in, but Lily, you looked so sexy tonight."

A smile snuck across my lips. I was pleased with myself for wearing something that turned his head. Okay. Okay. I was pleased with Mercedes for putting me in something that turned his head. The fact that I couldn't have given a flyin' flip what Jack thought of my clothes a few weeks ago was not lost on me, either.

"Will you wear that kind of thing again?" he asked.

If he was trying to change me into someone else, I wasn't too bothered by it. "You'll have to ask Mercedes. Those were her clothes." I laughed.

"Remind me to send her a thank you note." He was standing close, and he seemed hyper focused on my hair, twirling a loose strand around his finger.

Since I had been drinking, I knew he wouldn't be open to a proposition of *SexwithJack*. Plus, I was still a little weirded out about Ditch. So, I asked him to help me out of the cowboy boots, and then I went to shower off the beer residue. When I came out of the bathroom, he was on the couch finishing a Corona and scrolling through his phone.

"Want another?"

"Yes," he said and downed the last swallow in his bottle. I let him open both beers, as I plopped on the couch and began what promised to be a painfully comprehensive play-by-play of the evening's events. Ordinarily, he'd say something snide like, "This is a great story; is there a shorter version?" But he wanted specifics and asked a lot of clarifying questions in the process. It was as if he really wished he had been there and was reconstructing the scene so he could see it all clearly in his head.

I tried not to belabor my account of Ditch's behavior, but Jack needed details. When I told him Ditch grabbed my bruise on purpose, he absently rolled his right shoulder, like he was loosening up to throw a punch. I wasn't sure he was aware he did it until I saw him consciously pause, clench his fist, and then let the negative energy drain from his hand, arm, and body. Jack had amazing control when it came to stuff like this. A lesser man might have put his fist through the drywall to get the anger out.

Deciding to expedite, I jumped ahead to the most important part of the evening—the new lead. He agreed that the probability of bumping into the one person who used the same wacky phrase as Storie was infinitesimal.

"Maybe you should buy a lottery ticket tomorrow," he suggested. "The odds seem to be in your favor."

"Let's buy it on the way to Culpeper."

"You want to go tomorrow?"

"Can you?" After my experience at The Switchback, I wasn't even thinking about doing this part by myself. That was a considerable adjustment in my approach. I'd have to sort through the implications later, because I was slightly concerned that my overall independence was in jeopardy. I was no Stephanie Plum, but even I could see I needed some emotional backup at this point in the investigation.

"I can," he answered firmly. "I'm on at the firehouse tomorrow evening, though. If you find Storie's family and share the sad news of her murder, are you gonna be okay by yourself tomorrow night?"

I thought about that. "Probably not."

"Would you rather wait 'til Monday? I can change my schedule at the garage."

"Maybe. The problem is, I'll be coming out of my skin tomorrow with nothing to distract myself. I mean, I could spend time with Dad and 'em, but I'd still be antsy."

He lifted my forearm to his face and took a deep breath of my freshly washed skin. His love for oranges renewed, the fragrance of the soap triggered a soft moan. Talking more to my arm than to me, he said, "I can think of lots of ways to distract you. And I got all day until my shift."

He was clearly talking about his version of *SexwithJack*, or *SexwithLily* in other words. My version was something I found myself contemplating a couple times a day. Minimum. Still, when confronted, I didn't know what to say or how to act, which is why I said nothing, and I did nothing.

"You don't have to answer right now," he told my arm. "You can let me know what you want to do in the morning."

"Okay," I agreed. "I'll sleep on it." To get him off the oranges and the sex, I asked if he knew where Sanders' Ridge Farm was. He reluctantly set my arm down and picked up his phone. Plugging the name in, he threw himself into the search for what could very well be the last piece of this bizarre puzzle.

We found the farm and did a little online sleuthing. The business was started by a husband and wife, Jimmy and Beulah Sanders, back in the 1970s. The now-elderly couple appeared to be alive, or at least there was no obit that popped up to the contrary. Their small, picturesque farm was certified organic. The family was proud not to use any chemicals or genetically modified seeds and feeds.

Beulah and Jimmy had three grown children, two sons and a daughter. They also had two granddaughters, but we didn't find any names for the younger generation. It wasn't clear which of the three adult children parented the granddaughters, and it also wasn't clear if the two granddaughters were sisters or cousins.

There was a scrapbook of pictures on the website. In one photo, a dozen or so young people were horsing around while loading bushel baskets of vegetables into a junker pick-up truck. Two of them looked a little like Storie and Stella, but that could be my wishful thinking. Were Story and Stella the granddaughters? I thought maybe I would recognize someone else from the hiking group in the picture, but I didn't.

So now the question was how to use this information. Jack and I talked about possible approaches. He was uncharacteristically restrained, letting me propose all the ideas and not proposing any himself.

"Don't you have any suggestions?" I finally asked. That was, after all, the truly good part of having someone who was in on all the drama—there was a second point of view.

"Girl, I always have suggestions."

"I know. So why aren't you sharing them?"

"I told you I could be hands off. I'm giving you the discretion to do your thing. All it takes is a little self-control." It almost sounded like he was trying to talk himself into it.

Okay, that was new. I liked the freedom associated with it, but at the moment, I needed some good ideas to get things rolling. If I came out and asked him, that would be like flying a white flag of surrender. He wanted me to, I was sure of it, but give him what he wanted and I would effectively lose this measure of control. There was a lot more to Jack than met the eye. He had problems with control, sure, but when he made his mind up, it happened. Now, how should I play it?

"I like that you're letting me do my thing." That was my warmup.

"Well, that's what you told me you needed, right? It's kind of the one thing standing in the way of this relationship for you."

How we got onto the relationship, I had no idea. I sort of felt like it was a trick, so I moved carefully. "It is," I agreed. "However," and here I paused longer than I really wanted to. I just didn't know where to go.

"However…" he prompted and waited for me to finish the sentence.

"I could use some thoughts on how to go about this next step."

"I think you got this, Lily."

"Well, there's a curve here. And while I'm sure I could come up with a plan, I'd like to compare it to your plan. Kind of layer one on top of the other to see where they line up or if they completely diverge." I shook my head because it sounded like a lot of nonsense. "I don't want to screw this up. This is a big deal, you know?"

"I know. It is a big deal."

"So, I'll take your help on this."

"Are you positive? I'm trying to be hands-off."

"Yes. I'm positive."

Without any additional coaxing, he jumped in. "Here's what I would do—I'd roll right up to the farm, ask for the manager, and go from there. Just say you're a friend of Storie's. One of two things will happen—they'll be happy to meet her friend or things will go dead quiet. The response you get will dictate the next play."

"You're coming?"

"I'm coming."

"Thanks, Jack."

"You're welcome. Decide in the morning when you want to do this— tomorrow or Monday."

He lifted the back of my hand to his lips and placed a light kiss there, watching me as he did it.

We went to bed, and it was comfortable. I'm not sure if he was thinking about *SexwithLily*, but I wasn't thinking about *SexwithJack*. Instead, I was thinking how it felt nice to be safe at home. The Ditch slime was fading from memory, I was getting closer to solving a dark mystery, and I was on track to get back to school. This thing with Jack would probably get explored and resolved, one way or the other. And that's all I remembered thinking until Jack nudged me.

"Do you want another chicken lesson?"

"What?"

"It's time to feed the chickens."

I groaned when I heard the egg song that confirmed his statement. "I'd rather just let them starve."

"I'm sure Miss Delphine would appreciate that."

I groaned again. "I can do it if you want me to," he offered.

"No. I'll do it. You've been doing it a lot lately."

"Let's do it together."

"No. I'd rather use my method—one third indecision, one third self-doubt, and one third panic."

"So the same technique you employ when driving a Jeep off-road."

I didn't appreciate his attempt at humor this early in the morning, but to be fair, I wouldn't have found that funny any time of day. "Yes," I said, trying to put defiance ahead of sleepiness in my voice. "I find that technique works equally well for Jeeps and chickens."

Throwing back the covers, I dragged myself to a sitting position on the edge of the mattress. Before I could stand up, Jack pulled me backwards onto the bed. Disoriented, I flapped a bit before landing, at which point he used his body to anchor me.

"You're so sexy in the morning." He stirred my messy hair with his hand.

"What?"

"I know you might not be ready to fool around, but I had to say it."

"Jack," I stammered.

"Relax," he whispered. "Just a passing thought I have every time I see you. I'll feed the chickens; you go back to sleep."

He bounced up and was out the door before the final syllables hit my eardrums. I decided the least I could do was offer moral support from an Adirondack chair on the porch. I stepped outside just as he exited from the garage below with a scoop of scratch. I couldn't see McNugget any-where. She may not be obstructing his path, but I had a feeling she was ready to intercept him. I kept a keen lookout, creeping halfway down the steps in spite of myself.

When I spied her, she was poking along like the con artist she was—scratching here, pecking there, trying to blend in.

"I'm on to you, feather duster," I hissed.

Jack flung the food, and a few chickens raced toward that general direction, but McNugget continued to peck the ground disturbingly close to his feet. I watched, horrified, as he gently set the scooper down and then snatched the oblivious bird. He was so quick, I doubted that I even saw it happen. But the boy was standing there with the chicken in his arms, and I'm pretty sure she didn't fly up there of her own accord.

Jack and his friend ambled over to the stairs where I was frozen. He stood at the bottom, then kind of made like he was giving me a gift. I shook my head dramatically, rejecting his gift in the clearest way possible. He smiled up at me and motioned with his head for me to come closer. Again, I rejected this invitation. Finally, he put a foot on the bottom step.

"Stop!" I was emphatic. "There's no barrier between me and that pred-ator. I don't have a weapon."

"She's not a velociraptor."

"She may as well be."

"She's not hurting me," he explained calmly.

"Doesn't she freak you out?"

"Which part?" He asked. "Her intimidating size or her soft, snow-white feathers?" He took another step.

"Jack, I'm not kidding."

"I have her tight, Lily. You're not in danger. Let yourself be close to her in this safe way, and eventually your fear will fade."

"Are we back to the principle of proximity?"

I heard his deep, soft chuckle. "Yup."

I watched the chicken closely. The chicken watched Jack closely. Jack watched me closely. "Can I come up another step?"

My shoulders sagged, but I nodded. "I'm not holding her."

"That's okay. Will you touch her?"

"Probably not."

"Keep an open mind. You might surprise yourself," he said quietly, as he continued to climb the stairs toward me.

Reflexively, I took a step backwards. He stopped mid-step.

"Would you feel safer if we were on the ground instead of on the stairs?"

Hmm. I'd have more places to run if we were all on flat ground. "Yes."

"Okay," he said. "I'll back up so you can come down."

When he got to the bottom, he nodded. I took the steps like they were made of the thin crust of caramelized sugar on top of a crème brûlée, carefully working my way down. The faster I touched this bird, the faster I could go back to bed.

"You're doing great. You feel okay?"

I rolled my eyes, stuck between a genuine sense of disliking farm birds and a deep disappointment in myself for playing the helpless woman who needed to be saved from a farm bird.

Jack soldiered on, seemingly happy to be the one who got to save me from said bird. "She seems spastic, because she moves a lot, but right now she's really pretty calm."

Calm? To me, calm was the way an empty swimming pool looked before the first person jumped in. Jack apparently saw it as the lit fuse on a firecracker.

Once I finished slinking down the stairs, I stepped on the ground and prepared for another encounter that would permanently scar my psyche.

"Okay," Jack continued, "you can pet her head or her back."

Not wanting to aggravate her any more, I asked, "Which would she prefer?"

"Um," he pondered. "Why don't you softly touch her back."

She looked so small tucked in his large hands.

"Is she still growing?" I asked. "She seems small compared to the chickens in the grocery store."

"Two reasons," he started. "First, she's a layer, not a broiler like the kinds of chickens you get in the store. Broilers generally get a little bit bigger."

I stared at him, trying to decide if I was looking at a human being or a hologram programmed with the full breadth of Wikipedic knowledge.

He ignored my look. "The second reason," he continued, "is that Miss Delphine doesn't give these hens any growth hormones. This is the natural size of a chicken, not the size people have come to expect in the grocery store."

Absorbing all that information, I felt like my hand was too big a tool for petting a chicken, so I stuck out two fingers. Hovering close, frozen above her back, I waited for her to peck me, but she didn't. Jack turned a little so she was looking in the opposite direction, and I lightly touched her back. She looked around and made a little noise that sounded like a chicken's version of a purr.

"Awww. She liked it!"

"She did," he agreed. "That's the sound they make when they're content."

"Maybe she just likes being in your arms."

"A lot of women do," he said as his smile took on a decidedly erotic air. "You should try it sometime."

"Okay, okay," I attempted to draw his attention to the bird by running my fingers down her back again. She repeated the little purr sound, so I greeted her quietly, "Hey, McNugget," I said. "Maybe we got off to a rough start."

If I was expecting her to respond verbally, she didn't. Instead, she banged her beak into Jack's chest.

"Did that hurt?"

"What? That little nudge? No, that didn't hurt."

"Hmm." I weighed his response, trying to figure out if he was being truthful.

"She's not some steampunk half-bird-half-machine invention with an iron beak and rusty barbs for claws."

I smiled at the image, absently stroking her feathers one more time.

"Are you sure you don't want to hold her?"

"I'm sure I don't want to hold her."

"Okay. There's plenty of time for that. Are you ready for me to set her down?"

I glanced around, planning an exit strategy in case she turned mean again. "Go ahead," I said and took half a step back to give him room.

He gently placed her on the ground, and she looked up at me before walking toward her chicken family.

⤨ 🐤 ⤩

Standing at the kitchen window, Delphine smiled. "Cro, that boy loves our girl." Cro thumped his tail and made a happy sound. She set her coffee on the counter and reached down to scratch his ears.

⤨ 🐤 ⤩

Up in the apartment, Jack and I washed the biohazard off our hands at the kitchen sink. After the chicken lesson, I was wide awake, and he looked it, too. "You hungry?" he asked.

"Famished," I said. "Chicken school gives me an appetite." I let my tone take on an evil quality as I said, "KFC?"

He laughed. "Let's go over my house. I'll fix you cheese grits and bacon."

"You have bread for toast?" Because as far as I was concerned, grits were only half of the carbohydrate equation.

"I do. And OJ. And eggs if you want 'em."

"Sold." Looking down at my pjs, I said, "I guess I should change."

"Or grab some clothes and shower over there. Doesn't matter to me."

The desire to change gave way to the more pressing hunger pangs. I made a thirty second swipe through the place, stuffing necessities into my backpack—clean shorts and tee, panties and bra. I grabbed my toothbrush and threw in a new bar of my orange soap. Wait a minute. Why did I need my special orange oil soap when Jack had plenty of plain white Dial at his house? Oh holy House of Hamburger Helper. Would that fall under premeditated seduction? Thinking about it was one thing, but this went a step farther. I was planning it. Wow. Bold of me.

Chapter 17

Over his house, Jack went right to the kitchen where he started banging cabinets and rattling pans. I appointed myself Constable of Coffee, in charge of grinding beans and boiling water. For as many shortcuts as Jack took when it came to food, he always preferred to grind his own beans. I don't even know where that came from. His parents didn't do it. His brother didn't do it. Must have slept with a woman who liked it was all I could think. Not only did he grind the beans, but he didn't use a standard issue coffee maker like the rest of us, either. No. He used the pour-over method with a glass carafe. The only thing that didn't scream fancy pants coffee house was the fact that the hot water came from a beat-up pot on the stove.

With each of us working diligently on our respective jobs, the good smells of bacon and coffee took over the kitchen quick like. Grits were next. He never had the patience to make the grits the old-fashioned way, but instant were fine by me. Put enough cheese on them, and you could hardly tell.

Waiting for the pot to boil, I donned two lavender oven mitts, circa Candy Lady era, and reached in the cabinet for the despised Scorpion Welding mug. The money I stashed in the cup was gone, giving me a slight superiority complex.

He laughed. "Does that thing still bug the crap outta you?"

I threw him a hateful, you-know-it-does look and placed the cup on the counter.

"Want to make a deal?"

I tossed my head back at the suggestion. "Probably not," I said. "The deals I've made with you lately don't seem to serve my interests as well as they serve yours." I took the mitts off and reached for another, nonthreatening cup for my own coffee. My hand touched the cup just as his arms closed around my middle.

"I can see why you'd think that," he said, in a way that gave the sentence a consolatory tone.

With my right wrist resting on the shelf of mismatched mugs, I took a second to assess the situation. True, I felt trapped, but I wasn't frozen from shock the way I had been those times he came up behind me doing the dishes at the kitchen sink. Was his crazy principle of proximity working after all?

To redirect his attention, I asked, "What would the chief say if she saw you horsing around in front of a stove like this?"

"She'd write me up for sure. Luckily, we're not in front of a stove."

"Well, the water is boiling, so if you want coffee, you'd better let me get in front of the stove."

He made a sound that implied he was considering his options. "No," he finally said. "The coffee can wait. I like it here for now."

"Does this have anything to do with the deal you were proposing?"

"This hug? No. This hug doesn't have anything to do with that deal. I wanted to wrap my arms around you strictly for my own purposes. The deal had to do with mugs."

"Mugs?"

255

He kept his arms around me like it was the most ordinary thing he would do all day. The key for me was not to squirm or try to get free. Movement of any kind on my end could create an intense reaction on his end, beyond the definition of the so-called hug. "Yeah," he answered. "Coffee cups."

My interest was piqued, and I said, "I'm listening."

"Ahh. *Now* you're interested. Well, I had planned to propose a trade of sorts. You give me something of value, and in exchange, I'd get rid of trusty ol' Scorpion Welding."

At this point he had my full attention. I seriously hated that mug.

"What's my end of the deal?"

"Sorry, that deal is off the table."

"What?"

"You said you weren't interested."

"Well, I am now."

"Well, it's too late now."

With my hand still resting lightly on the shelf, I closed my fingers around a coral-colored cup and brought it down to the counter. If he was willing to part ways with Scorpion Welding once, he'd be willing to do it again. I just had to identify a trade with the right value. An alarm in my head, similar to the sound a dump truck makes when it backs up, alerted me to the potential for disaster. I didn't know who was driving the dump truck. Maybe Stephanie or maybe my seldom-seen friend Common Sense. I couldn't tell. It was good advice, though. The things that Jack sought before, a kiss on the lips or the chance to smell my skin, were not the high-value targets he was seeking now. I'd probably have to take my shirt off at this point. So, I put the idea on ice for the time being.

While I was distracted with my own designs, Jack took the opportunity to spin me around so we were face-to-face. Up until now, I had been patting myself on the back for doing a great job keeping a cool head during the whole unsolicited hug-from-behind, but I was starting to get a little nervous at this point.

"If you burn my bacon," I cautioned, "there's no amount of sweet talk that'll get you back in my good graces."

Jack had a weird way of making bacon in the oven instead of using a frying pan like every other normal person. Point being, he couldn't just look over at the burner to see if everything was okay. He sniffed the air and decided to check the oven. It wasn't burning, not even close to crispy, but the ploy worked, and the subsequent space it created between our two bodies was a huge relief. I usually wasn't so accomplished when it came to pulling on the puppet strings, and I found myself happy with this little victory.

"I know what you did there," he whispered in my ear as he passed behind me.

"Hmm?" I hummed quietly, pretending not to hear as I poured boiling water into the coffee filter.

With our feast nearly prepared, we started to move things to the kitchen table. Jack decided to elevate his toast and bacon to the level of a BLT and grabbed a ripe Cherokee Purple tomato off the counter. I assumed it came from his mama's garden, along with the lettuce he pulled out of the fridge. I put the bacon on a bed of paper towels to sop up the grease and brought the plate to the table. He went back in the fridge for juice and the industrial-sized jar of Duke's mayonnaise.

"You want a BLT?" he asked as he cut thick slices of the juicy tomato on his plate.

"No," I said, scooping out a huge spoonful of cheese grits. "But I'll take a slice of tomato."

He plopped one on my plate. I grabbed a couple pieces of the perfectly cooked bacon, surveyed my food to make sure I hadn't forgotten anything, and reached for the butter for my toast. With my dad's heart attack always present in the back left corner of my mind, I realized at some point in my life it would be prudent to start leaning toward a more heart-healthy diet. Just not this morning. Hoping for the best where my own heart was concerned, I took a big bite of grits.

The coffee was almost finished, so I jumped up to get the carafe and my cup. I went back for his, using a dish towel to grab hold of and hide from view the despicable scorpion.

"Your days are numbered," I hissed softly to the inanimate insect.

"What?" Jack looked over at me.

I tested a few rhyming phrases in my head—Your ways are encumbered…No clays for the lumbered…He plays with a gum bird…but quickly realized they weren't believable and fessed up.

"Nothing," I said. "I was talking to your mug."

He chomped into the sandwich and looked at me like he was evaluating the status of my mental health. "Sounds 'bout right," he declared when he finished chewing.

"Hey, I never claimed the bats in my belfry were playing with a full deck of marbles."

Laughing at my stupid mixed metaphor, he agreed. "I never did either. Sexy? Yes. Sane?" He gave a half shrug in response to the sane question then trained those blue eyes on me. It felt like he was exploring the sexy part in his head.

I took a gulp of juice. "We can get to the so-called sexy part later. For now, let's stick with the insane part." He poured coffee and waited for me to continue.

"I decided I want to find Storie's family today. I know I might have to deal with some strong emotions when you're at work tonight, but if we start fooling around and things progress…" I trailed off, not wanting to explicitly spell out *SexwithJack* in the bright morning light. I picked the thought up just on the other side and finished, "I'd have to deal with that while you're at work tonight. So either way, I'm dealing with something on my own tonight."

He seemed to be aware I was on a roll, and he didn't interrupt.

"So let's just get this part over with. The Misty-Storie part. You know?"

"Yeah. I know." He smiled a small, sad smile. "Lily, I'm sorry you have to go through this."

I was touched by his sincerity. He really did seem to understand that the feelings associated with this mess required muck boots at the bare minimum, if not full-on waders. If he was hoping I would have decided to wait 'til Monday, his face didn't show it.

He fixed himself another BLT. "After we eat and shower," he said, "I'm ready to go."

"Okay," I agreed, serving myself another scoop of grits from the pot on the table and one more piece of bacon. We laid out our strategy over the second cup of coffee.

When it became clear I had finished breakfast, he picked up the pot of grits and asked, "You done with these?"

"Yep."

He proceeded to eat them right out of the pot with the serving spoon. Then he polished off the last two strips of bacon, drank the rest of his juice, and said, "I'll jump in the shower first. Leave the dishes."

"Oh, okay." I slathered the words with sarcasm like I had slathered my toast with butter a few minutes before.

He picked up my wrist, circling it with his fingers. "If I need to keep an eye on you, I'll pull you into the shower with me."

"For the love of a blue footed booby in a bicycle helmet." I tugged at my wrist and raised my free hand in frustration. "Alright. Alright. I won't do the dishes. It doesn't make any sense, though, because I know you don't like to do them, and you know I do."

"I just don't want you cleaning up after me in the kitchen."

"Today?" I asked. "*Today* you don't want me cleaning up after you in the kitchen? I've been cleaning up after you since, oh, elementary school! Here's a newsflash, Jack—you in a kitchen is like a shark in a duck pond. Let's just say there's a lot of thrashing and destruction."

"Things are changing. We're about to be lovers." He smiled when my eyes went wide. "It'll go from something you don't mind doing, to a chore you hate doing, and I don't want it getting in the way of this relationship."

"A chore?" I searched for some phrase to express my frustration, but finding nothing, I said, "Knowing you is a chore." Trying again to free my hand, his other word landed. "Relationship?"

"Yeah, I said it. Relationship. It's gonna happen. And it will not be a one-night stand. Make your peace with that." He held my hand for a few more seconds then let go. On his way to the bathroom, he said again, "Don't do the dishes."

Silently, but using my most demonstrative mannerism, I mouthed "Don't do the dishes." When he stopped in the doorway to glance back, I was sipping coffee with artificial restraint. We stared each other down for three seconds, and I took the point since he turned away first.

Once I heard the shower start, I stood up to clear the table. *Stacking* the dishes wasn't the same as *doing* the dishes. Any first-year law student could get a jury on board with that. But once they were stacked, I decided to wash just the pot he used for the grits. That stuff would dry like cement if you let it. He'd never miss one dirty pot, especially since the crown jewel of dirty dishes was sitting on the counter—a cookie sheet boasting half an inch of solidified bacon fat. I washed then dried the pot, putting it away so there was no evidence in the dish drainer.

A few minutes later, the bathroom door opened in the hallway. I waited, ear cocked. When I heard him rummaging around in dresser drawers, that was my cue. Grabbing my backpack, I darted into the bathroom and closed the door behind me.

Fishing my stuff out of the bag, my hand landed on the bar of orange oil soap I had imported from home. I considered it for half a second but decided to go with the house soap instead. It seemed like orange-scented skin was a distraction we could do without today.

I showered as quickly as I could, which was still about ten times longer than Jack's shower. When I dressed and finished squeezing the water out of the wet mop I called hair, I opened the door and wandered toward the kitchen in bare feet. Jack was sitting at the table, drinking coffee and looking at his phone. The dishes were done. He must have just fixed me another coffee, because the steam was still curling out of the cup. As I was about to go all mushy because it was nice of him to fix me coffee and do the dishes, I spied the paper airplanes. Three of them. The ones I had made out of his fifty bucks. They were lined up on my phone like fighter jets on the deck of a tiny aircraft carrier. That little superiority complex I enjoyed earlier this morning came back to mock me.

I picked one up and launched it in his direction. The thing fell on the table with the grace of a Christmas tree on the receiving end of a curious cat. So I flicked it with my finger, and the plane skidded across the slick wooden surface, stopping right in front of him. He flicked it back. I grabbed all three, tossing them toward his head confetti style.

"These are yours," I said.

"No, they're not. I don't make airplanes that fly like walnuts."

"The aeronautical design is definitely mine, but the money itself is yours."

He stared at me. "Lily, you know what you're doing, right?"

"Giving you back the money I told you I didn't want in the first place."

"No. You're pickin' a fight you'll never win. It's a stall tactic. You're stalling because you don't want to face Misty-Storie's family." His words weren't critical, just honest.

I would have liked to think, on some level, I was evolved enough to know I was stalling on purpose. Nonetheless, his revelation shocked me.

"Don't beat yourself up," he continued. "Anybody would have a tough time with this one."

The money was forgotten. "What will I say to them?"

"The words will come. I think you'll probably want to reiterate that you don't have any hard evidence, but the tattoo in the picture seems familiar."

I listened as he spoke in his calm, firefighter voice.

"Remember, not everyone can handle that website. It might be too much for them. Maybe you take a screenshot of the tattoo, so they can see that without all the other stuff?"

"I can do that," I said, nodding.

"And maybe write down the contact info for the officer in Florida who's in charge of the investigation."

"Okay."

"One last thing. And I don't want you to misunderstand what I'm saying here." I looked up, waiting.

"I'm not suggesting in any way you should be ashamed of your relationship with Storie."

I tilted my head, taking him in as he expanded on that thought.

"Maybe keep the details to a bare minimum, though. You don't know how much of her life Storie shared with her family. This is probably not the time to reveal anything that could drive a wedge. Know what I mean?"

"Makes sense," I agreed. Not that I was planning to tell Storie's grandparents that she and I were lesbian lovers for three days, but this was a good reminder to choose my words carefully.

"You ready?" he asked, putting his hand on my arm.

His touch was reassuring.

I nodded and stood up.

In Jack's truck, I fiddled around with the screenshot and jotted down the name and number of the investigator listed on the case file. Then we rode without saying much for the hour and a half it took to get to the farm. He had the seventies station on, and I was lost in the playlist of silly old songs. When he turned onto a shady tree-lined lane, and I saw the hand-painted sign for Sanders' Ridge Farm, I started shaking my head "no" like I was answering a question that nobody had asked.

Jack slowed the truck and pulled over to the side of the dirt road. "You okay?" he asked.

"I don't think I can do this."

"You can, Lily. They may be looking for her right now. You have to tell them what you know so you can help them find peace. I'll be right there."

I took a breath, still not sure I had the strength for this.

He asked again, "You okay?"

I nodded, but no one was convinced.

Jack put the truck in drive, and we eased up to the first building we saw. It looked like it had once been a barn and was now a market of sorts. The building used to be blue, but the sun and rain had done a number on the paint, and the new color scheme was a cross between blue and the brownish-gray of weathered wood. A bell jingled when Jack pulled open the screen door, holding it for me.

"Howdy, neighbors!" a bright, somewhat elderly voice greeted us. "Y'all make yourselves at home. Let me know if I can help you with anything."

I scanned the room for the source of the voice and finally identified a tiny older woman. I knew right away she was Miss Beulah from the pictures we had seen online.

Jack, who probably saw the panic tingeing my body language, leaned over and whispered, "Remember, start by saying you're a friend of Storie's. See where it goes from there."

I reached for his arm, and he bent it at the elbow, like an usher escorting me to my seat at a wedding, or, I gulped, a funeral. Latching onto him firmly, I tried to skim some of his courage.

"Y'all from around here?" Beulah chattered on.

"Yes 'um," Jack answered, "just up the road a piece. Marshall."

"Oh, I know Marshall! Well, welcome to Sanders' Ridge. Come'ere'n try this jam." She was dropping tiny blobs of amber goo onto little square crackers. By the color, I guessed it was peach.

I reached for a cracker and handed it to Jack, then I reached for another for myself.

The human vacuum inhaled his before I even got mine off the plate. "Oowee, that's delicious," Jack said.

Laughing at his exuberance over jam, I popped the cracker in my mouth. Wow. He wasn't kidding. "That really is good. Did you make it?"

"My recipe, yes, but the kids do the work now."

Mention of the kids brought me back to the reason we were here in the first place. "Is this the Sanders' family farm?"

"It is, child. I'm Beulah Sanders."

"My name's Lily Barlow," I started. "I'm a friend of…"

I couldn't seem to get her name out because a weird thing started happening. I assumed the reaction was triggered by stress. My vision got dark around the edges and a low level of white noise invaded my brain, like the sound of the tide dragging tiny pastel-colored clam shells across the sand. I flashed back to last August, in the evening by the river. Storie's beautiful face shimmered in my head the way a mirage ripples in the heat.

Awash in wooziness, I swayed slightly. Jack, who hadn't taken his eyes off me since we walked in the place, stepped closer, giving me a solid timber to lean on. He was an expert at reading my symptoms, and I hoped he was silently preparing to perform some kind of resuscitation should I go into full cardiac arrest. Vaguely aware of all the cholesterol I had consumed at breakfast, I ping-ponged between the two possible types of attack I was having—anxiety and heart.

"Are you…" Before he could finish asking if I was okay, a soft voice called my name.

"Lily?"

"Miss Beulah?" I said aloud.

Jack, who had been focused on me, snapped his head up at the not-right sound of Miss Beulah speaking my name. By the expression on his face, he was either sharing the figment of my imagination or we were both looking into the face of a living, breathing Storie Sanders.

She hadn't stepped out of my memory after all; she was standing right in front of us.

Chapter 18

The woman who materialized before my eyes spoke again. "Lily Barlow?"

"Storie Sanders?" Jack asked, since I was incapable of baseline guttural noise, much less recognizable speech.

"I am," she affirmed, bypassing Jack to wrap me in a surreal hug. As she did, the helichrysum on her skin scented the air with honey, which will forever be part of my permanent collection of remembered fragrances. "Nana," she said over her shoulder, "this is a friend I met down Charlottesville way when we were hiking the Appalachian Trail."

I was aware that Miss Beulah had made an approving comment, but I had no idea what she said. I really needed to sit down.

"Storie," I reached for Jack's hand, and for some reason I'll spend the rest of my life trying to understand, I said, "this is my boyfriend, Jack Turner." I glanced at him, signaling with my eyes that I'd like him to play along for the time being. He signaled back that his role as "boyfriend" was not an act.

"Jack," she said in a throaty whisper, almost to herself. She studied his face and finally said, "You weren't lying, girl." She smiled and said to him, "You have beautiful eyes."

Had I told her about Jack's blue eyes? Why would I have mentioned Jack's eyes in the heat of all our passion? Why would she remember it after all this time?

"Thank you, ma'am," he said with a sweet note of modesty.

I glanced at the owner of the blue eyes and knew right away the third degree would be relentless, but his self-control in this moment was admirable. I raised my eyebrows and gave him an embarrassed smile along with a one-inch shrug before turning back to Storie Sanders.

Luckily Jack intervened with a pretty good suggestion. "Storie, is there some place quiet y'all could sit and catch up?"

Storie took me by the hand and drew me through the shop to a back door. With my free hand, I held on to Jack and dragged him along. Outside, there was a wide, shady porch with a big porch swing covered in blue and white checkered cushions. The sight of the comfortable swing brought on a wave of exhaustion so profound Sleeping Beauty would have been impressed.

Storie landed lightly on the swing and pulled me gently down beside her, never letting go of my hand. Jack asked if we wanted some privacy, but I said no, so he sunk down on the step with his back against a post, facing our direction. I could only imagine what classic porch-swing porn flick was running through his mind.

He smiled as if it was a favorite.

"Storie, can I see the flower tattoo on your ankle?"

Without asking why, she lifted her long, flimsy skirt and showed me the tattoo. It was identical to the one on the Doe Network. What was going on here? I looked over at Jack who could see the tattoo from his vantage point. The same questions were written all over his face.

"So, you might be wondering why I'm here."

She smiled. "I'm a little surprised to see you."

"I was afraid you might be…well…dead."

"Dead?" The emphasis she applied to the word was how I imagined she would respond if someone offered her something unappetizing, like licorice. Or Brussels sprouts.

"Murdered, actually. I saw a picture of your tattoo. It was on the body of a woman who had been killed."

"How do you know she was killed?" she asked. It seemed like she was trying to absorb the idea.

"The picture of the tattoo is part of a police report. It was listed as a distinguishing mark that could possibly help someone identify the victim." I took my phone out, brought up the screenshot, and handed it to her. Her face went white, like she was seeing her own dead body.

I didn't really know what else I should say, but at the same time, I didn't know how to shut up. I added, "To honor your memory and out of respect for the…special time…we, uh, shared, I wanted to let your family know. So they could bring you home. From Florida."

She kept staring at the picture on my phone.

I saw Jack shift positions. His body tensed which meant he was noticing something important.

"You alright, Storie?" he asked. No answer.

I put my hand on her knee. No movement. When she looked up, there were tears in her eyes. Jack stood but didn't approach.

"I have friends with this tattoo," she whispered. "There were six of us who got the same one in high school." She continued, more quietly, "We were only in the tenth grade, and it took a lot of persuading to get all the parents and some of the grandparents onboard."

I took a sharp breath in. Once I saw Storie alive, I felt a sense of joyful relief, like my heart was bouncing on a pogo stick. Where the profile on the Doe Network was concerned, I very quickly chalked that up to a sad case of mistaken identity. Misty still deserved justice. Obviously. But my part seemed done, and I was hoping it was helpful that I had narrowed the field by eliminating one possible victim.

It only took one more look at her pained expression for me to put everything in perspective. Misty would certainly be identified. She was one of five friends Storie had in high school, all of whom were close enough at some point to permanently brand their friendship onto their ankles. I leaned over and gave her a hug, awkward only because of the angle of my approach. She held onto me.

"How can we help, Storie?" Jack asked. He had come over to the swing, plenty large enough for the three of us, Miss Beulah, Miss Delphine, and all of Lucy's puppies and sat down on the other side of Storie.

You'd never know it by how he crowded me all the time, but Jack had a decent understanding of boundaries and personal space. He was close enough to lend comfort, but not so close he was giving her the sardine treatment. Storie pulled away from me and acknowledged his gesture with a weak smile.

"I see Scarlet and Shelby all the time," she said, "so I know it's not either of them."

"What about the other three?" I asked softly.

"Luanne's family moved when we were in the eleventh grade. I completely lost track of her. I haven't seen or heard from Dana or Pauline since before we hiked the AT. Dana got pregnant and left town, and Pauline went to Mexico, Costa Rica, to a place where they speak Spanish. A mission thing or something like that."

"We can help you look for them," Jack offered. "I know a cop who could do some checking."

"Let me see what I can find first." She looked down at her hands, as if studying her many rings.

"Storie," I said, picking up her hand, "when I thought it was you...it was really hard. You don't have to do this alone."

She laid her hand softly on my cheek, in a very tender way, and said, "Thank you, Lily. I'll call you once I sort through some things. This is... it's just a lot right now."

"One more thing," I said, not knowing how to proceed delicately. "The report didn't mention anything about the victim being pregnant, having been pregnant, or having given birth. By a certain number of weeks, I think that's something a medical examiner can tell. In other reports I've read, I have seen it mentioned as a way to help identify the person."

"You've read other reports?" Storie asked, focusing on the peculiarity of me reading police reports about murders instead of the fact that her friend, Dana, may not be the person who was murdered in this case.

"It's kind of…" The phrase 'long story' sounded like I was poking fun at her name, but what else would work here?

Jack, always a step ahead, supplied, "A saga. It's kind of a saga."

"Yeah." I nodded. "I'll tell you sometime, but it doesn't help right now."

The three of us slipped into silence. I felt the presence of Storie's high school memories filling up the porch and spilling into the yard under the tree. I saw Storie, Scarlet, Shelby, Luanne, Dana, and Pauline learning to drive, all crying when one got a broken heart, drinking beer, getting ready for prom, cramming for biology exams, buying the same new phone. Maybe they played softball, or chess. Maybe they cheered, or marched in the band. Maybe they rode horses, or dirt bikes. Maybe they just hung on the fringe, together.

Jack and I seemed to be in tune, and neither of us rushed the exit. This was Storie's nightmare, and she would let us know when it was okay for us to leave. I wasn't sure who started the swing rocking, but when I realized it was, I relaxed into the smooth back-and-forth of it. We could have been rocking for hours, I lost track. It was Miss Beulah who roused us from the shared silence.

"You three look lost in thought," she said from the yard. It seemed none of us had heard her approach.

"Hey, Nana," Storie said sweetly.

"I'm heading to the house, honey. Your daddy's in the store."

"Yes, 'um," Storie answered.

After Miss Beulah ambled out of earshot, Storie moved forward to the edge of the swing. That seemed like an invitation to me and Jack, and we stirred as well.

"Do you want my phone number?" I asked.

"Please."

I pulled up the keypad on my phone and handed it to her. "Call your number, then you'll have mine and I'll have yours."

She dialed. When she handed it back to me, I went into the log, clicked on the number she had dialed and saved her as a contact. Meanwhile, Jack stood up, and stepped back so the two of us could get off the swing. I hugged Storie again, half tempted to tell her I was glad she was alive, but I kept my big mouth shut knowing that someone she cared about was dead.

Jack leaned in for a quick hug and reiterated, "If you need help, call us."

"I will."

Instead of walking back through the store, she led us around the barn to the parking lot out front. I assumed it was to eliminate any introductions that might be required since her dad was inside. Smart. That's what I woulda done.

As Jack backed the truck up, I rolled the window down and lifted my hand in a half wave. She looked small and forlorn, like someone had taken the very gleam from her shining silver spirit. For a second I wondered if I should have kept the unidentified body a secret. After I confirmed it wasn't Storie, I could have just kept the rest to myself. But I knew, ultimately, it was the right thing to do. The victim deserved her identity back. As painful as it was for anyone who knew and loved her, it was nothing compared to the pain she endured in the attack that ended her life.

As we drove down the tree-lined lane, Jack reached over and took my hand. Without saying anything, he asked if I was okay. I looked over, squeezed his hand, and without saying anything, told him I was.

We rode quietly for about thirty minutes, until it occurred to me that I was dangerously close to starvation. One of the things I liked about Jack was that you never had to convince him to get something to eat. He'd eat at the most obscure reference to food. We did the drive-thru at the next greasy chain restaurant we came to.

At first, we were silent because of the mood. Then, we were silent because our mouths were crammed full of French fries and chocolate milkshakes. After the food had been hastily consumed, though, Jack broke the silence.

"I switched my shift tonight."

"Why?"

"Brian needed someone to cover him next Saturday. Anniversary, I think. But that's a technicality. If he hadn't asked to switch, I would've."

"Nice job of answering the question without answering the question."

Falling back to his usual, straightforward way of speaking he said, "I didn't want you to be alone tonight."

"Storie's not dead," I reminded him.

"Doesn't change anything."

"Jack, I'm fine."

"Okay. Then I'm doing it for me."

This was obviously going nowhere and taking a long time to get there. Much like the return of the paper airplane money, I would not change his mind. So why, in the name of donkey doulas, even pursue this line of questioning? I told myself to save my energy for something bigger and called myself by my last name, to show me I was serious.

"Alright. At least you're honest. So, what do you want to do?"

"I'm wide open," he said, then inventoried an extensive list of ideas. "We could go out to eat. I could cook you dinner. We could stop by and say hey to your Pop. The Nats are at home, we could go to the game. We could get the Ouija board out and try to contact Miss Brown. We could go down to the lake. We could go get drunk. We could keep on driving."

When I heard lake, I stopped listening. Ah. The Lake. Peaceful. Restorative. Generally speaking, the group didn't show up two nights in a row, so it would be quiet down there. I could use a shot of that powerful water therapy right now.

I looked over. "The lake," I said. "Let's go to the lake." He smiled, liking my choice.

We drove by my house then his to change into swimsuits and collect sunscreen, towels, cooler and water bottles. On the way, we stopped at Cumquat's for some sweet tea.

When we got to the spot, he pulled the truck down by the water. We were the only car there, and since this wasn't a place people could really walk to, we were completely alone. Which was good and bad. Good, because it was blessedly quiet. Bad, because there was no foot traffic to knock back the bugs I would encounter on the route. The lake ecosystem, especially along the path, was dense with insects. And not just spiders. Caterpillars, centipedes, millipedes, 'pedes of any kind, really. Flying things like hornets, wasps, yellow jackets, bees, both honey and bumble.

I had a problem with all of them. An ant. A single ant was the only insect I felt I could handle on my own. But if there was a long line of ants, forget it. I once ran screaming from an apartment I was renting near campus because of a stream of ants that poured through the window, across the kitchen counter, down the cabinet, and into a crack in the floor. Jack, in all his infinite bug wisdom, told me to wipe the trail with alcohol. He might as well have told me to rent an F/A-18 Hornet and join the Blue Angels at their next performance. I did not wipe any trails. Someone in the house more fearless than me got close enough to hose the site with something toxic. That strategy came with a whole new set of consequences, having now contaminated the kitchen surfaces with poison. I didn't stay in that house much longer.

At the lake, I always relied on the presence of other people to scare or squash the resident bug population before I arrived on the scene. With no one else around, I asked Jack to go ahead of me to bulldoze any spider webs laced across the path. Wearing sneakers-no-socks instead of flip flops, I picked my way along, avoiding any long-reaching plants that might brush my legs. When we got to the dock, I made him do a full sweep of the splintery boards and ladder before I stepped foot on it.

He stomped on the dock three separate times, killing bugs, or at least making me believe he was. When he certified the area bug free, I walked to the end and laid out two towels, pulled off my t-shirt and wiggled out of my shorts. He stood there, watching.

By way of encouragement, I asked, "You swimming in your shirt?"

"Nope. Just enjoying the view," he winked.

I put one hand on my hip and made a cheeky little turn, trying not to stump my toe in the process. He smiled and nodded.

"Nice."

I found it curious that he didn't try to kiss me but didn't spend any time interpreting it. I sat down, a little harder than I intended, and scooted into the water with a medium-sized splash. He threw his ball cap on the dock, ripped off his shirt, and did a colossal cannonball with a trajectory that put him three feet from me. Big splash.

He was tall enough to stand easily. I could touch bottom, but if I did, the water would cover my nose. I somersaulted backward to wet my hair. The water was perfect, the somersault was nearly perfect. I always felt so much more nimble in the water than I did on dry land. Water was my equalizer. We floated and treaded and splashed for a bit. I let the lake wash away the stress leading up to the visit with Storie.

"You wanna try the rope swing?"

"The rope swing?"

"There's nobody here. You might not be so nervous."

"Okay," I said, surprising the Jujubes outta myself.

I used the ladder to get out. Jack hauled himself up using only the strength of his upper body. *Show off.* I pushed my dripping feet into my sneakers and followed him to the old tree on the bank. When not in use, the rope was wrapped around an accessible branch. He unwrapped it and held it out.

"Oh, no. I'm not going first."

273

"Okay, watch me. I'll let go before the swing turns back to the bank and just drop in the water."

He stopped, looking at me as if he was putting something together in his head.

"What?"

"Lily, have you ever jumped into the water?"

"Like a million times."

"I mean, when you get into the lake, how do you do it?"

"You know how I do it." In my head I added, *numbskull.* "I sit on the dock and push myself into the water."

"Right. You're always sitting. Have you ever jumped from a standing position?"

"No. Why?"

"That's why you can't let go of the rope. You have to learn how to jump first. Let's go back to the dock."

On a mission, he grabbed my hand and pulled me back toward the dock. When we got to the end of it, he told me to jump in.

I surveyed the water, looked at him and shook my head no. "I don't want to."

"You know how deep it is. We were just out there five minutes ago."

"I don't want to," I repeated, a little louder this time because obviously the water in his ears was making it difficult for him to hear me.

"Will you watch me?"

"Sure, I'll watch you. But I won't do it."

"Okay, just watch." He didn't even take a step back for momentum. From where he was standing, he launched forward, sinking under then pushing up. When he popped back out of the water, he was grinning like Neptune at a mermaid festival. "Nothing to it."

I shook my head "no" again, so he bounded back up onto the dock.

"What is it you think will happen?"

"I never really dissected it before."

"So let's take it apart now. What could happen?"

What could happen? He didn't know? For someone I considered to be a smart guy, sometimes his intelligence ran way below the normal range. "I'll tell you what could happen, nut job. I could trip, hit my head, fall into the water and drown. You know I'm a klutz, Jack."

"You won't trip if you don't take a running start. Just stand here like I did."

"I don't have strong legs. If I don't push far enough out, I could hit my head on the dock, fall into the water, and drown. Or I could make a bad jump then crash into the water. People have gotten paralyzed that way."

"Usually," he started, speaking in his patient, let-me-walk-you-through-this voice, "when people get spinal cord injuries, it's because they dive into water where they can't see the bottom. They hit their head on something they didn't know was there, like a log or a rock. So you're right—never dive. But you're jumping here; it's not the same."

"It looks like it might hurt."

"It doesn't hurt. That summer you were learning how to dive down at the pool, and you did all those belly flops...when you hit the water like that, it hurts. Can we hold hands and jump?"

"No."

"Please."

"Jack—"

"Please," he cut me off. "We'll go in together. I'll pull you away from the dock, and if you make a bad jump, I'll be right there to fish you out," smiling, he added, "and give you mouth-to-mouth."

He took my hand and wove his fingers between mine in a tight grip before I even agreed. "Will you do it?"

"Oh for the love of a feather boa on a Burmese python."

"Please?" he repeated for the third time.

"I'll jump off the dock, but I will not go off the rope swing." It was more to shut him up than to expand my skill set by learning how to jump into water.

"The dock is plenty for today." He didn't give me any time to reconsider. "On the count of three."

With counts one and two, I unconsciously bent my knees and did practice pushes, likely because I knew I couldn't chicken out. It was a guarantee he was jumping on three. And if he jumped and I didn't, somebody could really get hurt. Somebody with the initials LB, and I wasn't talking about Ludwig Beethoven or Lucille Ball.

On three, I pushed off and Jack pulled. We went flying through the air, hand-in-hand, displacing a tremendous amount of water when we hit the surface. I guessed I had been holding my breath since the dock, because underwater I kicked frantically to get back to the surface. Splashing and gasping, strong arms lifted me up keeping my head above water. I took a big breath and laughed.

He joined in my laughter. I don't know if it was the thrill of the jump, the joy at not drowning, or the way his blue eyes flashed, but I came forward and kissed him. Without so much as a warmup on the lips, I went full tongue. He changed his support from holding me up and instead pulled me to him. With a swift movement, he lifted me again in a way that made it natural for my legs to wrap around his waist. I wasn't heavy, thanks to the magic of buoyancy, and we stayed like that for a very long time. When he pulled his lips away from mine, he laid his cheek on the wet skin of my chest. He was breathing hard. I could tell he wanted more.

"Jack," I said tentatively, "I want to do this."

"Do what, Lily?"

"Have sex."

He didn't say anything for a few seconds. Then, he shook his head and in a husky voice, he said, "I don't want to have sex. I want to make love."

"Does it matter what we call it?"

"Yes."

"Why?"

"Because this is the first time. We've done a lot of stuff together, but this is new for us. When we look back on it, I want to remember it was special."

"I don't want all the emotions that come with making love," I said, digging in.

"I do." He dug in on his side.

"Making love—" I started to explain that the term carried a lot of weight and therefore engendered a lot of pressure, but he cut me off with a kiss. The kiss was deep, dark, and wrapped in mysteries, so I just let it nudge me forward, away from my trivial, albeit obsessive, distinctions.

Still kissing, still with my legs around his waist, he walked us over to the ladder and set me on the rung. I climbed out ahead of him, but he was on my heels and spun me around for another kiss. In the water it was hot, but out of the water, the wet skin made it steamier.

"I want to lay down with you," he breathed.

"The dock is kind of out in the open," I noted.

"Bed of the truck?"

The truck was tucked away from any spectator that might roll in; we would hear someone driving up long before they would see us. It sounded like a more private option but less comfortable. Reading my mind he added, "I have a rubber sleep pad."

Smiling, I shoved my feet halfway in my shoes and wore them like clogs as I grabbed the towels, t-shirts, and my shorts. Jack grabbed the cooler and we raced to the truck. He rolled out a rubber pad that looked like a yoga mat on a protein diet. It wasn't the most luxurious mattress I'd ever rested on, but it was better than the boards on the dock or the metal ridges in the back of the truck. It was wide enough for one point five people, so he was half on and half off the mat. He didn't seem to notice.

Feeling a new wave of nervousness, I fell back on my old go-to, "I need to pee."

There weren't many options at the lake. With no formal port-a-john, over the years I had to come to terms with peeing in the woods or peeing in the water. The latter seemed like more effort, so I went around the front of the truck and found an open space that would hopefully have fewer spiders. I whispered a deal with my adversaries that I would try not to pee on them if they would grant me a pass this time. Since no spiders marauded, I assumed they were cool with that deal. Wrestling to get the wet suit back up, it occurred to me it would have been a lot easier to use the lake after all. No spiders, and the bathing suit would still be in place.

When I came back around, I half expected Jack to be naked. He was leaning back against the cab of the truck, but he still wore his trunks. Looking at him, I had a vague memory of how he wanted this first encounter to unfold, something about him taking a really long time to get me naked and twice as long to explore my naked body. Again, I noticed my nerves. It felt like they were oxidizing, and I was frozen in a state of oxidation.

He stood up, walked to the end of the tailgate and reached a hand to pull me up. When I didn't grab it, he jumped down, brought me back into a hug and asked, "Are you freaking out?" He took my silence as an affirmative response. "Tell me what you're thinking." No answer.

He sat on the tailgate and invited me to sit beside him. "If you're not comfortable here, we can go back home. Or," he pushed a damp strand of hair away from my eyes, "we can save this part for another day."

It was always my choice. He always gave me the gift of choosing. In that moment, I knew what I wanted to do. I felt our solid friendship, like granite blocks stacked around the truck. I scooched up onto the mat, and he followed. We looked at each other. I reached out to touch his face. He drew his hand down my neck to the strap of my suit and pulled it off my shoulder, then he started kissing my shoulder. That felt so good, I reclined more fully and he took the other strap down. I was naked from the waist up, and I realized I didn't care. He traced lines between my freckles and kissed my scars. When he discovered something he had never seen before, he gazed as if transfixed by its magnificence.

He asked me if he could pull my suit off. I nodded, but he waited for verbal permission. "You can take it off," I said, with the smile you smile when you've got a can of whipped cream and no one is watching.

He peeled it off too easily, and I briefly wondered how many suits he had peeled off other women while honing this talent. Three or four dozen? But it didn't matter. It was the two of us here in this moment.

I was naked, he was not, and I let him explore with his hands and mouth. His passion was contagious. I found myself exploring his body. When I got to his swimsuit, he asked, "Do you want me to take it off?"

"No," I said, enjoying the hint of turmoil that crossed his face. "I want to do it." He smiled a wicked smile and laid back. I tugged it off with no finesse whatsoever and continued my tour of his body. While we kissed, I lost track of positioning. When I took notice, I found myself under him, all his weight suspended above me.

He shifted to his side, lifted the corner of the mat and pulled out a shiny square. Jack's need to be prepared was never more appealing than right now when he produced a condom. "You still okay?" he asked.

"Yes," I breathed.

He made short work of the foil wrapper, perfected with practice as well, and it was in place smoothly and quickly. He asked again if I wanted to do this.

Yes, yes, yes, I wanted to do this. I wanted to do it more than pine pollen wanted to make people sneeze.

"Yes," I said, and in the back of his black pickup, I *MadelovewithJack*. The act swallowed us like quicksand. My orgasm came in second only to the universe's big bang. Letting go felt like I was running toward the end of the dock with the speed of someone who medaled in sprints. When I got there, I switched from a track star to a third-generation trapeze artist and launched skyward into a triple front flip, mocking gravity, before plunging beneath the surface, fearless.

If you are interested in the cause of naming and reuniting unidentified and missing people, please visit the Doe Network. With the exception of Misty-Storie's profile, the cases mentioned in this book are people who have been found but had not been identified at the time the book was first published. Misty-Storie's case was created for the purpose of the storyline.

About the Author

I once wrote in an online dating profile that I don't cook, gossip or panic. True enough at the time, I suppose. Although the idea of writing this author bio has got me in a bit of a panic. I was told my first attempt sounded like a resume, and not a particularly good one at that. So here's the skinny: I got a degree in language arts and then proceeded to use my skills to  write grants, newsletters, an occasional freelance article, and lots of IEPs. To be honest, it's not exactly what I had in mind when I got the degree, but it paid the bills.

In 2016, with the encouragement of my very supportive husband, I took a sabbatical from teaching to work on my first novel. It was love at first write. (See what I did there?) I enjoyed the process so much, I resigned from teaching special education and threw myself into my new career as an author. The hardest part has been making my peace with the fact that writing is only a tiny part of what authors have to do. There's plenty of things I'm not good at, but telling stories, that's something I am good at. I also love connecting with my readers in person and virtually. You can find me on Facebook at Carla Vergot's Back Porch.

A free ebook edition
is available with the
purchase of this book.

To claim your free ebook edition:

1. Visit MorganJamesBOGO.com
2. Sign your name CLEARLY in the space
3. Complete the form and submit a photo of the entire copyright page
4. You or your friend can download the ebook to your preferred device

Print & Digital Together Forever.

Snap a photo

Free ebook

Read anywhere

Printed in the USA
CPSIA information can be obtained
at www.ICGtesting.com
JSHW080728300923
49411JS00002B/17